Armorica

Armorica

Joseph Hughes

WHITE CLOVER

Armorica

Copyright © 2010 by Joseph Hughes

Manufactured in the United States of America.

White Clover

ISBN-13: 978-1-933651-63-7
ISBN-10: 1-933651-63-6
LCCN: 2009911084

Author contact information:

Joseph Hughes

jh@ARMORICAworld.com

www.ARMORICAworld.com

To my mother and father,
without whose support and guidance this work
would have remained on my computer
as nothing more than a document
full of grammar errors.

Acknowledgments

I'd like to acknowledge quite a few people, but the list starts with my mother who has helped me every step of the way. I'd also like to thank my friends whose names were used in the book—not that the characters are in any way based on you as a person but rather that you were around and a friend when I first wrote it.

Special thanks also go to just a few of the people who have supported this book, encouraged me in my writing, had a special impact on my life as a writer, or otherwise directly helped me. Without them, despite the goading of my parents, I probably wouldn't have bothered to stick with it. To name a few: Katie Hughes, my sister; Bee & Charlie Oldfield, my grandparents; Celeste DesOrmeaux; Lucas Driggers; Jaclyn Greenfield; Sue Jackson; Lori Martin; Emily Martin; Maria Palacios; and Ann Williams.

I would also like to recognize some of the talented professionals and friends who helped make this publication and the Web site realities: Cynthia Stillar, The P3 Press; Mark Devaster and Brewed Art; and Torrey Owens, Hand2Toe. Also: Amy Johnson, Celeste Mele, Will Turner, and Marilyn White.

I sincerely hope that you enjoy my creation and that you will be eagerly awaiting Book II!

Joseph Hughes
Dallas, Texas
22 July 2009
jh@ARMORICAworld.com

Primary Characters

HUMANS
The Empire
    Shadow Crusaders
        Boryn Mhinbron
        Wenval
        Laric and Calny (twins)
        Emily
        Ranton
    Lord Mhinbron (Algyer), Emperor and Boryn's father
    Scruffy (Edrick), the healer
    Belral, Emperor's sword master
    Hannah, adopted sister of Stevan
Knightly Realms
    Order of the Blood Knights
        Ramgis, commander of the Blood Knights
        Cadegray, healer of the Blood Knights
    Orders of the Raven, Serpent, Bear, Wolf, Dragon, and Horse
Rath, mercenary
Elemencia
    Marlok, the thief
    Quaswyn, the bumbling mage
Red X
    Luthor Mhinbron, Boryn's brother
    Dace, Luthor's second
Other
    Captain Yarrik of the Sand Ocean
    Lulz, the Force of Nature

ELVES

Moon Elves (also known as Noble Ones)
> Silvaros, Moon King

Flame Elves
> Xandon, Flame King
> Lentz, King Xandon's personal guard
> Prizzadar, archmage and advisor

Dark Elves (also known as Dark Ones)
> Lord Kelris and the Dark Lancers

Wood Elves
> Weskin, Wood King

DAEMONS

> Tarn, Daemon King
> Daemon Generals
>> Fernus, Glacius, Tharrus,
>> Thundrus, Aquus, Noctas

DWARVES (Ones-of-the-Earth)

> King Fazrin
> Boringer, the gladiator
> Bret, the brewer
> Rogma, forge master
> Stevan, the chef
> Kam, the betrayer

OTHER RACES and FORMS

Unknown: Morpheon, harbinger of carnage

Mihiran

The Four: Zalmani (Regret), Death, Destruction, Terror

Rapi (lizardmen)

Orcs, Golems, Olans, Goblins, Zombies, Tecn

Icon Key

 The Empire

 Shadow Crusaders

 Boryn Mhinbron

 Knightly Realms

 Rath

 Elemencia (Marlok & Quaswyn)

 Red X

 Moon Elves

 Flame Elves

 Dark Elves

 Daemons

 Dwarves

 Morpheon

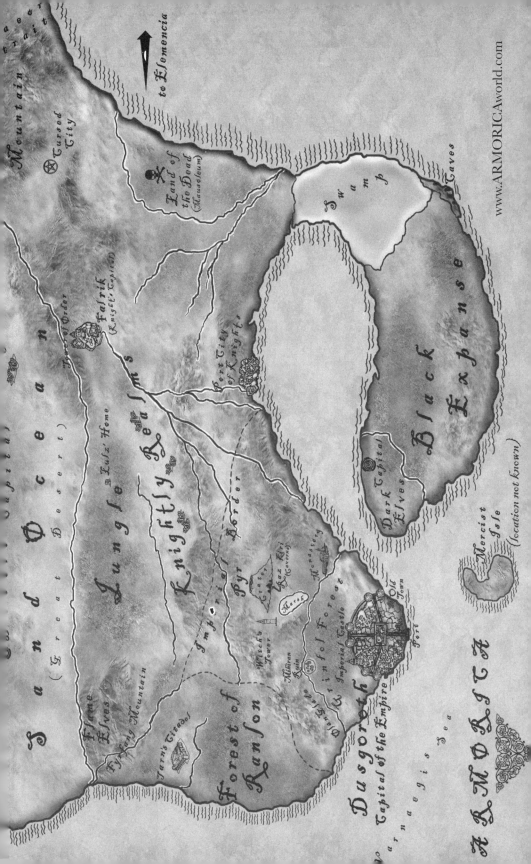

The world was formed
betwixt darkness and light,
between daemons and archons~
ever hungry to destroy one another.

Into this realm,
we humans were born.

Possessing will and imagination,
we choose our sides
~to protect or to destroy~
to live in fear or to die in glory.

Prologue

He stood staring at the crooked building. The wooden sign with the green cross that hung above the door creaked in the cold night wind. The boy ran long fingers through his black hair hanging lank and straight to his shoulders and sat heavily, leaning against the hard wall of the house across the street. He strained to see in the upper window where candles were still lit. A man with snow white hair and a long, fuzzy beard, or his shadow, moved purposefully around the room, and the boy could hear a woman who screamed in pain. *I'm happy I'm not a girl*, the boy thought.

His mother was giving birth to a child, and more like a commoner than nobility, she went to the healer to have her baby. *But that was the least of her reasons for leaving home*, the boy thought bitterly.

Luthor waited outside the healer's home worried and expectant. *I hope it's a girl. I couldn't stand a brother.* He rose again and paced in front of the door. *She'll have black hair and blue eyes; she'll be short all her life; and she will be weak. Yes, that would be a good sister.* He sat again, this time below the small window next to the healer's door, and drifted off, dreaming of adventures and of ordering his younger sister around.

He nodded awake, realizing the screaming had stopped. Unable to contain his curiosity, the boy jumped up, ran to the door, and began to knock anxiously. The scruffy old man he had seen through the window opened the door, his full, white robe billowing in the draft. With still clear eyes, the man looked up at the gangly boy standing before him. The boy's royal blue doublet with golden trim and his serious, green eyes seemed as worn and tired as the boy himself, and his face, neither handsome nor unpleasant, was clouded with concern.

"Yes?"

"I am Luthor. My mother, she stayed here last night."

"Yes. Come in, young man." He ushered the boy toward the room. "She's upstairs along with your baby brother."

"Brother?" asked Luthor despairingly.

"Yes, brother. Go see him."

Luthor hurried up the stairs, long legs taking the steps two at a time. *At least he'll have black hair and blue eyes.* Quietly, he opened the door to see a newborn baby sleeping in its tiny cradle. *Can't see his eyes yet.* He turned his gaze to his mother who slept as soundly as the infant, and then he crept out.

Not knowing what to do with himself, Luthor wandered through the darkened streets of Dusgoroth, the imperium's capital. The boy walked toward the city square past the empty market stalls, their vibrantly colored cloth awnings folded underneath for the night. Continuing through the square, he headed down the cobbled street that spilled to the sea. He roamed the docks, tasting the salty tang in the damp, chill air, and listening to the waves lick the shore on this strangely moonless night.

Despite his attempts at self-distraction, the boy found himself drawn back to the healer's house. It was quiet when he approached. *Still sleeping, I suppose.* He knocked gently, but the door remained untended. He tried the handle and, finding it unlocked, entered on his own. The calm from outside cloaked the frenzy within. The white-robed healer shuffled about the room gathering oddly colored potions. Luthor noticed something strange in the man's expression. Was it terror he saw behind the healer's eyes?

He sprinted up to his mother's room where two more healers, both in generous white robes, tended the woman, one frantically casting healing spells, the other applying ointments, and the woman bathed in perspiration.

"What's going on?" Luthor demanded.

"Watch out," barked a bent old healer as he brushed past Luthor to reach the mother. "Out of the way, lad."

The healers continued their work, ignoring the confused and scared boy. One hurried down the stairs, returning shortly with a bundle of new potions. Luthor slid into the chair in the corner to watch and wait. The candles burned low, their wild flicker adding to the disquiet. He stared, transfixed, until the flames grew long and tall and still, and Luthor looked up to see that the flurry had stopped. With a careful hand, the healer smoothed the bedclothes, and then the three, weariness in their eyes and bodies, moved toward the door.

The eldest, the scruffy one, stepped close to Luthor. "I have failed you."

"What are you talking about? She's fine, right? Just sleeping," the boy stammered, jumping to his feet.

"I am sorry. I couldn't save her," said the healer gently. "Our strongest potions and spells seemed powerless. There was nothing we could do." The healer placed a gnarled hand on Luthor's shoulder as if the hand alone might provide some comfort, and then the scruffy old man left the room.

Luthor stepped toward the bed, toward the tiny figure. She might have been sleeping beneath the smooth bedclothes. He reached down to shake her. "Mother, wake up. Don't sleep now." But when there was no response, his movement and tone grew urgent. Begging through hot tears, "Please, Mother, please get up." Then finally, he crumpled to the floor and wept until completely spent.

After awhile, the healer came up and forced Luthor to leave the room. He gave the boy some hard bread, but Luthor sat zombie-like, not eating. As a gray dawn broke, Luthor fell into fitful sleep, his dreams filled with memories of his mother: her gentle smile and lively green eyes; how she used one finger to brush the hair from his eyes; the way her supportive words and fantastic stews soothed the soreness after training with the sword master; and that she was always there to shield him from his father. And now she was gone.

The stairs creaked with each exhausted step as the healer climbed to tend the babe. Entering the room he noticed an odd stain on the tiny forehead. He bent low to inspect the red mark then gently wiped it away with a cottony sleeve.

"Now, how did you get blood on you?" he questioned softly.

A drunken cry from outside summoned the healer to the window. "Oy, howsss that, uh, lady of mine doin'?"

The healer leaned out to see a powerfully built man, flask in hand, stumbling toward the house. Foamy contents clung to his messy black beard and dribbled down his golden breastplate.

Hurrying downstairs, the healer met the man at the door. "Lord Mhinbron, you have a new son," the healer said, faltering. "But, sir, I regret that we were unable to save Lady Mhinbron."

The man blinked absently. Without a word, he turned to go, tottering toward the nearest tavern.

Luthor pushed past the healer and stepped through the doorway. "You bastard!"

The big man stopped and turned, his face red with drink and rage.

"You don't even care, do you?" challenged Luthor.

The father closed the distance between them, his breath nasty and hot on Luthor's face. "What? Your mother dying, your new brother . . . or having a girl like you for a son?"

"I hate you."

"What did you say to me?" Luthor's father grabbed the front of the boy's doublet and shoved him against the wall.

"Lord Mhinbron, please stop," begged the healer, wedging between them.

"Stay out of this," ordered Lord Mhinbron. He pushed the

old man aside. "I am the Emperor, leader of the greatest power in Armorica."

"I hate you!" repeated Luthor even louder.

"Aw, does the little girl want her mother?" taunted the man, a beefy finger jabbing into the son's bony chest. "Well, too bad. She's dead. It's just you and me—and that baby brother—now."

Luthor screamed as he slammed his fist solidly into the Emperor's ample gut. Lord Mhinbron bent double, surprised by his son's power. He reached out to grab Luthor's leg, but the thick cloth of the boy's breeches scratched through his fingers, and the boy escaped. Gasping for breath, the Emperor forced himself upright. Luthor waited while Mhinbron swallowed deep gulps of sobering air, allowing the father to think the fight was done. Luthor took a step forward, looking hard into his father's smirking face, then with the edge of surprise, smashed his knuckles into the man's yellowed teeth. Luthor heard a shallow cry as the man recoiled and grabbed his bloody mouth. The father rebounded, his fist aimed squarely for the son. At the instant before impact, Luthor dropped to the ground, grabbed the man's wrist and kicked up. A satisfying snap told Luthor the move was successful.

"You stupid child!" bellowed Mhinbron as he withdrew a sword with his unbroken arm.

Luthor pulled himself tall and tried his best to sound grown up. "Don't call me a child. I am a man!"

"Pah!" The father laughed from deep within his belly. "How might a man be a man without a single whisker?" Then, without warning, the powerful figure swept toward the son with his sword. Luthor jumped backwards but was struck with a sharp, slashing pain. And then another. Warm blood flowed from the two gashes that crossed his chest.

With visceral fury, Luthor powered forward, ramming his fist into his father's jaw. Lord Mhinbron's feet left the ground as the bone cracked, and he tumbled to the street.

"You are not my father. You're nothing but a stupid, drunken lecher who can't even rule his own city!" Luthor spat on the figure

Joseph Hughes

lying face down in the road, slimy waste from the gutter pooling around him. *A fitting place. Rot in hell.*

The old healer stroked his beard, deep in thought. He regarded the family lying in the beds of his house: one covered with a shroud; one out cold from blood loss; another unconscious from stupidity. And in the crib lay a baby crying.

The healer walked to the crib and extended a crooked finger for the tiny babe to grab. He smiled, lifted the infant, and cradled him in aged arms. "I shall call you Boryn," he said. "Rest, Boryn Mhinbron, rest."

Release

He could pick pockets before he could walk, and playing cat-and-mouse with guards had been a favored pastime ever since. Guards had tried to catch him in the act of stealing since he was little, but after so many years of practice, he was good, very good. Filled with the charm he'd cultivated in his fifteen years, and being swift with word, too, they rarely pinned him with a crime.

Oh, how he loved his free days, not working like everyone else around him. On days like today, he could explore the whole, beautiful city of Dusgoroth, and he imagined what he could get if he wanted it.

Enjoying the coziness of his sleeping place tucked beneath a market stall, Boryn stretched his lanky frame. Every day, his legs pressed harder against the confines of the space that he called home. In spite of his humble circumstances, it felt good to be back in the city after so many years. *Oh, yes, it will be a good day.*

Naturally quick, he scrambled up and dressed in a hurry to fight the predawn chill. Tattered black breeches, a dirty black shirt, and leather boots that stopped at his knees served as his only protection from the elements. In fact, these were the only garments he owned.

Using his fingers, he combed the tangles from his hair, full and long, hanging past his shoulders, and the color of sand on the beach. Boryn snatched up the leather satchel that contained his worldly possessions—a small black mask and whatever he had stolen the day before—and headed out, adventures calling.

Scarcely had he stepped into the open before he spied his first victim, a guard paying more attention to a pretty, young fruit vendor than he was to his satchel. Leaning heavily against the edge of her stall, the guard made miserable attempts to woo her, but the girl ignored him, staying busy setting up her stand for early business.

Boryn grinned and slipped on the mask, a strip of hide with two slits cut for eyes. With little effort to conceal himself, he chose the moment. Boryn glided behind the guard and knocked the man's elbow off its underpinning, sending the man crashing down face first. Boryn seized the satchel with his free hand and winked at the girl as he grabbed an apple from her cart. The guard cried out, and Boryn took off, picking up speed as he scooted through a maze of streets and out the city's northern gate. He bolted up a tree, its branches perilously close to the city walls, and waved the guard's satchel tauntingly.

"You there, thief, stop!" shouted the guard as he and his fellows converged on the culprit.

Boryn coolly observed their desperate attempts to climb the tree, but their iron plate made it impossible.

"Shall I come down for you?" he teased, a mischievous glint in his eyes, startlingly green even through the mask.

"You are wanted and hereby under arrest for thievery, vandalism, avoiding and resisting arrest, battery of a guard, trespassing, stealing from Emperor Mhinbron, and endangering the lives of our citizens!" ranted an enraged guard.

"There are two problems with that. One, you forgot conspiracy, and two, you can't arrest me until you catch me."

"Arrogant little—," sputtered one who finally gained a foothold and progressed up the trunk.

"You really are stupid," said Boryn. He drew back then released a leafy branch, swatting the guard like a fly and sending him hurtling. "Nothing to it," Boryn muttered to himself as he climbed higher. "Oh, and by the way," Boryn tossed down an iron rod the length of a man's arm. It landed heavily on the ground beside the men. They stared confused, but too late, it dawned on them. It was the pin that held up the portcullis.

The gate creaked and whined through the rust and grime accumulated during so many seasons of peace with neighbors and neglect from the leader. Gaining speed under its own weight, the gate shut with a heavy, dusty thud. The guards looked from one to another in horror, realizing their choices: one, they could return through the Emperor's gate, but that would not look good; two, they could walk around to the eastern gate, but then they would have to enter through Old Town, and they were definitely afraid of that; or three, they could wait.

"You're stuck out here, too," one of the guards blustered.

"Not quite."

Boryn clambered the length of a long branch and hurtled toward the city wall. He grabbed the ledge, slammed into the grey stone wall and pulled himself to the top. The young thief turned and waved to the guards outside before hopping down to a roof below and scampering free within the city walls.

He always thought it funny that there were so many guards and so little need. It had been twenty years since the rebellion, and the only crime around was, well, people like him. But the pay was good and the work easy, so many chose the profession.

He navigated the sloping tiles and thatch with agility, leaping narrow alleys and streets and completely losing any remaining pursuers. He doubled back toward the town square and squatted on a roof to observe the circling guards and enjoy a bite of his luscious red apple. *Fools.*

Just then two angry storks rocketed toward him to protect their nearby nest. As he dodged to escape, a roof tile gave way. Boryn slid and fell, bouncing once on the eave before landing directly atop an unsuspecting guard. "Greetings," Boryn spoke playfully. He poked the man in the eyes before scuttling around a corner and vanishing into an alleyway.

On the lookout for mischief, Boryn returned to the wall
to check on the tormented guards. He smiled impishly to see them
sitting on the road waiting for someone to open the portcullis. *Yes, a
good day it is.* The boy walked the parapet for a ways before kicking
off the edge to land within the city walls. He came out from a narrow
passage near the arena, an ancient marble structure built long before
Dusgoroth and the Empire existed.

The arena was enormous, blocking the sun with its bulk. In olden
times, it was used for entertainment. Captured slaves and dangerous
creatures fought to the death regularly in the days before men had
joined as one to rule the land. Now it served as a training center for
guards and soldiers. Even regular citizens, so long as they had the
coin to pay, could buy lessons in the way of the sword.

Beyond the arena stood another impressive building, this one
with a patterned tile roof. Once the mansion of an old merchant who
deserted it for a nearby island, it served now as a library containing
all the secrets of the old world.

Boryn made his way toward the library's doors, wooden and
heavily carved with creatures of all kinds. He entered, scanning the

grand space within. Around the hall were placards inscribed with the wisdom of the ancients. Shelves, fifteen feet high and holding the written legacy of mankind, lined the walls and defined cozy vestibules at each window through which light spilled across book-laden tables. Poring over them were students of history, masonry, metals, mythology, and even farming.

At the far end of the vast chamber, a double staircase wound up to a balcony filled with more books and tables. Boryn read the placard on the wall above the stairs: "Magic is governed by the limits of man's imagination and the power of his will." *Imagination and will? Guess that leaves me out. I don't have the patience.*

Taking the steps two at a time, Boryn bolted up, almost colliding with a mage whose pristine white robes identified him as one of the city's healers. Only those who had demonstrated special skills in healing were approved by the council to wear the honored white robe.

He propped himself atop the lustrous bronze banister to make way for the healer's passage, jumped down, and continued his run to the mezzanine. In the center of the room stood a large, round desk burdened with huge leather-bound volumes. Sitting at the desk was a slight, shaggy-haired boy of Boryn's age clad in a green cloak with red lining that flushed his pale skin.

The boy bent over an open book, entranced in his task, messy brown curls falling in his eyes. Boryn guessed that the work must be fascinating for the boy's cloak quivered, a telltale sign that his feet were jiggling. It always happened when the boy was deep in thought.

Boryn smiled, remembering how they first met not so long ago, when Boryn used the underside of the boy's table as a hiding place from the guards. He had scared the poor boy to death, a rocky start to an unlikely friendship. But Boryn, a man of action more than letters, was intrigued by the other boy's lively, thoughtful mind, so unlike his own impulsive one. And Boryn became a frequent visitor to the library to befriend the brilliant, fresh-faced scholar.

With uncharacteristic quiet, Boryn crept up close behind the focused learner before slamming his hands on the boy's shoulders. "Wenval!" he exclaimed.

The boy launched from his chair, nearly sending it tumbling. Wenval spun angrily, staring at the boy who stood almost a full head taller. "Not funny, Boryn!"

"What have you been doing, professor? You've been holed up in here forever! What, a week or more?"

"About that."

"What have you learned? Anything of worth in this dusty old collection of parchment?" Boryn inquired as he idly flipped through a volume.

"Actually, these books contain amazing spells. Unfortunately, most of them are in a different language. Some even use an unknown lettering system!" Wenval told him with excitement.

Boryn read the cover: *Legends and Lore.* "More of that nonsense?" It was, after all, the generally held opinion.

"It is not nonsense! It's written treasure. Watch!" Wenval extended his hand and turned his outstretched palm toward the open brazier. "*Fyr!*" he called. Instantly, a ball of flame shot from his hand through the open window and out toward the arena, blasting apart a stone statue and peppering startled passersby with fragments.

Boryn's eyebrows rose as high as they could go. "Now *that* was interesting," he grinned widely.

"Wasn't it?" Wenval agreed with a hint of pride. "I've learned several more spells and read about so many others most people can't even imagine! I figured it out with the help of *that*," indicating the volume through which Boryn leafed.

"So you have learned to use magic? I thought you couldn't read the books."

"I can't, but it's odd . . . the more I concentrate on them, the more I understand. I don't know why or how, but I know the result. I now have the ability to cast a few spells."

"Well, a life of the mind makes Wenval a dull boy. There's an entire world calling us out there! So get up, and come on!" Boryn's mood was playful and buoyant. "You can show off for the others; they'll love it!" He clamped onto Wenval's sleeve and dragged him toward the door.

"Wait! This mess——," Wenval referred to the books and papers littering the large table. "My parents will be furious!"

"No time to worry about that. Let's go find Ranton," Boryn said as he sprinted down the stairs, knowing right where to find the third boy. With only a breath of reluctance, Wenval glanced back to his table and then followed along.

"Remind me why I'm here again?" asked the tall, long-faced elf, scratching the head beneath his stark white hair.

"You know full well why we are here," said the shorter elf, though still taller than most humans, his bald head shining from the oil he used on it.

"I don't really understand the point."

Prizzadar twisted a golden staff between his bony fingers. "Think of it as our time for vengeance," suggested the elven archmage, his magnificent lapis robe shimmering like blue flame in the torchlight.

"If you say so. Shall we tell them we're here?" the Flame elf mumbled as he held one hand forward. A fireball formed which he launched toward the Forest of Ranlon. The tall elf watched it strike its mark, setting a tree ablaze. Almost immediately, horns blared, warning the Wood elves to protect their home.

The King of the Flame Elves turned, motioning a group of his golden-armored warriors forward. "Light it up."

"Soldiers! Open fire!" commanded one of the captains.

"And so the Flame elves march," Xandon said through a yawn, his voice sonorous and calm.

A black line fired out from the forest, whistled past King Xandon's head and struck the soldier behind him. A deluge of arrows followed. Xandon raised his right arm high, golden armor glimmering in the light of the flames, and then brought it down in a broad sweeping motion that left a screen of flame separating his men from the arrows and protecting their advance. The flames died, and the Flame elven warriors thundered into the burning forest, cutting with both fire and steel.

The elven king smiled confidently, a green scar that slashed his right eye glowing in brilliant contrast to the scarlet robe that showed behind his breastplate. By human standards, the Flame king should be old, but in the world of the elves, he was yet young, with strong, angular features that enhanced his regal bearing. Xandon held his hand forward, firing a flaming blade from his palm, and he stepped into the forest.

It took only moments for a leather-armored Wood elf to drop from the overhang intent upon sinking a blade into the Flame king's throat. But Xandon was quick. He jumped back and sliced his fiery blade through the assailant's neck, and the severed head dropped to the ground.

The Flame king advanced toward a distant clearing where he saw a stone temple, moss and decay threatening to overtake its walls. He whistled, a second troop formed up beside him, and he ordered the charge. The warriors hacked through enemy lines, clearing a path to the temple's pillared entrance. Xandon marched through the gap toward the portal, but a Wood elf, stouter and even taller than Xandon and clad in green-leather armor, blocked the way.

The Flame king smiled. "Guards, step back and make room so that the honorable King of the Wood Elves and I may begin our fight."

"But, lord—"

"I'm not going to lose!" Xandon said with annoyance. He watched the opposing king unsheathe a longsword and stand at the ready.

"So now you're the guardian of this accursed temple as well as of the Forest of Ranlon?" posed Xandon derisively.

"I, Weskin, King of the Wood Elves, shall guard this temple with my life!"

"Then lose it." Xandon nodded to his guards who formed a defensive ring around them. *Finally, a fight that might actually challenge me. It's been awhile.* Spurred by habit, he brought up his fingers to touch his right eye, feeling the scar's fiery green heat. He waited, circling Weskin, expecting the older elf to make the first move.

"I shall cut you down, Xandon, just as I did your father," Weskin taunted.

"My father was an impatient fool," replied the Flame king. "I have more important matters to consider."

Weskin rushed at Xandon and ripped his blade up, attempting to catch the Flame king with an unexpected low strike. Weskin felt the impact reverberate through his arms as his attack ricocheted off Xandon's blade of fire. The Wood king swept his longsword across Xandon's belly then reared back before lunging at the opponent's throat. Xandon stepped away from the first attack and then parried the stab, slapping Weskin's sword aside with the flat of his own fiery blade.

Weskin mumbled ancient words; immediately, roots fired out of the ground and wrapped Xandon's legs. Even motionless from the waist down, however, Xandon moved too fast for Weskin and blocked several hacking strikes. "Immobilize my whole body and leave only this arm free if it will help you," Xandon waved his flaming sword, flaunting it, taunting and annoying the Wood king. Before Weskin could respond, Xandon swooped with the blade to incinerate the roots binding his legs.

Weskin unsheathed a second blade, and with both blades swung simultaneously high and low. Xandon stabbed the point of his sword into the earth and ducked behind it, hiding himself, the low swing stopped by the blade, and the upper strike, slicing only air, sailing harmlessly overhead.

"Aim was a little high."

"You're all mouth, aren't you? That's why you never attack."

"Fine." Xandon extended his arm and charged. Weskin jumped

back to keep clear, but Xandon dropped low and brought a sweeping kick across Weskin's legs, sending him tumbling to the ground. In a flash, the Flame king was above Weskin, stabbing his sword toward the fallen Wood king's head. Terror flashed across Weskin's face.

A second before landing the blow, Xandon stepped back and allowed the Wood king to rise. Weskin stabbed both his longswords into the ground and turned eyes to the sky. Green light fired from his body, and the earth beneath him buckled. He lowered his chin and glared at Xandon, eyes burning with hatred.

"There we go! The power of the Wood elves, the woodland guardians. Hah! Seriously impressive," Xandon applauded.

"You will die in the name of the Forest of Ranlon!" roared Weskin.

Xandon's guards stepped closer, ready to bring their blades to their king's aid. Weskin shot forward and sliced toward Xandon's neck with both blades, but Xandon's flaming sword stopped them before they came even close to his head.

"Sadly, power is useless without skill," Xandon remarked before kicking up, jettisoning Weskin skyward. As the Wood king dropped, Xandon sliced through his neck. The head rolled across the temple yard before the corpse hit the ground.

Xandon's blade extinguished, he dusted off his red robe, and he paused to look at the soaring wooden doors that sealed the entrance to the temple. Then he turned away. "And the bad guys win again. Give the orders to fall back. We are going home."

"Yes, my lord," said the captain, who sounded a horn to signal the retreat.

"Prizzadar, do whatever it is you need to do here. I'm leaving."

"Yes, my king," bowed the blue-robed archmage, a satisfied smile creasing his aged face.

Boryn reached the central gatehouse to find the portcullis open and the guards nowhere in sight. He ran up the stairs to the wall-walk from which archers fired at practice targets along the edge of Grinfol Forest, and watched the swordsmen below battering their pells.

He heard a *thunk*. A straw dummy swayed, an arrow impaling its head. Boryn turned from the dummy to the tower from which the arrow was fired. Another shot zinged, hitting the target dead center again. Retracing his steps, he called down to Wenval, just arriving at the gatehouse and out of breath. "Ranton's on the watch tower."

"The tower?" Wenval moaned, eyeing the steep steps, but Boryn turned on his heel and ran ahead to the tower's door where spiraling treads led higher still, ending at the roof. Boryn's friend knelt behind a crenel, back to the stairs. Not usually so patient, Boryn waited, with only his head above the hatch, for Ranton to fire. The archer's shoulder pivoted, elbow back, his action smooth and his aim dead-on. An imperceptible shift of finger, a distinctive *twang* and the arrow whizzed forward. The boy stood, blinking his hazel eyes as if to refocus them, and lowered the bow.

"Nice aim," Boryn said, climbing through the trapdoor to the top.

Ranton turned, slinging the bow over his shoulder as if it was a part of his own body. The bow was long, its limbs almost as long as the boy's own, and its dark wood matched the color of his unruly hair. The two boys, Ranton and Boryn, were of about equal height, and both were strikingly handsome. But Ranton was substantial and muscular while Boryn was lanky. And Ranton's clothes, though tattered like Boryn's, were earthen green, a complement to his olive skin.

"Boryn! We've missed you the past few days," Ranton said happily. The skilled young archer bent to collect his unused arrows, slid them into his leather quiver and stood straight. "Where have you been? Fending for yourself finally? My mother asked yesterday why you haven't been around scavenging for food."

"Tell her that her foundling is well. But it's nice to know I can count on the spoils of her hunting in a pinch!" Boryn said with genuine appreciation and fondness, too.

"Wenval with you?"

Boryn walked to the tower's side that overlooked the city and pointed. Ranton tracked the finger's lead to the see their friend resting at the foot of the stairs far below.

"Ah. So, what's the plan? What shall we do today?"

"Um, we could explore Old Town," Boryn said without giving the matter much thought.

"Why would we want to do that?" Ranton wondered. "I've lived around here all my life, and it's been deserted the whole time."

"Well I haven't, and I'm curious. You never know what you might find if you look."

"There's nothing better to do . . . ," Ranton relented.

"What about the twins? They'd be up for it. Any idea where we can find them?"

Ranton had known the twins since the three of them were small, capering under the market stalls while Ranton's mother traded her game and hides and the twin's fishmonger parents peddled their catch. "Where they always are, I expect. There's training to watch this morning."

Boryn and Ranton hurried down the stairs and rushed past Wenval to the street.

"We're going to find Laric and Calny at the arena. And then to Old Town," Boryn called. "Come on." Ranton, surprisingly fast for his size, was already well ahead, and Boryn had to run to catch up.

Wenval groaned. "Enough . . . with . . . the . . . running!"

His friends laughed but made no effort to slow to the shorter boy's pace.

Boryn slipped past the man guarding the arena gate, Ranton at his heels. His long gait carried him up the stone steps; his eyes circled the near-empty stands. Across the way, he spied the twins, their matching shaved heads glistening in the warm sun. With identical chunky builds and slump-shouldered posture, it was impossible to tell them apart sitting side by side with dark eyes glued to the scene on the sand.

Boryn followed their gaze and noticed someone new in the ring today. The fighters used weapons, of course, but the skill with which this one fought was particularly impressive. Wearing a plain red cape over his armor, the fighter was tall, wiry, and appeared to be past his prime. His hair was steel grey, also wiry, and he held up a practice blade and waited, confidence in his stance.

Three young soldiers charged: one with a spear, another with a sword, and a third with a battleaxe. The man ducked with the agility of someone half his age as an arrow flew overhead, and he turned to see a fourth opponent, an archer, off to the side. The spear-wielding opponent chose that moment to stab. He bent low, hoping to catch the old fighter off balance, but the old one was nimble, jumping sideways to dodge the low jab. The sword-wielding soldier took the next swing, but the red-caped fighter blocked with his own and kicked both boots forward to collide with the soldier's knees and tumble him backward. Landing in a sideways roll, the fighter avoided an incoming chop with the axe, then came up with a wide sweep to fling the first soldier's spear wide. The flat of the fighter's blade swatted the other's face, and the spear-bearing soldier dropped to one knee, conceding.

Without pausing, the steely-haired man fought on. He spun to escape the downward path of the axe while simultaneously ducking beneath a sword that whooshed overhead. Red cape flying, he came around to smack the swordsman in the side, and the second fighter took a knee.

An arrow whistled in, slicing through the cape but missing the fighter. With a mighty roar, the old man charged the archer and used the flat of his blade to slap the archer's throat hard enough to make him cough; he, too, took a knee.

Only the axe master remained. The skilled warrior faced the final adversary with a smile. "Now, aren't you the lucky one?"

The axe man lifted his weapon, ready to chop, block, or swing. As if shot from a barrel, the fighter blasted forward, caught the neck of the axe with his sword, and sent it flying before flipping his sword's sharp edge around to tap the younger soldier's neck.

The old fighter tossed the practice blade aside and barged across the sand. "You are all pathetic," he said, exiting the arena.

Boryn shook his head and wound his way toward the two boys sitting in the stands, eyes glued to the ring.

"Amazing!" Boryn greeted them.

"I couldn't even follow that last move!" Calny marveled.

"Laric, a new weapon?" Boryn nodded toward the sheathed two-hander on the wooden bench beside him.

"Yep. I decided I like the feel of it the best," Laric answered then pointed at the fresh cut on his right cheek, the mirror image of his twin's. "But look at this. Nice, huh?"

"How'd that happen?"

"This blockhead," Calny said pointing to Laric, "was swinging the blade around and tripped, so I ended up with this lovely cut."

"Then he came after me while I was asleep."

"You started it."

Laric rolled his eyes. "At least you can tell us apart better now."

Boryn returned his attention to the ring where the outmatched victims of the old swordsman still rested. "Who was that man?"

"You've never seen him before?"

"No . . ."

"That's the sword master of the Empire and personal guard and assistant to the Emperor. He doesn't come into the ring much anymore," Calny said.

Laric continued. "Doesn't need to, he's so much better than everyone else. He used to lead the city guard but gave that up; said the guards were incompetent nitwits."

Boryn grinned, agreeing. But he said, "Seems to have himself on quite a pedestal."

"Those four are the best fighters of all the imperial regiments according to their battalion and weapon type," Laric said jerking his chin toward the arena. "And old gray-hair beat them all single-handedly—easy as that—which gives him full right to brag as far as I'm concerned."

"So what are you up to?" Calny asked.

"We're going to check out the thieves' dens in the deserted side of town? Want to come?"

"Yes!" Laric's response was instant and enthusiastic.

"Why?" Calny's squirm was not.

"No reason. Why not?"

"Sounds absolutely thrilling . . ."

The sun burned high and white in the cloudless sky as the armored horse crested the hill. The rider, despite the slight slump in his broad shoulders, made an imposing sight astride the mighty white warhorse. He was big and wore a blood-red plate trimmed in gold. In the bright light, his bald head shone, and his skin, weathered and dry, was coppered by the sun.

Looking into the distance, he squinted, deepening the lines at the corners of his eyes, and he wiped his nose, permanently misshapen from an old break. The clear, cool day gave for great visibility. The armored man frowned.

A handful of stone and thatched structures huddled around an open space, a disarray of houses, pens, sheds, and barns. On the flag standard in the center, a banner snapped in the breeze, its brown insignia clear against the purple field. There was no sign of the knightly Order of the Bear charged with protecting this village. Instead, it was being plundered by a band of marauding orcs while peasants and animals scurried, frantic in the face of the vicious assault.

An older companion, less grand on a dun-colored pony and wearing dusty white robes, waited beside the man.

"Mindless, chaotic destroyers," mumbled Cadegray, the one on the pony.

"Which? The absent Order, or the witless orcs?" the commander asked with a rueful smile. "I had hoped for a quiet patrol today, but I guess that's not to be," he said as much to himself as to his companion. "What are you thinking, Cadegray? Shall we spill some evil blood this day?" he asked.

"That would be our name, would it not, Ramgis? I'm behind you until the end, as are your men."

Ramgis signaled, and hundreds of armored Blood Knights topped the hill, crimson banners waving and golden armor shining in the bright light. The commander sighed. "Once more it seems the Order of the Blood Knights must come to the aid of the innocents."

Hatred in his eyes, less for the green-skinned horde's brutal assault than for the absent Order, Ramgis mused, "So where do you suppose the Bear might be?"

"As always, more occupied by personal riches than by those who rely on them for help," Cadegray replied.

Ramgis lifted his golden warhammer from behind his back and held it aloft. Its head, larger than one of the orc's huge feet, was solid steel, but Ramgis wielded the huge weapon with ease. He roared and charged down the hill, Cadegray's pony following in a valiant but futile effort to keep pace.

It took only moments for the green-skinned orcs to notice the line of armored knights galloping toward them. The slow but muscular brutes left their pillage and circled the village to fire arrows at the advancing knights.

Ramgis smiled as the first orc charged. He took aim and swung upward, clipping the orc's chin, its face crumpling, and sending it hurtling through the air. He swung down, splattering another's head like a rotten apple. A flash of blue lightning fired by, sending dozens of orc bodies smoking and twitching to the ground. *Thanks for the hand, Cadegray.*

Ramgis heard the war cries of the Blood Knight brigade colliding with the orcish line. He jumped from his horse as a heavily armored beast lumbered toward him. It roared and pounded its chest plate in challenge. Other orcs ringed the pair, facing outward, to keep the Blood Knights at bay.

"You cowards strike at the weak, and now your death comes by our hands," Ramgis shouted defiantly.

"We orcs cut you down," came its growled reply.

Ramgis stormed forward and smashed with the hammer, but the orc rolled aside. The ground broke apart where the hammer struck. Ramgis dodged as the orc's axe made a quick swipe for his unprotected side. He spun, bringing up the hammer to block, and the axe head whistled down. Catching the axe neck with his hammer, Ramgis tore it away then wheeled back toward the now-unarmed opponent. A powerful upward blow slammed the orcish leader's chin, and the beast landed in a heap at the circle's edge.

Ramgis approached the dying orc and crunched his armored boot through its skull. In response, the orcish noose tightened on the Blood Knight commander, but blue lightning fired from Cadegray's hand stopped them in their tracks. The whole bunch was wiped out; the outlying survivors fled. *They won't be causing any more problems.*

As his men helped the villagers bring order to the mayhem, Ramgis moved away and found a place to rest. He lay down on the grass, spent though strangely energized. A cool wind lifted the cloth he had tied to his hammer. *Such a simple fight, and such a grand victory.* A grin creased his aging face.

"So, Ramgis, we've saved the Order of the Bear's village, we've wiped out the orcish band, and not one Blood Knight died," Cadegray observed. "What shall we do next?" he asked with an easy laugh.

"When do we ever have casualties anymore?"

"True. But we haven't done much heavy fighting like we used to, either."

"The calm before the storm, my friend."

"What do you mean?" asked the old healer as he sank down beside his commander.

"Remember back before the Daemon War—it seems so long

ago now—there was an uneasy peace?"

"So?"

"Then strange things began to happen, like the rapi leaving their jungles . . ."

". . . and orcs coming together in larger war bands, attacking villagers until, out of nowhere . . ."

"Exactly. And then the daemons came and almost took everything from us."

"Is that what you think is happening now?" Cadegray's face darkened.

"All the signs are there. And this is my greatest concern: if not for the Alliance and the heroes who defeated the daemon king, we never would have managed."

Cadegray's eyes drifted, looking back to an earlier place in time. "A time of honor when victory was gained through defense by humans, dwarves, and elves together."

"But the Alliance didn't hold." Wearily, Ramgis shook his head. "Even we humans couldn't get along. And the heroes who fought beside us . . . most disappeared long ago. Call me old or crazy, or both," he chuckled, "but I sense we're heading for another war; it's only a matter of time. We killed Tarn, but I'm betting it was not the end of the daemons," he added, sighing deeply and shoulders sagging.

"Every age will have its heroes, just as we were once. If that kind of evil comes our way again, someone will rise up to stop it, Alliance or not. I have to believe that."

"I hope at least to meet the heroes of this age. Maybe even help them in some way."

"Fate is a mysterious thing. Perhaps we'll have the chance to be heroes ourselves again. You never know." Cadegray nudged the old commander on the shoulder.

"Ha! Old men like us? Well, we should move on." Ramgis took a long draught from his waterskin.

"Unless you have a better idea, perhaps we should take this opportunity to go and destroy the Dark elves—rid the daemons of a potential ally," winked Cadegray.

"Always looking for trouble, aren't you, Cadegray? We didn't form the Order of the Blood Knights to *make* trouble, but to stop it. But . . . if stopping the Dark elves will help with a coming war," Ramgis added with a grin, "then I say we go for it." *An excuse for vengeance at last.* Ramgis stood up before helping the healer and friend to his feet.

Prizzadar passed through the doors and entered the sanctuary of the ancient stone temple. Openings filled with colored glass lined the walls, and in every niche stood a marble statue. At the far end was a huge window that told a story of winged daemons, whips and blades in their red-skinned hands, flying above cowering, helpless humans. The shameless elven mage scraped mud from his boot on the base of a statue, and he looked up to rest his eyes on a painting of men and elves fighting together against the winged beasts.

Prizzadar approached the massive stone altar. The seal was there as expected, etched in the surface and glowing yellow with internal energy. He circled the altar, admiring the seal's exquisite craftsmanship, and he hesitated but an instant before twirling his golden staff and swinging it down. Stopping short, he tapped the heart of the mark. The seal shattered; the altar snapped.

"That should do the trick."

A moment of absolute silence was followed by an unearthly crack, and the ground began to rumble. The elven mage dropped his gaze; fractures snaked across the stone floor, widening, and insufferable heat spilled out. Prizzadar sat down and watched as the black fire of hell heaved from the bowels of the earth.

A sudden, loud pop caused him to jump, and his eyes shot upward. The temple itself rent in two, and the ceiling tumbled down, slamming into the floor, shattering the daemon window and showering the mage in glistening fragments. Through shards still clinging to the frame, he could see the ground outside buckling, chasms widening.

He heard a growl, and he turned to meet a daemon's evil grin. Just as pictured in the now ruined glass, the daemon was wild eyed, red eyed, and hairless, its skin the color of dried blood. It had naked-looking, translucent wings like a bat's, fangs, and deadly-sharp horns sprouting from each side of its head.

Prizzadar stared at the beast, unmoved by its fearsome appearance. Behind this one, another daemon, larger still, crawled from the fissure.

"You must be Tarn," the mage observed.

Momentarily, the fire faltered, hissing, and the daemon jumped aside. An enormous clawed hand fired from the abyss. Talons sank into the earth, and the creature being spit up from hell pulled itself higher. First came horns as large as a man, etched top to bottom with daemonic symbols. Then a hungry mouth, saliva dripping from bared fangs. Tattered, black, leathery wings flared up and flapped, lifting the enormous creature, five times the elf's height, from the depths. At its breast glittered a pitch-black gem the size of its extended hand.

"That would be me," the daemon king said, outstretching his wings and holding both arms aloft as hundreds of smaller daemons flew out from below. As varied in size and shape as the humans whose bodies many inhabited, the daemons swarmed and scratched and howled in a peculiar way that only daemons could howl.

"Go start your precious second war," sneered Prizzadar.

"I don't answer to a frail, pathetic elf," Tarn scoffed.

"You aren't answering to me, I assure you, Tarn."

Prizzadar left the cathedral ruins and considered the burning trees all around. "And so Ranlon burns in the flames of revenge."

The five friends shifted into single file when they entered the narrow streets of Old Town. Crooked buildings sculpted their path, bent and weathered like so many broken, old men, windows boarded up, and roofs collapsed. In some, walls had crumbled to be reclaimed beneath a blanket of dirt, rubbish and vines.

A soft wind channeled through the narrow passage, an old sign creaked eerily as it swung to and fro, and a crop of determined weeds sprouted through the paving stones. The afternoon sun cast long, moody shadows, and something about the quiet made whispering seem right.

"If we get robbed, you're paying me back," Calny said under his breath.

Laric held his sword at the ready, Calny, being the more timid of the two, staying very close behind him. "This is definitely creepy," the braver twin offered.

"Where's your spirit of adventure?" Boryn smiled. Wenval followed, continuing his reading and oblivious to the surroundings while Ranton brought up the rear, eyes in constant flight, taking in every detail.

"Judging by these houses, wealthy people used to live here," Boryn observed. "It looks like they left in a hurry. I wonder what happened. Hey, Wenval, what happened here?"

"All I know is some ludicrous fairy tale that drunks like to tell. At least, according to my father, that's where the story came from originally. Of course, since he hears all kinds of outrageous stories from people trying to find answers, could be he was simply trying to scare me away from this place." Wenval looked up and swallowed hard. "Always worked before."

"Mind telling?" Boryn urged.

"Well, they say there's a tavern here called the Blue Pixie. Simply the name is enough to disprove the tale. I mean, what kind of ridiculous name is that?"

"It's simply ridicurus," Ranton said playfully to get a rise out of Wenval.

"That's not a word."

"It is now."

"You can't just arbitrarily make up words," Wenval insisted.

"You do."

"Please continue," Boryn pressed.

"Anyway, they say the tavern was overwhelmingly popular, and the owner expanded the storage cellar, going even deeper, to make room for even more barrels and kegs. Business was great; the Pixie stayed packed.

"Well, then a strange thing happened. One night after closing, they found a body outside; things were far too busy to notice it when the tavern was open. But then it happened again and again, and then there were two bodies, and two more . . ."

Wenval's story held his friends' attention.

"So the owner hired some men to check it out. The next night, thinking they had found the culprit, the hired men grabbed him in the bar, pulled him from his seat and threw him to the floor, weapons drawn. No one knows exactly what happened next, except that the man went on a rampage and slaughtered everyone—not one person left the tavern alive. After that, the wave of death spread throughout this part of town, and people lived in terrible fear. They stopped coming to the Blue Pixie, they left altogether, or . . . ," he let his words hang long, "the legend says they went mad and began killing one another. Not a good place to be. And now . . . it's nothing but a thieves' den."

"How does anyone know what happened that night if no one was left alive?"

"As I said, a fairy tale, a myth, a bedtime story—like olans and archons." Wenval held up one of his books, a drawing of a winged man painted on the cover.

"Oooh, I love that one," Laric exclaimed with childlike glee.

"You said it was a fairy tale, right?" Boryn sought confirmation.

"Of course it is."

"All of it? Look." Boryn pointed ahead. A weather-worn sign with the faded words "The Blue Pixie" creaked in the chill wind. The little color in Wenval's already pale face drained. "Did the story ever mention *who* it was killing them all?"

"Nuh-uh," breathed Wenval as he started walking backwards, fully aware of his surroundings for a change. "But I'm ready to get out of here."

"It *is* getting late," Ranton said while glancing toward the darkening sky. The others agreed and turned to go, eager to make a quick escape. It was nothing that they saw, only something that they sensed.

That something lurked in the shadows nearby, grinning and licking its fangs with a pointed tongue.

The odd collection of friends each took a turn for home: first, Laric and Calny toward the docks where their family lived; then Wenval in the opposite direction toward the library where he lived with his parents; and last, Ranton to the northern gate and out toward Grinfol Forest where he lived with his huntress mother.

Boryn's gaze lingered on the road leading out of the city. Even in the dark, he could read the proud sign on the guard tower:

Dusgoroth, capital and port city of the Empire. Even though he had returned by this same route only a season ago, in some ways he felt as if he had never left, and the five years spent roaming from village to village seemed more dream than reality. He looked toward the Emperor's keep, warm light spilling from the windows. *Most people would kill to live there. And I'd rather die.* He chuckled at the irony.

Shrugging off the melancholy, "Well, home for me, too," and he drifted down the dark and empty street toward the market, a cold sea breeze whipping his hair. Suddenly, the clap of heels on paving stones crossed behind him. He spun, but no one was there. He turned toward the alleyway. A rubbish barrel teetered. Boryn reached into his boot and drew out a dagger. The boy pivoted slowly, looking. Ahead, light and laughter spilled from an inn and gave him comfort; he was drawn toward it, and he felt warmer the closer he came.

"Shouldn't you be home?"

Boryn jumped. A woman, dressed more skimpily than most, leaned against the doorframe. *Must work at the inn. She certainly is pretty.*

"Can you talk?" she teased, but her voice was soft and kindly.

"Oh . . . yeah, er . . . I'm going home now."

"Good. Well, make it safely, will you?"

"Definitely." He started to run and turned the corner and sat down against the wall considering the dagger in his hand. *Really, what would I do with this?* And he laughed in spite of himself.

"Is someone there?"

Boryn heard the barmaid's voice again. Then he heard a sharp scream that echoed through the dark, empty street. A cool gust assisted the chill sliding up his spine. He rose slowly, leaned around the corner to look, then spidered down the wall toward the alley across from the inn. A woman lay on the ground, her clothes torn away, and a dark, thin figure hunched over her.

"Hey!" Boryn blurted, not thinking what he was going to do.

The man, or so it seemed from behind, lifted its face from the woman's open chest and turned a fanged, bloody grin and haunting eyes in Boryn's direction. The creature left the woman's motionless form and moved toward him with long, creeping strides. As it approached, its limbs seemed to grow longer and more powerful, and its eyes looked menacing and red in the dim light. Boryn shook his head to quell his rampant imagination, but he held his ground. The creature came up close, a pointed tongue licking blood from its lips. It latched empty eyes with Boryn's, and Boryn was unable to break away from the stare, frozen with fear.

"I saw you earlier, and you looked like you'd make quite a meal." The thing touched Boryn's face with a clawed hand then traced his jaw line with a sharp finger, digging in, drawing blood. It reaped the blood and licked it off as if it was utterly delicious. Boryn squeezed the dagger still in his hand. *Move!* His arm shot up, the dagger stabbing right into the thing's throat. It growled, tore the dagger free, and tossed it aside. With force sufficient to send Boryn tumbling out of the alleyway, it punched him in the face. Boryn crashed against the wall of the inn, the air blown from his lungs. As the figure walked toward him, the boy struggled up, reaching for the windowsill above him. He pulled himself through and tumbled inside, landing in a heap on the floor.

"Help me!" he gasped just as the powerful arm, veins bulging, shoved its way through the window. The fingers grabbed like pincers until they caught the boy by the leg and began dragging him outside. Customers watched in stunned horror. The boy cried out, breaking the spell. Those nearest the door rushed outside while the ones nearest Boryn unsheathed swords to hack off the red-skinned arm. Boryn felt the clawed hand release and drop him, and he shot up.

"There's a lady outside; she's dying," he pointed toward the alley.

"Daemon!" was heard from outside, and it was now that chaos broke lose, and the massacre began.

"Summon the guards!" someone called.

Boryn rushed out to see victims of the clawed hands; he grabbed a sword from one of them. It was not shaped like a normal sword but instead was flattened and curved. He charged toward the daemon and swung with all his might, but the attack was easily blocked. The daemon backhanded the boy who spun to the ground beside the man whose sword he had taken. *I need another one.* He grabbed the man's second curved blade. *And the sheaths, too.* Boryn flew at the creature once more, ducking below one swipe and blocking another. Seizing an opening, he shoved one blade up into the thing's chest. It roared and stumbled backward, grimaced, then turned and disappeared into the darkness of the alleys.

Boryn looked down at the blades; he felt at ease with these in his hands, almost as if they were an extension of his own body. He had held blades before, but they had never felt quite like these. As townspeople tended the wounded and others prepared for the hasty burials required for the dead, Boryn searched amidst the carnage for the man whose blades he had borrowed. The man survived, so Boryn helped him to the healer's house where he knocked on the door.

An untidy old man answered Boryn's knock. Recognizing the boy instantly, the healer said, "Heavens, Boryn! When did you come back?" and then, "What did you do?" The healer helped the bloodied boy haul the more seriously injured man inside.

"I didn't do anything. I tried to save some lady from a daemon."

"A daemon! That can't be!"

"That's what everyone started screaming."

"And this man tried to save you?"

"He, along with others."

The victim, weak and bleeding, said to the healer, "There are people out there who need you far more than I do. Go help them."

The healer settled the man on a wooden chair and swept his arm across the man's body, and a wave of green light began closing up his wounds. "Time will finish your healing. Stay here and rest, and I will return soon." Then the healer turned kind, old eyes to the boy. He searched the boy's face but asked no questions before hurrying away to aid those in dire need.

"My blades . . . ," the injured man reminded the boy who still held the swords.

Boryn looked from the man to the weapons and shrugged. "I'll return them when I'm through with them." And he hurried out the door, disappearing in the gathered crowd.

Marlok's eyes walked up the narrow stone tower to the one lighted window. *Why must mages always build towers?* He studied the parchment in his hand. On it was a crude map and a drawing labeled "The Morpheic Orb" with a description: "Heavy, round, about the size of a helmet. Luminous purple glow. Use: Cre . . ." The rest was smudged out. *Why would someone want this silly, old stone? So long as I got paid, what do I care?*

The hired thief was counting his easy money already. He spun the grappling hook like a lasso then threw it into the air. It caught on the first window ledge, first try. The man smiled smugly. Next, he wrapped one callused hand with the rope and tugged. The grapple held true. He pulled himself upward, scaling the stone tower with skill, relishing the reward that was going to let him take some time off at last.

From the street below, several women watched. Using his free hand, the tough-looking character pretended to remove a hat with a grand flourish. "Good evening, fair maidens," he waved gallantly.

They tittered and returned the wave.

Maybe now I'll have time for some wenches, too. He reached the first window and set another grapple that he tied to his current line. *Don't want to become one with the street.* The thief continued to climb. He looked up. Only two more windows then he was going to have the time of his life. *No more contracts for awhile.* One more window. *I can see the women already.* A wry grin plastered his wide face. At the upper window, he pulled a dagger from his sleeve and used it to flick open the latch. The window creaked open, and Marlok hoisted himself inside. The room was empty; he saw no one and no glowing purple ball. Instead, a flicker, a slight movement reflected in his dagger blade, caught his eye.

He angled the blade deliberately and glimpsed a man above him, floating near the ceiling. The man had wild carrot-orange hair, wore billowy purple robes, and held a purple stone as big as his head.

"Heavens!" the hovering mage cried, and he lost his concentration and crashed to the floor.

Marlok felt a terrific outward blast as something very heavy and rock solid shattered like glass against his head. And he fell away into darkness.

Marlok bolted upright. *Where's that mage? I won't have him ruin this for me.* There was no sign of the mage, but the orb, strangely unbroken, lay to one side. *I thought that broke on my head.* He reached up, grimacing when his fingers found the painful knot on top.

"Why, it seems I'm moving!" came a startled cry from the mage.

That was weird. Marlok crawled toward the orb. *Ah, yes, the prize.* He picked it up and jumped to his feet.

"Oh, goodness!"

"Where are you?" Marlok spun, dagger drawn. *Wait. . . .* He gazed down in horror to see himself clad in blousy purple, his own grubby brown tunic wadded in a heap on the floor. "What the hell did you do to me?" he muttered, utterly confounded.

"I'm not really sure."

"Wait! No, no, no, no, no—no way . . . ," Marlok groaned.

"It seems that . . . we have become . . . one . . ."

"That's . . . disgusting . . ."

"I must concur. You are a rather filthy individual. Your hair is like a rat's nest," cried the mage as he sat heavily, inspecting himself in the reflecting glass.

"You made my hair orange . . . ," came Marlok's horrified exclamation, catching sight of himself, ". . . and black striped!"

"I certainly did no such thing! Can't you see it's black with orange stripes? And look what you did to my hands! They are covered in calluses! Oh, my beautiful, silky hands!" the mage wailed.

"Shut up . . ."

"My face! A scar! Ahhhh . . . noooo . . . !"

"Why me? Why?"

"It's what you deserve, you trespasser. I'm going to turn you in . . ."

"The guards don't know who I am, so that won't help you."

"I didn't mean turn you in to the authorities. I meant turn you into a squirrel!"

Marlok grimaced. "Let's think about that for a moment."

"What?"

"You can't turn me in to the guards . . . or into a squirrel."

"Well, why ever not?"

"I'm you, and you are me . . ."

"Oh, why yes. That appears to be true."

"You're a moron," Marlok grumbled.

"That's not helping your case, sir."

"I didn't do this. You did."

"I bet it was the orb," Quaswyn, the prissy mage, reasoned.

"And so the orb merges things? Interesting."

"Apparently. But didn't it break?"

Marlok rubbed the goose egg on his head. "Yes."

They stared at the orb, all in one piece, trying to imagine what had happened here.

They faced the tall mirror that stood on carved wooden feet. The figure staring back wore the purple robes of the mage and bore the scars from Marlok's dangerous work. Quaswyn ran their hand through their hair, stripes of black and orange.

"It looks like me . . . sort of," Marlok noted with a shrug.

"I look so . . . dirty! Oh, I simply must wash up." Quaswyn tried to rise.

"You're not going anywhere. Sit back down. Now, you're the mage. You tell me how, exactly, are we going to undo this?"

Quaswyn pondered. "I'm not sure, but this orb was brought to Elemencia from Armorica. It's called the Morpheic Orb after a creature from which its power was replicated. I was still in the process of unlocking its mysteries when you so rudely—"

"I don't care if it can fix my dinner. All I care about is getting out of this mess." Marlok's patience was short.

"If we take it to Armorica, maybe we can find the one who made it, and maybe he can fix . . . this horrid situation," Quaswyn sniffed. "I smell like a wet street dog . . ."

"To Armorica?" Marlok asked doubtfully.

"Do you have a better idea?"

"Pick up the orb, and let's get going."

"I'm not carrying it. It's heavy!" complained Quaswyn. "This is your fault. You should carry it."

Marlok stuffed the too large orb in his too small pack.

"It's too heavy . . . ," Quaswyn squawked about the shared burden.

"I know how to get to Armorica. Just be quiet on the way," Marlok muttered, accepting the distasteful necessity of this journey.

"I will not just shut my mouth!"

"You will if I do," Marlok said with a grin. He clamped their mouth shut, and a series of angry mumbles followed.

It was almost morning, still, quiet, and dark, and the dead were already buried. Seven new mounds lined the edge of the graveyard, six with weapons as their headstones.

Boryn looked at the grave without weapon or marker. *She died because she saw me and was worried. It's my fault. All of these people died because of me.* He closed his eyes. People always died around him: this woman, men from the tavern who had run to help him, even his own mother.

He heard someone coming and knelt behind a gravestone where he would not be seen. Head lowered and long auburn curls shielding her face, a girl entered the gated yard. She cradled a wooden marker against her chest, walked toward the unmarked grave, and fell to her knees. Reverently, she placed the marker on the mound of fresh earth and sobbed, burying her face in cupped hands. Boryn crept from behind the stone and walked toward her. He dropped down, knees on the damp ground. "I'm sorry," he said gently.

The girl stopped crying and turned smoky, lavender eyes toward him. She sat tall and straight as a reed, distant and hardened in her grief.

"Who was she?" Boryn asked.

"My mother. All I had left."

"I promise you, I'll kill that thing."

"You can't be serious!"

"I will kill the daemon with these swords," Boryn said holding out the curved blades.

"You're just going to get yourself killed, just like them," she waved toward the other graves, "and leave this world to those who will weep your passing."

"Only if I die."

"You're just a boy."

"Probably the same age as you." His laugh was soft and light, but confident.

"What do you know about killing daemons? Look what that one did to you already?" The girl touched the wound on Boryn's cheek.

He stood to leave but stopped and turned to her with dead-serious determination. "My name is Boryn, and I'll be back once it's dead. I'll find you then."

The moon dipped into the ocean as Boryn arrived at the still quiet waterfront. A light shone through the window of the shack that clung precariously to the shore. Boryn rapped on the door, and a burly man, hair like fringe around his bald top, opened it.

"Good morning, sir. May I see Calny and Laric?"

"Sure, hold on." The man's tone was gruff but not unkind when he called behind him. "Hey, boys, get out here!"

Boryn heard shuffling from upstairs, and his friends stumbled to the stoop, slightly pudgy faces still creased with sleep and pushing sleepy arms into uncooperative sleeves.

"It's hardly morning, you know," groaned Calny, tipping his head toward the dim blue sky. Laric swayed back and forth, almost teetering over, and rubbed his drowsy eyes with balled fists.

"I need your help," Boryn said, clapping his open palms against their backs, startling them awake.

"With what?"

"Last night, I fought a daemon."

"Yeah, right. And I slayed a dragon," Calny remarked.

"Really! It gave me this," Boryn proudly displayed the war wound, pointing to the gash along his jaw.

Calny's eyes finally opened, and opened wide. "Bloody hel—"

"Yeah, I know."

"How can *we* help with *that*?"

"I'll explain later. Let's get going. Calny, you go get Ranton. Then meet us at the library."

"Why me?" whined Calny.

"Because you run faster than we do," said Boryn, and he dashed off, Laric close behind.

A pattering sound intruded on his dozy sleep. Slightly disoriented to be still seated at the library table with a book for a pillow, Wenval sat up with a start. "Oh, no!" he moaned as he wiped away the puddle of drool with the sleeve of his robe. Relieved to see no damage, he turned his attention to the insistent knocking at the front door. He could see Boryn and Laric leaning against the window, hands cupped around their eyes to see inside. Wenval yawned and stumbled toward the stairs. *It's too early! Maybe I can pretend to be asleep.*

"I see you, Wenval," called Laric as if reading the boy's mind.

Wenval unlocked the door and cracked it open. "The library is closed now."

"You think we want a book?" asked an incredulous Laric.

"Of course not! Why ever would *you* want such an absurd thing?" clucked Wenval. "What happened to your face, Boryn?"

"They said it was a daemon."

"And I suppose you want me to tell you all about it?"

"It would be nice to know since I plan to kill it."

"You want to kill a daemon?" Wenval's eyebrows disappeared behind the curls dangling on his forehead. He opened the door wider, and Laric and Boryn stepped inside.

"Yes."

"I won't help you; you won't be able to kill a daemon."
Wenval was emphatic.

"I made it run away once already. I can kill it."

"That's preposterous."

"Come again, professor?"

"You can't kill a daemon."

"No? Look!" Boryn held out the unusual, flattened blades
smeared with strange, dark blood.

"You struck it?" Wenval's eyes grew wider still as he tried to
imagine how Boryn could have managed such a feat.

"That would explain the blood . . ."

"Where did you get the scimitars?"

"Is that what they're called? Took 'em from an injured man. I
look like a true warrior now, huh? Now, will you help me, or am I
doing this alone?" Boryn waved the blood-caked scimitars.

"Fine, I'll help you. I can't let you go alone."

"Perfect. Just what I had in mind," Boryn smiled.

"Tell me, what did it do, and what did it look like? Describe it all
to me. I need details if we're going to beat this thing."

"The daemon looked like a man but with sharp teeth and a
pointed tongue. It was eating this woman from out of her chest after
stripping her . . . uh . . . Then, he came at me. It had long fingernails,
like claws, that it used to fight, and it talked to me." Boryn searched
his memory to separate reality from imagination.

"Sadly, this isn't a possession."

"A what?"

"A possession. Daemons of this form are said to have taken
over a person's body. The daemon lives in the body and controls it.
Possessing a body weakens the daemon because it uses much of its
power just to control the human. But they do it in order to lure other
victims into deals or death, to drag their souls down."

"So if this isn't a possession, what is it?"

"Sounds like what scholars call a 'soulless.'"

"Explain please," Laric requested.

"When a human sells his soul to a daemon, the daemon removes the human spirit—kicks it out. It leaves the body to survive with only the most animalistic, primordial urges, like lust, and most of all, hunger. If it had been a real daemon, a pure form as it's sometimes called, it probably wouldn't have kept the human form in a fight, especially when injured."

Fleetingly, Boryn remembered his odd sense that the creature was changing as it approached him.

Wenval continued. "A real daemon would have *released*, which means transformed into its powerful daemonic form."

"Released?"

"From what I've read, true daemons look much like humans most of the time. But when they get angry or hurt or just want to be at their most powerful, they change to a daemonic form—wings, terrible horns, red skin. Never seen one. Hope I never do."

"That wasn't it."

"Thus, I would venture to guess that what you saw was a young soulless, weak enough that you had a chance. A mature soulless would have been like fighting an intelligent bear; there's no way a boy could have taken it on. But here's the bigger problem. If there are soullesses around, real daemons can't be far behind, so it leaves open the possibility that a real daemon is in or around Dusgoroth."

"That's a happy thought," Laric interjected.

"Who knows? Could be it's the creature from the Blue Pixie legend," Wenval added lightly. "The sooner we destroy this thing the better, because a soulless will become stronger over time. And as the soulless grows stronger, it becomes more and more like a pure daemon."

"You lost me on all that," Laric looked from Wenval to Boryn, frowning.

"Here's the point: baby soulless? Kill it before it grows up," stated Wenval as simply as possible.

"How do we kill it?"

"First we have to find it. Then we outnumber it."

Boryn jumped in. "Let me get this straight. Some guy sold his soul to a daemon, and this 'soulless' that I fought—it's what's left of the man?"

"That, or a true daemon somehow tricked you. There's one more possibility. Worst case, the man could have been cursed by a daemonic artifact."

"And that turned him into a daemon?"

"No. Humans cannot become daemons through physical means. They are segmented forms."

"Huh?"

"A person's humanity is completely separate from any daemonic energy which could eventually destroy that person. In other words, the daemon destroys the man's humanity, and the soulless is what's leftover. The garbage if you will. And about the artifact . . ."

The door crashed open, and they turned to see Calny standing in the doorway bent double, catching his breath. Ranton stood behind him barely breathing hard and a grin on his face.

"Bloody hunters run too much," panted Calny.

"See? I'm not the only one getting tired of your running!" Wenval pointed out.

"So, where do we start?" Boryn wanted to know.

"Let's hit the Blue Pixie first," Wenval suggested.

"Wait! We need a name," said Laric.

"He's right, you know," Wenval agreed. "In the days of the Daemon War, there was an unwritten rule that all the great daemon hunting groups had titles."

"Seems a bit silly to me, but hey, whatever you say. So what shall we call ourselves?" asked Boryn.

"I'm thinking 'The Holy Light,'" announced Laric, hands on hips and bowing from the waist in tribute to his own brilliant idea.

"No. That sounds like a storybook."

"How about 'The Doomed'?" groaned Calny, less than intrigued by this whole notion.

Thinking aloud, Boryn suggested, "The Shadow Crusaders?"

"Nice."

"It's got my vote," Ranton chimed.

"I liked my idea better," Laric protested.

"Sounds like you lose, brother."

"Shadow Crusaders, let's go get that daemon, er, soulless," announced Boryn.

The Shadow Crusaders left the library toward Old Town. The sun, still low in the morning sky, was just beginning to warm the air. Boryn looked at the creaky, wooden sign with its peeling picture of a trim, blue pixie. Dramatically, he kicked open the door, blades drawn.

He peered inside the dusky tavern, his eyes gradually adjusting to the dimness. A wall of spider webs blocked the way. He sliced through to see broken stools and overturned tables, edges softened by accumulated dust.

Laric turned to his twin, "Calny, you might not want to come in."

"Why not?"

"Lots of spiders and crawlies."

Calny sneezed and turned to wait outside, eager to comply. "Don't do anything stupid in there."

"Don't worry about me, little brother."

"I'm the same size as you, moron."

"Not if you count muscles," Laric said with a grin. "Watch this." He hoisted his two-hander upward but *thwanged* the blade into a crossbeam overhead.

Calny rolled his eyes. "Bigger muscles. Smaller brain."

Laric pried the sword free.

Calny had little interest in waiting outside alone and left for home, but Boryn, Wenval, Ranton, and Laric stepped deeper into the space. Remnants of life—mugs on shelves, bottles stacked in the corner, dishtowels rotting on the bar left hurriedly and long untouched—lay beneath a layer of dust. Boryn scuffed his boot across the wooden floor to bare evidence of blood spilled long ago. A spider web grabbed at Boryn's face, startling him, and he batted it away as he moved behind the bar. On the floor, a shattered trapdoor, split at the hinges, lay to the side, a dark, yawning hole beside it. Boryn leaned over, looked down, and without hesitation, began to climb down the shaft on wooden steps that creaked with every footfall. The air felt cold and damp as he descended into the darkness. He reached the bottom, Wenval and Laric following. Boryn heard mumbling behind him, and his swords began to glow. He turned toward Wenval who smiled.

"I love it when I have an excuse to use entertaining spells."

Impressed by his friend's handiwork, Boryn turned back toward the cellar now bathed in a white light. The space was hall-like and stretched far beyond the reach of the glowing blades. Wooden kegs stacked three and four high lined the walls, each painted with a code to identify its contents. The floor was cold, hardpacked earth beneath his feet. He found a loose pebble and kicked it, looking for the end of the space, but the stone clattered into darkness until it tumbled to a natural halt.

A creak. Just beyond the light's halo. Boryn froze, willing his eyes to see what was there. Then he heard a sound that made his blood run cold; a soft cackle echoed from deep within the chamber. It grew louder, drawing nearer. Two red eyes pierced the darkness, and shiny, wet fangs glinted in the light of the blade.

"Boryn?"

"It's right in front of us," the tall boy whispered.

"What?" Laric asked.

"I don't see anything, either," Wenval said.

"Staring right at me!"

"Watch. . . . *Fyr!*" cried Wenval, launching a fireball down the hallway. The fireball lit up the cavern. Boryn watched the eyes dissipate with the shadows and saw at the far end a rotted, wooden door hanging by a single hinge. With only a hint of hesitation, Boryn and Wenval approached the opening. At Boryn's touch, the hinge let go and the door clattered to the floor. Extending a glowing blade ahead of them, they looked inside. Nothing. Boryn stepped through the doorway, his foot making contact with the tread of another set of stairs. He took one step down. Something clawed and cold grabbed hold of his ankle.

"Staring in the mirror isn't going to fix it," growled Marlok. "Come on. We almost made it out the door earlier."

"Maybe if I try this," said the mage as he rubbed an ointment over the nasty scar.

"So what's your name?" asked one half of the fused being of the other.

"Oh, how rude of me! I beg your pardon. My name's Quaswyn. And yours?"

"Marlok . . ."

"Pleasure."

"Those can kill, you know," Marlok said gesturing toward the mirror.

"Mirrors?"

"Truth. I killed a man with one once. Got him to stare into it 'til he starved," chuckled Marlok.

"You are one repulsive human being," Quaswyn crowed.

"Being a sell-sword's kept me fed; plus, the man wasn't exactly a sterling example of humanity. Why else would someone pay to have him murd . . . um . . . dispensed?"

"You still kill for money?" Quaswyn asked with disgust.

"I steal as well."

"Rogue."

Marlok replied, "You're just mad that you have a scar on your face."

"It's your fault. Get rid of it," Quaswyn whined.

Marlok found his bag, pulled out a small, yellow container, and squeezed a dab of greenish paste on their finger. He rubbed the masking paste on the scar. "There. Gone. So can we go now?"

"Oh, my!" exclaimed Quaswyn with genuine delight. "You absolutely must show me how to make that. It's incredible!" he said straining toward the mirror for a second look.

"We're leaving!" Marlok tore them away and moved toward the door.

"Fine . . ."

"First, we need to head toward the mountains—"

"And which mountains would those be?"

"The Draeor Mountains, of course. We're going to Armorica, remember?"

"But that's such a long walk . . ."

"Well, I don't have the coin for a horse. How about you?"

"Why, yes," said Quaswyn, happily withdrawing a silken coin purse from beneath their robe.

Marlok's eyes ignited with anticipation, but then, he groaned, "It's . . . purple!" at the sight of the offending object.

"And?"

"We are going to use my bag," Marlok said as he dumped the coins into his shabby leather one. "And this is not nearly enough for a horse."

"No taste whatsoever."

"This is never going to work. Obviously, one of us has to be in charge," announced Marlok.

"My pleasure. Thank you."

"I didn't mean you, you bloody fool. I'm the one who knows the way." Marlok leaned out the window where the grappling line waited. He smiled and raised a leg to climb out.

"What are you doing?"

Marlok hurdled out the window, grabbing the rope with one hand, Quaswyn screeching the whole way down. Marlok tightened his grip to slow their descent as they neared the street, landing softly on the cobblestones, grinning.

"You, you . . . knave!"

"Shh. They'll think we are crazy." Then Marlok smiled and whistled jovially as they headed west toward Armorica.

First, he felt the cold, then the tight grip on his wrists, some force holding him up. He swam back to consciousness to find himself shackled to a wall. A lone candle flickered on a table, spitting pungent black smoke into the airless stone cell. Laric, unconscious with a gash across the side of his head, and Wenval, his feet jiggling, lost in thought, hung on the wall opposite.

"Wenval!" Boryn's whisper bounced off the hard walls.

"Lower your voice. We want whatever that creature was to be gone for as long as possible."

"Did you get a look at it?"

"No, but there's more than one, and you were right about something moving at the other end. They knew we were coming and caught us perfectly off guard."

"All I remember was being grabbed by the ankle."

"Hmm . . . What!" Laric startled awake, exclaiming loud enough for their captors to hear.

"Well, that should end our planning time." Wenval snapped his fingers. "*Is,*" he said, and the shackles blasted apart. He then snapped with both hands pointed toward Laric and Boryn while repeating the word, and their chains fell away.

"Where's Ranton?"

"That's what I was trying to figure out."

Breathlessly quiet, Boryn, Laric, and Wenval stood beside the door and waited. Scrambling sounds outside drew closer.

"First, we need to find our weapons. Then we will find Ranton."

Just then the door flew into the room, and Boryn barely dodged out of the way before it slammed against the cell wall behind him.

"I found our weapons." Boryn pointed toward the two creatures standing in the doorway, one holding his scimitars and the other holding Laric's two-hander.

"Soulless?" Boryn, under his breath, asked Wenval.

"Best guess, yes."

"Glad you could join us," said one of the creatures, its voice silky smooth. "We were about to make dinner."

The companion added, "Sadly, your friend won't be joining us. He's a bit tied up." Both of them cackled.

"Where are the others?" Wenval had noticed that neither of these matched what Boryn had described.

"Who said you could ask questions?" challenged one soulless as it hurled a scimitar toward Wenval's head.

Wenval closed his eyes, ready for quick death, but heard a clap instead. He opened his eyes to see Boryn standing in front of him, the scimitar hilt in hand.

"Let's get them." Boryn shot forward and swung upward. The soulless holding his other scimitar blocked as the one with the two-hander took a swing at the boy's open back. Boryn exploded forward, out of the longsword's reach, and forced the blocking scimitar back against the wielder's chest. On instinct, Boryn ducked as the blade shot overhead and the second blade zoomed in from the opposite direction. The blades of the soulless creatures collided, ricocheting with tremendous force, and giving Boryn the chance to roll out of the way. The daemonic beasts roared. The boy sprang, stabbing upward through the ribcage of one, piercing its heart. It let out a horrendous bawl and fell backward while Boryn spun in a circle with

54

a backhanded slice through the other's neck. The second corpse splashed into a puddle of blood on the cavern floor.

"Bravo!" came an eerily calm voice. Boryn looked the length of the hallway and recognized the creature as the one he had fought in the alley, although its skin was clearly red now. It stood in front of a roaring fire, and behind it, over the fire, Ranton was suspended like a rag doll.

"You know, I actually didn't think you would beat those two," the daemon said. It lifted a clawed hand, enjoying the giant shadow it made on the wall. "A shame, though. Fools who sell their souls are hard to come by nowadays."

"Boryn, this isn't a soulless," Wenval whispered. "You never mentioned the eyes."

"Yeah, they were red."

"Important detail. Red eyes? Daemon. Real daemon."

"How right you are, lad! I'm the real deal. Flesh and blood daemon at your service, for a price of course. What can I do for you? I have humans offering up their souls for the most trivial of reasons. Like that one?" he pointed to a decomposing corpse. "He wanted his wife to survive some deadly disease. And over there? He wanted enough money to keep his family fed. Ah, humans are pathetic creatures. Like animals, acting on instincts, foolish really," the daemon rambled.

"You're a beast yourself," said Wenval. "You aren't even strong enough to give yourself a human appearance—just a pretender that can't even fool a child."

"You humans know nothing of daemonology. Sadly, you won't have the chance to learn."

Boryn recovered his second scimitar. "If we humans are so lowly, wouldn't it make your kind lower still to have been beaten by us in the Daemon War?"

"You have no idea what the Daemon War even was, boy." The daemon continued, "But fear not, for soon you shall learn. Soon the whole world will know!"

"Let's get him."

"No, no, no," tsked the daemon, shaking its head. "You and me alone. Your friends have their own opponents to deal with," the daemon said as two more soullesses emerged from the shadows. "Kill those two," the leader inclined its head toward the boys in back. "The one in front is mine."

Following the command, the two soullesses rushed Wenval and Laric. With a cocky grin, Boryn stepped in their path and swung but felt his blades strike something hard. Before him stood that daemonic thing, its claw pressed against the intersection of the blades. The underlings ran by and dragged Wenval and Laric kicking and screaming into an adjoining chamber.

"Your fight is with me, Mhinbron," it said with a grin.

"How do you know my name?"

"If you're lucky, you'll die before it matters."

"Sorry. Not happening."

Xandon followed the narrow stairs from the throne room to the volcanic cavern below, a hall containing the remains of honored Flame elven ancestors. The only light in the oppressively black space came from the scar on Xandon's eye and from the eternal flames placed upon each crypt and before every grave.

Lowering himself to a stone bench in front of one vault, the Flame king fanned his scarlet velvet cloak. It was exquisitely tailored to fit his long, lean body and stitched with white flames running up from the bottom where it was cut like so many banners. Impassively, he fingered the hem, darkened where it had dragged the ground.

"Your Highness?" came a voice from behind. A golden-armored Flame elf stepped into the Hall of the Eternal Flame.

"Lentz, how long have you been my personal guard?"

"Seventy-five glorious years, sir!"

"And I hope it will be one hundred more." Xandon paused, "Am I a poor king because I don't despise the other races for what they did to us?"

"In my opinion, sir, no. I think it very smart of you to avoid war despite what most of our kin desire. War would only cause our fire to burn out," the levelheaded guardian advised.

"What of Prizzadar? Our archmage . . ."

"Prizzadar, you ask? The one who pretends to be your advisor? I wouldn't trust him within light's reach of you, my king."

"Call me 'king,' 'my lord,' or 'sire' one more time, and you, sir, shall be reassigned as Prizzadar's personal messenger," Xandon laughed then turned serious. "This . . . graveyard is the result of my father's rash actions, his lust for power and war. These tombs represent only a small fraction of our bloodline lost in that war alongside the daemons; think of the hundreds of soldiers killed. I ask you, what did we gain by joining the daemons?" Xandon scanned the cavernous, crypt-filled hall, a burdened expression never leaving his face.

"An ally against our former brethren and a chance to avenge our brutal treatment. Flame elves are raised from birth hearing sordid tales about our persecution. We are never told the details, only the cruelties dealt upon us. What do you expect them to believe?" Lentz asked.

"I wish they would listen to reason rather than stories," Xandon muttered.

"You expect far too much of society, Xandon. A compelling speaker could even convince us that the Race of Stone isn't extinct." They both laughed at the preposterous suggestion.

"It's a shame Prizzadar's such a captivating speaker."

"Indeed."

"If you put your mind to it, King Xandon, all would follow you and trust you over him, should it come to that."

"Well," Xandon said as he moved to rise and end the conversation on a hopeful note, "I'm sure that whatever Prizzadar is up to will help us all in some way."

"That, my lord, is a wish that's far too hopeful."

"Not if I stay a few plays ahead of him. Either way, Prizzadar's plan is sure to become very . . . interesting."

Boryn stabbed upward and watched as the daemon dodged with unearthly speed. Claws shot out, and Boryn retreated, but still he felt the daemon's claws rake his chest. He yelped and fell to his knees but instantly rolled aside as the adversary slashed again with the deadly claws, scarring the cavern floor instead of rupturing the boy's head. Boryn popped to his feet with a fast horizontal slice, nicking the daemon's arm but taking a backhand to the face that sent him reeling into the wall.

The daemon laughed. "I'm going to cut you apart just like that bar whore," and then it expelled air and deliberately licked its fangs.

Boryn remembered the woman waving goodbye. He heard her scream and saw her corpse. Then there was the girl, her eyes overflowing with sadness and despair, staring at the wooden marker she had made and taken to the grave. Fire burned through his body, and he brought up his sword to block the incoming, taloned hand.

Face bloodied and bruised, Boryn looked into the creature's dark red eyes, finding nothing there. "The thing being butchered here is you," he raged. With astonishing speed and immense purpose, he ducked beneath a wild swing of claws and hauled back to prepare for a strike. In one brazen maneuver, he sliced with both scimitars to sever first the creature's legs and then its arms, ending with his blades crossed in an X at the thing's throat, capturing it under the chin in midair.

"Burn in hell." In a final, willful gesture, Boryn brought the blades across, cleanly removing the daemon's head and releasing an unearthly screech that echoed through the cavern.

Boryn hurried to the adjoining chamber where lay Wenval and Laric's victims, the two fallen soullesses, one cleaved in two and the other perforated with smoking holes. The hint of a smile crossed Boryn's face, and he sat down, chest still pounding. *I did it!* He admired the scimitar blades then wiped his face against his shoulder to remove the blood. He lifted his shirt; nasty gashes, more painful than penetrating, striped his stomach.

Before the boys had time to catch their breath, they heard a voice. "If you don't mind, untying me would be nice," Ranton called from around the corner, flames licking the soles of his boots.

"So the boy killed it . . ."

"So it appears."

The creature with blood-red eyes beheld the sight before him: the monks of this holy place, corpses now, torn and hardly recognizable, macabre under any circumstances but especially so enclosed by the austere beauty of the monastery. "There's nothing more thrilling than slaying those who think they're safe."

Despite the human form, this cruel creature was clearly a daemon. He kicked one body, muscles bulging beneath the fitted white cloak of a daemon general, sending the bloated corpse into the wall with a disgusting splat.

"Brother, tell me, who is this boy who killed my subordinate?" the general asked in a high-pitched, nasal voice.

"A Mhinbron. I'm sure you remember that name, Tharrus. Perhaps we should end him."

"I'd much rather waste his entire city," said Tharrus with a dark smile.

"But where to find an army . . . ," sighed the brother.

"I can handle that request. No need to fret," Tharrus chuckled.

The daemon general snapped his fingers, and roars erupted from outside the monastery walls.

The room was spartan: a single bed, a bookshelf, and a rickety wooden stool. Boryn sat up and leaned against the familiar planked wall. *Hard to imagine I was born here.* He heard a knock, and a white-robed man with rowdy, white hair and beard entered the small room.

"Scruffy!" cried Boryn with clear affection.

"When are you going to get past that nickname?" chided the healer.

"I rather like it. I think it's yours forever."

"You really took a beating this time," said the healer, concern in his tone.

"Yeah, I know," said Boryn inspecting the bandage wrapping his middle.

"Oh, while you were out, I took care of that frightful slice across your face, too."

Boryn's fingers felt the almost-healed skin at his jaw line.

"But tell me, what foolishness possessed you to take on a daemon?"

"A girl," he said with a dumb grin and a quick flush.

"Why does this not surprise me?"

Boryn laughed. "It was for revenge as well, so it all works out in the end."

"Oh, really? And how is that?"

Boryn gazed out the grimy window, miles away.

"I need to ask you a question," said the healer, summoning the boy back to the present. "Where are you staying these days?"

Boryn looked surprised. "What does that have to do with anything?"

"Will you go back?"

"Nope."

"Five years is a long time to be gone. I wish I could say things have changed at the Emperor's keep, but sadly, nothing has. How long have you been back in Dusgoroth?"

"A season, maybe two. Does it matter?"

"So where are you sleeping?"

"I sleep under the stalls in the market."

"That's horrible."

"Nah. I gather all the cloth covers, pile them up. Makes a fine bed. Of course, before market opens I get a rather rude awakening if I'm not up early. But it's better than breaking into inns at night to sleep."

"I had something better arranged for you when you left."

Boryn shrugged. "I guess I had to find my own way."

"Willful." The old healer said it fondly.

Boryn smiled crookedly and scratched his head.

"By the looks of your eyes, you aren't sleeping much, period. Your living arrangements can't be comfortable. Is that what's bothering you?"

"No, it's not that. But I've had a strange feeling the last few days . . . ," Boryn tried to explain, ". . . I can't put my finger on it. Like something is wrong, or really different, or both."

"Probably just lack of sleep. You should be better now; your wounds were not as bad as they looked, and you've had a little rest. But promise me you'll come back here to sleep tonight; you need more."

"If you say so," said Boryn as he rose from the bed, put on a new black tunic Scruffy had laid out for him, and grabbed his satchel. He sheathed the two iron scimitars he now considered his own and ran out the door, the afternoon sun on his back. *Aw, I slept a whole day away! Maybe she's at the graveyard.*

Despite the lingering catch in his side, Boryn ran through the streets. He made the turn toward the northern gate but was surprised to find it closed and the portcullis lowered. *Great . . . I guess they've heard about the daemons.* A horrifying bellow from outside the walls and afterward a shrill scream sent him hurrying up the stairs. He topped the wall, jumped across to his favorite tree, and smelled it before he saw it. *Why is a bear so close to town?*

He followed the line of the animal's gaze where he saw the girl from the graveyard backed against the wall. A huge black bear stood on its hind legs and roared viciously. It never crossed Boryn's mind to stop and think before he leapt from the tree. He hit the ground rolling, ending his tumble upright with blade extended.

"Oy!" Boryn called, caution not his strong suit. The beast turned toward him and charged. Boryn jumped sideways but a claw clipped his shoulder and sent him spinning. He slammed hard against a tree trunk but regained his footing swiftly. While Boryn clambered up the tree, the bear grabbed the trunk and shook mightily. Holding tight, the boy crawled out on a limb so that he was above the bear then pounced onto its back, stabbing down between its shoulder blades.

The beast dropped and rolled, but Boryn jumped away before being crushed under its weight. On the rebound, Boryn heaved his scimitar deep into the animal's chest then turned to the girl he hoped to save. The enraged beast reared. A clawed paw plowed into Boryn's back and sent him into the dirt. Shaking his head to clear it, he heard the hiss of an arrow and felt a spurt of hot blood. A pointed shaft had impaled the animal's eye.

Boryn's head snapped toward the forest. The shack was there that Ranton shared with his mother, and in front of it, the young bowman planted his feet, set his square jaw, and took aim again. Boryn grabbed the girl's hand and led her running toward the croft nestled in the wood's edge. Ranton's shot hit its mark, but the bear barely slowed.

Boryn pulled the girl faster, her soft shoes skidding on the dirt. Ranton locked eyes on the target and calmly discharged the fatal strike; the arrow pierced the bear's skull, and it collapsed in a heap.

Ranton threw his arm around his friend's shoulder. "We can call it even now; you saved me from being dinner, and I've just saved you from the same."

"I'll take that deal."

"And who is this?"

In unison, Boryn and Ranton turned to the auburn-haired girl.

"I'm Julia," she said, shaking both of their hands and smiling. Her face was enchanting, her smoky, lavender eyes mysterious and catlike.

Ranton called toward the house. "Hey, mother, come see the bear that almost killed Boryn."

A tall, slender woman wearing a loose cloth shirt and short pants came out of the cozy cabin.

"Where is your usual hunting outfit?" Boryn asked with friendly familiarity.

"I'm done for the day." She welcomed Julia to her home then turned to Ranton. "Help me butcher and dress the bear. We need to make the best use of it we can."

"I'll help," Boryn offered, eager to appear the conquering hero. But Boryn didn't have the slightest idea what to do with the beast, and Ranton and his mother knew it. So Ranton swatted Boryn on the back of the head and told him to take the girl inside and keep her company until the task was done. Boryn's smile gave away his delight at the unexpected turn of events.

It occurred to Ranton while walking away to call back to Julia, "I'm Ranton, by the way, and your would-be savior is Boryn."

Once inside, Julia moved toward the window and watched, oddly fascinated by the task going on outside. Boryn sat back, unsure how to make the most of this opportunity and even less sure how to simply make small talk. Finally, Ranton returned to the house. "It's getting late," he said. "Do you want to stay here for the night?"

Boryn considered for a moment and, more interested in staying with Julia than honoring his promise to Scruffy, he said, "The gates were closed when I left. I guess word of last night's attack is out. So, seeing as our choices are in here or out there with the wolves and his furry friends, I'd go for here," laughed Boryn.

"Agreed," said the girl nodding thanks toward Ranton.

Ranton and Julia exchanged a look which Boryn caught. Boryn sidled toward his friend and spoke in a muffled voice, "Back off; she's mine."

Ranton nailed him with an irritated look. "Boryn and I will sleep down here. Julia, you can take my room or stay down here with us if you don't like it. Let me show you where it is." Bending to clear the ceiling, Ranton led her up the tiny stairway to the two rooms where he and his mother slept.

Boryn, meanwhile, rummaged for something to eat. He found a round loaf of dark, crusty bread and broke off a piece, eagerly stuffing it in his mouth. "I'm starving," he said as Ranton returned. Boryn sat down on the floor near the fire where several thick hides were piled.

"Most people ask before they take other people's food."

"So I'm a thief. Can't help myself," Boryn said with an impish grin, lobbing a chunk toward Ranton.

"What happened?" Ranton asked. He used the bow he was cleaning to point to the dried blood on Boryn's shoulder. Craning his neck to get a look it, Boryn muttered, "That would be the bear. What about your bow? Where did you get it?" Boryn wanted to know as he tucked one hide underneath his head and pulled another on top and lay back.

Ranton carried the bow across the room and hung it on a peg

next to his mother's. "My father left it for me. At least that's what my mother said."

"Where is he?"

"Don't know. Never met him."

Could be worse. You could know him and despise him. Boryn closed his eyes.

Ranton continued, "But I'm sure I will one day." He sat down beside Boryn. Playfully, Ranton yanked away the hide rolled under Boryn's head, spread it across himself and settled down for sleep.

Quaswyn threw himself face down across the top of a large, smooth boulder. He panted dramatically then flipped face up, arms outstretched. "I can't go another step. How much farther?" the mage asked while looking down the mountainside at all the ground they had covered.

"Shouldn't be too far," Marlok promised as he forced them to their feet and marched. "Keep your eyes open for a cave."

"There's one over there," Quaswyn pointed. "But why would we want to find a cave?"

"It's that or dragons. Take your pick."

Quaswyn shuddered. The gloomy entrance yawned. "There's no way I'm going in there!"

Marlok stopped, hands on hips. "Look, there are only two ways to Armorica. One is through the caves; the other is going over the mountains through draconic lands."

"It's dark and dank, and well, there are probably bats and all sorts of nasty vermin in there."

"You forgot about the unusually large spiders," Marlok egged.

"I've had it. That's it. We are going home." Quaswyn felt peevish and turned to leave.

"Waaaait a minute. We are going . . . to fix . . . this ridiculous . . . situation, remember? And now, how about making yourself useful. Surely you know some kind of spell to give us light," Marlok said as if speaking to a child.

"Do you have any idea how hard it is to cast a spell when I have only half of the control?" Quaswyn complained.

"If I gave you all of it, you'd have sprinted off long ago."

"I won't. I promise. Give me a chance!"

"Fine."

Quaswyn fumbled around inside their robe then mumbled. A ball of light grew in his hand. "Happy?"

"Just kidding. We don't need it," said Marlok as he ran toward the mouth of the cave, tossing the lightball behind them and plunging into the darkness.

"Ah, nooooo!" Quaswyn hollered in despair, struggling to stop the forward charge.

Marlok's strength prevailed, and before they knew it, they were deep within the cavern, so deep that daylight was no longer visible, and they stood in total darkness.

"You villain! Now we are completely lost!" Quaswyn spluttered.

"Pipe down and give me some time!"

"We're going to die! Starve! Be bitten by poisonous bugs! Be lost forever!" Quaswyn stomped his foot like an impatient tot. Marlok shut their eyes tightly and reopened them. Slowly, the hollow in which they stood became dimly visible in shades of blue.

"Oh, my!" said Quaswyn, seeing through new eyes.

"Thankfully, our unfortunate union did not damage my glyphs," Marlok replied with growing confidence. He pushed up their sleeve to show a glowing symbol on their forearm.

"You tattooed us?

"Think of it this way: without this mark we'd be lost forever," Marlok remarked.

Quaswyn straightened himself, curious. "What is this vision?"

"The glyph enhances the eye's ability to see in darkness. At first, we'll only be able to see the lightest objects. But in time, we'll see more."

"It's rather cold and spooky."

"Everything will be shades of blue. That's how it works."

"I think I see something . . . it's a . . . *spider!*" screeched Quaswyn. He stumbled backward, pointing.

Marlok bent toward the place where the finger pointed to see a tiny, white spider. Marlok's face registered disgust.

"Where there is one, there are hundreds," Quaswyn justified.

"Shut up until our eyes adjust and you can really see."

Ranlon burned, and the last of the Wood elven groves were destroyed. Tarn watched from above, hovering over the forest, a smile creasing his evil face. Task finished, the daemon king returned to the earth to move on to the bigger job. First, he stilled the flames so that they no longer consumed but only burned, an ongoing inferno to herald his presence. Then, he stretched his tattered wings and tensed his powerful red-skinned arms. He extended one hand toward the abyss from which he had come and raised his long arm toward the sky. At this command, a massive fortress followed, rising from out of the earth with a thunderous rumble.

Tarn's citadel, a mighty, walled fortress of jagged black steel, pitched up from the depths of Ranlon and swallowed the remnants of the old temple. Along with it, daemons poured out in staggering numbers. Waves of heat rose, filling the sky with soot and black smoke, and boiling magma poured into the moat. Tarn breathed in deeply, savoring the sulphurous smell of destruction.

"The new fortress of the daemons," Tarn announced with pride and entered his presence chamber.

It was huge and echoey, filled with distinctive daemon howls, and lit by one soaring window. The king ascended the throne, spotlighted under an upturned bowl of stained glass in the ceiling, patterned with red and blue flames.

The throng massed at Tarn's feet, and he began his address. "Welcome back to Armorica, my friends. Our time for vengeance is at hand. The races of the Alliance will be no more, and the first to fall shall be the Moon elves. Daemons, go and rip them apart." Screeches and cheers reverberated across the Forest of Ranlon, a crushingly fearful sound to any unlucky enough to hear it.

Tarn turned away from the dispatched horde, but a blue imp flittered like a gnat near his face. Giggling madly and circling the giant horns, it awaited orders.

When none were forthcoming, it spoke. "My lord?" Its tiny head twitched from side to side.

"Instruct the generals by order of Tarn, Daemon King, to return to Ranlon at once."

"Yes, sire," snickered the imp as it took flight, following the river now flowing with lava, through rings of fire that burned without consuming, and disappeared into the distance.

Boryn yawned, stretched, and sat up. Across the room, Ranton's mother took her bow from its peg, preparing to leave. He grinned stupidly, appreciating the woman's taut leather jerkin and leggings. Without noticing the boy's admiring gaze, she walked out the door, quietly closing it behind her. *Oh, the joys of waking early!* He felt a swat on the back of his head and turned to see Ranton awake as well.

"No."

"You know I wouldn't," said Boryn.

"You know you *couldn't*," laughed Ranton.

"I have some, uh, skills."

Ranton shook his head groaning. "Dreamer."

"What are we going to eat?" Boryn asked.

"Don't know. Do you always worry about food?"

"Well, if I'm hungry then what would you like me to think about? What have you dragged in lately?" Boryn asked.

"Other than a bear? There might be some venison left." Ranton moved toward the corner that served as a kitchen and began shuffling through the cupboard. "You just had to finish off that bread, huh?"

"Hey, I'm a wounded hero!" Boryn exaggerated boldly. "It soothed a weary spirit!"

"Here's some jerky. Try it." Ranton peeled away a hunk of the dried meat and tore it in two. He tossed half to Boryn and bit into his own. "We used hot spices on this one. What do you think?"

"Nice! You know me too well."

"Enjoy it while it lasts. Those spices are expensive."

"Since when have you worried about that? I thought game sold well at market," Boryn said between mouthfuls.

"It always has, but coin is getting tight nowadays. Selling isn't the problem, finding the game to sell is. It's the strangest thing. The deer and boar seem to have vanished from the forest; only the scavengers are left, and the bears and wolves. Even the birds are gone for the most part."

Boryn listened carefully. "Has this been going on long?"

"I don't know exactly, but long enough. We've talked to some of the other hunters, and they are noticing the same thing."

"That must be why that bear was so close to the city; he was looking for food, too."

The stairs creaked behind them, and the boys turned to see Julia creeping down.

"Morning!" Boryn said happily.

"Hello." It was almost a whisper. "I need to go home now. Ranton," she said as she came up behind the young hunter, draping her arms across his shoulders, "will you go with me and protect me?"

"Uh . . . yeah, sure," he stammered. He took a quick look toward his friend.

"I'm leaving, too," Boryn bristled then added, "and I'll come up with some money to help you."

Ranton smiled, guessing what Boryn meant. "Thanks, Boryn. My mother will be grateful. Oh, by the way, Wenval wants us to meet him at the Pixie around midday."

"I'll see you then," Boryn slung his satchel across his chest and left ahead of Julia.

By the time Boryn reached the city, the portcullis had been raised. He hurried through the gate toward the marketplace busy with buyers, sellers, and traders. Finding a viewing perch atop a sloped, tile roof, he sat back, wondering what Wenval had up his sleeve. He looked at the sky. Only half the morning was gone; there was time to waste.

Boryn reached into his bag for the black leather mask and strapped it on. *Who first?* He noticed a richly attired man harassing a merchant, the man's fat, blotchy face ugly against his blue, silken robe. The man swatted the poor merchant with his laden pouch, pocketed the trinket he had selected, and left without paying.

Boryn capered across the rooftop and waited for the man to round the corner. He jumped down, rolling to break his fall, but winced when his wounded shoulder hit the cobbled road. He pulled the dagger from his boot, crept up close behind the man, and with the stealth of a master, sliced through the back of the man's voluminous robe.

The rich man felt nothing more than a slight tug, but still he spun. Seeing nothing, he continued ahead, checking to find his coin purse where it should be. The man shrugged and muttered and sputtered about bloody vandals and what this town was coming to.

Boryn was back on the rooftop, lying down, head resting at the ridge. He cocked his head to keep an eye on the man while he fingered the object clutched in his palm. The man out of sight, Boryn held up the trinket; it glittered extravagantly in the sun. Boryn bit it and grinned. *Pure gold.* If anyone other than an advisor to the Emperor had stolen this, he would be hunted down by the guards and thrown into chains.

"You. Boy."

Boryn let his head loll backwards. The silhouette of a tall, wiry man came between him and the sun. As his eyes adjusted, he could see steely hair and a weary, red robe. *It's that fighter from the arena!*

"You will be returning that."

"To the merchant, sure," Boryn said casually, rising slowly while evaluating his options.

"It belongs to the Emperor's advisor. Now hand it over, Black Mask, or I shall take it from you," said the swordsman.

"You seem to know my title, yet I don't have the pleasure of knowing yours," he stalled. The alleyway below was empty. *Perfect.*

"I am Belral, sword master from the Daemon War, and trainer of the Emperor's elites," the man spoke without a glimmer of humility.

"Impressive," Boryn clapped. "You must have practiced that!"

"I won't wait much longer. Return the gold, or draw your swords." Belral reached as if to unsheathe his.

"All right, all right, since you itch to hack someone." Boryn released like a spring and landed on the tip of a beam supporting the slightly rickety roof. The roof gave way, tiles sliding to the ground, Belral with them. Boryn waved as Belral, clipping his chin on the eave, tumbled and fell.

"Patience is a virtue," Boryn mocked. He vaulted down into the street and turned to make his escape but instead found himself face-to-face with a pair of enchanting green eyes.

"Hi," he said scratching his head with one hand, a silly grin on his lips.

The girl laughed merrily, flicked him on the mask and vanished around the corner without a word.

"Guards! After him! The one with the black mask!" Belral barreled up the street, nose bloodied and lip swollen. Boryn scampered down a side street and turned into a narrow alley. He jumped, grabbed a window ledge, and propelled himself through the opening, landing noisily on the wooden floor inside. A young man and a young lady sharing the bed and very much awake, and Boryn, all squealed in surprise. Great. The guards' shouts trailed off, and Boryn nodded pleasantly toward the startled couple and crawled out the window, slamming it shut behind him.

Now those eyes. I have to see them again! He removed the mask and shoved it into his satchel along with the new trinket. He juggled a sack of coins he had lifted from hand-to-hand—this should help

Ranton out—before tucking it in as well. Work done for the day, Boryn returned to his rooftop vantage point in hopes of glimpsing the girl. The hustle and bustle of Dusgoroth, the imperial jewel, was in full swing: boatloads of fish arriving at the docks, townsfolk in the streets bickering and bartering, and merchants barking the benefits of their wares.

Boryn searched the crowd for the girl. She would be instantly recognizable not only because she was beautiful but also because of her black hair cropped short like a boy's and her unusual clothing. *Like Ranton's mom.* He spied her entering the market from the opposite side. Boryn tracked the bobbing head through the maze of people. She stopped at a fishmonger's stall, and even from his distant vantage point, he was beguiled by those amazing green eyes. *Tall, too.* Seriously distracted, he lost hold on the tile roof, slipped and managed to catch himself, but not before losing sight of the pretty, black-haired girl. Anxiously, he scanned the square to no avail. He dropped to the street; a small but firm hand clutched his shirt front and pulled him aside.

"You, mister Black Mask, are a nuisance."

Startled, Boryn could muster nothing better to say than a lame, "Uh, hey there."

"You are the Black Mask, aren't you?"

"What are you talking about?" Boryn feigned innocence.

She shot him an annoyed eye and turned to go.

"Wait! What?" He reached to stop her.

"My name's Emily. What's yours?"

"Boryn Mhi . . . Boryn."

"Oh!" Recognition showed on her face. "Are you the one who killed the daemons at the Blue Pixie?

"Word travels fast," he grinned a stupid, cockeyed grin.

"You and your friends are the talk of Dusgoroth! Shadow Crusaders, isn't that what you call yourselves? We can sleep better at night knowing there are heroes like you around to protect us."

Boryn was unsure just how much she was teasing him.

"Thanks to you, the daemon scare is over before it even begins!"

"There was only one 'real' daemon," Boryn admitted with rare humility. "The others were soullesses, or at least that's what my learned friend Wenval said." He laughed lightly, hoping to keep the conversation flowing.

"Too bad. I've always admired daemon hunters."

"They were close enough. Surely I qualify!"

"How about this. You take me into the Shadow Crusaders, and I won't let it slip that I found the advisor's coin purse in your bag." She dangled it in front of him and met him eye-to-eye with a challenging stare.

She's a thief, too! "Um, sounds like a deal," stammered the surprised, willing, and very intrigued boy.

The time for battle arrived sooner than expected—sandwiched between a narrow neck of the swamp to the front and vengeful orcs to the rear. Assessing his options, Ramgis looked down from the hilltop while the Blood Knights waited. Dark elven ships lined the beach, and well-armored Dark elf forces protected the swamp. The orcs, in an unusually large war band, roared and beat their chests with exaggerated ferocity.

"Cadegray!"

"Yes, Ramgis?"

"What should our plan be? Have you any tactically enlightening ideas?"

"These orcs and Dark Ones are no friends to each other, of that I'm sure. But give me a few moments."

"We are running out of those—not to rush you."

"Our cavalry should handle the orcs and prevent any more naval landings. I want the first through third companies with me. The great swords go with the heavy mounted toward the orcs. The archers are to split into two groups; each watches one beach and shoots at anything in range. Shall we move out?" asked Cadegray as the mounted banner bearers carried the tactician's orders toward their companies. Cadegray turned to Ramgis and said quietly. "We need more men."

"I am aware."

A scout on horseback approached. "My lord, a rider comes fast this way. Shall we allow him by?"

"Let him do as he pleases." Ramgis looked in the direction and saw a lone rider breezing past the orcs toward the Blood Knight army. The brave—or foolish—man tossed off a few lazy shots with his bow and picked off several of the green-skinned beasts. The horseman wove through the Blood Knight ranks and stopped directly in front of Ramgis. Ramgis took stock of the rider, shocked to see that he lacked the protection of iron but rather was simply clad in leather and green cloth.

"Commander, sir, my leader has taken note that you are in need of assistance," the dark-haired rider said. His hazel eyes were clever and carried the hint of humor.

"If he would grant it, I should be much obliged," said Ramgis skeptically.

"If the coin is right, Sir Blood Knight."

Ramgis hefted his golden warhammer and pointed it at the rider. "Return to your master and tell him that war is no business. People die, and beliefs should not be trivialized with money."

"So you really are the commander whispered about with such admiration!" laughed the rider, and he turned and galloped away.

"I hope an orc gets him," Ramgis muttered.

"Are we ready to move out, sir?"

"Yes. Tell the archers to fall in behind, company one with me, two to your group."

Cadegray acknowledged. "If you say so, my lord."

Ramgis held the warhammer high, a signal to battle. From the vantage point of the troops, the hammer was silhouetted by the setting sun, a powerful symbol of honor, of countless Blood Knight victories. To Cadegray, he said, "We need to win this by nightfall, or we are all dead." With that, Ramgis charged toward the swamp where the Dark elven patrol was reported to lie in wait.

Silver glinted in the falling light at the marshy tree line, and a protective force of Dark elves emerged. Spiked, black armor over gold robes covered their tall, slender forms. Ramgis dismounted, preferring the agility of foot battle, and swatted his horse to send it away. Down the hill he ran, warhammer high, and armored Blood Knight warriors breaking ranks to charge behind him. The pale-skinned Dark elves raised their spears and marched toward the confrontation with the human army.

Cadegray watched the unfavorable scene unfolding: more Dark elven boats unloading on the shore; an orcish force closing from behind; and an old commander as brave as he was determined. He signaled the rest of the knights to charge the orcs, galloping after them as fast as his pony would carry him. A fireball rocketed toward them. Cadegray mumbled, casting a spell that threw up a barrier protecting the knights and ricocheting the fireball back toward the orcish forces. *We need to hit them fast and turn back to the swamp because Ramgis is in trouble already.* "Hit them once then turn immediately toward the swamp. The raiders have already made landfall," Cadegray commanded the banner carrier.

"But what of our orders?"

"That plan is falling apart." Cadegray sped toward the Blood Knight archers. "Move in behind Ramgis. If you can get off any good shots on the way, do so."

"Aye, sir," said the flag carrier as he swung the crimson, hammer-emblazoned banner toward the bottom of the hill like a pointer directing the assault.

Cadegray turned to see the knights collide with the orcish line, cutting through with deadly force. Several knights fell from their horses. Cadegray held out his hand, and a blast of lightning shot from his palm, slaying the orcs that tore knights from horses. With his other hand, a second blast extinguished another group. The orcish shaman, deep in concentration, prepared another fireball. Cadegray smiled. He released another bolt of lightning, and the shaman's smoking corpse hurtled into the air.

A unit of elite infantry carrying massive swords formed up behind Cadegray. He turned to them. "Cover the retreat, but move your formation toward the swamp."

"We'll cut 'em all down," said one of the elite swordsman with a grin.

"Do not charge. If they charge you, attack. Otherwise, stand clear and move toward the main force to regroup."

"Understood. Men, let's move out."

Dark elves lowered their spears, prepared for battle. Undeterred, Ramgis ran toward them, turning sideways and spinning, spears rattling off his armor. Ramgis smashed his hammer into an enemy helmet, crumpling it and the elven skull within. Another spear glanced off his armor. He sent his hammer rocketing down into the wielder's head.

At last, the infantry arrived to back up Ramgis and his smaller force. Clanging swords. Screaming voices. Ramgis smiled as the tide began to turn. *The time of Blood Knight revenge is at hand.* His knee fired up; an elf fell to the ground, and Ramgis stamped down, snapping the evil thing's neck.

Just then a bolt of blue lightning zoomed past Ramgis' head. *Damn. Cadegray's breaking orders to help me. Now we're going to be crushed by the orcs, damned green-skinned bastards.* He glanced toward the sea; more Dark elves were unloading. Ramgis' hammer launched an elf skyward.

A high-pitched horn blared. Ramgis turned toward the sound to see a lone rider crest the hill, waving his bow as if to say hello.

"Bloody mercenaries!"

Calny was scrubbing the bar clean, and Laric was rearranging the freshly polished furniture when Boryn entered the Blue Pixie with the pretty, green-eyed girl.

Boryn began the introductions. "Everyone, this is Emily. Calny's behind the bar. And the one with the scar on the right, that's Laric, Calny's twin." Wenval hovered over a table, engrossed in the task of mixing liquids in assorted vials and cups. "That's the professor." Wenval shot him an annoyed glare. "Also known as Wenval." An arrow zinged by, narrowly missing Boryn and sticking a spider to the wall. "And that would be Ranton," he pointed to the hazel-eyed boy at the top of the stairs. "So now you know the Shadow Crusaders. We're pleased to be at your service," Boryn bowed grandly. "Welcome."

Emily rolled her eyes and chuckled at Boryn's antics. "So this is the famous and legendary Blue Pixie." She looked around the room.

"I wouldn't call it famous exactly. More like infamous," Wenval corrected.

"So why exactly did you call me here, Wenval? And why all the cleaning?" Boryn asked.

"I was curious who owns this place so I asked around and learned something very interesting. Seems it's been deserted for so long that according to the regulations, no one owns it anymore. So I thought we could clean it up, claim it, and do something with it," Wenval explained.

"What do you have in mind?" Boryn asked.

"We could start our own inn," Calny suggested rather casually.

"That's crazy!" Laric exclaimed.

"It will never work," Wenval agreed. "What do we know about running an inn?"

"Sounds like a great idea to me. I like it," Boryn said, not one to be dissuaded by practicality and reason.

"Just a few problems with that," Wenval outlined. "First of all, we need customers, and everyone in town is too afraid to come to Old Town. Second, we need workers; they won't come here either; and third, we need coin to get started."

"I can help with that," Boryn pulled the moneybag from his satchel and jangled it.

"And we'll need drinks," Laric added, "a specialty of our own, since the best taverns always have one."

"That part won't be a problem," Wenval admitted, coming around.

All eyes turned toward him.

"What do you think I've been doing over here?"

"We might want to change the name," Calny observed.

"Good point. Hey, Wenval, what's your drink taste like?" Boryn wanted to know.

"Um . . . sort of like strawberries."

"The Strawberry Patch!" Laric cried, pleased with his idea.

"No . . . ," Calny protested.

"What's wrong with it?"

"It sounds really dumb."

Warming to the notion, Wenval offered, "We should retain a sense of youth to the name but avoid a childish cliché."

They stared at Wenval, awaiting the translation.

"We need to have a younger-sounding name just not one as foolish as that," Wenval restated.

"The Strawberry Mug?" Emily suggested.

"That could work."

"Let's vote on it," Boryn said. "Laric, how do you vote?"

"No," he pouted.

"Yes," Ranton chose.

"I'm in," Calny said bubbling at the prospect, eager to run such an establishment, and eager to beat out his brother. "You lose, Laric!"

Wenval laid out a plan. "Calny and Laric, it's your job to figure out how to get customers here and find workers, and Boryn," he rolled his eyes with a knowing smile, "we know you'll take care of the money. Oh, by the way, I made these for everyone." Wenval gave each boy a leather strap from which five crystals dangled. "Sorry, Emily, there's not one for you."

"What is it?" asked Ranton as he inspected the chiseled pendants.

"Each one of the stones is engraved with one of our initials. The stone will allow us to keep up with one another, to make sure we're all safe. For instance, if Boryn decides to rescue a damsel in distress and is about to get himself killed, we'll know soon enough to rescue him. These stones can read a situation better than you can."

"How do they work?" Boryn was curious.

"The color will change according to the situation. Black means mortal danger, green means being healed or in need of being healed, um, blue is troubled, and red means engaged in battle. That's all I've done so far."

"That's amazing," said Emily, more surprised than the others but no less impressed.

"You never know what to expect from Wenval," Boryn answered her while Wenval preened at her compliment.

"The stones are grand, Wenval, and I can't wait to see how they work. But let's get back to the plan for the Strawberry Mug," Calny said. "Boryn, what do you have in mind for getting the money?"

"Do you really want to know?" Boryn waggled his eyebrows.

"Let's see. Right now, it's peak market time, so I think we should take advantage of the opportunities."

"Ah! The Black Mask returns," chuckled Wenval.

"Didn't know he ever left," Boryn winked. "A mass thievery should do the trick."

"And how might we pull this off?" Emily inquired.

"Easy," and he began to outline his plan.

Coal-black hair and black cape billowing, the man sat motionless on his dark brown horse, a weary, old bridle lank across his palm. A bone horn hung from his belt, and a claymore was tethered to the horse's flank. A wide, flat sword, this one was twice as large as most. The sword was unadorned but for an X of red stones on the crossguard. Almost handsome, though ill groomed, the man turned his ear away from the wind.

Another man, smaller and stouter than the first, whose board-straight hair hung like strands of pitch draped across his scalp, parted from the waiting army. It was a ragtag assortment composed of disenchanted rebels numbering a hundred or more. The black-haired second rode toward the leader. "What's the matter?"

"Don't you hear it?"

"Hear what?"

"Orcs. A great number of them."

"Not good. Which way shall we go to avoid them?"

"We're advancing toward them."

"Sir?" Dace questioned. "I've ridden beside you for how many years? And I still can't figure you out."

Luthor offered a cockeyed half smile. "Listen. They sound riled, and they're moving in the direction of Dusgoroth. Some bloody shaman must have called a religious war to bring such a large group together."

"May I ask why the Red X is saving a city from which its leader is banished?"

"Because there's someone in Dusgoroth I need to protect."

"Ah! So there is a heart beneath that hardened crust! Who is it?"

Luthor chose not to speak.

"Great. Risk my neck in a bloody battle for an unnamed 'someone,'" Dace grumbled, fingering the hilt of his katana.

"Tell the men to mount up and the others to start running," Luthor said with a knowing smile.

"Aye," obeyed the unhappy rider.

Wenval observed the scene in the square with the cool eyes of a strategist, playing it out in his mind's eye. He nibbled the inside of his lower lip. *Distraction you want? I can't wait.* He tied a square of soft, black leather around his face. It was cut with holes for eyes and a smile. He searched the street for Calny, finding him near the melon vendor just as planned.

Calny reached to dislodge a melon. Someone bumped into him and knocked him to the ground. When he jumped up, he kicked away one of the stall's legs, sending the tidy stack of melons avalanching to the street. People tripped and fell; Wenval watched and smiled. Just then, a flurry of arrows shot through the crowd, severing the ropes on coin purses.

Perfectly timed, Boryn and Emily swept past, snagging bags of coins before they hit the ground. Boryn tripped a man in front of him, swiped the heavy golden necklace from around the man's neck, and pocketed it. He smiled to see Emily dressed in typical lady's skirt and tunic, disguised to blend in.

From his rooftop perch, Wenval started to chant silently. A cloud formed around him. Wenval threw his arms wide, and the glistening mass dispersed. A thunderous sound poured from the swirling mist, reformed in the shape of a dragon. Flapping its mighty wings and buffeting terrified townsfolk, the vaporous beast slammed down into the market square. The dragon lifted its head and roared; pandemonium ensued. Befuddled guards shook impotent spears. The dragon opened its mouth and let loose a jet of cold water that sent guards crashing into a wall. Boryn smiled. *Not bad, Wenval, not bad.*

Beside the baker's stand, a bald boy wearing a black mask cut with a crying face stuffed a bag with freshly baked treats. With his own bag full to overflowing, he snatched more coin purses before hapless owners realized what was happening.

Warning horns blared from the main guard tower, summoning reinforcements and ending the skylark. Boryn sprinted toward the wall and scuttled to the roof.

"Wenval! What was that?"

"A mist dragon, my friend, created with water manipulation along with an illusion spell."

"Amazing! No time to waste now; we're pulling out."

"As you command, sir," Wenval saluted. Hand extended, "*Lux,*" he said, and a flare of light signaled the Crusaders it was time to retreat. The two boys scampered across the roof, and Boryn hurdled to the next. "Come on, professor, you can do it," he encouraged his less athletic friend.

"*Graev,*" Wenval said then blew into his hand. A vortex of air whirled at his feet, carrying him across the gap. "How was that? A rather civilized way to travel, don't you think?"

"This magic nonsense seems to be going to your head!" Boryn teased, and laughing together, they hurried toward the Strawberry Mug.

"When shall we attack?"

"You have made general now. You tell me," said the red-skinned brother who hadn't bothered to assume a human form.

"You are older and wiser—but had no interest."

"And you are more ambitious, Tharrus." Elaborately, the elder brother shrugged his bony shoulders, batlike wings in tow.

Tharrus smoothed his white general's cloak and fingered the black trim that lined its edges. Then his fingers moved toward the new general's weapon sheathed at his side but stopped short of touching it. *I don't want some rotting, old daemon spirit messing with my mind.* And he pulled his hand away like a finger from fire. Then he snarled. *And why did they give me a scimitar? I hate scimitars.*

Through the foliage the gray wall of Dusgoroth rose. The daemon turned to the army of orcs amassed and milling behind him, and now he grinned.

"Ha!" Tharrus announced in an unpleasant, nasal snort, pointing into the foliage. "What a nice surprise! I didn't even notice her." The daemon came to rest crouching on a limb behind the leather-clad huntress. Undetected, he moved close to her ear. "Good hiding spot," he whispered. She froze. "How very clever—the way branches conceal you from all sides yet you still have a perfect view for observing your prey," the daemon praised, "unless, of course, approached from behind."

Terrified, the huntress sprang from the branch, fired an arrow into the foliage, and took off toward the gate of Dusgoroth.

"Quit toying with her and kill her," the brother groaned, weary of Tharrus' games.

"We should let her go back to the city. Tell everyone what she saw. Worry the townsfolk a bit," Tharrus sneered.

"You intend to let her escape?"

"Not in one piece," the sadistic creature said behind a fanged grin. Tharrus pulled a spiked whip from his belt. *So much more fun than a scimitar.* He appeared in front of the woman with a vicious smile and snapped the whip forward. The whip cracked across her shoulder and sent her spinning to the ground. With a clipped shriek, she hit the dirt and started to crawl.

"I thought you'd have more fight."

Suddenly, she lunged toward Tharrus, impaling her dagger into his knee, but the daemon only laughed. "There we go."

Stepping back, he let his whip fly again, this time coiling it around the huntress' arm. He grinned as he jerked it back, the spikes ripping through the thin leather and the flesh beneath. She screamed, her shredded arm freed. She staggered to her feet and stumbled toward the city gate, leaving a crimson trail. Tharrus sighed and pulled the dagger from his knee. He raised the bloody blade, twirled it, and released it spinning. The dagger hit its mark, striking the woman in the back, and she collapsed. The daemon vanished while guards rushed to the brutalized woman's aid.

Calny nursed a broken leg. Laric sampled from his horde of stolen sweets. Wenval was back in business filling dozens of kegs with his special drink. And Emily, who had stolen almost as much as Boryn, was counting the take.

Not a bad day, Boryn thought. "Where's Ranton?"

"I haven't seen him since we were in town," Laric mumbled through a mouthful of jelly filled pastry

Boryn remembered the gems tied to his belt. One shone green; its initial was *R*. "What does green mean again?"

Wenval answered without looking up. "He's at the healer's."

Boryn jumped up from the table and sprinted out the door and down the dusty streets of Old Town. When he rounded a corner near the market, he saw guards blocking the way.

"Hey, you! Stop! We're questioning everyone about the dragon sighting."

Ignoring the command, the boy ducked down a side street and climbed atop a barrel. The guards sprang in pursuit, and Boryn waited then hopped, vaulting off the first guard's helmet to land behind him. Using surprise to his favor, he dashed between two more and made it into an alleyway that led to the back door of the healer's house. Boryn threw open the door and ran upstairs. Staring vacantly, Ranton sat on the single wooden chair, his mother in the bed beside him.

"What happened?"

"Look at her arm."

Boryn recoiled at the sight. Shredded skin. Protruding bone. Still unbandaged to receive the healer's care, much of her body revealed a savage torture. *What in hell's name would do this?*

The white-bearded healer entered. "Scruffy," Boryn turned to him. "This is horrible. Can you heal this?"

"I would feel more confident if her wounds responded to my spells, but these are very strange. My magic seems powerless. So I am resorting to older remedies like herbs and ointments."

"But will she live?"

"She should."

Boryn rested his hand on Ranton's shoulder. "Do you know what happened?"

"Nah. When we were leaving the market, I happened to see the guards carrying her here."

Emily and the others arrived and stopped at a respectful distance, shocked by the mangled woman's appearance.

"What can we do to help?" Boryn asked the healer.

"I can think of only one thing," Scruffy said. "I can't imagine that it could work, or that you will be successful . . ."

"Tell us. We'll do it. Anything," Boryn blurted.

"Wenval, have you heard of the Mihirans?"

"A race that goes back to the beginning of time but extinct since the Daemon War, if I remember correctly. Supposedly, they had a temple in Grinfol Forest, but no location has ever been found."

"You may also know," added the healer, "that the Mihirans were known for their skill in the forbidden art of alchemy, a powerful magic feared by many but one that allowed them to become very advanced in the healing arts."

Wenval's eyes widened. "Weren't they persecuted for those same practices? Because it was a powerful but dark magic?"

Scruffy laughed, but there was no humor in it. "Mihiran persecution was driven by fear," the healer's tone was certain. "People often reject that which they don't understand." He paused, and no one spoke, then he continued. "Since my magic seems to be powerless against these wounds, I want you to try to locate the temple. See if you can find anything that might be useful," Scruffy explained. "That, and time, are our best hopes."

Wenval protested. "But no one knows where the Mihiran lived. How do you expect us to find it?"

With heavy steps, Scruffy moved to a shelf on the wall and withdrew a rolled parchment. He held it toward Wenval. Without looking away from the healer's eyes, Wenval took the roll.

"Some history is best left locked away. But I suspect we are facing a new enemy. Perhaps it is time to extend our resources wherever possible."

Wenval glanced from son to mother and said with more confidence than he felt, "I'm sure we will find something."

"So much for opening tonight," mumbled Calny. The others shot him daggered looks.

Boryn asked, "Ranton, are you coming with us?"

"Sure. There's not much I can do here." He paused, reluctant, then left the room.

Scruffy reached for Boryn's arm and whispered urgently. "Boryn, you must find the elixir."

"I thought you said she was going to be fine."

"*Should* is not the same as *will*. Without that medicine, she will likely die."

"So we are relying on a legendary medicine of an extinct race from an unknown location to save her?" Boryn shook his head.

"A long shot, perhaps, but our best. You have what you need to find it," Scruffy gave Boryn a reassuring pat on the back.

"And if we don't?"

"I will press my skills while you search for the lost Mihiran temple, and the cure."

"Good luck, Scruffy. Keep her safe until we return."

The mood was somber despite the fast clip at which they moved through bustling streets toward the northern city gate. Ranton joined them in body, but his spirit was elsewhere, lost in his own private fog. Wenval unrolled the sheaf and began to try to decipher its cryptic marking. Moved by the sight of Ranton's mother, Emily stayed quiet. And Laric, oblivious, swept his new blade back and forth idly as if scything wheat.

Calny asked again, "So what about opening tonight?"

Boryn stopped and turned cold eyes to Calny. "If you can't think of anything else, why don't you just stay here and open the inn tonight?" With long, angry strides, Boryn stomped ahead.

Laric lagged with his brother. "How are we going to drum up customers?"

"Here's my idea. I'll tell the guards we have quarter-priced drinks and ask them to spread the word," said Calny, thinking aloud. "Even if they're afraid of the neighborhood, they'll show up for cheap drinks."

"Quarter-price?" Laric asked.

"Yep, we'll start the night at quarter-price, but as it gets later, we'll up it to twice the price!" said Calny with a satisfied grin.

"Not a bad idea." Boryn fought the desire to smile. He stopped and said, "All right. We don't all need to go look for this Mihiran place. In fact, Emily, I'd rather you didn't." She started to protest, but Boryn help up his hand. "Wenval, Ranton and I will handle this. Emily, Calny and Laric, stay in Dusgoroth. Open tonight if you can; it will give us something happy to come home to."

Calny was thrilled to agree. Laric and Emily put up a small fuss but ultimately broke away with Calny toward Old Town.

"What are we looking for exactly, Wenval?" Boryn asked.

"White stones, or if we're lucky, a pillar."

"Anything else?" asked Ranton, snapping from his trance.

"Rubble, or a slice or crevice in the ground—anything unnatural."

Foraging through the forest, Boryn was struck by the quiet. A month ago Grinfol Forest bubbled with sound, but now it was utterly quiet, without even the squawk of a jay. *Could this have to do with that daemon's threat?*

"So what's the story on this race, the Mihiran?" Boryn asked while they walked. "I've never heard of it."

Wenval looked up from the scroll. "At the moment, all I know is that they died out shortly after the Daemon War."

"Seems like a lot of change hinged on that war."

"You could say it reshaped our entire world. The number slaughtered was horrific; whole races reached the brink of extinction, and only the strongest survived. In a way, it was also the Daemon War that ultimately led to the Empire's break from the Knightly Realms."

"The scroll says all that?"

"No. I knew that already."

The foliage grew thicker and the light dimmer, but they plunged ahead, following Wenval's lead. A hawk's cry pierced the silence, and Ranton's head snapped up. He shouldered through the thicket, pointing. "Over there!"

"Where? I don't see anything."

The others squinted through the dense underbrush. Finally, a pile of rubble came into view.

"How do you do that?" Wenval asked.

"Do what?"

"See something that's practically invisible?"

"Good eyes. Now let's hurry."

Branches swatting faces and arms, the three boys shoved into a small clearing. Stubs of stone pillars rose from the brambles, their tops toppled on the ground and overtaken by vines. Boryn entered the open ruin, surprised by its small size, more like a stable than the grand palace he had envisioned.

"How does this help us? There's nothing here," Boryn blurted.

Wenval ran a finger to the center of the parchment. "Look for a circle of stone in the earth, and near it, a switch of sorts."

Ranton brushed away a pile of decaying vegetation to uncover a circular slab, a platform about as broad as he was tall. Boryn stepped up on it and ran his hand around the base, searching for a clue, when suddenly the slab shifted beneath him. It began to rotate. It stopped turning and dropped a bit, like tumblers in a lock falling into place. Twice more it moved. Turn, drop. Turn, drop. Boryn leapt off as the stone began to fall away, releasing a gust of air, stale and dusty.

Boryn peered into the shaft hoping this might be the entry into the alchemists' lair. Just enough light penetrated the dense canopy of trees so he could make out the contours of a few chalky, stone treads spiraling down into darkness.

"This doesn't seem right somehow," Wenval observed.

Ranton interrupted. "It doesn't matter. Let's stay focused on our job; we need to find the medicine," and he rushed past them down the stairs.

Uneasy, Wenval scanned the area.

"What's the matter?" Boryn asked.

"I don't think these are undercity ruins. The set up is wrong, and these symbols on the circle," he bent down and traced the chiseled characters with his fingers, "these are human magic symbols—from another time, yes, but certainly not Mihiran."

Boryn shadowed Ranton. He unsheathed one scimitar, and in response to Wenval's spell, it began to glow brilliantly white.

"What are these, Wenval?" Carved into the rounded wall was an intricate pattern of teal-colored symbols.

"Could be symbols for protection."

"From?"

"The Mihirans perhaps," Wenval guessed.

At the bottom of the stairs was a long hall, still and cold. Compared to the stairway, the hall seemed almost new. Eerie blue light glowed from more symbols etched into the white chalk walls, and the three advanced through the gloom in awe and wonder.

Two massive slabs of stone, also covered with glowing symbols, formed a doorway at the far end of the hall. Boryn pushed one of the doors; it would not budge. Ranton and Wenval added their power to the effort, and the door creaked. With a grinding sound, the hinges broke free, and the door glided open. An enormous chamber opened beyond. In the center stood an iron pedestal, and upon it, a gigantic crystal, rectangular and smooth, almost as tall as the three boys combined. Boryn walked in and circled the opalescent vessel. It seemed to capture light and spill it back out in a radiant, blue green halo.

"This is definitely not an undercity," Wenval whispered, the softness of his breath alone sounded loud against the airless quiet.

"So no medicine here?" Ranton asked in a similar tone.

"Most likely not."

"I don't like this room," Ranton said under his breath, his hunter's instincts alerted. "We are in light while surrounded by darkness." He stepped forward, raised his bow and nocked an arrow while Wenval stepped back.

"The Mihiran are supposed to be dead, remember? So don't worry over it too much," Boryn advised.

Silently, the gigantic door began to move. It picked up speed then slammed shut with a resounding boom. Wenval ran to the door, but found the back sides to be perfectly smooth. No lock, latch, or finger hold.

Turning his broken leg to profit, Calny attracted the attention of two fine, young ladies standing at the fringe of the activity. He grinned and hobbled toward them. "How would you ladies like to make some money?"

"Sorry, but I think you're a little young for that," a buxom one with pretty yellow curls giggled.

Momentarily confused, he blushed red. "I had something else in mind. Do you want a job, a real one?"

"What *do* you have in mind?" the other, her long hair dark as night, asked playfully while patting Calny on his bald head like a cute pup.

"Barmaid."

"Where?"

"The Strawberry Mug. Opening tonight. Quarter-price drinks."

"What will you pay us?"

"I'll give you a portion of each night's sales."

"Sounds fair. So where is this Strawberry Mug? Never heard of it," the dark-haired one said.

"Ever hear of the Blue Pixie? The Mug is where it used to be."

"In Old Town? Are you crazy? I'm not working there! Everyone died!"

"Aw," said Calny dismissively, "that's just an old tale. Did you ever meet anyone who died there?"

The girls passed a serious glance between them and shook their heads.

"So you see, nothing to worry about. And besides, with quarter-priced drinks, we'll have plenty of business, and that's money to you. Now, go spread the word. Quarter-price drinks!"

With good-natured shrugs, the girls agreed. "All right. We'll see what we can do and meet you there after awhile."

Calny grinned and stood a bit taller, never before having experienced such success with women. *That was easy. Now all I need to do is hook the guards.* He limped toward one, an ever vigilant sentinel of the law, asleep across the top of a barrel. Calny tapped the guard's shoulder with his walking stick. No response. He poked him hard in the chest, but this one was out cold. Next, he picked up a rock and threw it at the roof tiles hanging from the eave above. The rock bounced off, so he tried again, throwing harder. This time, the edge gave way, breaking the dam that held back the tiles, and the roof load slid, crashing down, burying Calny along with the snoring guard.

"Great. Now we're locked . . ."

"Such vanity! You humans believe you can solve any problem the instant it arises without concerning yourselves of the feasibility." The voice was deep, filling the chilly void to its darkest recesses, and also pompous.

The boys spun in the direction of the voice. A shadowy figure lurked just beyond the light's reach.

Ranton spoke next. "Who are you?"

"One of the last of my kind. One of the few who survived the vicious butchering, though none of us escaped unscathed," said the figure sadly.

"You're a Mihiran?"

"The shadow of one. A husk if you will. What I was, the humans destroyed. What we are now is far different." The figure moved into the halo of light. It was a tall, hairless creature, slender, humanlike but with pasty gray skin and two slits where a nose should be.

"What are you talking about?" Boryn spoke with indignation. "We did nothing to you."

"*Your* race! The mindless *humans* who hunted us down and

103

massacred our peaceful race for no reason other than intolerance for our practices—which were really none of your concern."

"So you've stayed hidden here? For how long?"

The being's laugh was particularly hollow. "Your impudence is surpassed only by your ignorance. We are not sequestered here by choice. Rather, we have been trapped here since the end of the Daemon War when human magic sealed our door. Every day for many years I have waited expectantly for the moment the humans would forget that we were here and, then, release us. And now, you have brought us our opportunity for revenge."

Boryn turned to see two more Mihiran bookending the first. "Revenge on whom?" he dared to ask.

"Humanity will burn."

"Are there more of you, or just the three," Wenval asked.

"Only three. But we will go down covered in the blood of your insolent race."

"Boryn, Ranton, back up," Wenval whispered.

"Why?"

"Just do it!" Wenval insisted before turning back to the Mihiran. "I challenge the three of you to a battle of minds. A duel of magic if you will. Spells only. No enchantments, curses, or glyphs. If I win, you give us what we need, and we leave peacefully."

"A human against a Mihiran? Three Mihirans? You must be daft." The other two wagged their heads in agreement.

"Let's find out, shall we?" Wenval spoke with incredible confidence.

"As you wish. A battle of magic and magic alone," laughed the leader. "I hope you are ready to feel your flesh burn from your bones, you meek-minded child."

Wenval smiled as the three Mihirans readied their spells.

"*Fyr.*" A fireball formed in each of Wenval's hands.

"*Zulon!*" the Mihiran intoned. Three bolts of lightning discharged from their hands just as Wenval threw one fireball.

"*Is!*" Wenval swept his empty hand up, palm flat, casting a shield of ice between him and the lightning. The bolts struck the ice wall, shattering the wall but dispersing the lightning as well.

One of the Mihirans stepped behind Wenval. Boryn noticed that this one wore a loose leather jerkin and trousers, unlike the robes of the other two, and its legs and arms were dressed with bandages as if wounded. Suddenly, this one threw wide both arms, palms out, and two beams of light fired downward forming into the shape of swords. The creature charged Wenval from behind.

"Watch out, Wenval!" Ranton warned.

Instinctively, Wenval sidestepped, avoiding the blades of light. He swept his arm behind him creating another shield of ice. "Swords? That could be pushing the magic-only rules."

"You don't have the right for rules," the sword-wielding Mihiran spat as it jabbed at the boy.

Boryn withdrew his scimitars and charged forward. "You want a sword fight, you get me."

The Mihiran looked toward Boryn smiling, and Boryn swung. It dodged and made a swipe of its own. Boryn stepped in to block and watched as the shafts of light passed through his blades unhindered. He leapt backward but not fast enough. Searing pain shot through his shoulder.

"What in hell's name?"

"Surprised? You assume these swords can be blocked. But such is not the case. These are pure light energy, and you cannot stop them—with anything."

Boryn ran at the Mihiran and swung low at its bandaged legs. He planted his front foot and pivoted, landing a solid hit to the creature's back with the flat of his blade. "Gotcha."

"Pah. You don't stand a chance. . . ." The being dematerialized before Boryn's eyes but reappeared behind the boy instantly to smash its elbow into his spine. Boryn shrieked as he slammed into the cold, stone floor. "You see," the Mihiran continued, "when I focus my energy into a single spot, I can channel it into different parts of my body for incredible power. And if I really want to make it hard for you, I can phase. That's what happens when I appear to disappear. In reality, I am simply moving faster than your feeble, human eye can see. And phasing makes it impossible for you to hit me. So I ask, little boy, what possessed you to dare enter our temple?"

"We want medicine," Boryn groaned, rising to his knees and taking in what the Mihiran had told him.

"Ah! You mean the very medicine for which your race damned us?" asked the Mihiran as it kicked Boryn in the ribs. "How ironic!"

"So you have it?"

"Of course we do! Our people have guarded it, used it well for hundreds of years."

Boryn rolled across the floor and slowly stood. "How about if I beat you, I get it?"

"In the far more likely scenario that I win, what will you do for me?" the light bearer laughed.

At that moment, fireballs from the hands of the Mihiran sorcerers flew toward Wenval. He dropped and rolled. *Think, think, think.* Something intruded on his concentration, an odd burst of energy. He turned to the source; it was Boryn, his eyes tightly shut, facing the Mihiran adversary. *No way . . . is Boryn channeling?* Wenval spun back toward his magi opponents to be face-to-face with another fireball.

"Is!" The novice mage's frozen hand shot up to take the brunt of the blast.

The Mihiran leader looked at Wenval and sneered. "Sorry, boy, but I've lost interest. I must end you so we can pass and take care of our business in your pathetic world."

Boryn's eyes remained closed, focusing intently, and the bandaged one phased out again, vanishing then reappearing behind the boy, to stab toward Boryn's spine with its light blade.

"Farewell," it said blandly.

The blade struck air as Boryn copied the Mihiran's trick. Sensing the incredible energy it required to phase, Boryn focused fully on the act and successfully shot behind the Mihiran at an unearthly speed, and the bandaged creature coughed blood as a scimitar penetrated its chest.

"Nice trick! Thanks for the lesson." Boryn nodded to the falling Mihiran.

"No!" roared the leader who stooped and slammed his hand

against the floor. *"Pleg Fyr!"* Flames exploded from the leader's hand, knocking human and Mihiran alike from their feet.

Boryn scrambled up and glanced at Wenval who was patting the singed ends of his hair. Boryn became aware that the remaining Mihirans were standing very close.

"You will understand what it is like," the master said.

"What do you mean?"

"To be despised for *what* you are, not *who* you are."

Boryn considered the Mihiran's omen. "What makes you so sure?"

"Your blood." The creature's eyes flared with intense, searing blue light, and then it dissolved into the darkness, taking the dying one with it.

"Wait! The medicine!"

The last one, the leader, shook its head.

"And what did he mean 'my blood'?"

"Take it at face value," the Mihiran replied. "And your friend," jerking his chin toward Wenval, "he knows the medicine," this one said as it, too, faded away.

Boryn and Ranton spun toward Wenval, the question hanging in the air.

"I don't know." Wenval shrugged.

"You must know. What could he have meant?" Ranton insisted.

Suddenly, it dawned on him. "The crystal. It's the crystal!" Wenval moved to the center of the room. "It's not a crystal at all. It's a vessel, and it emits light due to the liquid within. What causes the aura I'm not sure." Wenval reached out to touch the smooth, cool surface.

Wide-eyed, the young bowman looked up the towering container. "How do we get it out?"

Wenval ran his hand along the crystal and with the other took the flask from Ranton. He flicked the glass and a ripple slithered to the top. With a firm grasp on the bottle, Wenval closed his eyes and pushed. His hand penetrated the peculiar casing, and the flask filled instantly. Wenval extracted his hand and corked the bottle. The glowing vessel sealed without a drop being spilled.

"Whoa . . . ," Ranton took the proffered container which glowed like its larger counterpart.

"Wenval, what do you think they meant by 'my blood'?" Boryn asked.

"I haven't the slightest idea. It's not like you're anyone special."

Boryn's brow furrowed, but Wenval didn't notice. "If you figure it out, will you let me know? And the Mihirans, where did they go?"

"It's said that Mihirans can flow in and out between the physical and the spiritual planes, so I'm guessing they fled the physical. Wouldn't be surprised if we run into them again."

"Now how are we getting out of here?" Ranton asked.

"If you will step away from the door, I would love to try a new spell." Wenval stepped forward and slammed his palm flat against the smooth, stone door. "*Pleg Fyr!*" He repeated the Mihiran's chant. Fire blasted from his hand, demolishing the door. Wenval held up his palm and pretended to blow smoke from it. "After you, good sirs." He turned to Boryn with a wink. "You weren't the only one to pick up a few new tricks."

Boryn grinned crookedly but admitted to nothing.

"Reminisce all you want, but I'm taking this to my mother," Ranton said cradling the precious vial, and he sprinted down the hall, up the stair, and out into the forest.

Images emerged in shades of blue—colorless skeletons, skulls, and assorted bones strewn about the large, damp cavern. Water, green and mossy, slithered down the chalky wall. Marlok shuddered at the sight of one particularly large skull from which curved two deadly sharp horns carved with symbols.

"I told you we should go *over* the mountain, not *through* it!" Quaswyn complained.

Marlok ignored him. "What do you suppose happened here?"

"My guess is this is where the Daemon War ended—the ancient capital of the dwarves."

"Where Fyr Bill fell? You know the story of this place?"

"Indeed, I do. I'm well learned; it just takes time to remember when you're sharing a mind with a thief."

"So what happened?" Marlok asked with genuine interest, idly lifting a bone and dropping it clattering into the pile.

"Well, the daemons were at war in Armorica, and after they utterly destroyed that land, they moved our way, to Elemencia. As the daemons came through the mountains—they didn't want to face the dragons, either—they fought a forgotten race, thought to be extinct. Fyr Bill and his companions joined the forgotten ones and slew the daemon king and brought an end to the daemons' reign of terror over Armorica. Lucky for us, the daemons were stopped before they reached Elemencia," Quaswyn explained.

"What of the hero? What happened to Fyr Bill?"

"The story says he fell in the battle; only a few of his companions left the cavern alive."

"Odd," Marlok thought aloud as they continued to explore the surroundings.

"And just what do you mean by that?"

"You would think the survivors would have brought out the hero's body, honored it even, considering what he did for the world."

"True, but everyone was convinced the place itself—this place perhaps—had become possessed," Quaswyn's voice dropped very low. "They were afraid of bringing out the possession with him."

Marlok heard a rattle behind them. "What was that?" They stopped and listened, and Marlok peered warily into the dim blue distance.

"What are you doing?" Quaswyn demanded.

"Quiet, before we attract more attention."

"From what?"

"Something has been trailing us for a while."

"Hey, come out!" Quaswyn called in a loud but friendly voice while moving toward the sound, seeing nothing. "We know you're there! We don't want to harm you or anyone!"

From out of a darkened recess in the cavern wall, an axe whooshed. Acting on instinct and in one swift motion, Marlok pivoted. Dagger. Spin. Block. Knee. The assailant flew back into the stone wall, grunted, and struggled up. With considerable sputter and fuss, the foe rose to his full height, slightly more than half that of Marlok. *Was that a nose I crunched?*

"This is holy ground, ye idiot!" the short, barrel-chested man roared as he charged them again. It was now that Marlok noticed the beard, bright and wiry, like spun gold, and the horned helmet atop the low head.

"A dwarf!" Quaswyn exclaimed.

"Shut it, Quaswyn."

The dwarf screwed up his face, penetrating blue eyes beneath bushy, yellow brows, and demanded, "Did ya jus' talk to yerself?"

"Well, to be precise . . ."

"Shut up, Quaswyn . . . ," the thief said through gritted teeth.

"I will not. It's impolite to ignore this gentleman's question."

"I'm sure he'd rather not know."

The dwarf observed in befuddled silence.

"Of course he would," Quaswyn insisted.

The dwarf's axe raised high. "Wha's wrong with ye?"

"I'm Marlok. The other voice is Quaswyn. We were fused into a single person thanks to some stupid orb . . ."

"An important, magical artifact," Quaswyn corrected. Rustling for their satchel, he offered, "Would you like to see . . . ?"

"Oy! Both of ye, clam it."

The two obeyed.

"Why are ya here?"

"We are trying to reach Armorica."

"Why didn't ya go over," the dwarf gestured toward the mountaintop, "like ya humans are suppose' ta?"

"I personally find ghosts preferable to hungry, fire-breathing dragons," Quaswyn explained conspiratorially, trying to make the dwarf warm to them.

"Argh, so they're still around? All right, I'm takin' ya outta here. But before I do," he raised a finger and waggled it threateningly, "don't ye be comin' back in here. It's holy ground, I tell ye." The helmed dwarf slapped the axe handle into its carrier, thrust his hands deep in his pockets, and forged ahead with fiery determination.

"Really?"

"Aye. Now shut up and follow me."

The happy barmaids returned to their generous customers, and Calny remained behind the bar, leaning against his walking stick. Grinning stupidly, he rubbed ruby lip marks from his cheeks. *I think I like this job.*

Every table overflowed with boisterous guests, a den of laughter and music, the jingle of coins being tossed in friendly wagers, and mugs clanking in gay salute. *Not bad for a first day. And best of all,* Calny gloated, *they're too drunk to notice the rising prices!*

He raised his own mug in tribute to his senseless customers. Then he called out, "Oy!" The room hushed, and bleary eyes turned to the young, bald bartender. "It's because of the Shadow Crusaders that this place became a reality. How about a toast to them?"

"Hurrah!" a man cheered and fell over, clipping his chin on the table. Only for a moment the patrons paused before the gaiety resumed, more cheers and upraised mugs. *Wenval, this drink is genius.*

"If the Mihiran elixir is so potent," Boryn wondered aloud, "why did we dislike them for it?"

"Humans tend to fight what they don't understand," Wenval replied as they rounded the corner toward the Strawberry Mug.

"Like magic?"

"I suppose. The physical we get; the spiritual scares us."

A shout arose from inside the Mug, and the boys ran toward the sound and the light. From outside looking in, Boryn saw Emily carrying an armload of rubbish toward the back door. *She is really beautiful.* He loved it that she wore her hair short—few did—and that she wore the clothes of a hunter rather than dressing in skirts and tunics like most of the girls. Even wearing breeches, she maneuvered among the rowdy crowd with the grace of a princess.

Wenval returned by the door, but Boryn had a different idea. Grinning mischievously, the boy made his way to the alley. As the door opened and Emily stepped out, Boryn leapt behind her and grabbed her. The girl squealed, spun, and slammed her sharp elbow into his nose, sending him *thunking* against the hard door.

"Oh!" Her hands shot to her mouth. "I'm so sorry! Are you all right?" She bent to help him up.

"Other than my bleeding nose, definitely," quipped Boryn, rising slowly.

"Well, just a thought, but maybe you shouldn't sneak up on girls in dark alleys," she teased. "Did you find the temple?"

"Yes. And Ranton has the medicine. I hope he made it in time." Boryn grabbed the crystal strand at his side. "Ranton's stone is clear. Hopefully, he'll be along with good news soon." Boryn took Emily's arm.

"What are you doing?" she asked.

"Come with me."

"Where?"

"Just follow me. You'll like it; trust me." Boryn handed Emily a piece of cloth. "Cover your eyes. It's a surprise."

"But the Mug is packed! I can't just leave . . ."

"Sure you can. I'll take care of it with Calny later."

She shrugged off the last measure of reluctance while Boryn secured the blindfold over her eyes. Holding her arm and gently guiding her, Boryn led her through the lantern-lit streets of Dusgoroth.

"So where are you from?" he asked. "I'm sure I would have noticed you before."

"I come from a village in the Knightly Realms."

"Just visiting?"

"No. Here to stay, for a while anyway."

"Why did you leave home?"

"There was nothing left. Orcs swarmed the village, came through butchering and burning everything in their path. Everyone either fled or died that night."

"I'm so sorry. What about your family?"

"As soon as I can, I plan to go find them."

"So you think they survived?"

"Honestly, I haven't a clue."

"Why didn't your Order protect the village? Which was it?"

She stopped walking and, from behind the blindfold, let out an empty laugh. "The Serpent? Protect us? What a joke."

"Lucky you met us, then. The Shadow Crusaders will protect you!" he offered gallantly.

"But you have lives of your own here. Families, things to do . . ."

"What could be more important than helping one of our own?"

"Thank you. I can earn my keep, you know."

"Yeah, I saw in the market. Nimble fingers you have!"

She bobbed her head in acknowledgment and stumbled over the raised threshold. "Where are we going anyway?"

"You'll see."

She could tell when they entered a building; instead of stone, she felt first smooth wood and then the pad of a rug under her shoes and heard the echoey sound of a large room. A door creaked. Around a corner. Up some stairs. Boryn whispering to stay quiet. Down a long corridor and up a few more stairs. The aroma of rich food reminded her that she was hungry and told her this was a place of wealth. Emily giggled, enjoying the intrigue. Another door creaked. Cool night air brushed her face, and she smelled the salt in the breeze.

Boryn reached to remove the cloth. The revealed sight was breathtaking. Before her, bathed in moonlight, lay the great city of Dusgoroth. Her green eyes danced from the city warmed by candlelight to the lush treetops of Grinfol Forest and around to the sea tumbling peacefully against the shore.

"It's so beautiful!"

"Amazing, isn't it? This is our home, Dusgoroth," Boryn said with pride.

Emily was stunned; the view was more glorious than any she might have imagined from her tiny village in the hills. Her eyes swept the scene trying to discover what place could provide such a splendid vista. As she turned, Boryn inched toward her. His hand brushed hers as he moved closer still, and he felt the warmth of her skin against his. He slid his long fingers between her small ones. Emily did not resist but instead grasped his hand and leaned close.

A sudden flash of thunderous lightning raced across the cloudless sky, shattering the moment and causing Emily to jerk away.

"What was that?"

Boryn noticed a roiling bank of clouds building in the north. "I'm not sure." By the moment, it grew more threatening, pulsing with a ruddy-red glow.

"Boryn!"

Boryn rushed to the edge of the parapet and looked down. Wenval, panting, and Ranton looked up.

"How did you know I was here?"

Ranton held up the crystal strand Wenval had given him. "These things are creepy," laughed the young hunter. "Apparently Wenval has added an enchantment so we can find one another."

"Boryn . . . something . . . isn't . . . right," Wenval said between breaths.

"Do tell," said Boryn, eyes locked on the onrushing clouds. "Hold on. We're coming down."

"You brought me through the Emperor's keep?" Emily guessed, wide-eyed by the opulent surroundings as they retraced their steps.

"Shh! Later," Boryn said.

They spilled out the door, into the courtyard, castle guards on their tails, and out to the street beyond, where Wenval and Ranton waited. Outside the city wall, they could see angry black smoke boiling against an intensely orange backdrop. With eyes glued to the sky, the four of them rushed to the public stairs.

"What's going on, Wenval?" Emily asked.

"Can't you feel it?"

"Feel what?"

"A weird, oppressive . . . presence."

Boryn asked, "So you feel it, too?" He felt oddly comforted to know that he wasn't alone.

From the midst of the gathering storm came the bellow of a horn. The sinister sound repeated and grew louder.

"That's an orc horn!" Wenval recognized the deep, mournful tone.

"The bastards that attacked my mother," Ranton speculated, his rage palpable. Emily shivered remembering the poor woman's wounds.

"Ranton, go back and get Laric and Calny. We'll need all the help we can get to hold off this attack," Boryn urged. Thunder and lightning sounded as one, the storm was close, and the sky opened with a powerful burst of sharp, stinging rain.

"These may be orcs, but I think there's more to it than that," Wenval frowned.

Boryn reached the top of the wall first to see billowing flames, unfazed by the pouring rain, swallowing Grinfol Forest. Just then, the head of a creature, silhouetted against the fire, popped up from the outside of the wall. Only its beady red eyes were visible. The creature clambered to the top and poked at Boryn with a simple spear. It was about half Boryn's height and lankier than an orc with a long, pointed nose and a mouthful of needle-sharp teeth. Now Boryn could see that its skin was green.

"That doesn't look like a daemon or an orc." Boryn left the question open to Wenval.

"Goblins. Those red eyes are natural."

Boryn gripped the wet handles of his scimitars and unsheathed them. He swung them both hard but was surprised to see the goblin block the strike. It kicked out at him, hoping to catch him in the stomach, but Boryn spun left of the kick, fiercely slashing sideways with his scimitar, neatly amputating the creature's leg. It howled, now crippled, before Boryn kicked it backwards off the wall. Boryn turned to the sound of creaking wood and saw the top of a crude rope and wood ladder. He waited until the next goblin poked its head over the wall. He lunged with his blade, easily piercing its head. With a grunt, he kicked the ladder backwards, tumbling several more goblins to their deaths.

Laric and Calny had arrived and were facing their own adversaries. Calny *thomped* orcish heads with a heavy club, cringing with every blow. Laric used his advantage of reach and speed to hack at a band of goblins that had managed to surround him, their crude wooden spears aimed at his torso, as he kept them at bay. A fireball launched by Wenval came to Laric's rescue, striking down the group of goblins, incinerating several and blowing the others into a heap a few feet away at the base of the watchtower.

A mad screeching drew Boryn's attention. At the base of the wall he saw Emily spinning like a dancer, her arms spiraling gracefully. She dipped and swept, bending like a willow in the breeze, while around her, orcs and goblins dropped into pieces. It was beautiful to watch, yet morbid . . . entrancing.

A grunt came from behind. Boryn's head snapped up, and he reeled back to see an orc hovering, blade upraised. Boryn stepped back, raising his scimitar to block but was saved instead by an arrow that pierced the thing's skull.

Relief flooded the boy, but just as suddenly, he felt a heavy, ominous weight descend upon him, pressing him to the ground, and the rain stopped. Instinctively, Boryn looked up. Two hooded figures floated above him, one in black and one in white. Except for its red eyes, the one in white looked human. *Who or what in the name of hell are they?*

At the moment Boryn's eyes met those of the hooded figure, a barrage of brutal images seared his mind: humans burned alive or butchered by red-skinned creatures and screaming in terror and pain. His mind seemed overtaken by the images, but abruptly, they stopped when the figures turned and walked through the stormy skies directly toward the Emperor's keep.

They need to be stopped. Boryn turned to Wenval. "Try not to let anyone die."

"Where are you going?"

"You were right. There's something wrong here." Leaving the Shadow Crusaders to hold off the greenskin assault, Boryn jumped from the wall with a somersault landing and dashed back toward the castle.

Lightning flashed across the sky, fracturing it like glass. He raced through the streets dodging rain-drenched citizens cowering beneath the raging firestorm and orc assault. Boryn waved his scimitars to clear the way.

He rushed up the hill toward the darkened keep; an eerie horn sang out, different from the one he had heard earlier. *Maybe the rain dampened the sound.* Afraid to hope, Boryn charged ahead. When he reached the fortress gates where guards should be, he saw instead blood splattering the iron posts. The castle portcullis was rent and hung in jagged shreds. *This is not the work of an orc.* With growing dread, Boryn hurried into the courtyard to find a morbid and terrifying scene. Blood mixed with rain to puddle on the ground. He nearly retched seeing the desecrated corpses strewn about the sodden courtyard. Boryn picked his way toward the great wooden door that had protected the castle for ages, now splintered like kindling.

It was then that a chilling cackle cut through the hush of the night, freezing him in his steps.

The white-hooded figure loomed over the whimpering, drunken Emperor. "Such a cowardly swine," Tharrus said to his brother in a high-pitched, nasal whine. "Let's stamp down on the bastard." He trailed the ruler who crawled across the polished floor of the throne room, desperate to escape. But the cruel daemon laughed at the pathetic attempt, absently twirling a black cord weighted by a large, pitch-black amulet.

Tharrus' brother, concealed beneath a black cloak, ordered impatiently, "Quit playing around. Just slay him so we can go find the one you really want."

"But toying with your prey is the best part," Tharrus snorted when he laughed. The daemon slid the necklace over his head before seizing the Emperor by the throat and dragging him to his feet.

The Emperor turned terrified eyes to the daemon. "You attacked the woman outside the gate, didn't you?"

The daemon did not reply but rather backhanded the Emperor's face, spinning him back to the ground.

Lightning flashed across the sky. Torrents of rain splashed on the window ledge and spilled to the floor inside.

"You mean the bow huntress? Why yes, I did a nice job with her, didn't I?" The daemon bared his teeth and withdrew his whip, displaying the spikes and serrated blades that ran its length.

"Stop."

Tharrus spun from the Emperor toward the window. A scimitar-wielding boy, his sandy hair plastered against his face and shoulders, stood backlit against the threatening sky. The boy held the window frame, ready to vault into the room.

"And you must be Boryn, the one who killed my underling at the Blue Pixie."

"I am."

"Wonderful!" exclaimed the daemon. He flicked the whip, enjoying the sport of it. "How convenient that you joined us!"

"Thar . . . rus," brother called like a mother summoning a wayward child.

"What?"

"You're letting the Emperor escape." Brother raised a taloned finger toward the Emperor who was slinking toward the servant's door.

"Oh, so sorry, your highness. How rude of me to forget you!" Tharrus snapped the whip, coiling it around the Emperor's fat leg. The man cried out. First the blades dug in, and then they tore free with a ripping sound as the daemon jerked back the whip.

The Emperor turned pleading eyes to the boy in the window. Recognition flickered across his face. "Why are you . . . ?"

"I'm not here to save you. I'm here to kill the daemons." Despite Lord Mhinbron's suffering, Boryn made no effort to disguise his hatred for the man.

"Fantastic. Now for the head," said the daemon as it recoiled the whip and cracked it forward. Metal against metal, the whip clanged, encircling a scimitar injected into its path. The daemon frowned while the Emperor looked at the boy, shocked but newly hopeful.

The boy lowered the blade; the barbed whip slid to the floor. Then he held the blade up, ready for the daemon. "You will harm no one else."

The daemon snorted, amused by the boy's useless show of bravery. "I was planning to play with you for a while anyway. Oh, my name is Tharrus, general of earth, just so you know."

From behind, the black-cloaked brother slashed with his longsword, patience depleted. Boryn ducked, unsheathed his second blade, and spun low, slicing behind him. The daemon jumped out of the way but rebounded, and as the boy came around, it slammed its knee into Boryn's face. Boryn tumbled; the sword-wielding daemon reacted, feet planted, longsword high.

"Farewell, young daemon hunter," the daemon lunged forward.

"You two must be pathetic if you have to team up to defeat a child," challenged a red-caped, steely-haired man who slammed down into the spot where the brother had been standing. Belral, the Emperor's sword master, pointed his longsword toward Tharrus' brother. "Let us learn who is the better, you or I. We will take our fight outside."

"So be it. Brother, handle the boy while I deal with this one."

"My pleasure," Tharrus smirked.

Boryn wiped the blood from his nose and rose, holding both scimitars out from his sides. "You are going to pay, Tharrus."

"Ha! Look at the blade you used to stop my whip."

Boryn watched the whip crack again, this time connecting with Boryn's blade full force. The blade shattered in a spray of metal that cut his hands and peppered his face. He dropped the useless hilt and ran at the daemon, the remaining blade held low.

Outside, roars of green-skinned orcs competed with the booming thunder. Boryn looked toward the window, and the daemon used the momentary distraction to his advantage. A heavy, black boot swept wide beneath the white cloak and slammed into the side of Boryn's head, sending him hurtling across the throne room, knocking the gilded chair from its dais. In desperation, Boryn flung his remaining sword sideways like a boomerang, but Tharrus nabbed the spinning blade with a smile.

"The end, Mhinbron."

The daemon cracked his whip at the boy's unprotected thighs.

Boryn jumped sideways; the stone floor split where the whip struck. Boldly, foolishly, Boryn rushed in. Tharrus laughed, cinched the boy's forearm and threw him across the room. Boryn crashed through the paneled wall and landed in a heap in the corridor. A bloody gash snaked down his shin; he tried to stand, wincing in pain.

A horn blared outside, shrill and eerie; it was neither that of an orc nor a watch guard. Now Boryn remembered; it was the same horn he had heard when he left his friends for the castle.

At that moment, a man, black cape slinging water, leapt through the window much as Boryn had before him. The commotion drew Belral and the daemon brother back to the throne room just in time to see the broad-chested man use two hands to thrust his long, flat blade toward Tharrus' throat. The daemon's eyes travelled the length of the blade to the intruder's face. Hair the color of coal, slicked with rain, reached his shoulders and framed a square-jawed face, the chin darkened by several days' growth. He wore a weathered leather cloak and brandished a claymore twice as large as most, a ruby X on its crossguard. A bone horn hung from the man's waist strap.

"Morning," the man said, absurdly, pleasantly. Holding the massive claymore in two powerful hands, he lunged, the tip of his blade striking the black gem at the general's neck. The amulet cracked then shattered.

Tharrus dropped his whip. "Look what you did! Now my storm is gone!" he cried as a ray of light pierced the dissolving clouds and fired into the room.

"Sorry to bring your dream to an end so soon." The man jabbed again.

The daemon of earth stumbled backward to evade the blade's assault, and he whined like a spoiled child. "You broke my toy, so I'm leaving." He fingered the string that once held the black crystal.

The older daemon said, "The orcs are failing anyway."

Tharrus tried to escape by fading to black but found his powers too weakened. So brother grabbed the scruff of Tharrus' white cloak and dragged the humiliated general into the darkness with him.

Belral greeted the newcomer with a broad smile. "Good to see you again!"

"That wire you call hair is getting grayer by the day," teased the black-haired man to his former teacher, though his eyes remained dark and serious.

"Now where did the Emperor go?" asked the sword master without real concern.

"The coward must have slithered out while you fought." The man approached Boryn, who had settled back against the wall. "You, you're Boryn, are you not?"

Belral looked from one to the other, surprise on his craggy face.

"Do I know you?" asked the boy.

"Ouch. That hurts," the man pretended to wince. "Don't even remember your own brother—but since we've never formally met, I suppose you have a good excuse."

"Luthor?" Boryn tried to stand but fell back grimacing. His face twisted from pain, or was it from the shock that this stranger might be the brother he had never known?

"In the flesh." Luthor turned to a guard who had taken refuge behind the throne's heavy drapes, "You, take the boy to the healer's. And Belral, give my regards to my pathetic excuse for a father."

"Gladly. I'll forget the part about you being in town, however," laughed Belral.

"Good plan." Then back to Boryn he said, "I'll be back, but now I must get my men out of town." With a practiced move, Luthor dropped the claymore into a sheath on his back, offered a two-fingered salute, and before Boryn could speak, Luthor bounded through the window to vanish into the city below.

Ramgis rested near the fire observing the well-tanned, hazel-eyed man across the encampment. The young man's dark hair was tied back with a thin, leather strap from which it made many daring escapes. He was muscular and healthy—strikingly masculine, but lean rather than bulky. His leather garments showed the scars of age, and he carried a polished ebony bow like part of his own body, slung over one shoulder. Comfortably, he stood among the knights drinking and laughing at their tales and celebrating the win alongside them.

Ramgis studied the mercenary. Why had he appeared at such a coincidental moment? He recalled seeing the man top the hill as the first barrage of arrows rained down on the orcs, but that was the last he remembered. Instinctively, he reached up and touched the bandage wrapping his head.

"Sadly, it was only a skirmish, but he saved us, and he hasn't even asked about payment yet," Cadegray praised the mercenary's work.

"Remind me what happened." The aging warrior rubbed his forehead. "And why does my head throb so fiercely?"

"You were knocked cold by an elf that smacked your face with its shield. Put a nice gash across your forehead, too. I always tell you to wear a damned helmet," Cadegray chided, sounding a tad motherly.

"And I always say I don't have one."

"No excuse. When you die from a strike to your thick skull, we will be the ones weeping, not you."

"Tell me about that man," Ramgis redirected the discussion and tilted his chin toward the visitor, "and why does he annoy me so?"

"He's the leader of the mercenaries. Lucky he showed up when he did. We needed him."

"He seems a good enough fellow," Ramgis observed while reclining on one elbow and continuing his frank appraisal.

As if he could feel Ramgis' eyes on him, the mercenary turned and deliberately met the stare. He walked toward the fire and Ramgis and extended his hand. "The name's Rath."

"Ramgis."

"Pleasure, really. I've heard all about you."

"From?"

"You are legend! First, a hero from the Daemon War, and now, guardian of innocents! Protector of the Realm's villages left defenseless by their disinterested Orders! The Blood Knights alone stand ready to save the day!" Rath laughed before continuing. "See? Your reputation precedes you. It's not as if your efforts are unnecessary! My men and I just rode straight through the Order of the Serpent's lands—without a problem!" Rath took a long, thirsty draught from the flask dangling from his fingers.

"Why are you here?"

"I felt the need to help you."

Ramgis raised an eyebrow. "And why might that be?"

"Possibly because I saw you running toward certain death, so I thought, why not help out an old warrior and his army?"

"And you expect to be paid for this service, no doubt."

"Call us helpful fighters who much appreciate compensation," Rath suggested with a broad and sincerely friendly smile.

"Like I said, bloody mercenaries. Well, don't expect any payment from me," grumbled Ramgis.

"We have no better battles to wage just now. So use us as your own, General Ramgis of the Blood Knights. All I ask is food for my men," he tried to take a swig from the flask but realized it was empty. "And drink for me," Rath offered in good-natured exchange.

The crowd parted to let the revered old man pass. Wearing a crimson tabard emblazoned with a golden hammer, he walked through the busy streets of Falrik, the capital of the Knightly Realms, toward the Tower of Order at its center. As he crossed the market, people stepped aside to show respect. He passed through the outer gate of the Tower and crossed a vast courtyard filled with fountains and sculpted gardens. At the inner gate stood two guards wearing heavy, black armor, a white raven encrusted on the breastplate, holding similarly emblazoned black banners.

"Welcome, Grandmaster of the Blood Knights." The sentries bowed deeply then swung open the massive doors for the esteemed arrival.

"Thank you," the man nodded, proceeding across the inner court to the marching grounds patrolled by elite Raven Knights. From this vantage point, the mighty Tower looked quiet. But years of experience told the crimson-robed visitor to expect trouble inside. *Ramgis, why did I let you get me in to this?* The man chuckled, shrugging. *We were too young to know any better.*

The doors to the Tower were opened by two more guards.

"Welcome to the Table, Grandmaster of the Blood."

"Greetings to you, Knights of the Raven." The Grandmaster climbed the majestic stairs with surprising ease for one of his age to still another pair of doors, these tall and wooden and standing open to a spacious, round hall. In the center of the chamber stood the resolute Table from which the Knightly Realms were governed. It mirrored the shape of the room and was encircled by seven thronelike chairs, each draped with the colors of its Order. Above the wooden table, a massive chandelier blazing with one hundred candles provided the only light in the windowless, stone space.

Seated at the Table in their heraldic finery, the Grandmasters of the Knightly Orders made an impressive sight. The Grandmaster of the Dragon, protector of Falrik, a huge man to begin, wore white armor, ever ready to defend the capital city, and over it draped a white tabard elegantly embroidered with a golden dragon. Opposite the Dragon, armored and draped in black, sat the Grandmaster of the Raven, moderator of the Table. Between them and colorfully attired were the Grandmasters of the landed Orders: Serpent, Bear, Horse, and newest, the Wolf. And then came the Grandmaster of the Blood. Furious eyes turned to the late arrival.

Without hesitation, the old man moved toward his seat. "Good day," the newcomer nodded. "I apologize for my tardiness."

"How nice of the Blood Knights to join us—finally," the Grandmaster of the Serpent sniffed, fingering his blue tabard.

"You are in no position to seek pardons," growled the Bear. "One might have expected you to be on time since you bring a matter before the Table."

The Horse, too, railed at the new arrival. "Your army is out of line. The Blood Knights march freely through our lands—as if they had a right—and snub direct orders from this Table!"

"Ramgis and his merry band of marauders think they are above the law!" came the Bear's outburst.

"Your men are endangering our way of life!" hissed the Snake.

The Grandmaster of the Blood, ignoring the ire thrown his way, took his seat and said wearily, "Calm yourselves. The Blood

Knights moved through your lands cutting down ravaging bands of orcs—and protecting your people. I fail to see how eliminating our mutual enemy—how did you put it, Grandmaster of the Serpent—'endangers' your way of life."

"When on our lands, the orcs are our problem. We are fully capable of handling this on our own."

"If I'm not mistaken, Grandmaster of the Serpent, your army was eliminated by the Dark elves. Under the circumstances, I'm unclear how you intend to do such a fine job of protecting your own," the Grandmaster of the Blood Knights said with measured words.

Turning from the Grandmaster of the Blood Knights toward the others, the Grandmaster of the Wolf rose deliberately, drawing all eyes to him. "Gentlemen, my Order may be young, but even so, it is obvious your arguments are outrageous. The Blood Knights help us, all of us! Perhaps you others should ask Ramgis for a lesson in protecting your own people."

"You upstart! That your Order has recently risen in the ranks gives you no right to dictate to us! Your word is not law here. In fact, your vote should carry less weight than the rest," the Grandmaster of the Serpent snapped, his tone acidic. The Bear and Horse nodded in agreement.

"I never dictated a thing. I only meant you are mindless fools," was the Wolf's sober reply.

Heads turned to the Grandmaster of the Horse when he spoke to the Blood Knight Grandmaster. "Since your lands were put under control of the Ravens, you Blood Knights have worked tirelessly to turn our subjects against us."

"Bring General Ramgis under control, or you will be removed from the Table, and your knights will be hunted down as rogues."

"And who will you throw out next? Knights of the Wolf or perhaps the Order of the Serpent?" the Wolf challenged. "That should buoy your spirits; you would have no one to vote against your ridiculous positions."

"You have the gall, you pup!"

"And your tongue darts like a viper, Grandmaster of the Serpent. Perhaps you should be wary lest a heel crushes your skull," howled the Wolf. The room erupted in a volley of insults.

Finally, the Raven interrupted the argument. "Grandmasters, let us check our tempers. Recall that we are the rulers of the Knightly Realms, esteemed leaders of our people, not bickering children," he upbraided.

"Indeed, we must address the request the Blood Knights bring before the Table," said the equally powerful Dragon.

"Pah! The Blood Knights bring no matter of interest to me. I'm leaving. Inform me when true business arises," threatened the Grandmaster of the Bear.

"The Dark elves recently attacked one of the Knightly Realm's most profitable port cities, one of the Serpent's, and Ramgis now marches toward the Black Expanse to take the fight to the elves. The Grandmaster of the Blood Knights requests our assistance," the Raven reiterated.

"Let the Blood Knights die! One more problem out of the Horse's hair!"

"Our troubles will only grow if we ignore the problem of the Dark elves. Many more problems will be on your hands without the Blood Knights protecting your back. The Order of the Wolf pledges its support."

"Thank you, fellow Grandmaster," the leader of the Blood Knights replied.

"Both of the upstarts shall die—General Ramgis as well as the General of the Wolf," the Snake predicted, relishing the thought.

"Our general may be but half the age of most, but he is the reason we sit at the Table respected more than your backstabbing Order will ever be," snapped the Wolf to the Serpent.

"The Knights of the Wolf and the Blood Knights are hereby commanded to move for vengeance on the Dark elves," announced the Grandmaster of the Dragon.

"Your General Ramgis has more experience with the Dark elves than we, so I offer my men to serve under his command." The Wolf bowed toward the Blood respectfully.

"Now, anything else?" asked the Grandmaster of the Raven. The room fell silent, whether from anger or resignation, indifference or triumph, it was impossible to tell.

"Well now," said the Grandmaster of the Bear, rising and planting his palms flat against the Table's waxy surface, "our meeting is adjourned. Let us feast!" As if awaiting the cue, servants swarmed in, delivering a lavish banquet. The feast was laid: mouthwatering lamb; aromatic chowders; fresh, hot bread; and wine-filled chalices.

"Our peasants honor us with such delicious fare; we should dine in homage to them," toasted the Horse with thinly veiled sarcasm.

"You appreciate no one but yourselves and nothing but lining your own pockets. Your people are simply pawns in a disgusting little game for power and wealth," declared the Grandmaster of the Wolf.

"Silence!" roared the white-clad Dragon. "This is not the place to wallow in petty rivalries. It is a time of war."

"A few orcs and Dark elves wreaking havoc, and suddenly you call it a war? Overreacting a bit, aren't you, Grandmaster of the Dragon?"

"Our world will be gripped in the flames of war as long as rapi, elf, and orc roam free."

"Paranoia from an age long gone."

"Even if there is war, our armies will keep us safe, hidden away in our comfortable fortress."

The Grandmaster in the white tabard rose and walked to the door. He stopped, turned, and announced to the gathered Table, "It seems I have no appetite." And he left, the Grandmasters of Wolf and Blood Knights at his heels.

The short shadow spilling from window to floor told Boryn it was midday. He sat up scanning the room, finding it comforting and familiar. *I've been here too much lately!* Stiffly, he rose from the bed, and noticed at the foot of the bed his usual black garb, mended, washed, and neatly folded beneath his satchel. He smiled at the healer's special attention, brushed his sandy hair away from his face, and dressed.

A surprising sight greeted him when he opened the door. The usually quiet home was crowded to overflowing with wounded guards and civilians. *Emily!* He searched among the wounded, in every room, and did not find her. Unsure if that was reason for worry or relief, he ran out the door and all the way to the Strawberry Mug.

The tavern, too, was filled, by those with only minor injuries. Behind the bar stood Calny, a heavily bandaged shoulder countering the splint on his leg. Instead of his usual broad grin, Calny greeted Boryn with a weak smile.

"Hey, Calny, what happened to your shoulder?"

"A, uh, keg hit me. Where have you been, Boryn?"

"Scruffy's. Where is everyone else?"

"Upstairs." Calny motioned toward the rickety steps. "There's a healer with them."

Boryn hurried up. Guards flanked the first door, and inside Boryn saw the Emperor whose leg was shredded in the same way Ranton's mother's had been. Belral and Scruffy tended the man. Without emotion, Boryn continued down the narrow hall checking every room. In the last one he found Ranton and his mother dabbing Wenval's forehead with a warm cloth.

"What happened to him?"

"He seems to have overspent himself with too much magic energy. He should be better soon."

That 'should' word again. Boryn turned to Ranton's mother. "I'm glad to see you are up and about. You look . . . ," he smiled, "as good as always."

"Thank you. And thank you for finding the Mihiran elixir." She gestured with her heavily bandaged arm. "Now there is hope," she said, genuine warmth in her weary eyes.

"Where's Laric? And Emily?"

"Laric took a spear to the back and is sleeping but will be fine. Emily, though," Ranton told Boryn, "we haven't seen."

"I'm going to go find her." He left the tavern-turned-clinic and headed toward the market looking in every sidestreet and alley. He rounded a corner and turned into a narrow passage, but the way was blocked. Taking a backward step, he bumped into something solid though yielding, and he was grabbed by the arms. He pivoted to a pair of eyes turned glistening pink.

"Julia?" Surprise and confusion registered in his expression.

"Hey, handsome," she said bringing her face close to his.

He swallowed hard and tried to back away. *This is very peculiar.* She slid the back of her hand across his cheek. "Don't you want to kiss me?" she cooed.

Try as he might, he could not turn away from her eyes. He felt her warm breath on his lips.

A shout from the street broke the spell, and Julia released her hold. "I have to go, handsome, but I'll be seeing you later. I have to get ready; my friends are coming tonight." She winked before scurrying away.

When she left, Boryn felt as if a weight had been lifted from him—he could move again. He fell to the ground, feeling disoriented and light. *Whoa! What was that?* He leaned against the side of a building, and his mind skipped to the other girl. *What if she's dead . . . ?* He took a deep breath and let his eyes close.

"Hey," called a warm, friendly voice.

His face snapped up. "You're safe!" he said with a growing smile.

"Of course I am. Otherwise you would have found me among the injured, wouldn't you?"

"True."

"So, how are you? You seem shaken."

"I'm all right, thanks. What were you doing last night by the wall? That dance, it was amazing. Dazzling, really."

"Oh, these?" Emily held out her small hands. Resting in the palms were the thin metal loops from which dangled tiny strings. Pea-sized silver weights, sharpened like razors, were connected by the finest silvery filament Boryn had ever seen. She slid the rings on her fingers, let the ingots drop and then flicked her wrist, demonstrating the lethal cutting motion.

"How can something so small cut through something as solid as bone and metal? It looks like a string," Boryn said.

"I'm not sure. My mother taught me how to do it."

"Is it skill, or magic?"

Emily massaged the question for a moment. "A little of both, I suspect."

"I'm sorry I left you so suddenly. There was something I had to do."

She smiled and gave him a fond hug. "You took the worst of it from what I heard."

"I carry luck in my pocket." A lopsided grin crossed his face.

"Could be there's a higher-up on your shoulder," she teased.

"So tell me what you saw. I'm still trying to piece it together, make sense of it all."

"After you left, the orcs and goblins were pouring over the wall. I thought sure it was the end. But then, an army under a black flag with a red X across it crashed into the back ranks of the orcs. In a matter of minutes, the men in the Red X army had the orcs and goblins running away as fast as their stubby green legs could carry them. What happened with you?"

"Two men, er, daemons were on their way to kill the Emperor."

"You went to save him?"

"No."

"What, then?" She paused. "And come to think of it, how did you get in the castle last night?"

"I'll be back in a little while," Boryn deflected, turning to leave.

"Where are you going?"

"You reminded me of something important. I'll see you later at the Strawberry Mug." Boryn tapped Emily on the arm then took off for the northern watchtower, the tallest building in the city.

Despite the joy of having resisted the unusual attack, it was a somber day in Dusgoroth, as if a heavy burden had settled, comfortably, ready to stay awhile.

Distracted by the clean up, guards failed to see Boryn enter the tower. *Good thing. Don't think they'd be happy to find a young thief in their headquarters.* He flew up the stairs to the attic where a wooden hatch opened to the flat roof. Boryn scrambled up the rungs clinging to the stone wall and shoved open the covering. He propelled himself up and took in a sharp breath at the sight of Grinfol Forest. Large patches were burned, leaving only blackened skeletons of once magnificent trees, some still smoldering. Beyond, he scanned the plains and harrowed fields that rolled into the distance like gentle waves but found them empty, with no sign of retreating armies. And to the south, the sea lapped the shore, as if nothing at all had changed.

"Already back to breaking the law?" The wiry sword master hoisted himself through the hatch.

"Why are you following me?"

"I came to see if you need my help."

"Like last night?"

"Something like that. You fought surprisingly well."

Boryn tipped his head in acknowledgment.

"I knew you would come back one day."

"What are you talking about?" Their eyes met and held.

"I recognize you. Black Mask. Boryn Mhinbron." Belral said the name pointedly.

"Does he know I'm here?"

"The Emperor? I doubt he even remembers."

"Shall we keep it that way?"

"If you prefer."

"Is my brother gone?"

"Luthor left as soon as he knew you were safe."

"But I wanted to talk to him. Find out where he lives, *who* he is, even." He sounded a bit like a needy child.

"Your paths will cross again."

"How do you know?"

"Trust me. I know Luthor well; eventually, he'll be back to confront his past."

"How do you know him?"

"I trained him, or more accurately, raised him—at least until he was banished."

"You trained my brother? Maybe you and I could fight sometime, and you can tell me which brother is the better fighter," suggested the naïve and confident boy.

The sword master merely laughed and leaned out to see guards converging on the tower. "You should go. The guards will return for their dinner soon."

Boryn looked to the sky, painted with copper and gold. *What a day.* He jumped down through the hole to make his way back to the Mug.

The door to the alley was propped open, and Boryn could hear the den of voices inside. Emily stepped out; from a distance, unseen, Boryn enjoyed her beauty, her warm smile, the day's last shaft of light playing like fire on her black hair.

The light died, and the alley fell to dusky gray; Emily's expression shadowed, too. Boryn tracked her gaze to see a black cloud swirling beyond the rooftops. *Already?* He climbed to the roof to get a better look. The mass was enormous like the first, but this threat was far more menacing than greenskins. A flash of lightning cracked the sky behind thousands of winged silhouettes.

"Emily!" Boryn called. "Tell everyone to hide in the cellar! Now!"

Emily rushed to the task. Boryn saw Scruffy in the distance, heading out of Old Town. He hopped from the roof and trotted after him, catching up at the healer's doorstep and pushing through the door behind him just as ferocious rain drops began to splat like eggs on the stoop.

"Scruffy, we need to get everyone to safety."

"What is it?"

Boryn recalled the images that spiraled in his mind when the beefy daemon Tharrus first looked at him. "Daemons! They're coming."

The healer hurried to the window. Lightning flared as the creatures neared. "Boryn, help me get some of the wounded back to the Strawberry Mug. They'll be safer in the cellar." Scruffy sprang to action. He swept an armful of potions and herbs into a rucksack while Boryn rushed upstairs to start the rescue. Straining under the weight, Boryn heaved an injured guard onto each shoulder and blasted down the stairs and off toward the Mug.

The rain washed his eyes, almost blinding him. He noticed a man leaving and called out to him for help. The man summoned others from inside, and dozens of men swarmed from the Strawberry Mug to pitch in.

"We need to bring the wounded from the healer's house and get them into the cellar. And warn as many people as you can. They're almost here," Boryn was breathing hard; he shifted the guards' weight.

"They?" asked one of the men.

"Daemons! A skyful of them!"

"Daemons in Dusgoroth? Not since the war," said a skeptic.

"Pah! It must be the orcs again. Daemons never travel in groups."

"Just do it!" Boryn ordered.

The men raced toward the marketplace to shoo those still out to the relative safety of their homes. Boryn placed the injured soldiers at the cellar entrance. "Calny, get these men downstairs. I'm going back for others."

"Shall I come with you?"

"No. You'll be more help here. Keep everyone below."

The minute Boryn stepped outside, he felt the weight again, the strange pressure on his shoulders he felt when the daemons had hovered the night before. Today it felt even more oppressive. The daemons' distinctive howls mixed with screeching to make peculiar, discordant music, alone enough to drive a weak man mad.

"You, sir, over there and be ready to shut that door," Boryn commanded a passerby. The man recognized the boy as the leader of the Shadow Crusaders, so he took the order seriously.

A heavy figure splashed into the wet street. The daemon was red-black, winged, and fanged. Boryn unsheathed his remaining scimitar. Using his left hand, the boy slashed, reaching out as far as possible. He felt the razor-edge slice the daemon's chest. Two more swooped toward him. He bent his elbow and steeled his arm with the blade edge in front of him, ready to block.

From nowhere and just in time, Belral swept into the fray. Daemon necks spewed blood, and beheaded bodies dropped.

"Boryn, go inside."

"I'm going to fight."

"I said, go inside!"

"I am going to fight."

"So you wish to die?"

"Of course not, but I am willing to put my life on the line if it is necessary to protect others."

Boryn turned his palm and held the blade up, jabbing upward with perfect timing to impale a landing daemon. He slid the blade free and spun toward a noise behind him. Daemons ripped tile from roofs, windows from frames; anything destructible was going to ruin.

Seeing a pair of daemons enter the Strawberry Mug, he chased after them. He heard screams as one rushed behind the bar as if it knew exactly where to find the cellar door.

Boryn vaulted across the bar, plowing the daemon into the wall, but it grabbed Boryn by the head and tossed him across the room as smaller daemons flew through the windows. Two more fell at Belral's blade; the loyal fighter helped Boryn to his feet.

"They found it," Belral mumbled, fear and frustration in his tone.

"Of course they did."

Calmly, in stark contrast to the chaos, a huge, white-cloaked daemon crossed the threshold followed by a smaller, hunched daemon draped in black.

"Well if it isn't the young Boryn!" the large daemon snorted, the tone not nearly as friendly as the words. "Look, brother, our friends are here waiting for us!"

"Tharrus," Boryn said through gritted teeth.

The novice general strutted across the room, eager to show off the prestige of his position. Although he was careful not to touch the black blade sheathed at his side, he drew back the cloak to display it, feeling powerful just to know it was there. "All of you back off," said Tharrus. The daemons surrounding Belral and Boryn obeyed, making way for the figures who were clearly their seniors. "I believe it's time we finish what we started last night. Shall we have some more fun?"

Boryn glared at the daemon. "I'm not losing this time."

The cruel daemon tossed its cloak aside, and its skin reddened. It grew taller and more powerful, muscles rippling and veins bulging. The face elongated, fangs appeared, and points sprouted on its ears. Then it howled as two curved and deadly-sharp horns burst from its blood-red skull.

"You see these?" Tharrus said, pointing to his horns. "They mean you are going to die."

Witnessing the change from human to daemonic form was more than Boryn had ever imagined, but still he spoke defiantly. "Now you're just as ugly as the rest of your kind."

"You know nothing about daemonic hierarchy, do you?"

"I know I just hacked up a few of your friends. Don't worry; you'll be joining them soon," Boryn pledged with the bravado of youth.

The creature shot forward with unearthly speed, slamming its horn into Boryn's chest. Boryn coughed blood as the daemon extracted the vicious weapon, letting the boy fall to his knees in blinding pain. "That's what a true daemon can do, no problem!" His head fell back with laughter.

"Boryn!" warned Belral as the black-cloaked brother underwent a similar mutation and charged him. Tharrus grabbed Boryn by the neck and held him while his brother drew a sword, ready to strike. Belral brought up his blade, halting the fast but wild assault then swung his blade out, forcing the brother's longsword wide before stabbing forward. But the daemon dodged. Belral lunged again; the creature laughed, spun with blade outstretched to block, and brought its foot across the sword master's face. Belral tumbled to the floor, his face gashed by a clawed foot.

Brother stepped aside to give Tharrus the floor. "Now, little daemon hunter, it is your turn," said Tharrus as he lifted Boryn with an enormous clawed hand and let him dangle by the neck. Boryn dropped his blade and, with both hands, clutched at the red-skinned fingers, desperate to pry open the grip, but instead the vice tightened. He couldn't draw in breath, and he started gasping. *Wenval, Ranton, Scruffy, Emily, Laric, Calny . . . I failed you all.*

Whirling at the edge of unconsciousness, he noticed the blade sheathed at the daemon's side. He felt lured by this scimitar. The draw was almost magical, swirling with the colors dancing before his eyes. With will beyond measure, Boryn lifted his numbing arm toward the hilt. It hung barely out of reach. Somehow he knew that blade would be his savior.

A bolt of lightning cracked the sky and provided the instant of distraction Boryn needed. His arm shot out, and his hand seized the hilt. Even as the daemon squeezed tighter, nearly snapping his neck, Boryn tore the blade from its leather sheathe. An icy chill coursed through his veins as if something foreign had slithered into his body. Yet just as suddenly, the disturbing feeling vanished and something powerful washed over him. He realized he felt . . . *immortal*.

Suddenly, an incredible force blew the daemon backward, through the wall of the inn and into the house across the street. The roof blew off. A tremor of shock swept the tavern in response to the power emanating from the boy. Boryn chased the daemon into the street, where Tharrus, rising slowly, saw it: the scimitar in the boy's hand. *Touching that blade should have been enough to kill him!*

Shock turned to fury. The daemon's red eyes nailed the boy; the stupid child was simply staring at the ground in front of him. The daemon smiled, lay claim to the opening, and charged. "That's my blade, you fool!" The general cackled and cracked his whip.

Ignoring him, Boryn held the blade aloft. For an instant, or was it many long moments, he looked up, inspecting the gleaming shaft, admiring its heft and exquisite craftsmanship. It shone like a diamond but was obsidian black, chiseled from a single stone. Boryn's eyes lowered with the blade, and when they did, Tharrus froze; the golden yellow eyes did not make sense. *How can a human boy have enough power to withstand the blade?*

Tharrus cracked the whip, but Boryn dodged and grabbed hold of the whip high on the cord and spun to rip the handle away. Like a sidewinder, the whip slid across the floor. The daemon glared at the human and howled like a stormy sea, then unsheathed his other, plain sword. Rocketing forward, the daemon of earth slashed, but an easy sidestep, and Boryn was out of the way.

"Fight! Quit dodging like some pathetic dancer!"

"If you insist." Boryn rushed to the daemon's side, sliding past to grab his dropped iron scimitar. Then with a swirling leap, he sliced both his old and his new black scimitars across the thing's back, sending it roaring to the ground. Boryn shut his eyes and focused energy in order to phase, seeming to dematerialize in preparation for a finishing strike.

"Brother!" Tharrus bellowed for help.

With a gust of air, the older daemon appeared. His sword pointed precisely where he knew Boryn would reappear, and suddenly, Boryn found himself vulnerable, his throat at the tip of the older daemon's blade. "The boy seems to have done very well at garnering the power," the older brother coolly observed.

Tharrus scowled at the black-gem blade in Boryn's grasp. Anger replaced the cruelty in his eyes. "That's my sword! Give it back."

Boryn flung the blade in a low sweep, blood trailing and splattering the ground. "And that's your blood."

"He took something of yours, so we take something of his, brother," the wiser, older daemon hissed. The tavern door flew open, and a black-haired girl rushed out. The daemon snapped its fingers, and a black coil shot out of the ground and twisted around the girl's legs. A clutch of lesser daemons held her; one cocooned her slender, young body in its batlike wings.

"Emily!" Boryn swung the black blade. A blast of energy fired into the sky slicing one of the daemons in two.

"Good luck finding us," said Tharrus as he and the others lifted to fly away.

"Help me, Boryn!" Emily screamed.

Boryn jumped to the roof and ran after them, leaping from roof-to-roof. But there was nothing he could do.

"If you want her back, you will find us in a holy place," Tharrus called.

The brother swooped and slammed a knee into Boryn's chest. The boy felt the air blown from his lungs, and he tried to keep his eye on Emily, but he lost her in the mass. And then he blacked out.

Wearing his helmet like a hard hat, the golden-bearded dwarf trudged along the ancient cavern corridor well ahead of Marlok and Quaswyn, determined to keep his distance.

"Oy!" he called, pointing to a side passage.

Marlok hurried to the place and looked; light sliced in at the hall's end.

Quaswyn galloped toward the opening and, with childish delight, skipped into the sun's glare.

"You're making us look stupid."

"I'm so happy to be alive *and* in the light *and* out of the cave," he sang.

"Ye certainly are pretty damn strange," said the irritated dwarf as he exited the cave.

Quaswyn frolicked across the grass waving his arms in celebration. Suddenly, a nasty, green goblin leapt from behind a bush. Quaswyn screamed as a small, spinning axe cracked through the little thing's skull.

"Nice throw," Marlok praised.

"Aye."

"So where do you go now?" Marlok asked.

"Away from you."

"You don't like us?" asked Quaswyn, sincerely hurt.

"Ye're just annoyin', all righ'? Now, I'm leavin'."

"Please, sir. . . . Remind me your name again?" Quaswyn tried to be friendly.

"Didn't say," came the curt reply.

"May I have the pleasure?"

"Boringer."

"Will you please stay with us, Master Boringer."

"No."

"Then, where should we go from here?" Quaswyn pressed.

"How woul' I know? Ye were the idiots tha' wanted ta be here in the first place." His mouth was virtually invisible, nested in the brambly beard.

"Where are _you_ going?" Quaswyn tried.

"Nowhere you will ever go, ever." The dwarf stomped away.

"I just don't know what we did to—"

Boringer stopped, turned, and raised a wagging finger. "An' do no' be followin' me. An' Marlok," he added, softening, "will ye please make that idiot quit talkin'."

"Trust me, I'm trying."

"Rude," muttered the mage pulling himself up straight. "Boringer, I pray we meet again in our travels."

"I pray we do no'," Boringer mumbled as he thrust his hands into his pockets and trudged off through the woods, horned helmet bobbing.

"Great," Marlok said like a sour raincloud.

"What?"

"Now what do we do?" The thief threw up their hands and paced.

"Well, I'm hungry," Quaswyn complained.

"If we follow that road we're bound to come across something," Marlok decided.

A dusty trail rolled across the countryside. They followed it, leaving the mountains behind.

"Do we have any food?" mewed Quaswyn. "Even one small crumb?"

"No."

"Why not?"

"Because you ate it all, you pig," snapped Marlok. "If you make me fat, I won't be happy."

"I am not fat!"

"You're pushing it though," Marlok teased, grabbing the added girth at his waist and enjoying the rise he was getting out of Quaswyn.

"Impressive for a human boy . . ."

"No, impressive for the power of the *blade*," corrected the daemon messenger. "The boy is as naïve as he is arrogant."

"Is it not true that when most humans merely *touch* those weapons, the massive energy rips them apart, body and soul?"

"That doesn't matter now, Xandon. You have orders."

"Why am I taking orders from you fools? If I should answer to anyone, it should be Tarn himself," complained the Flame king.

"You insulting—," the daemon messenger's words cut short, a blade of fire pressing against his throat.

"So what are my orders?"

"General Fernus wishes to meet with you to discuss them."

"Why are you wasting my time if I am waiting on Fernus, anyway?"

"I'm to make sure this hole of yours is presentable, you know, worthy of the daemon general's presence."

Xandon scowled, scanning his cavernous throne room. The magnificent black marble chamber was the masterpiece of the Flame elven artisans. Artificially formed stalactites and a scarlet red carpet formed an aisle leading to a polished, black marble throne. Towering braziers spilling fire into troughs flanked the Flame king's chair and illuminated the space with swirling, symphonic light.

"I should think the general of fire will find my palace quite accommodating."

"You might want to remove that disgusting flag from your walls." Above the door hung a black flag crested with a green flame. It did, in fact, seem somehow out of place in the red and black den. "Makes you seem even more repulsive than you and your kind already are."

Xandon thrust out his hand, summoning the flaming blade. He used it to stab upward, gorging the daemon's throat. While the blade died black, blood spurted from the messenger's chin. "Now, who's not presentable?" And the Flame king walked out of the room, leaving the corpse slumped on the floor in a pool of red.

Boryn Mhinbron. Well, well. Xandon shook his head. *Here we go again—only fifty years later.* Xandon looked down the marble hallway and wondered how long it would be before Tarn realized his messenger would not be returning. *Damned daemons think they deserve to command everything. They don't even realize they're just puppets in another's disgusting little game.* He snapped his fingers and burst into flame. The fire engulfed him, but it was comforting rather than painful.

He reappeared in the center of a jungle, in a blighted pocket enshrouded in heavy, hot moisture, in a land long forgotten. Ahead was an ancient stone temple where tribes ruled until the Empire tried to claim the land and execute the natives. At Xandon's feet, a headless human skeleton lay partially swallowed by the undergrowth. *Humans . . . greedy cowards. Think they have the right to own everything, even the lives of their fellows.*

"Come out, Morpheon. I know you're watching me."

"Back for another fight?" The voice was like nails scratching glass.

"Not this time. I thought you ought to be warned of the new management. From the high daemon king," mocked Xandon.

"Oh, really?" A raw-boned, manlike creature, stringy gray hair and pasty skin stretched taut like rubber across sharp features, stepped from the dense underbrush. Unperturbed by the fact that it was utterly nude, the mean little being licked its fingers clean and appraised Xandon with intense purple eyes.

"Yes. Apparently Tarn is in charge for the moment."

"We are all going to die with that simpleton commanding us," the pale being rasped offhandedly.

"Tarn is a fool, but for the moment, there's really no choice. I suspect the daemons have plans that will keep you happily entertained for a while, so you might want to complete the task of finishing off your once-heroic race before the daemons find you."

"Ah, yes, my few remaining brethren. Finally, all those who might know how to kill me will be gone, and my revenge will be complete."

The gray creature smiled. Feathers burst from its waxy skin, the color of a grub worm freshly uncovered, and slowly, it transformed into a dark gray carrion bird. Eyes darting, piercing and purple, it flew away.

Xandon shook his head and leaned into the bushes where Morpheon had been. A scene of carnage: pools of blood and chunks of human remains. *What a disgusting creature . . .*

His back pressed against a rigid, splintery surface, and his hands were tied behind him. Distant cries impinged on the soft buzz of his awakening mind. He opened his eyes slowly and bobbed his head to clear it. The wooden cart in which he rode rattled along the cobblestones while crowds lined the street, cursing him. A rotten tomato splattered against his face, and he felt slimy pulp slide down his cheek and chin.

He was tied to a pole rising from the cart's bed. He wrested against his bonds, struggling to free his hands, while trying without success to avoid another hit to the face.

"Cursed daemon, we don't want you here!"

"Burn him!"

"Leave him to the wolves!"

What did I do? What happened? Where are the daemons? His mind swirled in confusion at this wild dream. At his feet, he saw the black crystal blade, reminding him that this was no dream. Images from the night before flashed before him: the daemons, that sword, the power and . . . *Emily!* She was in serious danger, and it was his fault. Boryn writhed, desperation mounting.

The cart continued its clattering journey, and a man grabbed the side rail, threw himself aboard, and unsheathed a short sword. Boryn shut his eyes as the blade sliced his side. He cried out, and the crowd jeered as guards tackled the man and pulled him away. Warm blood trickled down Boryn's side, soaking his shirt and then dripping to the floorboards.

The cart rolled through Dusgoroth's seldom-used eastern gate and bounced along the rutted, earthen road beyond. The city walls grew distant, the townspeople held within by the guards, and the charred Grinfol Forest drew nearer with each rotation of the wooden wheels.

Suddenly, realization dawned on him. Tied to a pole. Being hauled out through the eastern gate. *I've been . . . exiled!* The cart lurched forward as the horse was unhitched and led away. *On whose order? I was only trying to help. . . .* A sword hacked through the ropes that bound him, and he dropped heavily to the ground. The daemon's black-gem scimitar slid to rest against his boot; his hands went to the sheathes at his side, the right one empty. *The black sword, the daemon's sword. They must think . . .*

He looked up to see arrows trained on him, guards backing toward the gate. Once inside, they quickly shut the portcullis then the wooden gates and left Boryn alone outside. Confused and a little scared, Boryn forced himself to his feet, one hand covering his wound. He retrieved the daemon sword and began walking. The setting was bizarre in its familiarity yet so completely different. He was an outcast for reasons he could not imagine.

"Wenval, Ranton, Calny, Laric!" he called in despair, sticky blood crusting his fingers. *I need to patch this up. . . . Ranton's house is not far from here.* He turned down the lonely path through the forest. The scuff of his boots on the hardened earth seemed loud against the silence; not even the coo of a dove broke the breathless quiet.

The roll of distant thunder called him. Turning, he saw a city still burning, smoke from the daemon's destruction still rising from behind the walls.

Where are my friends? Have you turned on me, too? Boryn clenched his fists as a tear of bitter frustration rolled down his cheek. *Or have I failed you, just like I have all the others who have fallen around me.*

He remembered the daemon's words: 'If you want her back, you will find us in a holy place.' He replayed the memory. *Emily. I will find you . . .*

He whipped the black scimitar from his side as his rage crested, the daemon's face in his mind's eye. *The monastery? That has to be it; it's so close to here.* Boryn stared at the crystal blade then down the road. In the distance, he could make out Ranton's house.

Certain that no one would be home, Boryn still tapped on the door before entering. The iron bolts creaked as the door arced inward. Boryn pulled the cloth from the table, ripped a strip from one end, and wrapped it around his middle like a wide belt over his shirt, hoping the injury was not as bad as it looked.

Thunder, a short clap and then another, closer, introduced a splatter of raindrops outside. Across the room he saw a black cape hanging from a peg. It was soft, old, and well-oiled and would provide some protection. Boryn threw it around his shoulders, grabbed a half loaf of crusty bread from the cupboard and stepped outside. *I'm coming, Emily, and those daemons are going to pay.*

Moss-draped trees stood like ghostly sentinels in the thick, low fog. The horses were tethered in a holding place while the Blood Knights advanced.

"I hate this swamp." Ramgis watched as his swordsman cut a makeshift path, carefully picking his way from one spot of solid ground to another.

"It's not so bad. Just think . . . ," Cadegray said, "once we are out of this reeking swamp, we will be in the beautiful, open wasteland of the Black Expanse and the glorious home of the Dark elves!" His words dripped sarcasm.

"These lands are cursed."

"Fitting for the previous inhabitants," Cadegray reminded Ramgis.

"But why did the daemons desert it and why, of all races, would they choose to leave it to the Dark elves?" Ramgis' lip curled with disgust as he viewed the stagnant water. A single misstep would spell the end, horse, rider or foot soldier sucked into the repulsive depths.

A sudden movement startled him from his musing; something darted between two trees, the mossy tentacles quavered. Then a splash.

"To arms!"

Ramgis ran ahead toward a cluster of trees with knotted roots that rose like knees from the bog and trapped soil to form an islet. A few knights followed, forming a tight circle in the center. Suddenly a cacophony of cries and screeches collided with the thickening fog. An arrow whistled past Ramgis' bare head; he heard it ricochet off the helmet of the knight behind him. *Maybe Cadegray is right. A helmet might be a wise idea.*

Ramgis watched as Dark elves, jeering and cackling, rose from the swamp, surrounding them, and held out their weapons, dripping with slime. Ramgis cracked a knowing smile.

A ring of fire shot up, encircling the elves and the Blood Knights. The Dark elves charged toward the knights, but another ring erupted like a shield, separating the two, Ramgis and his knights at the core and the Dark elves trapped between two fiery walls. With his metal gauntlet, the human commander tapped the metal shoulder-guard of the soldier beside him, the signal to duck. The signal was passed, and knights dropped to the ground.

A storm of arrows flew into the rings of fire where the Dark elves were trapped, and screams flew out. It took less than a minute for both fire and screams to die.

"That certainly seemed to work well, didn't it?" Rath said as he entered the quieted ring.

"Our advantage that you warned us of this ambush," Ramgis nodded, counting the elven bodies bobbing like corks in the murky water.

"The only terrain we can't ride is a cliff. Even then I consider it merely a slight challenge," joked the engaging mercenary.

"You saved many lives this day," said the old commander.

"By the way, the dark bastards charged the infantry at the rear as well."

"What!"

"They never quite reached it, so all is well," Rath grinned at his pointlessly alarming comment.

"See, you do something good, and then you ruin it by making me mad again." Ramgis shrugged, wavering between anger and intrigue, and turned back toward the place where the horses were tied.

Cadegray held back with Rath. "That's his way of saying thank you."

"I know."

"Do you enjoy annoying him?"

"Might be," Rath grinned.

"You seem to be everything he dislikes in a single person."

"What can I say? I'm the full package," Rath chuckled.

Cadegray decided to let that comment lie. "Do you know how much farther we must march until we're out of this swamp?"

"We'll reach the Black Expanse soon enough, then the Dark elf capital—if we survive that long," noted Rath grimly.

"What do you mean?"

"It seems the Dark elves are trying to block us in. These ambushes are designed to buy them time to prepare defenses."

"Can we go around them?"

"We'd be going through the caverns."

"And how heavy are these defenses, Rath?" Cadegray inquired.

"We saw mounted ballistae, traps, camps, and riders."

Eavesdropping, Ramgis rejoined the conversation. "We are expecting reinforcements from the Knights of the Wolf. Have your scouts seen any sign of them?"

Rath shrugged. "Nope. No wolves here."

A question crossed Ramgis' brow, and he moved away to untether his horse, leaving Rath and Cadegray alone.

"Did you see amongst the defenders a rider in white armor riding a particularly large mount—black scales, gray underbelly, golden spikes on its long tail?" Cadegray asked with concern.

"I seem to recall seeing one fitting that description."

"Looks like we'll be going through the caverns."

"Why?"

"Ramgis has a history with that Dark Lancer. Best to avoid him for now," Cadegray noted, his mouth set in a grim line. "That Dark elf is feared mightily in the Knightly Realms; he has single-handedly exterminated many of the Knights' generals. He also led the attack on the Snake's port city and took out nigh all of that Order's forces."

"Sounds like a swell fellow!"

"What do you have against those vipers? You are a mercenary."

"Never mind. What's this Dark elf's name?"

"Lord Kelris," said the elven messenger as he poked his head through the tent's flap.

The Lancer stood next to his white, golden-trimmed armor. His skin was sallow, his features pinched, and a dark golden robe concealed his thin but powerful build. He turned beady eyes to the visitor and said sourly. "Yes?"

"Her Majesty the Queen requests an audience."

"I shall meet with her as soon as I cut down these advancing humans," replied Kelris.

"Sir, she demands an audience immediately. I fear you have no choice."

Kelris lifted the golden-spiked helm and turned to the messenger, biting each word. "Tell her I am on my way."

The Dark elven leader, second only to the Queen, dressed carefully in the white plate and left the commodious commander's tent. Tied outside waited a reptilian creature almost three times larger than a steed. It was saddled and scaled, as terrifying as it was magnificent. It had massive, muscular legs and clawed hooves that pawed the ground, but most fearsome of all were its cruel orange eyes. Kelris touched the amulet at the beast's neck then stroked its forelock before climbing onto its back.

Looking down his nose, Kelris turned to the camp staff. "I'll return soon," he announced, "and when I do, any who have not completed their assignments preparing our defenses . . . well, Krixlus seems a bit hungry." He patted the beast's thick neck, and it slapped the ground with its golden-spiked tail. Kelris dug his heels into Krixlus' side, clucked as the soldiers picked up the pace, and bolted across the ashen Black Expanse toward the Queen's capital.

Tharrus lolled across the broken altar, resting his head on one arm. With the other, he held out one long finger and pointed at the decomposing body of a monk. He raised his hand, and the corpse lifted into the air like a puppet on a string.

"Humans aren't nearly as much fun dead. Even so, this is rather entertaining." He moved his finger in a quick circle, watching the limp body twirl. He sighed and waved as if flicking away a pestering fly, and the bloated corpse rocketed toward the wall, splattering and shattering what bone was left.

The sadistic daemon gazed out at the limestone sanctuary. Flanking a wide, center aisle were rows of wooden pews. At each side, stone pillars soared to support ribs that vaulted across the space and beyond formed a colonnade of prayer shrines lit only by a few candles. High in the nave, clerestory windows pierced the arches and admitted sharp shafts of light filled with idly drifting dust motes.

Tharrus let his head roll backward, and he stared at the little circle, a small bell tower, that penetrated the ceiling above him. Lazily, he rose and ambled toward the colonnade, to the wall where the girl was suspended. She was terrified but unharmed, her glare boldly meeting the daemon's.

"What? Am I not as pretty as you?" He assumed a half-form—red-black skin, fangs, and claws—and approached the girl. Deliberately, he sliced his own face with his claw then used his power to seal it. In an unpleasant nasal voice, he asked, "I wonder if you can do that?" He reached out and touched a cool claw to her cheek.

"Stop," ordered the brother as he walked into the sanctuary.

"Look at her! She can't even talk! Ahhahaha!" Tharrus cackled.

"She's not bait if she's dead."

"I only plan to mangle her. She'll still be alive," Tharrus turned pouty. "But then that boy will think you're ugly and won't care to save you." He traced the claw along her jaw line without breaking the skin, unable to contain his mirth.

The hand dropped. He roared as something sliced down his back. He spun, back against the wall, surprised to see the boy there.

"Well, you came it seems." Tharrus pulled a bloodied hand away from the wound on his back, making no effort to conceal his testiness.

"I won't let you hurt her," Boryn blurted.

"What a hero!"

"You think you can save her in a place of our choosing?" laughed the older brother. "So very foolish."

"You are the fools," growled Boryn.

Tharrus boasted, "Do you know what it means for a daemon to be awarded a black-gem weapon? It means the daemon has the power of a general. Meaning, my abilities far surpass yours, boy."

Boryn held out his swords, both the iron and the black-gem one, and used them to push Tharrus against the wall. "Then why is it that I can beat you?"

"You can't. You only think you can because we didn't unleash our full power." The older, wiser daemon explained. "Generals and other particularly strong daemons are required to withhold, meaning we are not allowed to fully unleash our powers without permission because we would cause far too much damage. Only in very rare cases might one fully release, but only because it has learned to control the inconceivable energy and because it has been given permission to do so for that moment."

Tharrus added, "I am yet to gain full control of my power. So if by accident I'm pushed so far I can't resist . . . well, it's quite amazing."

Tharrus' brother unsheathed his sword and backed Boryn against the wall. "Humans misguidedly view temples and churches as safe from us. Daemons cannot sense what's inside of a holy place in the same way that we can elsewhere, so we usually don't bother with them. As a result, fighting a daemon in a holy place is like handing us your head, because we can let loose—release—and our leadership will never know."

"And that is what I plan to do right now," Tharrus threatened. "We will ever-so-joyfully destroy both you and your little girl over there." The air rippled around the daemon. "No one and nothing can stop me."

"Thank you for that lesson in what generals can and cannot do." A deep voice came from one of the prayer alcoves, and a figure stepped from the shadows. A droopy cowl was raised over his head, concealing most of his face, and he wore a voluminous white cloak with a white overmantle, both edged in black. At his side was sheathed a black-gem longsword.

"General!" stuttered Tharrus as the energy around him dissipated.

"You are going to fight this boy normally, and if you decide to 'let loose' . . . ," the general appeared in front of Tharrus, his hand pressed against the novice general's throat. "Do we have an understanding?"

"General Fernus, I am sorry, please," begged Tharrus, his voice whiny in hopes of receiving mercy from the most powerful of the daemon generals, the ruler of fire.

With a long, refined hand, Fernus brushed back the white hood. His skin was ghostly white, and his wild, wavy hair matched the color of his eyes—fiery orange. "Fight fairly, or I kill you both now," Fernus said simply as he reclined in a wooden pew to watch.

"Fear not, brother, it's still two to one," Tharrus whispered to his brother.

"Actually. . . ." The daemons' eyes shot up. It was Belral standing in the open clerestory. Smirking, the sword master leapt to the ground beside Boryn.

"Why are you here?" growled Tharrus.

"I have friends here, and when I don't hear from my friends, I get worried."

"You pick weak friends," Tharrus laughed, snorting, as he kicked one of the monk's bodies toward Belral.

Belral stepped out of the way toward Boryn. "I'll take the sword wielder if you prefer the role of avenger," he said, then nodded toward Tharrus, "That's the one that tortured . . ."

"Sounds good. This is for Emily and for Ranton's mother," Boryn said raising both his old, iron and his new, black-gem scimitars.

Fernus looked from the black blade to Tharrus to the limp sheath at Tharrus' side and began to chuckle. "Where is your blade?"

"The boy took it."

"So it would seem." Fernus laughed aloud.

Furious at being ridiculed, Tharrus roared, skin reddening and fangs baring, as he yielded to the drug of full, daemonic power, and the transformation began. Undeterred, Boryn charged even as Belral pointed his longsword at the brother, and the two began to circle one another.

"You're released, too, aren't you?" Belral suggested to his opponent.

"Caught me. I just learned to control it," the brother said calmly but with a slight grin.

"I wonder who will win this one," Belral toyed.

"I shall, obviously."

"Umm, seeing that I am a sword master and you've yet to see my techniques . . . ," Belral bragged.

"Ha! A feeble, old man defeating a released daemon?" the brother laughed.

"I might be old, but I still have a few tricks up these sleeves." A wide grin spread across Belral's narrow face.

At that instant, Boryn saw Tharrus' whip fling toward his face. He shot the black scimitar into the whip's path and watched the whip coil the black shaft. Then, he jumped sideways, letting the daemon hurtle past as it made to tackle him. The daemon's forward momentum provided an opportunity. Boryn spun in the opposite direction and jerked back with his sword hard to tear the whip from Tharrus' grip. He lowered the blade tip so the whip would slide free. The daemon regained his footing and charged again. Boryn felt a blast from behind. He winced, finishing his spin with two scimitars upraised just in time to block as the daemon's claws fired toward his face.

"You released! Now you're in trouble," teased Boryn.

Fernus interceded. "I'll address that after the battle. But for now, I'd love to see how this plays out."

"Good bye, kid," chortled Tharrus in his grating, nasal voice.

The daemon kicked high, smacked its clawed foot into Boryn's chin, and propelled him into the air. Tharrus reached for the boy's head, intent upon pulverizing it against the monastery floor.

Boryn managed to slice down, severing the daemon's finger, and the daemon recoiled in time for Boryn to catch himself. Momentarily, the daemon was stunned. Seizing the chance, Boryn spun, slicing the daemon with the black blade while impaling the general's shoulder with the iron one. Tharrus sniveled and swung away but continued to bring around powerful, bulging arms, clipping Boryn, unbalancing him. Shaken, Boryn staggered. The daemon sneered, tore free the iron blade and held it forward. Boryn grasped the hilt of the black scimitar with both hands. A sudden blast of energy blew Boryn into a pillar, but where there had been a sword in the daemon's hand now there was merely molten metal dripping from a hilt.

Tharrus dropped the useless weapon, brought his fist back and stormed toward Boryn. At the instant of impact, Boryn rolled to the side and watched as Tharrus' daemon-charged fist collided with the stone pillar, shattering the stone like glass. Boryn stabbed at the arm before it vanished, and something grabbed his hair from behind and tugged his head backward. The daemon's malice-filled eyes met Boryn's.

Images of incredible power flashed before Boryn's mind's eye. An odd sensation coursed through his body as if a dam to an immense source of energy had opened. And he knew. *All that power is mine.*

Boryn chuckled while sneering at the daemon.

"What the hell is so funny? I am about to rip your head from your shoulders!"

Boryn's self-satisfied expression did not change.

"You're infuriating!" Tharrus roared, plowing a thumbless fist into Boryn's face. Boryn's hand shot up, grabbed the fist, and stopped it midair. He pivoted, snapping the daemon's wrist, then, raising the black scimitar high, gripped it with both hands, flipped it downward, and stabbed. The daemon's chest took the brunt of the blow, and the chiseled, black blade skewered him. Boryn yanked the blade free and spun, angling the blade to cleave head from shoulders.

General Fernus rose, applauding.

"What are you so happy about?" Boryn asked, wiping the bloody blade on his pant leg before sheathing it.

"I'm honestly impressed. To see your bloodline awaken was impressive. Grand timing as well. Unfortunate for Tharrus, however. If only he'd used a bit more self control, he'd still have his head," said Fernus as he regarded the daemon's lifeless form with benign disinterest.

"What are you talking about?"

"Your power. How else do you explain stopping a 'released'— albeit only partially—daemon?"

Boryn tried to make sense of Fernus' words.

"The power of the Mhinbrons. Ha! Truly amazing!" Fernus seemed genuinely amused.

"What are you babbling about?" Weary of Fernus' cryptic talk, Boryn drew the black-gem blade and trained it on the orange-haired general.

"You know I consider that a challenge," Fernus remarked.

"You're a daemon, so you deserve to die."

"Ah, well, in that case—"

Boryn felt a sudden pain in his chest, and a cold edge pressed tight against his throat.

The powerful daemon general bent close, orange eyes blazing. "As you can see, you are far from ready to present a true challenge. So why don't you run along, let your little girl down, and escape." Fernus moved back and made a display of sheathing his black-gemmed longsword.

Boryn remained motionless, unable to understand what had just happened.

"Until then, Boryn Mhinbron, get stronger. One day you might prove an entertaining fight. I'll see you at Ranlon."

The daemon disappeared in a flare of his black hell fire.

I didn't know he'd moved until the blade was at my throat.

Boryn hurried toward Emily who appeared to have passed out during the fight. He untied her and gently let her down. He turned to see Belral standing over the corpse of the other daemon.

"Do you know what he meant by my 'bloodline'?"

"I believe so, yes."

"Well?"

Belral hesitated. "When the strongest among us, usually a hero, has a child, the child is often born with special powers and abilities. When the child is young, the powers are locked away, never evident, so it is impossible to tell who carries the 'bloodline' and who does not. And then, at the coming of age, some experience of particular danger triggers the initial release. After that, the power is unlocked in times of crisis." The explanation was very matter-of-fact, but the implications were far from it.

Boryn struggled to comprehend. "My father's only skill is immunity to sobriety."

"The power of the bloodline can skip generations. Or, it may be that your father has never faced a true challenge. But for now, you must be careful. This is known as the period of initial release; it's like getting an extra boost which may be hard to control. But even then, you are not as powerful as you will be. Just a few days will make a difference. You must work your way back up to this point and beyond. And you must be very careful."

Boryn held out his hands, inspecting them as if he'd never seen them before. *So that's what I felt.* He turned to Emily who was slowly sitting up. He offered her a hand and helped her to her feet. "Are you all right?"

"Boryn," she smiled. She put her arms around his middle and hugged him tightly. His face reddened in an awkward grin followed by a grimace.

"What happened there?" She touched the bandage tied at his waist.

Boryn unwrapped the dressing, lifted his shirt and was surprised to find the wound sealed. He tossed the bloodied bandage aside. "Do you suppose this is this part of my bloodline?" he asked with a crooked smile.

"I'm glad you weren't hurt," he said. "I was . . ."

"We need to return her to Dusgoroth." Belral stopped him. "Actually, I need to do it myself since you still can't go near the place."

"Why does she have to go back?"

"She will be safer there than with you, of that I'm sure."

Boryn felt Emily's hold tighten. He patted the back of her head. "I'll be fine. You just stay safe until I return."

"If you insist, Boryn," she said playfully.

Belral interrupted again. "Boryn, you must leave this place before nightfall, or you'll find yourself surrounded by a force of very riled peasants. The fact that you were exiled for being evil and you're in a monastery full of dead monks will not look good."

"Where should I go?"

"Go to Mount Pyr."

"And do what?"

"Get stronger. You told me you were willing to fight to the death so long as it protected others. Go out and prepare to prove it. I fear that our battles are just beginning."

Boryn nodded as Belral and Emily left the monastery, framed in the doorway against the setting sun. A dazzling array of color bathed the room in somber hues, and a beam of sunlight, scattered through a stained glass, illuminated a scene of flames licking a star-speckled sky. *And so it begins. . . . A journey to protect the ones I hold dear.*

Visions

"Looks like we get to eat again."

"Oh, goody," exclaimed Quaswyn. "I have an idea!"

"What?"

"Before we go into the city, let's change our name to 'Marwyn'," Quaswyn suggested.

"You are a dunderhead."

"Why? Then they won't think we're crazy."

Marlok shook his head and moved forward with purposeful strides toward the wooden-walled city ahead. As they neared, it became clear this place was far from prosperous, walls rotting and not a person in sight.

"You won't eat the food we save this time, right?" Marlok sought a promise.

"Yes, yes, I won't." Quaswyn wagged their head needlessly.

Marlok approached the unguarded and open city gate and entered. Inside, buildings tumbled to ruin; weeds sprouted through ruts in the road; neither human nor beast stirred the quiet. The thief shuddered.

Quaswyn raised a finger. "I'll bet this is the Cursed City I read about. The place where the four dead ones arose."

"The who?"

"The Undead Four: Death, Destruction, Terror, and . . . I think his, er, I suppose, the leader's name was Zalmani, also known as Regret. If this is the Cursed City, the Four annihilated it and cursed the poor souls of this town to remain trapped here forever. That's why it is also known as the 'haunted city of the dead,'" explained Quaswyn.

"Are the Four still here?"

"Let's hope not! Fyr Bill defeated them once. And it's definitely a power we don't want to arouse," Quaswyn shivered.

"You have seriously made me mad this time." Marlok stomped forward.

"Why?" asked Quaswyn, accompanying involuntarily.

"You brought us to a nothing town in the middle of nowhere where everything is dead!"

"And that's my fault . . . why?" Quaswyn pouted. They passed a dilapidated house. Something caught Quaswyn's attention. Marlok moved to go, but Quaswyn jolted them to a stop, squinted, and leaned close to the wooden wall. It looked as if a screaming person was trapped within the grain, the flattened, terrified face of a wraith. Quaswyn spurted forward.

"So what do we do now?"

"Humans still live here—mainly priests trying to break the curse so the souls may find their eternal fate. We should find a priest and ask him; he'll tell you about places they call heaven and hell," said the mage.

If Marlok could have looked at Quaswyn and scowled, he would have. Instead, exasperated, Marlok exploded. "Heaven and hell? Unless they are nearby, have food, and know a bit about defusion, I couldn't care less. Now let's get moving. There's nothing for us here."

"At the very least, you should carry this orb for a while. It's heavy, heavy, heavy; and I'm sick to death of lugging it."

Marlok rolled their eyes skyward and marched on.

Luthor gazed across the gently rolling plains that spanned the Empire's outer territory. He seemed tranquil, comfortable in the well-worn saddle of his horse. But the scene he had happened upon was far from serene. As the Red X drew near, they realized that the mounds marring the landscape were in fact rotting human corpses. A ragged imperial flag flapped in the breeze, the only sound to be heard. A gust rippled the thick grass and lifted the tail of Luthor's cape. *So much for finding a peaceful spot to rest.*

"What were they fighting?" Luthor wondered if his second would recognize the signs.

"Not daemons," Dace reasoned aloud, black eyes narrow like slits. "They wouldn't bother clearing their tracks, nor would they fight in a fashion that would leave no tracks. Can't be orcs in that case, either. Too dumb. Not elves. They leave their arrows as a warning. Not the knights. No horse hooves. No sign of a boot print, so that rules out bandits."

"You have no idea, do you?"

"I did find what appear to be tracks of a giant lizard. The tracks were under a body so I guess they were overlooked," Dace continued.

"That would mean rapi, correct?"

"Ah, yes, the lizardmen."

Luthor crossed his arms over his horse's mane and leaned against its neck, thinking.

"Where shall the Red X army head now, Luthor?"

"All the signs are here. My bet is we're on the verge of another Daemon War. I plan to help with that. Then it might be time to settle down, build ourselves a nice little fort . . ."

"The Red X in a Daemon War?" Dace's brow arched.

"You're right. Bad idea. The damned imperialists can deal with their own problems. Let's go find a place to settle. Nearly fifteen years as a nomad is enough."

"You always make the right decision, my lord."

"So where should we start?"

"Good question. The Empire is out, the Black Expanse inhospitable."

"Let's just ride until we find a place that looks good."

"Splendid idea, sir."

"Please stop for a while," Luthor said, feeling irritable.

"Stop what?"

"Talking. It bothers me."

"Sorry, sir."

"Commander," a Red X scout rode up beside the leader.

"Yes?"

"The Blood Knights are on the move again, doing what they feel like. That leaves some villages open for . . . if you're interested."

"Looting the Knightly Realms has long been a favorite pastime. Yes, let's do that." Luthor lifted his hands to the sky in mock reverence. "Thank you, General Ramgis, for leaving your post as self-appointed guardian of the countryside, or whatever your current game might be." Then he turned back to the scout. "Do you know where Ramgis is now?"

"His army is moving through the dark swamps. We think he will attack the Dark elves. They have skirmished already."

"The nasty bastards who shattered the Alliance between the

humans, dwarves, and elves?"

"Yes. The Dark Ones are his target."

"Men, with Ramgis otherwise occupied, we are in for some fun," Luthor announced, visions of pillage in mind.

Boryn crouched in a bent, old tree, concealed in feathery foliage. Below him, a creature slithered on its belly through the marsh. It was like a man but sickly, warped, and twisted, a being no longer human. Boryn waited, immobile, as it crept through the slurry. When it was directly below, Boryn dropped from the crooked limb, his black scimitar puncturing the thing's back.

He tore the blade free and wiped the blackened blood against the tree's hairy bark as something grabbed his ankle and yanked his legs from under him. Boryn landed face first in the smelly bog then flipped over to see the thing looming over him, upright now on short, back legs. It lashed out. Boryn's blade flew to block the swipe, severing the hand in the process. Groaning, the creature reeled, and others like it rose from the swamp water, intense, black eyes locked on Boryn. *Fantastic . . .*

"Abominations! Your end is at hand!" came a cry from behind.

A short figure, the essence of motion, blasted in. Halberd in one hand, a round shield in the other, the man sliced one creature from shoulder to hip; it dropped with a piercing screech. Another charged the stout, fuzzy-bearded man. Red hair flying like a puff of cinnamon dust, the man shot up like a coiled spring, cleaving the head of one and, on the downswing, slicing another in two.

"You got to chop 'em into pieces!"

One more creature remained. Scrambling to his feet, eager to help, Boryn held his blade high then jumped forward, his cape sailing behind him. With the chiseled blade, he slashed down, halving the beast in midair. Its body splashed, twice, into the swamp. Boryn landed to face his unlikely savior. The man was barely waist high to Boryn, but thick and powerful. His hair and chin-rimming beard were neatly trimmed. When Boryn looked the man in the face, he realized the man was only a few years his elder.

"The name's Stevan." A friendly hand was extended. "And what would yours be?"

"Boryn."

"Wonderful name. Where are you from?"

"Shouldn't we be focusing?" Boryn tilted his head toward another creature emerging from the marsh.

"Pah! If you insist." The bearded man chopped the last of the creatures and kept chopping until it fell into many pieces. "Damn zombies . . ."

"What are they?"

"Undead, as in stuff that should've stayed buried, but some witch, liche, or warlock gave them new life as hungry, flesh-eating beasts."

"I have no idea what you are talking about."

"Come with me. I'll explain it over dinner. You hungry? I left some meat over the fire, so I need to get back and brush a bit more seasoning on it."

"You cook?"

"What's wrong with me cooking?"

"You just don't seem the type," Boryn shrugged.

The little man lifted a zombie lying half on the solid ground and half in the water and smashed it with a head butt. "An' why is that?" Stevan turned to Boryn, grinning with gore dripping down his face.

The Strawberry Mug was packed, but the mood was unusually subdued. Instead of lively chatter and boisterous laughter, only warm light spilled from the windows to the streets. Most of the repairs were complete after the daemon rampage, and the Mug profited since Dusgoroth's other inns were not even close to being ready for business.

Alone, Ranton leaned against the outside wall at the margin between light and dark. He reached for the leather strap hanging from his belt; the crystal etched with a *B* was clear, no indication of trouble. He squeezed the stones in his fist and turned his eyes toward the stars as if they could provide the answer. *Where are you, Boryn?*

"Why the long face? You look like you could use some company." A silky voice wafted from the shadows. Ranton wheeled to see Julia standing very close.

"I'm worried about my friend."

"He's a daemon—everyone saw it!"

"Boryn is no daemon. It was the darkness of that sword."

"Darkness is evil, the power of daemons. Why is it, do you

suppose, that humans insist on so much light?" she motioned toward the bright tavern window.

'Humans'? That was weird. "I never thought of that. But still, the darkness we saw wasn't Boryn. I'll never believe that."

Julia rose up on the tips of her toes. Ranton could feel her breath on his face, but something made him tense. "You know, we could find him with your crystal. Learn the truth."

"Pah! We don't even know what's beyond our forest and the monastery."

"Do it for your own peace of mind if nothing else. Find out what he truly is—an evil being, or just another foolish boy."

Ranton stared into her smoky lavender eyes, his own glazing over as if entranced, possessed. "Yes. You're right. That's what we should do. I'll get the others."

Long strides closed the gap to the inn's door, and Ranton threw it open, light bathing him. Shouldering his way through the crowd, he found Calny and Laric at the bar. "Get your stuff together, and tell the barmaids they're in charge for a while."

"What are you talking about?" Emily stopped her work to listen.

Ranton held up the crystal with the *B.* "This is where we're going."

"You want to go find an exile?" Laric asked.

Wenval stepped up from the cellar, wiping his hands on the rag tied at his waist. "Ranton's right. Boryn's our friend. We should stand by him, not hide in this pathetic, little inn."

"That's what I've been trying to tell you!" Emily added.

"If he's a daemon, he would want us to stop him before he kills anyone," Ranton said with dazed certainty.

Wenval's head snapped toward Ranton. "What are you talking about? Boryn's no daemon! When we see him, you'll know."

Ranton's reply was emotionless. "Yes, we'll see."

Emily and Wenval exchanged a concerned look while Calny and Laric shared a shrug.

"And the Shadow Crusaders are on the march again," Laric said.

Wenval added, "Grab our gear and meet back here. There's no more time to lose."

Boryn followed the stout little man who waddled down the hill. The man stopped at the base of an ancient, sprawling oak. He stabbed the end of his halberd into the ground and twisted. There was a click, a trapdoor opened, and the man dropped. Boryn jumped after him. A coiled wire pulled the hatch shut as Boryn landed in a dust cloud, and a click signaled that the lock had re-engaged. Before his eyes could adjust to the dimness, a door opened, and flickering firelight filled the small space.

Climbing to his feet, Boryn shadowed Stevan into the adjoining chamber. It was a cavern, circular and hewn from the stone with two sets of sleeping platforms chopped into the walls. In the middle was a thick, wooden table cluttered with bowls and spices, scraps and plates. Beyond, opposite the door, was a huge fireplace carved directly in the stone. Boryn noticed bunches of dried leaves hanging from the ceiling and jars filled with powders and liquids lining niches chiseled into the stone. A sizeable boar roasted on a spit over the fire; the man slathered it with a thick, gooey concoction that smelled wonderful when it hissed into the fire. Boryn watched curiously.

"Your name's Stevan, right?"

"You're right with that."

"What are you exactly?"

"What do you think I am, you simpleton? Just because I don't have the horrid speech impediment of the others doesn't mean I'm not one."

"Not one what?"

"Honestly, what are you humans told today?" Stevan waggled his head in dismay.

"You can't be a dwarf!"

"And why ever not?"

"Because that race is extinct."

"That would appear to be incorrect," the dwarf responded indignantly.

"Then why are we told your race is dead?"

"Because you humans are dead to us after what you did. So we ceased all communications, and now you are foolish enough to think we are gone. Most of us live away from humans altogether. Only my clan lives 'out here.'"

"What did we do to you?"

"You left us to die. The daemons ravaged our capital and wiped out most of our race, but you humans were too busy defending yourselves to help us. Don't you know your history? The Alliance was a joke. The humans, elves, and dwarves only agreed to *not* fight each other while each defended themselves against the daemons. Imagine how many lives might have been saved if we had really worked together! But that was a long time ago."

Stevan turned back to his boar, hacked off a chunk, and bit into it. Licking the juice from his fingers, his youthful face ignited with joy.

"So tell me about those zombies." Boryn cleared a place in the table's clutter and helped himself to a seat.

"There's a witch north of here, in a tower of course. She captured and imprisoned my whole clan, including my sister Hannah. These zombies are her work, I'm sure of it."

"Have you tried a rescue?"

"Yes, but the witch uses cheater's fighting. My clan attacked her, but her magic beat us off. Then she hired mercenaries to capture us. Probably planned to sacrifice us in some nasty ceremony." Stevan shuddered then shrugged. "Luckily for me, I was away collecting potatoes for my newest creation." He lifted a large iron pot filled with sizzling oil from the rack above the fire. He drained the oil into a hole in the floor.

"Here, try this." Stevan handed Boryn a crisp, golden disk.

"What is it?"

"I call it a chip, because it reminds me of the stone chips I used to shape the stones of this world."

Huh? Boryn placed the chip in his mouth and crunched down. "Not that bad."

"Pah! Not bad? Here, try the boar." Grinning widely and wielding an enormous cleaver, he slammed a chunk of steaming meat onto the table.

"That's just a little scary."

"It's been awhile since I've had anyone around, so my manners might have slipped a tad." Stevan tucked a cloth into his collar where it hung like a windless sail. He took a large bite, juice sliding down his fingers and dripping onto the table. "So tell me, what were you doing in the marsh anyway?"

"Headed to Mount Pyr."

The dwarf seemed skeptical. "What for?"

"Not sure exactly. I was told to go there . . ."

"Well, you're here now. So what do you plan to do?"

"Er, I don't know. You saved me at the marsh, so how about I help you rescue your clan?" Boryn blurted without giving it a moment's thought. "This is really delicious, by the way," he said between mouthfuls.

"Now there's an idea for you!" Stevan bobbed his head happily. "Have you seen the witch's tower and her mercenaries?" Stevan took another large bite. "This is good, isn't it?"

"I don't care if they are ogres. We will save your clan." Boryn slammed his open palm on the table, sending up a clatter.

"Well, aren't you feeling heroic today."

Boryn and Stevan crouched in the scrub and observed the guard at the wooden drawbridge. The man was heavily armored in black, not a bit of skin showing, powerful and foreboding, in stark contrast to the unkempt courtyard and the rickety old tower behind him.

"This was a much better idea from inside your cave," Boryn whispered.

"I prefer 'abode.' Makes it sound more welcoming and homey."

"Who—or what—is that man?"

"He's one of the knights hired by that bloody witch. Used to be of the Raven Order, but now a renegade faction—a bunch of dirty, sell-sword, soulless rats, if you ask me."

"He's huge!" Boryn studied the spiked, black plate and mail, the black, cylindrical helmet, and the golden sword at the knight's side. The man stood as large and immobile as a column, eyes trained on some unseen point in the distance.

"We have some boys patrolling," Stevan elbowed Boryn and jerked his head toward a group of mounted knights advancing toward the tower. "I'll take care of them. You handle the big guy until I'm done."

"You against four knights?"

"I'll be fine. You worry about yourself."

Boryn sprang from the bushes and crossed the distance to the sentry in a heartbeat. He withdrew the black-gem scimitar and channeled energy into it. In slow motion, the black knight unsheathed his blade and raised it toward the boy, lifting his shield with the other hand. Black energy fired from Boryn's blade, struck the shield and scattered. The knight lunged at Boryn, swinging his sword upward and kicking dirt into Boryn's face.

Boryn rolled backward then reversed thrust to power forward. The knight smacked his shield against Boryn's face, snapping the boy's head to the side, toppling him to the ground. The boy flipped face up and blocked with the side of his blade as the guard's sword crashed down. The blades collided. The force of the blow crushed Boryn's elbows into the ground. Boryn shoved up and rolled aside; momentum carried the guard's heavy, golden blade smashing to the earth. Back on his feet, Boryn jumped back as the knight's sword came up in a slicing S, narrowly missing him.

The boy glanced toward Stevan who was surrounded by knights with only one downed. *This was a bad idea.* Boryn refocused energy, channeling it into his blade, and exploded forward. He dove beneath a powerful swing and somersaulted back to his feet. He spun out of the path as the guard's shield whooshed toward him. Boryn channeled more energy but this time forced the energy to stay within the blade. He sliced downward across the incoming shield. He watched as the charged scimitar cleaved through the shield, the gauntlet, and the knight's arm. There was a roar of pain and anger as the knight recoiled from the glowing, black blade.

Boryn wheeled to his right with a high-to-low slash, releasing a crescent of energy that cut from the knight's left shoulder to his right foot. Blood sprayed through the armor, and the knight careened backward and stumbled against the drawbridge rail. The weight of his armor flipped him into the moat. A single bubble gulped at the surface, and the water stilled.

Boryn turned back toward Stevan, all four assailants downed, poking his halberd to send off a riderless horse. Boryn smiled and whistled, but when Stevan turned, waving happily, the skittish mount kicked the dwarf and sent him flying. Boryn ran to give Stevan a hand up. They exchanged looks that combined "what in the world are we doing" with "we can do anything," and the improbable duo clattered across the drawbridge's warped planks. They reached the vine-covered tower and threw open the tired, studded door. Voices, loud and unintelligible, spiraled up the stair shaft.

"Stevan, you go downstairs. It's likely your clan we hear. I'll go up." Boryn started up the twisting staircase; a fresh eruption of yelling bounced up the stone hollow behind him. The stairs ended at a small landing under a conical turret. He paused momentarily at the crooked, wooden door. Then, he kicked hard, and the door flew open, cracking at the hinges.

"Oh!" An old, bent woman with wild, gray hair and knurly hands hovered over a sea green orb which floated before her. Backed against the wall and watching wide-eyed was a very pretty, human girl. Her clever blue eyes complimented both the corn-silk hair that hung in gentle curls at her shoulders as well as her jade-colored dress.

Boryn ducked through the arched, stone doorway. "Your schemes are at an end, witch!" Without a thought, Boryn flung his scimitar at the orb. The ball shattered, and the witch shot out her arm, two fingers pointing, and an invisible force plowed into Boryn's chest. He flew back to the stone wall where he was stuck, pinned by the witch's power.

The old witch raged, outstretched arm trembling but holding its mark. "Daemon spawn sent to free the powers, is it?"

"Who? Me?"

"Don't play the fool! You disgust me," shrieked the wild-eyed woman. She brought her other hand forward, a ball of light forming in the palm.

Boryn protested. "Are you mad? You're the one creating zombies and locking up innocent people!"

She stopped, confused, her fury melting away along with the ball of light in her hand, but she did not lower the pointing fingers. "This orb was keeping *that* from happening!" She inclined her head toward the window. Boryn looked out. A mountain was framed in the opening. Black clouds boiled at the peak and tumbled down the slopes.

His eyes asked the question.

"That's the work of a daemon general. I've held him bound on Mount Pyr with the power of the orb that you just broke."

"So you . . . ," Boryn puzzled it through. "But why are you holding the dwarves?"

"The fools tried to break the orb. I couldn't let them unleash the daemon and endanger all the races, because that daemon—," lightning flashed from the cloud, "—controls storms."

"What do we do now? Can we stop it?"

"Without the orb, only killing Thundrus will stop him."

"I'll do it."

"Pah! You're just a child, and a stupid one at that."

"I've fought a general before, and I've killed one in training. How else would I have that blade?" It lay among the orb's shards.

The witch looked down, and the wizened old face sparked with surprise. "A daemon blade?"

"So let me down; I'm going to go kill it."

"Do as you please."

The witch gave in, and Boryn dropped to the floor. He stood, unsteady from aftershock, and his knees buckled again. The girl approached him and held out her hands. An emerald green light floated down, wrapping him in its rejuvenating aura. Then, with urgency in her voice, she turned to the witch. "Let me join him. I can help with the magic you've taught me."

"Hannah—"

"Please, teacher, allow me this chance to prove myself."

"All right. But be careful."

Boryn retrieved the crystal scimitar. He rushed out the door and wound down the stairs, running headlong into Stevan.

Stevan wheeled to follow. "Did you find her?"

"Yes," Hannah answered, appearing at Boryn's heels. "And the witch is on our side."

"No. It's a trick," Stevan insisted.

Boryn said, "The witch was using an orb to control the daemon general of storms. We have to stop what I just released. Let's get to the mountain."

They burst from the tower, pursued by a rabble of untidy dwarves. Thunder rumbled down Mount Pyr and across the void.

"Sorry we can not help you, human," said a sour, old dwarf. "We are not allowed up the mountain."

"I am. I'll go with you," said Stevan.

"Stevan, our clan, was banished," reminded the old dwarf.

"*You* and the others were banished—because you wouldn't stay away from the humans; the king was only trying to protect our people with that restriction." Stevan glanced toward Boryn with a smile. "But because the king liked my cooking, I was given the option . . ."

"You'd turn your back on your own clan?"

"Hardly."

Boryn shoved past the dwarves and across the drawbridge, Hannah and Stevan close behind him.

I wonder if this is what Belral had in mind.

Moments before, the shady grove had seemed the right place to rest. But now, Xandon felt less sure. Uncertainty hung like a heavy blanket in the hot, damp calm.

"Xandon?"

"Fernus." Now he understood.

"Did you ever get your orders?" Fernus asked the Flame elven king.

"And what would those be?"

"To kill the boy."

"Ah. Your ignoble goal."

"Rescinded. Instead I want you to distract him while I take care of his friends. I'm interested in seeing how he fares against Thundrus."

"Is it just me, or do all you generals have names ending with 'us'?" Xandon posed the irrelevant query.

"A second name is added depending upon one's abilities."

"Thundrus . . . Lord of Thunder, eh?"

"Storms."

"And so you want me to keep the boy busy? What if I kill him—by accident?" Xandon put forward, folding his arms across his chest.

"If young Boryn can't hold his own against you, he'll be no challenge for Thundrus. So fine, kill him," replied Fernus simply.

"Understood."

"By the way, these orders start now."

"The courtesy of your advance notice is well noted."

Mount Pyr towered in the midst of squat, little knolls, its foot cradled in oaks and its peak blasted away in some ancient, volcanic event. Usually, its jagged rim was distinct against a clear sky, but this day the crater was shrouded in swirling darkness. Wind and rain battering them, Boryn, Stevan, and Hannah sprinted up a gravelly path that climbed toward the summit. Lightning struck an outcrop; rocky shrapnel rocketed through the air.

Something inside Boryn screamed for him to jump backward. He did at the very moment an enormous plume of fire shot from earth to sky. It died down, burning away the rain and leaving in its wake a tall, slender, white-haired elf wearing intensely red robes. A green scar slashed across the elf's right eye. Boryn unsheathed his black scimitar.

"Aren't you excited for a fight?" chuckled the elf. His voice was melodious, as oddly smooth as a raging fire's deep roar.

"Who are you?"

"Xandon's my name. You'll want to remember it so next time you hear it, you'll know to run."

"Hannah, Stevan, back away. This one's mine."

"Righteous, aren't you, little Mhinbron?"

"How do you know who I am?"

"Not important."

"What do you want with me?"

"Honestly, I'm bored," Xandon said, raising his voice to be heard above the storm. He glanced over the boy's shoulder to see Fernus advancing toward the other two.

"I can take care of that." Boryn rushed the seemingly defenseless Xandon and swept up with his black daemon blade, expecting it to cut right through the annoying elf. Instead, the scimitar recoiled, striking something hard. A blade of fire shot from the elf's hand, unaffected by the sheets of rain, to block Boryn's black sword. The boy reeled back as the Flame elf slashed with his fiery blade. Boryn reached for the dagger in his boot and grinned. *Easy.* He charged Xandon then veered, rolling low beneath the flame blade. He came up slicing with his dagger toward the elf's side. The strike fell short, and a knee connected with the center of Boryn's ribcage, blasting the breath from his lungs. He fell to the soggy ground, mud spattering his face.

"Well, that was fun." The elf was tediously nonchalant. "Farewell, Boryn. Enjoy your fight with Thundrus."

"Where the hell are you going?"

"Home."

"Our fight isn't over . . . ," Boryn was back on his feet.

"But this round is. Until we meet again, Mhinbron," laughed Xandon as he vanished in a blast of orange flame.

"Hannah! Stevan!" Boryn doubled back, but they were nowhere to be seen. The wind picked up; towering cedars that climbed the hill bent nearly to the breaking point. *Xandon must have taken them.* Boryn faced the top of the mountain, to the source of the churning black clouds, and dashed upward, zigzagging to elude the crackling energy that seemed to target him. His foot scarcely left the ground before an aggressive strike blasted the muddy imprint. His hair stood on end.

Marlok turned watchful eyes to the darkening sky. "Well, this is certainly nasty weather for traveling."

"If you hadn't made us lost . . ."

"Me? You're the featherhead that said there was a shortcut."

Lightning fingered across the sky.

"Oh, my goodness, that was close," gasped Quaswyn, hinged at the waist, hands on knees and breathing heavily.

"Let's find shelter at the base of that mountain to wait this one out. If we hurry, we might make it before the rain starts." A hissing bolt of lightning struck the earth beside them.

"Aim's off. It would seem the daemon's been locked up for a while."

"What do you mean?" Marlok demanded.

"This is the work of Thundrus, daemon general of storms."

"Ah, and he would live on the mountaintop, wouldn't he?" Marlok noted with dawning clarity.

"Daemons are not the most creative and original of creatures."

"Like you should talk."

"I beg your pardon!" Quaswyn sputtered. "I am far more

inventive than you ever dreamt of being!"

"I'm a thief, and a good one at that. That's about as creative as you can be. How else do you think I can get into towers like yours?" boasted Marlok.

"A door? A key? You know, like a normal person."

"You're such a feeble-minded fool, you'll never get it. But now, we need to get out of this daemon's path."

The bottle shattered as it struck the throne room wall. Wine splattered the stone, drooled down the wall and puddled on the flagged floor.

"Why was my son here?"

"How should I know?" the frizzle-haired healer replied.

"You were entrusted with his care." The Emperor wobbled toward the throne and lowered his slovenly form to the padded seat.

"No. You lost your temper and threw him out. I found him and did my best to help him." Scruffy eyed the Emperor with disgust. "But no matter. That was five years ago and has no bearing on the present circumstance."

"How long has he been back?"

"Boryn is old enough now to care for himself. He need not be tied by a string."

"Why did he return in the first place?"

"Not likely to pay a visit to his loving father."

The Emperor raised his chalice, and finding it empty, sent it clattering across the room. "I had a right to be notified he was living under my nose. I am his father!"

"And for that privilege, he received but a single gift. What caused you to be sober that day is a mystery to me. In every other way, you are a miserable human being who owes both of your sons a profound apology."

The Emperor pushed himself up using the carved arms of the throne for support. He descended the dais, but reeling from drink, he tripped over the hem of his robe and fell. The healer made no move to help him though the chamberlain stepped forward. "He's in no danger. No physical danger," the healer held off the hesitant assistant then ushered him out the door. When it was closed, the healer spoke as if the Emperor was not the only other person in the room. "Perhaps it's time for him to get a taste of his medicine."

The bulge of the Emperor's belly lurched beneath his clinging robe. He spewed time and time again, convulsing and choking. He gagged for air and pulled at his soiled garment, fighting to regain some semblance of control, his indignity complete. After a long spell, the Emperor flopped over to his back. "You bastard."

"Some might say the same of you," the healer replied placidly. "Boryn lived through ten years of hell under your roof—without even the protection of a mother—until you did him the favor of tossing him out. I am honored to have been of special service on that fateful day. I found him shivering, and hungry, and hiding under a market stall. Then you had the audacity to try to take him back so you could prove to him that running wasn't an option!

"I sent your young son to the farthest reaches of the Empire—to protect him from his own father! And what happens? He becomes a dirty, ragged thief, living on the streets." The healer looked at his toes and shook his head. "And when he returns—almost a man," he straightened and glared at the sniveling ruler, "you find an excuse to exile him—just like you did his brother before him.

"Afraid your offspring might interfere with your tenuous little reign? Your cowardice is staggering." The healer moved to leave.

The Emperor sat up, wiping his mouth on his sleeve. "Edrick, wait."

The healer stopped without turning.

"It's not what I intended."

"Ah! And that should absolve you?" The healer's voice was thick with irony. He turned full face to Lord Mhinbron. "If you discover repentance in your make up, Algyer, don't give it to me. Talk to your sons." Soft soles scuffing across the stone floor, the healer left and latched the door behind him. A chair crashed against the back side of the door, but the healer continued down the hall and out the keep.

Boryn batted his way through a swirling wall of black clouds that ringed the top of Mount Pyr. He broke through the vapor to find himself on the rim of a crater, the air dead calm, the eye of the storm. In the bowl, he saw a red-skinned, winged daemon, electric energy crackling from its horns and fingers and spilling over the crater's edge. A sneer painted its terrible face, and jagged bolts of black lightning streaked its shirtless chest and arms.

Thundrus looked up at the boy and smiled as if pleased to see him. "Boryn Mhinbron, correct?"

"And?"

"So you killed the trainee. It will be interesting to see how you fare against a real general."

Boryn unsheathed the black-gem scimitar and held it up against his forearm, cutting edge toward the daemon.

"Ah, yes, a battle of the blades to begin. We'll let the brothers battle it out," the daemon said, withdrawing a black-gem blade identical to the one Boryn brandished.

Perfect. Boryn held his blade higher. *Once I take that blade, I'll be back to fighting my way . . . a blade in both hands.* Boryn launched at the daemon and focused energy into the blade as he swept it down to slice the creature's shoulder. The daemon blocked, but Boryn pulled the sword back, spinning in a circle, bringing the sword whistling back to cleave the daemon's unprotected midsection. Boryn shifted his aim when Thundrus moved to block. The daemon's thumb flopped to the ground, and Boryn seized the hilt of the second black scimitar, wrenching it from the thumbless grasp. His hand tightened around the grip, and suddenly, he felt washed by the same cold sensation he'd felt when he first touched a black scimitar—only it was stronger this time, more menacing.

"You've ruined my hand! That is unforgivable!" Despite the plaintive words, a fanged grin creased Thundrus' face, and he held out his hand and opened the palm. "Now die." A bolt of lightning slammed Boryn's chest. Both blades dropped as Boryn fell to his knees, sucked in sharply, and clutched his chest. "That bolt just fired straight through your heart, so you'll be dead soon enough," Thundrus said, first chuckling then laughing outright, a low, booming sound.

The pain was horrific; it felt to Boryn as if his heart was in a vice with thousands of tiny daggers stabbing into his chest. He almost wished to die. It turned cold, frigidly so, and his body wracked with involuntary shivering. *You're helpless. . . .* In the instant he heard that strange voice, the pain ceased, vanishing altogether. His heart began to beat again, and slowly, he pushed himself to his feet.

"Still able to stand? Allow me to help you back down," the general of storms taunted, preparing to fully release.

Before the daemon could make good on his threat, the ground buckled beneath him. While Thundrus toppled, Boryn bent for the black blades and lunged. Thundrus swerved sideways, regaining his balance, although the movement was so fast Boryn was unable to register it. Acting on sheer instinct, Boryn ducked to miss a lightning-fast fist that whooshed overhead. He wheeled around, blades wide, nicking the daemon's knees. The general shot in and kicked, a blade skidding one way and the boy spinning the other. *I can't beat him; he's too fast.* Boryn reversed direction to round on the daemon. With his free hand, Boryn grabbed the daemon's cocked fist. With the other, he swept inside with the scimitar, slicing edge up. Thundrus countered the move, jerking back. Boryn sailed past, stooping to retrieve the dropped scimitar. He forced the energy from the blades into his entire body; he felt light and quick. With a smile, he wheeled toward the daemon. Thundrus ran at him, firing a lightning bolt from each hand, but the boy vanished.

"Where are you, you—." The words stopped short, and the daemon fell, clutching his throat. Blood flowed freely from a clean, deep slice. The daemon general threw out a trembling arm in a final attempt to finish his adversary, but the outward power was reduced to a frizzle of static. The storm cloud ringing the crater turned its destructive energy inward, and lightning fired into the bowl. Boryn felt the ground beneath him crumble, then he tumbled into darkness.

The crystal etched with *B* changed from black to its normal clear white. Relief crossed the faces of the Shadow Crusaders, except for Ranton whose face registered nothing. Wenval led the way, following the crystal in search of Boryn, Emily close behind.

Already their journey had taken them well past Grinfol Forest into unfamiliar lands. They now wandered through woods at the base of the peakless mountain known as Mount Pyr.

"I wonder who almost killed him?" Ranton thought aloud, shoving away a branch that encroached on his path. Julia trailed, not saying a word, after Ranton had insisted she be allowed to accompany them.

"A daemon, probably," Calny remarked.

"Maybe Boryn's the daemon," Julia said, and then whispering to Ranton so that no one would overhear, continued, "and if he is, he must die, right?"

Uncertainty flashed across Ranton's face. Julia reached out to slow him, lagging behind, and then stepped to face him, locking eyes and stroking his cheek. "You know the truth. Don't let them get to you."

Appalled even by the girl's earlier comment, Wenval protested,

"Don't be ridiculous! We are going to find Boryn, and we will all know. We're not hunting him down."

"That black blade was cursed. Don't you remember that power?" Julia suggested rather calmly. "Maybe he traded his soul for it."

"Boryn wouldn't do that. Ever." Wenval stood in front of Julia, defiant, instincts prickled.

"He might, to save his beloved city," she laughed unnaturally, and her eyes flared.

"Boryn is not a daemon. The crystals I made only work for humans. I tested them," Wenval insisted.

"You're even more dull-witted than you act," Julia snipped.

Wenval held out his hand, a ball of fire forming; Julia smiled at the intended assault. Ranton jumped back, arrow locked on his friend; Laric placed his blade at Ranton's throat, and Calny moved to lower Wenval's arm to point the fireball at the ground rather than at the girl.

Wenval looked hard into Julia's eyes. *She smiles when a fireball is aimed right for her face. And the hold she seems to have on Ranton . . . there's something peculiar about that one.*

"Look, the storm's gone." Emily stepped between them, pointing toward the mountaintop. "We should keep moving. And Ranton, put down your bow right now."

Hesitantly, he lowered the weapon but did not remove the scowl nailing Wenval and the twins. "You threaten Julia again, and you'll have an arrow in your arm," Ranton growled.

"And your whore of a girl won't have much of a face left."

Ranton's fist slammed into the smaller boy's jaw. Wenval's head snapped to the side, his satchel slid from his shoulder. Ranton backed away, awaiting Wenval's response.

Wenval reached down and grabbed the bag strap. "Let's keep moving." A metallic taste filled his mouth; he spat blood onto a rock beside the path.

"Why don't you try healing it?" Emily suggested, but the curly-haired boy in the green cloak started up the mountain without another word.

Ramgis stood next to his warhorse at the narrow mouth of a tunnel. The entrance was bracketed by sheer cliffs dropping to the sea below and an impossibly steep hillside shooting toward the sky. Eternal blue torches lit the opening and cast an eerie, dim glow that fingered into the distant recesses of the cavern, inviting the Blood Knights in. Or was it a warning to stay away?

The old commander considered his army, a mix of Rath's mercenaries and his own men. He turned to Cadegray. "Why are we here again? I don't like this."

"Rath's men scouted heavy defenses ahead of our position if we had continued straight through the swamp."

"Doesn't mean we need to go through this cave we know nothing about. We could take a different route through the swamp into the Black Expanse, and from there easily reach the home of the Dark elves."

"Rath advises otherwise."

"Any word of Kelris?" Ramgis turned to Rath.

"The rider of the big, ugly beastie? Last seen riding across the Expanse toward the Dark elves' capital."

"And the reinforcements from the Order of the Wolf? Any sight of them?"

"I'll let you know."

"Let's double our pace," Ramgis ordered. "I'd like to be knocking on the Dark elves' gates in a few days' march."

"Ramgis, do you think it wise to wear the men down?" Cadegray, the levelheaded one, mentioned.

"Let's pick up the pace!" Ramgis reiterated. He remounted, spurred his warhorse into a gallop, and plunged into the mouth of the cave, his voice echoing off the stone walls. The Blood Knights followed. Inside, the cavern was much larger than it had appeared, and the entire Blood Knight force was swallowed into its void.

Cadegray lagged at the rear with Rath. "Obliges for telling him you saw Kelris." The sarcasm was overt.

"He'd find out eventually. Truth told, I'm not a big fan of the caves either. Messes with my vision," Rath said, rubbing his eyes. Rath stalled to let the knights and infantry pass and Cadegray ride ahead. The distant sound of dripping water made Rath feel especially edgy as he waited for the army to round a bend and become lost to view. Alone, he rode back toward the mouth of the cave. A hawk flew in, the flap of its wings noisy in the echoey space. Rath grinned and held out his forearm. The mighty bird of prey came to rest on the leather gauntlet.

"Where ya been, huh?"

The hawk rubbed its head on Rath's shoulder then extended its twiggy leg. Rath pulled a small roll of parchment from his pocket and tied it to the meatier upper part with a bit of cord. He smoothed the feathers on the bird's back. "Don't eat too much on the way now," he chuckled. Rath turned toward the spot of light at the opening and lifted his arm, the signal to take flight. The bird pushed off and flew toward the light. Rath reversed direction and kicked his horse into a gallop to catch Ramgis.

"This is no place for an army." Ramgis looked around the

cavern, his whole face twisted into a scowl. "We should have blasted through those Dark elf defenses rather than crawl around in the shadows like they do."

"Your men thank you for sparing them such a prideful order, I am sure," Cadegray reassured Ramgis as Rath rejoined the leaders with a playful salute.

Wishing to dispel a palpable sense of unease, Ramgis ordered, "Rath, Cadegray, ride to the rear and make sure the troops are moving along."

Before the two could move out, one of Rath's riders approached, galloping toward them at full speed. The rider was wide-eyed and breathing hard. "Dark elves are charging the rear, and we noticed some outcropping tunnels. The bastards are coming in from there as well."

"So we go full speed forward?" Cadegray asked Ramgis for confirmation.

"No. We will simply ride back and crush them before we continue the advance . . ."

". . . and at the front, Kelris and his huge force of Dark Lancers approach," the scout amended.

"How do you know this?" Ramgis' eyes narrowed.

"Rath's scouts reported it," the rider said.

"Your instincts were correct, Ramgis," the old tactician advised. "We should turn back and break through the rear attack."

"No, Cadegray. We will go forward and fight this fight today."

Cadegray moved to protest, but Ramgis drew his mighty, golden warhammer and roared, "Blood Knights, to me!" The crimson-clad force, almost two hundred strong, formed up around the commander.

"Men, today is the day we have long awaited, the day for which we have trained—our chance to cut down the Dark Lancers of the Dark elves!"

A cheer of support, deafening in the mountain's cavity, erupted.

"Let's show them we are the greatest of all riders!" Ramgis' voice was loud and strong and filled with purpose. Turning his steed, he cantered toward the exit, a spot of light in the distance. The Blood Knight army spilled from the damp, dark cave and into the blinding, black starkness of the Black Expanse. Across the plain, Ramgis could make out a cloud of ashy black raised by the rush of Dark Lancers. And leading the pack was the black-scaled beast and its fearsome, white-armored rider.

"Kelris . . . ," Ramgis growled under his breath, his hand tightening round the hold of his warhammer.

The Dark elven commander smiled at the sight of the Blood Knights assembling before him. *Time at last to put an end to these human pests.* He saw one, the leader no doubt, thrust a particularly large, golden hammer into the sky. *Ah, my old friend Ramgis . . .*

Riding next to Cadegray, Rath observed the Blood Knights in awe. He had never seen them so solemn and focused. "There's more to this than meets the eye," Rath fished.

"Shouldn't you be preparing to fight?" Cadegray said while continuing to issue orders to his men.

"Why are the Blood Knights so determined to fight the Dark Lancers?" asked Rath, slowing his horse to stay alongside Cadegray's much smaller pony.

"It goes back to the very beginning, when Ramgis and I were young. We lived in the same village along the coast under the Order of the Bear. Our village was viciously attacked by the Lancers before the Dark elves were even known. They slaughtered everyone in sight, and Ramgis, little more than a boy at the time, watched as his family was butchered. Other than the two of us, there were few survivors.

"The Knights of the Bear, who should have been protecting us, were, of course, away. The people struggled to support the Order's excesses while barely eking out a meager livelihood for themselves. On that very day, Ramgis decided to form a new Order, the sole purpose of which would be to protect the people rather than its own personal interests.

"The Blood Knights have trained from the start for the day they would wipe out the Dark Lancers."

The Dark elf infantry came in range. Rath nocked four arrows and launched a salvo, striking four. "This will get ugly."

"Where's that daemon who nabbed us? The one with orange hair?" asked the girl.

Xandon lazed against a tree, his elbow resting on a low, bare limb. The girl and the dwarf were tied to the trunk of another. "I don't know."

"Why do you answer to him?" the pretty, young girl said, more accusation than question. She flipped her head so the wind would blow her corn-silk hair away from her face.

"I don't." *Sure, Fernus, leave me as babysitter.*

"Who are you? What do you want with us?"

And how did she get the rag out of her mouth? Xandon stood straight, smoothed his cloak with elegant, long fingers and squished across the sodden ground toward the dwarf. Hesitating, he removed the gag so that the dwarf's angry mumbles spilled out as actual speech.

"You seemed to be taking his orders. Why are you keeping us here?" Stevan spoke up.

"Let us go!" demanded the girl.

The Flame king cupped his hands over his ears as the peppering continued.

"Where's Boryn?" the dwarf wanted to know.

"I don't know."

"You fought him," the dwarf pressed.

"It honestly wasn't much of a fight," chuckled Xandon.

"Did you hurt him?" Hannah asked.

"It was a fight. People tend to get hurt." Xandon plopped down on a boulder, the flame-cut tails of his scarlet cloak fanning.

"If you don't want anything from us, just let us go."

Xandon proceeded to pound the heel of his palm against his forehead in response to the incessant barrage.

"What are you, anyway?" asked the girl. "Dark elf?"

"No!"

"Wood elf? Noble elf?"

"No. No."

"Moon elf?"

"Same as Noble."

"Oh . . . What are you, then?"

"I think he's a Flame elf," puffed the dwarf. "From what I remember, they sided with the daemons against us and the humans in the Daemon War. Been our enemies ever since. Spiteful little bastards."

"Sounds like us," grinned Xandon.

"You don't seem that bad except for tying us up and fighting Boryn . . ."

"I'm not as simple minded, nor as caring, as the rest of my race."

"Why is that?" the girl wanted to know.

"Lentz," groaned Xandon, summoning his golden-armored, personal guard.

"King Xandon! You're soiling your robe!" exclaimed the larger, more serious Flame elf, surprised to see his fastidious king perched on a mossy, old boulder.

"It really doesn't matter at this point." Xandon waved his hands.

"How may I help you, highness?" asked the royal guardian while scrutinizing the captives.

"Will you untie those two?"

"Why don't you do it?"

"One of them is a dwarf, and dwarves are quite the fist fighters. And that girl strikes me as a biter," Xandon quipped.

"Coward."

Xandon snapped his fingers, and the ropes that bound the two sparked into pieces, singeing the captives' wrists. "Go find Boryn and help him."

"You're letting us go?" Rubbing her wrists, Hannah turned penetrating blue eyes toward Xandon.

"I've changed my mind about what I'm doing, so quit asking questions and run."

"What about that daemon?"

"That's my concern. And Boryn? He was last seen on the mountaintop. Go there."

"Perhaps you should explain your intentions, Xandon?" came a calm voice from behind the elf. The words were cold but blistering. A figure stepped from the foliage. His ice blue hair was combed straight back and hung perfectly straight to his shoulders. The face was young with frosty blue eyes. His black-edged, white cloak barely cleared the muddy ground.

"What hell spit you out?" Stevan lifted his halberd.

"Glacius." Xandon's voice was rock hard. "It's been a long time."

"Who is he?" demanded the dwarf.

"A daemon general." The fire in Xandon's eyes never left the ice of Glacius'. "Lentz, escort those two to the mountaintop, and help them find their friend. I'd rather not have anyone in the way."

"A long time, indeed," laughed Glacius. "Since you were not more than . . ."

Rage burned in Xandon's eyes, the green scar pulsing. He clenched and unclenched his fists.

"Are you betraying us, Xandon, your loyal allies? Friends of your father?" goaded the daemon general of ice.

"Regardless of my intentions, these 'prisoners' are no threat to me. They're a waste of my time."

"And you give me an excuse to finish what I started so long ago," said the daemon with a grin as he withdrew a spear that had been lashed to his back.

"Earned your general's weapon at last, have you? My congratulations," Xandon said upon seeing the chiseled, black spear.

"And I know how to access the power inside."

"Well, we shall see which is the stronger—fire or ice." A swirling blade of fire shot from Xandon's hand.

Stevan struggled to keep up with the long-legged elf and Hannah.

"Why is Xandon fighting for us?" Hannah asked Lentz.

"For you? This has nothing to do with you. Xandon has an old score to settle with that one, going back before the Daemon War."

"What happened?"

"Ancient history not yet finished." Lentz' tone made it clear he would say no more about it.

"Why is he letting us go?"

"He found you insufferably annoying."

At that moment, a blast of energy bolted up the mountainside buffeting Stevan so that he nearly fell flat on his face. Stumbling, he spun to see the daemon general and elven king, weapons sparking. Ice clashed fire, and frozen spikes shot out from the daemon's back and shoulders.

"We should help," Stevan looked to Lentz.

"Don't even consider it. That daemon would rip us to shreds before we even got close."

Glacius reared back then lunged; the black spear shot forward, its icy tip narrowly missing Xandon's chest as the tall elf swatted the spear aside with the flat of his own fiery blade. Next, Xandon charged. He leapt into the air, spinning his blade to form a twister of fire. The twister shot forward like a coiling whip, encircling the daemon. Xandon jerked his hand back; the spiraling rings straightened like the recoil of a rope, converging inward in a powerful blast. Chunks of flying rock erupted toward the sky as Xandon's blazing blade whipped back and reformed. Knocked from his feet, ice spikes shattered, the blue-haired daemon sprang up, bringing with him new icy spines that fired up from the charred ground.

"Ready to die?" laughed Glacius, sorely tempted to release.

Just then, another white-cloaked daemon, a white cowl concealing much of his face, appeared in front of Glacius, the tip of his black blade at Glacius' throat. His voice was slow, controlled, and all business. "Glacius, go fetch Thundrus' body and return it to the citadel. He couldn't even stand up to the boy!"

"Don't move, Glacius. We're finishing this fight now," Xandon ignored the intruder.

"As you command, Fernus," Glacius hissed through gritted teeth, angered to be taking orders from a presumed equal but too spineless to stand up to the general of fire.

"Get out of my way, Fernus!" Xandon roared.

Stevan and Hannah watched from a distance, wide eyed. "Stay here!" Lentz ordered and rushed toward Xandon.

"I said move!" Flames erupted from the elven king's sword, some spinning back and swirling around his own body. The green scar that slashed across his right eye pulsed. Xandon held out his other arm, a dark chaotic flame starting to form.

"Xandon!" Lentz tackled his king, shoving him to the muddy ground, the chaotic, black flames doused

"Get off . . . ," Xandon's tone seemed resigned.

Lentz helped the young king to his feet.

"I don't want to have to stop you two again," Fernus said looking from Glacius to Xandon, "or I'll join the fight myself." Fernus glared at Glacius, "And you have a job to do."

Glacius glowered back with frosty eyes then darkened and faded into his own shadow until he was gone.

Stevan and Hannah approached Lentz where he stood beside Xandon who seemed on the verge of keeling over.

"Go to your friend," Lentz barked the command. "We are your enemies."

Hannah seemed confused. "But . . ."

"Get out of here before Fernus decides we should recapture you."

Fernus looked away as if not paying attention. Hannah and Stevan looked from face to face, and then, hesitantly, they doubled back toward the mountaintop.

"Let's go, Lentz," said Xandon, slumping from exhaustion.

"You stopped something, Lentz. What was it?" asked Fernus, raising his brow in curiosity.

"None of your concern."

"But I'm intrigued. It looked as if . . ."

Lentz snapped his fingers, and he and Xandon vanished in a burst of flame.

Instantly, Xandon and his second reappeared in Xandon's volcanic throne room. A daemon messenger had helped himself to the throne, where he lounged, awaiting the king's return. Startled by Xandon's sudden appearance but unwilling to show it, the messenger settled into a long, lazy yawn.

Then, with slow and deliberate disrespect, the messenger rose and approached the king. "I bring orders from . . ."

A fist blew into its forehead chased by a searing rod of fire that bored through the daemon's skull and struck the marble wall behind. The daemon's corpse, a smoking hole in its head, fell backward as if in slow motion.

Lentz shook his head as Xandon let his fist drop.

"I really didn't care about any orders he might bring."

"Clearly."

"I still wasn't able to destroy Glacius."

"Not the way you were headed. Unless you want to be burned by the black fire of hell, you must keep control of yourself. Xandon, how do you think Fernus keeps control of the others if not by their fear of his hell fire?"

"There must be a way to control that other fire."

"Soul fire? The white fire that burns from the soul? The most powerful of all? Doubtful. Fire by nature is chaotic; the fact that we control it at all is a miracle."

"But that fire—"

"Soul fire is not only the most powerful but the most destructive as well—even more so than the Fernus' black hell fire. You know that from experience."

"There must be a way to control the soul fire."

"It will kill you first, highness. Many of our race die in training alone. Controlling such chaos and destruction is nigh impossible."

Xandon left the throne room through the massive iron door. He drifted down the marble corridor and descended the dimly lit stairs into the Hall of the Eternal Flame. The glow of the green fire at his eye, along with the ever-burning candles, lit his way. He reached the gate, its iron twisted and warped into the shape of raging fire. A single flame burst from his fingertip, and he slid it into a slot on the lock. The gate clicked open.

As always, Xandon paused to admire the magnificently sculpted statues that adorned the marble crypts along the walls before moving to the One. In the center, in the place of highest honor, rested a simple vault, smaller than most, under a carving of a young elven girl. Xandon moved toward it, his head low. *I have failed again. The creature that executed you . . . I may never get another chance.*

"Xandon, you must not regret what you *might* have done. Just prepare for what you *will* do," Lentz advised. "You will have your vengeance on Glacius one day; there is no question. And no matter who we must fight, I will always be here to help you."

"How am I to defeat him?"

"You'll find a way; you always find a way to come out on top. As the humans measure it, you would be old and bent by now. But you are yet young. There is plenty of time for you to prepare for your revenge."

Oww . . . **Boryn moved,** every part of his body aching. He opened his eyes. *Where am I?* Several room heights above, he could see a jagged pinpoint of light, the bright opening through which he had fallen. *No wonder I hurt!*

He rolled over, rose stiffly, and stretched. Relieved that nothing seemed broken, he turned attention to his surroundings. It was a circular stone shaft with a hard, earthen floor. Perfectly smooth pillars carved at regular intervals aligned the walls. In the center of the space stood a pristine anvil covered with glowing symbols. *Way too fancy to be an ordinary cavern.* On the side wall, he noticed a single wooden door. Then he remembered. *The scimitars!* His hands went to his sides, to the empty sheathes. As his eyes began to adjust to the dim light, he saw the two black swords on the floor near the door. He went to them, but as he bent to retrieve them, a staff smacked up into his face. He careened backwards.

"Who are ya?"

"What in hell?" Boryn held his throbbing nose.

"I said, who are ya?"

"Boryn."

"Wha' are ya doin' with these?" the dwarf asked, using his long wooden staff to poke at the scimitars as if they were poisonous snakes ready to strike.

"Those are my weapons."

"Pah! Ya should no' be playin' with knives, much less these."

"I'm a warrior."

"Prove it."

"Huh?"

"Hit me with yer fist, an' I'll believe ya."

Boryn surged toward the provoking dwarf and took a low swing at the shorter man's head. He felt his fist crunch against the staff, the wood skinning his knuckles. The staff flipped bottom up, baton-like, clipping Boryn in the chin, knocking him off balance, before it boomeranged back to whistle toward his crown. Boryn's hand shot up to fend off the blow. He seized the staff and tried to tear it away, but the dwarf twisted it down, wrenching Boryn's arm until he had to let go. The staff came around to swat him in the face, and the impact sent him reeling sideways then tumbling to the dirt. Boryn stared up at the short man, the room spinning.

"A warrior, eh? Bwahhaha!"

Boryn rose unsteadily. Regaining his footing, he charged the dwarf who waited in a solid, defensive stance. With Boryn in range, the staff stabbed up toward his throat. He spun, grabbed the staff behind his back and continued the spin, bringing his fist around at the same time. He felt the staff leave the dwarf's hands, but an iron fist clamped on his wrist, stopping it. With a jerk and a flip, Boryn hit the ground. He hopped up, firing futile punches. The powerful fist caged Boryn's and tightened, crushing the boy's hand and grounding him again.

"Ya need some work."

Boryn tugged his hand free, flexed his fingers and winced. "Technically, I hit you with my fist. Give me back my weapons."

"Nah, I'm no' even lettin' ya hold a knife 'til ya deserve it."

"And how might I do that?" Boryn demanded.

"I'm goin' ta train ya. I go' ta hold on ta ye anyway. Make sure we can trust ya."

"What do you mean 'hold on to me'? You have no right," Boryn protested. "And who says you can train me?"

"I do. Would ya rather rot in a dungeon?"

"Given the choices, I'll take training. But why don't you trust me?"

The dwarf looked at Boryn as if he was very dense. The dwarf's eyes looked overly large behind two glass orbs suspended in front of them by wires strapped across his nose and ears. Boryn looked back. *Never seen anything like that.*

"Yer a human. Humans aren't too high on our list o' folks to rely on fer help. Anyways, we've lived down here fer almost fifty years without bein' bothered, so we really are no' interested or used ta havin' ye around."

"We?"

"Come with me." The thick dwarf, gray-laced hair and beard neatly trimmed, grabbed Boryn by the belt and led him out of the circular room, leaving the black scimitars behind. A short passageway led to an enormous stone door, its surface glowing with artistically etched symbols. Boryn noticed that the leather-vested dwarf jangled as he approached the door. The dwarf closed his eyes and held out his hands. The ends of his fingers glowed a bright golden color, and he drew symbols in the air. With a loud click, the door opened.

"How did you do that?" Boryn asked.

"Wha'?"

"Those symbols. And what is it with your fingers?"

"Runes."

"What's that?"

"Dwarven business. None o' yers."

The dwarf stepped across the stone threshold, Boryn behind, onto a ledge high above a cavern of unimaginable scale. Below them was an entire city—building, homes, roads—built of cinnamon-colored stone. In the center stood a white marble arena from which cheering and roars echoed. Above the entombed city, an enormous luminous ball created the illusion of sunlight and melted the expected underground chill.

"What in the world . . ."

"Welcome to Raz Kiri, the last bastion o' the dwarves, no thanks ta you humans."

"It's incredible!" Awestruck, Boryn scanned the space.

"Aye. Wha's yer name again?"

"Boryn." The dwarf studied the boy, almost double the dwarf's height. He looked from the boy's big feet to his long, fair hair.

"Wha's yer family's name?"

"Mhinbron."

The dwarf nodded, thoughts clinking into place like pieces in a puzzle.

"What do I call you?"

"Me name's Rogma. An' keep yer head down; we need t'avoid attention."

"Why?"

"We dwarves are no' particularly fond of ye humans, as I just told ye."

Rogma led Boryn down the well-tended wooden ramp that wound to the cavern floor and ended at a stone-paved street.

"This place is huge!"

"The only remainin' haven o' the dwarves. Why else do ye think everyone believes we are an extinct race?"

"Why do you hide down here?"

"Hide? It's not hidin'! We're simply avoidin' you humans an' all th' other equally annoyin' races."

"Why?"

"Ye're no' ta be trusted."

"I still don't get it. What did the humans do? I thought we were allies—along with the Moon and Wood elves—against the daemons during the Daemon War?"

"Aye, *were*."

"So what happened?"

"Now's no' the time fer a history lesson. Put yer hood up. And walk low; yer too tall here."

Boryn looked around. The streets were empty. "Why?"

"Just do it. And quit ye arguin'.'"

Boryn raised the hood and tried to shrink within his cape. The pair moved through the streets toward the arena without meeting a soul. Then they rounded a corner.

"How ya doin', mate?" Seeing Rogma, the friendly dwarf threw his hands in the air. He ran over and rested his arm across the older dwarf's shoulders.

"I'm all righ'. Tryin' ta get home." Rogma's tone was brusque.

Suspicions aroused, the dwarf probed, "Who's yer friend?"

"No one. Found 'im in the tunnels."

The inquiring dwarf moved close to inspect the stranger, rising to his toes, peering into the stranger's eyes. He turned to Rogma, sputtering with contempt. "Is tha' a . . . human?"

"Aye . . ."

"What in hell fire's name are ye doin' bringin' a human here?"

"He was no' really in the tunnels. He fell inta the Heart."

The dwarf's eyes grew big. "How did he ge' in?"

"He fell in . . ."

"A daemon blasted the ground right out from under me," Boryn blurted.

The dwarf put his hands on his hips and turned to Boryn scowling. "If I wanted ta listen to yer lies, human, I woulda asked ye in the first place. So shut yer trap."

"Tone it down, mate." Rogma held out a calming hand.

"Boringer's goin' ta hear abou' this. An' he'll know . . . ," the dwarf marched off, muttering fierce oaths.

"Now what?" Boryn was genuinely curious.

"Nothin' lad, do no' worry abou' him."

They came to a circular building that seemed to be carved from a single piece of rust-colored rock. It jutted from the side of the arena. Rogma lifted a large ring that hung at his side and jangled with dozens of keys. He found the proper one and unlocked the door.

Boryn ducked through the doorway behind Rogma and into the spacious, round room. A shimmering ring of coal glowed in the center. Hovering above the fire pit like an open mouth was a huge chimney that pierced the domed ceiling. Around the room, tables were littered with tools and weighted with anvils of sundry sizes and shapes. "Is this a forge?"

"Aye. Now get rid o' tha' cape," Rogma said. "Ye won't be needin' it while yer livin' here."

"Live? I don't want to live here!"

"I am no' askin' what ye want."

"Is there a room?"

"Aye. Two beds upstairs, but while yer stayin' here, ye work in the forge, and ye learn ta fight."

"I already know how to fight."

"Ask yer hand. See if it agrees."

Boryn cradled his swollen fist in his good palm.

"Ye know how a forge works?"

"Nope."

"Well, yer goin' ta learn."

"My lord, rapi lie in wait beyond the next rise, in the riverbed," announced the scout, approaching at full gallop.

"How many?"

"A patrol—twenty or so—from the main tribe of a couple hundred."

"Tell the men to hang back, stay quiet and await my signal," Luthor ordered as he dismounted. "We're evenly matched now, but I'm going to work to upset the odds."

"Aye, sir. As always."

Luthor reached into his saddlebag with one hand while unclasping his shirt with the other. He let his shirt slide away and pulled from the bag a battered iron shoulder guard. He slipped it over his head and tightened the strap. Pulling back his long hair, he tied it with a red strip of cloth. Next, he withdrew the claymore tethered to the horse's flank before swatting the horse away to join the waiting Red X forces. A cover of trees shielded his advance so that he neared the river undetected. He squeezed the grip of his waist-high blade, the ruby X embedded in the crossguard glinting in the afternoon sun.

Once he reached the open, Luthor took aggressive strides toward the riverbank. A spear zinged in his direction. Unconcerned, the Red X commander batted it aside with a wide, flat sweep of his long blade. He broke into a sprint as agile lizardmen, weapons aloft, slithered up the muddy embankment, intent on ambushing the lone man. The long rapi bodies were scaled and colored like a chameleon, but they balanced upright on short legs. Their long necks and waists were festooned with necklaces and belts made with feathers, fangs and bits of hide. They hissed like snakes and issued a tribal chant, their fanged mouths twisted in evil grins.

Luthor slowed and held his position, luring the rapi closer. When the rapi came in range, Luthor slammed the diamond-hard sword tip into the rocky path. On impact, the earth cracked and buckled, throwing the rapi warriors off balance. With two hands, Luthor lifted the massive sword and swung wide, slicing lizardmen's throats. A beast jabbed with its spear, but the razor edge of Luthor's blade glided through weapon and skull, cleaving both in two.

The surviving rapi backed away, making way for one wearing a colorful, feather headdress and holding an elaborately carved spear. "The rapi march at the direction of our prophet," the leader intoned, stepping forward.

"Honestly, I couldn't care less about your mission or your prophet, but your presence offends me."

"So speaks the Sun God through our prophet. Dusgoroth must fall, be it this day or the next." It hissed as hundreds more rapi rose from the rushing waters.

"Your numbers and your prophecies mean nothing to me, rapi."

"Nothing?" it hissed.

Luthor lifted a bone horn and blew, a shrill and eerie sound resonating across the hills. "I, Luthor, Leader of the Red X, defy you and your prophet." He held the sword high, light flashing from the ruby crossguard, and the thunder of horses' hooves rolled toward them.

"Then you will all die." The rapi leader lowered its spear as the Red X force crested the hill and galloped full speed toward the rapi.

The rapi hissed and screeched and shook their spears.

"You are mine to fight, commander against commander. You will die by my blessed hand," challenged the rapi leader.

"Ah! So, you are special, too?" Luthor pressed the ruby X, "Let's find out which is better, a blessing or a curse." His laugh was hollow as he pounded his foot on the ground, and red replaced the normal green of his eyes.

"Wake up, ye lazy lout!"

Boryn eased his eyes open. *What in the world? Oh, yeah.* He slowly sat up, rubbing his face with his hands, both the good and the bandaged one. He yawned and stretched as strong, callused fingers grabbed his ankles. A determined grip tore him from the pallet where he had slept. Boryn hit the stone floor, hard and cold. The boy groaned and tried to sit up, only to be dragged farther, to the top of a half-flight of stone stairs. It was Rogma who had him.

"Hey, lemme go!"

"Next time, ge' yerself up on time," said the dwarf as he flung Boryn down the steps. The boy somersaulted across the floor before colliding with the wall. He climbed to his feet and shook away the cobwebs.

"Get some food, an' meet me in the forge."

Boryn turned to the table where lay a loaf of dark bread, a hunk of cheese, and a strip of dried meat. His stomach grumbled, and he ripped off the crusty end of the loaf and stuffed it in his mouth. Tucking the rest under his arm, Boryn moved toward the adjoining room where the forge fire already poured out heat. A dozen or so dwarves, wearing leather aprons and holding an assortment of rasps, tongs and other tools, lined up in front of Rogma. The sturdy forge master, tidy in comparison to his smiths, wore a leather vest, the strange, glass disks over his eyes and an unusual pendant at his neck.

"Everyone, this here is Boryn. He is goin' ta be learnin' from us. Just don't be too hard on 'im, all right?"

"You're lettin' a human into our forge?" Murmurs of surprise filled the room.

"Aye."

"We do no' want 'im."

"It's not yer choice," snapped the forge master. "Those o' ye who object, feel free ta leave. I'll give ye three days to return, or do no' trouble yerself ta come back."

"Oy, Rogma!"

"Boryn, go get more ta eat."

"Why?" Boryn mumbled while stuffing an overlarge bite in his mouth.

"Now!" ordered the no-nonsense dwarf, and Rogma, jangling, nudged Boryn back toward the food table.

The forge door slammed open as a heavily armored, barrel-chested dwarf stormed in, his wiry yellow beard glistening with droplets of foam.

An eager smithy couldn't wait to break the news. "Boringer, Rogma's bringin' a human ta work in th' arena forge!"

"A human?" The dwarf's bushy golden eyebrows crept up to disappear behind the lip of his horned helmet. "Le' me see 'im."

"He's eatin'."

"I don' care."

"Boryn, come out 'ere."

Boryn stooped through the door, holding cheese and meat and chewing rudely, and ambled back into the forge, his frame appearing especially lanky in the dwarven surrounding.

"Ye've touched daemon blades, 'aven't ye?" came the slightly slurred accusation from a mouth shielded by moustache.

"More like wielded, but yeah."

The dwarf rolled his eyes in disgust then raised one of the ten throwing axes he carried in a pouch on his back. He waved it at the boy. Boryn scanned the room for a possible weapon. A fire poker rested in a bucket of coal a few feet away. He sidled toward it, the dwarf's axe following every step.

"Boringer, stop," pleaded Rogma.

"Which weapons were they?" demanded the mighty, golden-haired dwarf.

"Two scimitars."

"Scimitars . . . ," Boringer seemed confounded then wagged his finger in the visitor's face. "I'll be watchin' ye."

"Have fun trying."

Enraged by the audacious comment, Boringer charged the boy, only to have a stone pillar fire up in between them. The dwarf teetered backwards and turned hot eyes to Rogma whose fingertips glittered with golden light.

"Protect 'im all ye want," Boringer snarled, "but ye know we'll 'ave ta kill 'im one day. No humans can leave this place."

Seeking to cool tempers, Rogma held his hand out to the pugnacious warrior. "Give me yer helmet, Boringer. I'll fix those dents before yer fight tomorrow. So run on now, an' come back later."

Boringer lifted the helmet, uncovering a golden bird's nest, and handed the cherished possession to the master smith. Then, Boringer shoved his hands deep into the pockets of his trousers and blustered out the door.

Rogma moved toward an anvil and motioned for Boryn to follow. "Ye're goin' ta learn ta do this." Long bars of iron were stacked beside the roaring fire pit. "Grab one."

"If you say so." Boryn crammed a yeasty remnant of bread in his mouth and lifted the long, thin bar. The too-large bite and the too-long rod did not mix. He let go of the bar with one hand but the unbalanced iron seesawed and clattered against the floor. He fumbled to rebalance, bread hanging foolishly from his mouth. Rogma reached up, tore away the whole bite and threw it in the fire.

"Hey!"

"Pay attention."

"There are starving people who would kill for that food!"

"So why're you eatin' it, ye greedy pig?"

"Because I'm starving!"

Rogma rolled his eyes. "Take the bar, poke it inta th' fire."

"With what?"

"Your hands."

Boryn held the rod close to the blaze and nothing happened. He inched it closer and into the licking flames. The rod heated and glowed brilliant red. The hairs on his forearms curled and singed; the heat scorched his face. Boryn extended his long arm as far as possible and turned sideways to increase the distance between his face and the inferno.

"What're ye doin'?"

"Trying to keep my face from melting off."

With his staff, Rogma swatted Boryn between the shoulder blades causing him to straighten up and step in.

"Learn ta take pain. Quit tryin' ta hide from it. Ya might wan' ta take it out o' the fire now."

Boryn withdrew the iron; the end glowed yellow-white and sparked. "Whoa . . . ," he said, impressed.

Rogma grabbed the bar and tossed it clattering into a pile of obvious rejects.

"I did what you told me!"

"Heated it too long. If it sparks, ye've ruined the metal and ye go' ta restart."

"Oh."

"Here's what yer goin' ta want ta do." Rogma thrust a rod into the blistering white coals. The dwarf waited and then removed the bar, placing the heated tip on the anvil. After several skillful strikes with his smithing hammer and a repeat of the process, the dwarf held up the clear makings of a dagger which he inspected with large eyes. "Ye see?"

The Blood Knights thundered across the Black Expanse toward the lizard-riding Dark Lancers, the mounted regiment of the Dark elves. A cloud of ash billowed and stung the charging warriors' eyes. The knights lifted their warhammers high as the Dark elven riders lowered their barbed spears. Some of the knights rose up and crouched above their saddles ready to jump. When the Lancers drew near enough, Blood Knights sprang toward them, tackling one and sometimes two to the hard, black earth.

Ramgis, impressive in his blood-red plate, was single focused. An equally impressive, white-armored opponent, Kelris, charged head-on astride Krixlus, his formidable black-scaled mount. Ramgis kicked his warhorse, feeble in comparison to Krixlus, into a gallop, his golden warhammer held to the side.

Ramgis stood in his saddle eager for the assault and roared, "Kelris!" He leapt toward the Dark elven commander, rounding the hammer up and clipping Kelris' chin guard, smashing it and nearly unseating the Lancer. Ramgis sailed toward the charred earth, and rolled aside, plate clanging, to soften the landing. The armored spikes on Krixlus' tail slapped at his face, then the nasty beast wheeled, saliva frothing from its maws. The Blood Knight commander was doused, but he managed to dodge the tail and the gnashing teeth.

Coming around, Kelris thrust his spear, scraping Ramgis' plate with the serrated blade edge. Ramgis reared back, away from the attack, but Krixlus' powerful tail collided with his back, swatting him forward. The snapping teeth, like so many daggers, were ready. The beast bit. It pierced Ramgis' thick shoulder plate then tossed him aside like a rag doll. Ramgis struggled to stand, his arms outstretched for balance. Kelris spurred Krixlus to charge again, and the Dark Lancer slanted his spear and jabbed downward with all of his might. Ramgis felt the cold steel enter his shoulder and exit his middle, and a horrid scream escaped his lips. Kelris reached down and yanked the protruding spear, pulling Ramgis off his feet and dropping him to the ground. Ramgis coughed; blood dribbled down his chin. He looked up at Kelris, the Dark One's face invisible behind the white faceplate. *That dreadful helm* . . . The screams of the villagers, the cries of his mother, and the anguished pleas of his father. His baby brother run through with the spike of that helm and held aloft like a trophy. The village ablaze, smoke masking the stars from view. *This Lancer caused it all.*

Fueled by rage beyond comprehension, Ramgis raised a bloodied hand to the spear. He squeezed the shaft until he felt it snap. He rose to his feet. A dark, new fire burned in his eyes. He swung back with his hammer, a full swing, and launched a pulverizing blow to Krixlus' thick skull. The beast stumbled and fell, nearly pitching Kelris. Stunned, the beast lurched, roared angrily and ran at Ramgis, snapping and grinding. Ramgis veered to one side to elude the jaws, and with a spin, brought his hammer whistling into the opposite side of the lizard's head. It pitched away while whipping its tail. Ramgis dove to avoid the deadly metal spikes but looped back to bound onto the off-balanced beast's back. Holding tight to the reins with one hand, Kelris used his other to cuff the intruder's face. But Ramgis held his footing, and with an emotional roar, swung his hammer down into the Dark elf's face. The Dark elven leader stood in his saddle, unsheathed a sword and slashed out to throw the hammer wide. On the rebound, he kicked Ramgis backward off of his mount.

Suddenly, a pillar of black fire shot into the sky, blasting a hole in the clouds and momentarily commanding all attention. Recognizing the signal, Kelris shook his head, and behind the mask, his lip curled with disgust. He kicked his mount and charged away across the blackened, flat plain. A horn trumpeted three times and, abruptly, the rest of the Dark elven riders broke from battle to follow Kelris.

Ramgis tried to stand but wobbled back, stumbling over fallen knight and elf. He held his hand at his middle; warm blood seeped through the joints of his plate. *What called Kelris off and ended my chance to settle our score?* The invincible, old Blood Knight slumped to the ashen ground. *I would have gladly gone to my death in the effort.*

A flaming torch at the top of a tall pole lit the windowless room. Boryn stood opposite Rogma whose arms were draped over the accursed staff resting across his shoulders, the glass disks removed so that his eyes appeared normally sized.

"Ready for yer first lesson?"

"Not really," Boryn shrugged.

"Who trained ye ta begin with?"

"No one." Boryn circled the room, absently kicking a small rock on the hard, sand-covered ground.

"Tha's problem number one. Did ya always fight with a weapon?"

"Yeah."

"Well, ye're goin' ta learn ta figh' without one. Then I'll le' ye carry a weapon," Rogma outlined.

"What proves I've learned to fight without a weapon?"

"When ye're able ta beat me."

"And let me guess, you get to use that rune magic stuff."

"All dwarves can, but I will no' this time."

"What about your stick?"

"Aye."

"That's a rather unfair advantage, don't you think?"

"All battles have th' one with th' advantage. Ye must learn how ta regain it."

"Shouldn't we start on even ground so it's easier?"

"Fights that're even are the most dangerous of all."

"How so?" Boryn asked skeptically.

"Enough talk. Let's get to it."

Bringing his staff around, Rogma charged at Boryn. Boryn dropped onto his side, stretching long below the sweep. Then, on the rebound, he pushed up with one arm, while kicking into the dwarf's face with the upper leg. Rogma's stick *thwacked* Boryn's incoming shin then shot on, the heel planted. The bulky dwarf used the pole to boost himself into the air and crash into Boryn's legs. Boryn yowled even before the accursed staff came around to whack the bridge of his nose, snapping his head against the ground.

"Ye're no' even tryin'. Get up." Rogma backed off.

Dazed, Boryn sat, face like a rain cloud, green eyes dark with anger. "You have a stick; I have my fists." He held them up, one heavily bandaged.

Rogma thrust the stick up between the displayed hands to clip Boryn's chin and send him flying. Boryn rolled over, spat blood and struggled up. Then an idea sparked. Boryn stilled and focused energy into his legs. He vanished and reappeared behind the dwarf with his good fist cocked and ready. He torpedoed it forward but the staff intervened, and he cried out when the staff stung his cheek and then came around to his head. And he dropped to the floor, unconscious.

"An' there ends yer first lesson," said the dwarf to no one as he walked out the door.

Boryn roamed in the fringe of consciousness, head buzzing, fingers plying the grit of sand. He blinked his eyes open and pushed himself up. In front of him was an iron gate, and beyond it, blackness. *What in hell's name?* He heard a low growl and shook his head to clear it. Two intensely yellow eyes, shot with blood, emerged from the gate's darkness. *Big, bulky, green skin, long pointed teeth . . . an orc? Where am I?* Boryn looked up. *The arena!* Dwarves filled the encircling stands, but the place was absolutely quiet; without a sound, the audience stared.

The orc broke the silent spell. It roared, beating its wide chest and banging its cleaver against the rails that separated them. The gate creaked. *Not good.* Boryn scrambled up and searched for a weapon.

"Ye did no' wan' ta focus when we fough', so now ye can train or die," said Rogma from behind the irons. Boryn glowered. As soon as the gate rose high enough, the orc heaved underneath. With surprising speed, the beast barreled into Boryn, throwing him off his feet. Then it squatted low, close to the boy's sand-planted face, and released a windy exhale, its pungent breath causing Boryn to gag. Boryn flipped and punched. Unfazed, the creature grumbled and slammed its head into Boryn's injured fist, crashing it against the sand. Boryn rolled to the side then kicked in a wide arc, spinning. The orc stumbled in an awkward pirouette, and Boryn snatched the chance to regain his feet.

The orc charged. Its rusty weapon whistled toward the boy's head. **Focus.** Boryn shut his eyes and dropped low. He listened as the cleaver whooshed past. *What is my advantage?* In a heartbeat, he knew. Energy pulsed through his limbs, and Boryn's fist blurred by. The burst of power collided with the metal cleaver, shattering the old blade and sending pieces of rusty steel skittering across the sand. *Whoa.* Boryn was almost as stunned as the orc. The orc roared and tossed the useless handle aside, though it was clearly not finished with the fight. The lumbering creature balled its fist and took a wild swing at Boryn's head. The boy hunched against the force, steeling himself, then he fired his good fist again, upward into the orc's rock-hard chin. He winced and recoiled, but the blow was fierce, and the orc was stunned.

A battleaxe, the handle alone more than waist high, skidded across the sand to stop in front of the orc. "Can no' have ye fightin' on even ground now," laughed Rogma, the only voice amidst the spectators. Effortlessly, the orc lifted the formidable axe, roared and made a full swing toward Boryn. Boryn sidestepped. The axe bit deep into the sand. The orc tugged, but the blade held tight in the grip of the hard earth. Thwarted, it heaved and bellowed. Boryn smiled and bounded up the axe's long haft. The orc let go to ready its beefy fist; the fist shot forward. Before the punch struck, Boryn back-flipped, the toe of his boots collided with the orc's chin, and the orc rocketed skyward. Even as the orc flew, Boryn landed hands first on the haft and cartwheeled down to the axe head. With perfect timing, he vaulted up and around the handle, flipped the orc face down and slammed it head first into the ground. The orc lay still.

Chest hammering and proud of his victory, Boryn jumped from the unconscious orc's back and let his eyes circle the stands. The dwarves made no move but rather continued their soundless stare.

At last, "All righ'. Time ta get ye off th' sand," chuckled Rogma.

"That's it?" Boryn replied with no small measure of arrogance.

"Jus' get out o' there an' come with me."

"If you keep stopping we'll never reach the top," Ranton nagged as Wenval rested on a boulder.

"Weakling," snipped Julia.

Ranton nodded, grabbed Wenval by the cowl of his green robe and pulled him along, increasing the pace. The top of Mount Pyr was too close to stop now.

"Ranton, give him a break. Wenval's not too good at physical stuff," reminded Laric in defense of his friend.

"He's just stalling."

"Shut up!" Wenval opened his hand and pointed his palm at Julia. A needle-fine beam of light splintered out, piercing her shoulder. She screeched. Ranton cocked his fist and slammed it into Wenval's jaw again, sending the smaller boy toppling to the ground. Laric tackled Ranton and walloped the archer's face until he stopped flailing, consciousness lost.

Laric glared at Julia, fed up seeing his friends fight because of a girl. "I'm sick of you, too. If you don't muffle it yourself, I'm going to gag you," he growled.

"If we want Ranton back, we need to kill her," grumbled Wenval under his breath while using the edge of his cloak to wipe blood from his lip. Laric looked up, shocked.

"Kill her?" Calny was aghast.

"Yes."

"No, you won't," Julia smiled, but while her mouth looked pleasant, her teeth began to lengthen into fangs and her skin pulled taut and shiny and turned lightly purple. Her auburn hair turned raven black as wings, thin and dark like a bat's, fired flapping from her back. Julia held up her hand admiring the transformation as her nails turned to claws. All except Wenval stared wide-eyed.

"She's a daemon?" whispered Emily.

"A succubus is the correct term," Julia cackled behind now pink eyes. Laric unsheathed his two-hander, Emily slipped on her rings and Calny moved out of the way.

Emily turned to Wenval. In a low voice, she asked, "What's a succubus?"

Julia cackled again. "Watch, and learn."

"What have you done to Ranton?" demanded Laric.

"I've done nothing, though he is under my spell. He'll do whatever I want, and when Boryn comes through that passage at the mountaintop, Ranton will be the one to send an arrow through your esteemed leader's heart."

"Die!" roared Laric as he ran at her, sword held high. Julia shot forward, a black cord forming in her hand. She snapped the whip, coiling it around Laric's middle, pinning his arms to his side. He struggled to break free but lost his balance and fell to the hard ground. Julia dropped to her knees and bent close over Laric's face. He writhed against the cord, but it would not break. She leaned lower, her lips a breath away from his.

"Do you know what will happen if I kiss you?" she whispered.

Calny blasted forward to tackle her from behind at the same moment Laric slammed his head up, butting his forehead against hers. She was thrown to the side, screeching like a spoiled child, and it was Emily's turn to charge.

"Whore," Emily growled.

"Succubus, please!" Julia laughed.

Emily flicked her wrist and sliced the cord holding Laric. He brushed away the bindings and clambered to his feet, sword pointed at Julia, inches from the gruesome yet alluring face.

"If you Shadow Crusaders think you can slay your first daemon without your leader, go ahead. Come and die," Julia taunted.

As one, they ran at her, but a column of black fire shot up, engulfing the succubus' form.

"You revealed yourself." The Shadow Crusaders overheard the disapproving voice from inside the roaring pillar.

"They were going to figure it out anyway," was Julia's curt reply.

The black column of fire died away, revealing a white-cloaked figure with fiery orange eyes. He pushed back the hood and ran a hand through his flame-colored hair. "I'm disappointed by your lack of control. You've made this more difficult."

Julia sagged. "That one," Julia pointed at Wenval who stared in horror at the daemon general, "is making us take forever."

"Fortunately, Boryn won't be leaving the mountain anytime soon; you are not the only wrench thrown into our plans," the general informed her. "Hold them here until it is time."

"Time for what? Who are you?" Laric demanded.

"Someone you shouldn't irritate."

Laric heard fingers snap and felt cold earth on his face.

Boringer, boots clacking, marched past the guards, through the anteroom and straight up to the dais where sat the dwarven king's throne.

"O King, I am here ta represen' the populus o' the clans of Raz Kiri, and we wan' tha' human executed. Only dwarves're allowed th' honor o' the arenas!" Boringer fumed, waving his arms.

King Fazrin stoked his white beard with one hand while holding up the other to silence the indignant subject. "Who put the boy inta th' arena?"

"Rogma."

"Is no' Rogma one o' those in charge?"

"Jus' because he's the master smith does no' give 'im the right . . ."

Again the hand came up. "I'll no' be executin' the human. Why ye're all so hungry ta watch the human bleed, I do no' know. But ya migh' let 'im stay in th' arena. If ye're lucky, he'll ge' killed, eh?"

"But yer highness, since the dawn o' time, th' arena 'as been a privilege fer dwarves alone."

"Did we no' once figh' alongside humans both in th' arena an' on the battlefield?"

"We fough' against 'em as well."

"I will speak with Rogma as well as the Master o' the Bets an' decide whether or no' the boy will be allowed onta the sand again."

Boringer's generous eyebrows shot skyward. "Ye migh' allow this?"

"Aye, Boringer."

Boringer threw his hands into the air and stormed from the room. Outside the palace, he elbowed through the angry mob.

Spying Boringer and knowing exactly where the hot-tempered dwarf was heading, a wiry dwarf with mothy-brown hair and wearing a drink-stained apron broke away from the crowd. He trotted down a back alley, a shortcut to the brewery pub to beat Boringer there.

Like most of the buildings in Raz Kiri, the brewery was circular in shape with a copper dome for a roof. Along the side was a row of windows and a planked door. Boringer stomped into the courtyard, boiling like a thunderhead, and plowed into the tavern's wooden door, snapping it from its hinges. He tripped over the stone threshold and landed with a splat, face first atop the falling door.

"No' agai'!" groaned the baggy-eyed brewer.

"I saw ye outside the palace. Wha' were ya doin' there?"

"Wanted ta watch all th' dwarves bitch 'n' moan," laughed the brewer, his shaggy brown beard bobbing beneath an especially thick accent.

"Well, Bret, if ye was 'ere workin' like ya shoulda been, I would no' o' had ta smash in yer door," grinned Boringer as blood dribbled from his nose to his moustache.

"Wha' can I ge' ye ta drink, eh?" Bret asked sliding behind the bar.

"Wha's new?"

"Uh . . . I 'avn't really brew'd nothin' new lately."

"Wha' drink did I 'ave the las' time?" Boringer asked, working the length of the bar and checking mugs for leftovers.

"T'was da 'Pretty in Pink.' Bwahahaha."

"Ye ever though' about learnin' ta talk."

"Ever think tha' takin' tha' axe handle out o' yer arse is a good idea, eh?" Bret laughed as he turned for the storeroom.

"Yer goin' ta die, Bret."

"Jus' cause ye're insecure 'bout some li'l human stealin' yer glory, ye should no' be takin' it out on me!" Bret teased as he closed the storeroom door behind him.

Luthor looked down at the shredded remains of the rapi chief. *Fool.* In the distance, he saw a body of men moving toward him, a knightly band under a mossy-green banner with the insignia of a horse, and another, colors indistinguishable in the hazy distance. Ignoring them, Luthor squatted at the river, laid his claymore on the ground beside him and dipped the red cloth that had tied his hair into the cooling water. He tied the rag around his forehead, holding back his stringy black hair.

A rider approached followed by another. The men pulled their mounts to a halt a few feet from where Luthor crouched. "Luthor Mhinbron, you and your men were banished from the lands of the Knightly Realms long ago. You are hereby ordered to leave immediately," demanded the general of the Order of Horse.

Luthor made a point of looking to the ground and then up to the knight. "I'm fairly sure this is imperial soil."

"If I remember correctly, you are banished from that as well."

"May I ask what has prompted your visit to our fair land, general?" Luthor's words dripped sarcasm.

"I saw a Red X flag and felt like weighing down my coin purse

235

with the reward for your head."

"Sorry to disappoint, but we had our fight for the day. Though I appreciate the offer." Luthor grabbed his blade, stood, and gave a two-fingered salute as he turned to walk away.

"You turn your back on us? You impudent fool!" The general of the Order of the Bear swung his arm forward, and he and his small band of knights converged on Luthor with spears lowered.

"You really don't want to mess with me right now," Luthor warned.

"Oh, I really do. Skewering you will do me good. Especially with all the gold on your head."

"You might find going for that gold to be rather . . . expensive."

Luthor continued to walk away then reversed direction and nailed the Bear commander with a wicked glare. Eyes flaring red, Luthor raised the two-hander. The horses, sensing a change, grew skittish and backed away. Wisely, the Bear commander and his knights followed the animals' lead, turned tail and rode off.

Luthor's eyes cooled to their normal green though he winced and staggered to his knees. Dace hurried to his leader's side, caught him under the arms and, with the help of an aide, carried Luthor toward the main army.

"Are you all right, sir?" asked Luthor's second.

"Dace, every time I use it, that power is harder to control."

The bleat of a horn reverberated across the plain. Luthor craned his neck in the direction of the sound. He could see nothing, but the thunder of hooves signaled trouble.

"Leave me here; I'll take the lead. Move back with the men and wait." His tone was urgent; he wanted his men out of the way.

"But Luthor, sir . . ."

"Now."

Dace and his helper lowered Luthor and left to assemble the men for battle, having no intention of waiting as instructed.

Grimacing, Luthor forced himself to his feet. A banner broke the ridgeline; he recognized the purple and brown colors of the knights of the Bear who marched beside the soldiers of the Horse. The regiments were magnificent, emblazoned banners flying, mounted knights in a block formation flanked by infantry.

Luthor closed his eyes and tensed his fists. The earth seemed to pop beneath him. He opened his eyes, red again, and reached over his shoulder for the sword sheathed in a widemouthed, leather back carrier. With both hands, he thrust the blade high into the air and flung it upward—a call to battle. The weapon spun and flipped, and the hilt dropped into Luthor's readied grip, the ruby-studded cross brace caging it, the gems glowing like burning coal.

The two Realm armies charged, knights in front, infantry behind. Luthor waited as his opponents drew closer. He heard the Red X riders close in behind him. Mouth twisted into a cruel smile, he sprinted toward the oncoming knights. While the knights advanced, spears were lowered, ready for battle.

The Horse and Bear generals held their position at the rear.

"Damned plain. There's no higher ground to watch our armies rip the Red X apart," complained the general of the Bear.

"This rise is the best we can do. At least it hides our presence," the Horse said as the two commanders slipped into a copse that capped the mound like a tuft of hair. "At last, Luthor will be run down by our soldiers and his men captured or killed," bragged the Bear.

"Ah, yes, the reward for his head shall be quite enjoyable," the Horse commander agreed while pulling a jug from his saddlebag. "Fruit of the vine to celebrate?"

"Indeed! Victory is assured."

An inhuman cry erupted from the battlefield. Luthor slammed his blade tip into the ground, and a fissure exploded out, splitting the knightly ranks. A chill flared up the Bear commander's spine, and he swiveled to face the field of engagement. A raging fury on foot was cutting a decimating swath through the ranks. *How could one man make it through those forces?* The deadly wedge sliced through to the rear of the formation, and the two generals beheld a pair of blood-red eyes.

"Retreat!" ordered the cowardly commander of the Bear as the commander of the Horse stared slack-jawed, the jug of wine still dangling from his fingertips. Suddenly, Luthor was face-to-face with them, slicing and slashing. The wine jug crashed to the earth, shattering, its crimson contents spilling with the blood from the Horse general's chest.

The commander of the Bear dropped his weapon and held up his hands, but Luthor paid no heed. The devastating blade tore through the Bear's skull.

Luthor raised his bone horn and blew into it before calling out to the surviving Horse and Bear warriors. "Drop your weapons and your colors and join the Red X, or you will die here and now." Swords, spears and banners clattered to the ground.

Red X men swarmed the losers, and Luthor faltered, knees buckling. Dace and another Red X soldier bounded from their horses to come to their leader's aid.

"Three . . . times in a day . . . bad idea," Luthor gasped, wholly spent.

"By absorbing these soldiers, you have likely doubled our numbers. At least that's good news."

"Doesn't help me much right now . . . ," Luthor's laugh was weak.

"We're setting up camp," Dace said then turned to the aide. "I'll get him to his tent. You go find a healer to meet us there. Luthor will need him after today." The loyal second boosted Luthor across his mount's back and led it to his leader's tent.

"Thank you . . . my friend," Luthor said to Dace as he settled on a cot. "I rest well knowing your blade is protecting me." Instantly, he fell into a deep sleep.

Dace stepped from the tent to see the army arriving and the camp springing to life. Soldiers cooked, cheered, and celebrated while "kindly helping" to acclimate the lowly, new inductees into the Red X.

Then Dace considered the man he served, his respected leader. *Why would Luthor sacrifice so much of himself to protect the lives of his men?* Even after so many years, it remained a mystery. *So much for finding a fort and settling in for war.*

The dagger rasped against the file. Boryn held up the blade, inspecting its sharpened edge. He smiled. *Perfect.* He carried it to Rogma who leaned over a work table, glass disks over his eyes, engrossed in plans. Boryn extended the blade by the tang, a crooked grin on his face.

"How's this?"

Without even a glance, "Spine's curved."

"No way." Boryn held the blade close to his face and sighted down the shaft.

"Ye'll also have dents in the blade. You were no' wipin' th' anvil clear o' fire scale."

"This is, what, the fourth dagger?"

"An' ye will no' make a weapon fer yerself 'til you make one useable in th' arena."

"What do you do with all these rejects?"

"Melt 'em down an' try ta repurify the metal. Now throw tha' in the rubbish pile with th' others."

"How long until training?"

"No' until ye ge' yer first dagger righ', but ye've got a figh' in a bit, so hurry it up."

"A fight?"

"The arena."

"Who or what am I fighting this time?"

"A very vicious opponent to start with." Rogma turned big eyes to Boryn and snickered. Then he shooed Boryn toward the fire and anvil.

The crowd clucked, buoyant with anticipation.

"Wonder how our poor human frien' will handle such a terrifyin' beast," called out a spectator to the delight of his companions.

Boryn measured up his opponent: a goblin, about the size of a dwarf, with pointy, green ears that drooped around its face. Annoyance crossed Boryn's face. He walked toward the creature, and it dropped to the ground cowering. He nudged it with the toe of his boot. The thing rolled into a ball and tumbled to the side shivering violently. Boryn turned to face Rogma who observed from the stands, his genial expression giving nothing away. But the sniggers of the crowd made it clear the boy was being played the fool.

Boryn held up his hands, the bandaged and the good, and shrugged. "What?" he seemed to say.

Just then, Boryn felt something land on his back and grip with vicious claws. He dropped to the sand. "You bloody, little goblin!" Reaching behind him, he grabbed the goblin's hands, tore them free and slung the beast across the arena. Slowly, it rose on its haunches, trembling.

Then suddenly, the goblin cackled and pounced. Boryn made a high, wide sweep with one foot, kicking it in the neck. He accelerated then tornadoed around, his other foot smacking the goblin's head. A staccato crack, and the thing fell limp, the bout clinched. Boryn landed awkwardly, catching himself with his injured hand. *Bad idea.* He stood up cradling it. *No way I'll be able to hold a sword any time soon.*

"Congratulations on yer surprisin' victory, human" the

announcer called. "Now please make yer way out the gladiator gate, so a true warrior can battle a *true* beast."

Boryn stepped toward the gate. A heavily armored dwarf waited to enter the arena. Opposite, at the opponent's gate, stood a grayish-green beast of an unfamiliar sort. It was taller than Boryn, standing on two longer, lankier legs, but it slumped and looked as if it was half starved. *Heh.* Boryn ran at the dwarven fighter and kicked him backward. The dwarf tumbled into the gatekeeper who released the switch, dropping the gladiator gate. *My beast now.*

The stands erupted with a roar of outrage. Boryn smirked, confident that this opponent was as outmatched as the last. The skinny creature skulked from its gateway. Slowly, it raised its head and sniffed, crinkling its nose as if catching a foul odor. Then, it bellowed and pounced, exploding across the sand. Boryn lunged sideways to avoid the claws that raked the sand and grooved the stone below. The crowd laughed, amused to think that the human might very well die.

An instant later, Boryn felt pain rip through his chest, his shirt front shredded. He fell backward and landed with a thud. ***Focus.*** The word came from outside of himself yet inside of his mind; it wasn't his own but rather as if someone had implanted the word there.

He hobbled out of the creature's reach. Shutting his eyes and concentrating, Boryn saw himself standing in the center of the arena. The ground below him had vanished; all he could see was himself and the beast. All he could hear was his own rhythmic breath syncopated with the low growls of the creature. The adversary hurtled forward, flailing with long arms. But Boryn dove beneath the claws and came up chest-to-chest to the creature. He hooked his arm around its skinny neck, and with it trapped in a vicious headlock, he pivoted while bending low.

He used his injured hand, which suddenly, magically, felt healed, to crush the creature's face into the blackness where sand should have been. The neck popped, and Boryn heard the creature whimper. He released his hold and stepped back, hammers in his ears, breathing hard. The creature gave an involuntary shudder, rose, squared and lumbered toward the beast gate at which time the sand reappeared, and Boryn saw through his own eyes once again. From the crowd, he heard whispers and an occasional catcall. Boryn smiled. *I don't know what that creature was, but I put it on its knees.*

On all fours, Marlok perched on the jagged edge and peered down into the blackness.

"It seems to open into some sort of cavern. I can't even see the bottom," Quaswyn quivered.

"That storm must have blasted it open," Marlok mused.

"That was no regular storm."

"You think something is down there?"

"Maybe," said Quaswyn, leaning a little farther. The earth cracked and gave way. Quaswyn yelped as they were swallowed by the void.

"Whoa! You emptyhead!" bawled a frantic Marlok.

"I'll save us. Just give me a second to remember." Quaswyn put their hand on their chin as they tumbled headlong.

"Hurry up."

"The more you think, the less brainpower I have."

"Floor . . . ," said Marlok as the bottom zoomed up.

"*Guarda!*" Quaswyn blew into their hand; a swirling orb of air formed. He enclosed the fluffy ball in their palms and threw it down. It burst out like a cushion. They bounced, rebounded, and landed safely on their feet. Quaswyn preened.

Marlok blinked furiously, willing their eyes to adjust to the gloom. He pushed up their sleeve to uncover the glowing arm glyph.

"A temple of some kind," Quaswyn judged from the blue-hued pillars encircling the space. An elaborate anvil, its surface covered with glowing symbols, rested in the center, and the single door was similarly etched. "Look at the runes. Dwarven, I'd guess . . ."

"Great, lost in ruins again . . ."

"*Runes*, you, you . . . barbarian. Not *ruins*!"

Suddenly the door flew open, "Where in the world are all ye humans comin' from?"

Pointing upward and with a friendly tone, Quaswyn said, "I'm afraid you have a hole in your roof."

"Who are ye?"

"Marlok."

"I'm Quaswyn."

The dwarf stopped and stared with big eyes, confounded. He removed the glass disks that hung on his nose and wiped them on his shirttail. Carefully, he replaced the wires over his ears and looked again. "Which is it?"

"Oh my! Are those spectacles you're wearing? I've heard of them. May I see . . . ?"

"Quiet. I'll not be askin' ye another time. Who are ye?"

"Quaswyn."

"Marlok."

"Two names."

"Yes, you see, we had a little accident with an artifact, and, well, as you can see, it merged us into a single form. Most unpleas—"

The dwarf struck the stone floor with the heel of his staff, and a glowing golden rune appeared. Marlok felt the stone beneath their feet begin to flow like water.

They splashed down into the eddy of liquefied stone and sank up to their chin while the dwarf scribed sparkling runes in the air.

"Runic magic!" Quaswyn exclaimed.

"Shut it," Marlok barked.

The stone rehardened and cracked, and amidst screeches of

wonder and dismay, they floated up from the ground, trapped in a block of rock.

"Oh my, an encasement spell! You must be a master to *make* the runes as well as *use* them!"

Another rune caused the cavity in the floor to refill, and the dwarf jangled out the door. From the hall outside, they heard rumbling like a rockslide. A stone golem, a brutish figure made of chunks of rock, lumbered in, a grin lighting its face at the sight of the poor human trapped in stone.

"Grab it, an' follow me," the tidy, old dwarf ordered the chunky assistant.

"Aye." The voice sounded like grinding pebbles.

The golem flipped the cube on its side and raised a solid fist. It smashed the bottom of the block, freeing the prisoner's feet. Nabbing the feet like a handle, the golem flipped the block upside down. Merrily thundering down the hall behind the dwarf, the golem swung the block from side-to-side like a boy with a lunchbox.

"Urp . . ."

"Hold it in, Quaswyn."

"I think I feel our lunch."

"There. I shut our eyes. Now shut up, and keep it down."

"I can't. The swaying . . ."

A rock-laden slurry spilled from the encasement and solidified over their mouth.

"Now maybe ye'll keep quiet," said the aggravated dwarf as he hurried ahead.

The knife cooled, the intense orange glow dulling to gray. Boryn held it out and sighted down the straight spine. *Finally, I can move on.*

"Anyone know where Rogma is?"

"The Heaven Forge, the Heart." Boryn detected a note of reverence in the apprentice's reply.

At that moment, the door to the forge flew open, and Rogma stamped in.

"Boryn, come outside. Hurry."

The boy laid the dagger beside the grinder and followed the forge master outside. A giant golem was swinging what appeared to be a man encased in rock.

"I'll be removing stone chips from my clothes for days," droned Quaswyn.

"How'd ya get yer mouth unsealed?"

"We were lucky enough to hit the wall, thanks to your careless courier."

"Boryn, d'ye know this, this . . . human?" Rogma sputtered.

"Never seen anyone like him."

"Good dwarf, I'd be ever so appreciative if you could you ask your lovely friend to set us upright. All the blood has rushed to my head, and I'm feeling a touch woozy."

"Put 'im down," the dwarf directed, ". . . but do no' drop . . ." The golem gulped, flipped the block head-up and propped it against the forge wall.

"The las' thing I need is another human," Rogma moaned.

"Let me out of this rock, and I'll be out of here like that," Marlok bargained.

"A'mighty damn," groaned a voice behind them.

Rogma turned to see Boringer scowling at the odd man with only his scarred face and orange-and-black striped hair visible above the stone.

"You know this human?" Rogma asked.

"Can ya cover 'is mouth?"

"I already tried."

"Trus' me. It is worth tryin' again."

"Boringer!" Quaswyn exclaimed.

"Shut up, Quaswyn."

"How have you been since we last saw you?"

"I woul' be better if ye humans woul' stop droppin' in on us."

"We didn't choose to be here; we fell through a blasted hole," Marlok piped up.

"But we are *so* happy to see you again!" Quaswyn enthused.

"Maybe Boringer should take care of him, seeing as they are good friends and all," Boryn laughed. Boringer's hooded eyes shot darts at the boy.

"My, yes, it would be interesting to see how you dwarves live here!" Quaswyn exclaimed. "Speaking of here, where are we, may I ask?"

Boringer buried his beefy hands in his pockets and stepped toward Boryn.

Goading him, Boryn addressed the irritated dwarf. "Wasn't that your cousin's troll I took in the arena today?"

"Aye, an' I am 'ere ta kill ye fer it."

"Good luck with that," was Boryn's cheeky reply.

"You an' me in a figh'," Boringer challenged.

"When?"

Rogma interceded, "When his trainin' with me is over, then he will figh' you—an' feel free ta tear him ta pieces if ya want."

"Oh, Rogma, I finished a dagger, straight spine. No fire scale, either."

"You can show me later. First, we need ta decide wha' ta do with this blockhead."

"We could just leave 'im there," Boringer suggested.

Quaswyn asked, "You wouldn't happen to have anything to eat, would you?"

Luthor eased his eyes open, squinting in the bright light. He heard a sound. A scrap. Metallic. Fully alert but without moving, his hand wrapped the side rail of a crate next to his cot. Springing the trap, he flipped the crate into the path of the incoming iron. The blade *thunked* into the wood, and a knight cried out.

Luthor jumped up; he was surrounded. *My blade's on the other side of the tent, and if I go all out now* . . . A slit. Another. In the canvas above. Dace dropped through the X, crouching, hands low, his deadly curved katana—a relic of his water country ancestors—gripped underhanded and extended behind him.

"You shall not touch Luthor," Dace said to the gathered rebels still intent on collecting the price on Luthor's head.

"Dace . . ."

Dace stood and jerked his hands up so that the sword's back aligned his forearm, cutting edge out. One knight ran at the swordsman, blade held high and ready to bring it slicing down. Dace raised his elbow and swept sideways, slashing the sharpened edge across the assailant's throat. Without stopping, Dace jumped back, righted his grip then sprang forward, his blade slashing another rebel's chest. *Two.* A brilliant light shot from the hilt to the point of Dace's curved blade, charging it with energy that brightened at the tip. Dace vanished. The knights charged Luthor, but Dace reappeared in front of one, his blade deep, stomach to heart. *Three.* Next, blood spurted from a clean slit across another's throat. *Four.* Dace landed between two more; one took a slash through the spine. *Five. Six.*

Luthor heard shouts from outside as a Red X soldier rushed in.

"Drop your weapons or die," the soldier commanded.

"Assassins deserve only death!" Dace cried.

"We've been through this before, Dace," Luthor said calmly as the remaining knights gladly exchanged weapons for lives. The soldier led the knightly prisoners out of the tent.

"Are you sure, sire?"

"Yes, I'm sure. Now tell the men to pack up. We're going to Falrik, to the capital of the knights."

"Why, my lord?"

"These rebels will be nothing but trouble. Let's take them back and leave the problem with someone else."

Dace asked with genuine concern. "Luthor, are you up to it?"

"Yes. I'll be fine. Prepare to move out immediately."

"Oy, Morpheon! I know ye're here." The dark, squat dwarf scanned the withering jungle, a smirk on his wide, flat face. "I'm guessing you got 'em!" He whistled happily, unmoved by the grisly scene on the road beside him.

Morpheon stepped from the thicket. "Kam, it's good to see you. And yes, I finally finished off my old friends. The last of my competition gone, and my revenge complete. What could be better," it said pleasantly, making no effort to conceal its nakedness and brushing back its long, mousy hair with a dramatic gesture.

"Well, now. I'm needin' yer help."

"With?" said the raspy-voiced creature as it stepped in front of the dwarf.

"I'm charged with killin' the rest'a me people, just like you were yers."

Morpheon looked up, surprised. "You think you can do what I did?" Morpheon scoffed. "Good luck with that."

"Aye. I 'ave more power than ye think," Kam blustered, "but I was hopin' ta get yer help. Think o' it this way. You in the center o' Raz Kiri, free ta do whatever ye wan'. The last o' the dwarves, all

251

yers fer the takin'.'"

"Intriguing." The gray-skinned creature twisted a lock of stringy hair on a long fingernail then turned purple eyes to the sky. Its waxy gray face broke into a rapturous smile, wet fangs glistening. "Sounds like quite a party. Who else are we inviting?"

"We 'ave been given a few Flame elven regulars and a handful o' daemons."

"When do we leave?" Morpheon breathed.

"As soon as we get the rest o' our orders."

"In the meanwhile, may I return to my feast?"

"Ye're still eatin' this?" asked Kam kicking a skull half covered with flesh and straining the buttons on his too-tight vest in the effort.

"It would be such a waste to leave it."

The blade was as long as his arm, gracefully shaped, smooth, and razor sharp. Boryn held it up, admiring its balance and heft. At last he had made a half-decent scimitar. He walked over to Rogma and presented it.

"Good timin'."

"For?"

"Ye do no' have any more fights fer a few days, so you and me, we're leavin'. I just finished me plans."

"For what?"

"Me masterpiece. Me grand finale. The best work I will ever produce." Rogma looked at Boryn and smiled.

"What is it?"

"No' yer concern."

"Tell me about those glass things on your face. Will your masterpiece be something like that?"

"Oh, no. Nothin' like that." Rogma removed the contraption. "These are just spectacles. Help me old eyes ta see."

"Can I try?"

Rogma held the wires and hooked them over Boryn's ears.

"Whoa!" Boryn stood straight then bent over the table, tilting his head up and down. "Awesome! What about that necklace you always wear?"

Rogma's fingers went to his neck. "Was me son's."

"You had a son?"

"Aye. A long, long time ago. Seems like another lifetime. . . . I made this fer 'im when he was a little one." Pulling the silver pendant forward, Rogma showed it to Boryn. "A man of stone."

"What happened?"

"In the Daemon War, a greedy louse by the name of Kam betrayed us, his own people. Stupid, he was, trustin' the daemons to give 'im power if he turned on us. But still very damagin' ta the dwarves. Our capital city was destroyed; most o' the warriors died tryin' to help their families escape. My son was one o' those brave warriors. I los' me son; go' nothing' but the pendant back. I wear it ta keep 'im with me forever . . . ," the forge master paused, a world away. "Now, grab yer things. We're goin'."

"Going where?"

"Tell me, wha' did we do with tha' Marlok an' Quaswyn fella?"

"Ha! You'll like this . . . ," Boryn followed the old master from the forge.

"What do you want now?"

"Is that any way to address the Emperor?"

The white-haired healer remained silent.

"I'll come directly to the point, Edrick." Lord Mhinbron paused and sighed grandly. "I should like to reconcile with my sons."

Still the healer did not speak.

Mhinbron paced the lavishly appointed room, twisting his hands in agitation. Scruffy observed the man, taking note that his words were less slurred than usual and his eyes less bleary.

"You see, I've given considerable thought to this, and well, I now see the error of my ways."

Unmoved, Scruffy replied, "So you hope to turn the page and change the story?"

"I don't know what you're talking about."

"Then tell me why it is that you wish this reconciliation. And why now?"

The Emperor stopped pacing, moved to his throne, and sat heavily. With a deep, resigned sigh, he leaned to the side and rested his head in his palm, his elbow propped on an arm of the throne.

"You have to help me," Mhinbron pleaded.

"No. I don't."

"It is important that my successors be . . ."

"Or could it be that you have daemon hordes breathing down the neck of your city and mutinous advisors who'd like to use this crisis to their own advantage?"

"It's nothing of the kind! My council is loyal."

"If you say so, Emperor."

"I've heard that a purging can cleanse the soul of past misdeeds. Is it true?"

"Yes."

"Then I want you to purge me."

"I won't do it."

"I command you."

"I won't succumb to your threats."

"I will exile you."

"Seems that's what you do best to those close to you." Scruffy paused so that the inference would be clear then continued with conviction. "It won't work. Something more than pride and power must be at stake."

"Are you saying, Edrick, that your skills are inadequate?" Mhinbron parried.

"No. Your motives are."

Boringer banged his forehead against the wooden bar. Bret leaned against the back wall struggling to keep from bursting out laughing.

"He never, ever shuts up," groaned the dwarven gladiator.

"I think he likes ye."

"Shut up, Bret."

"Wha' can I get ye, eh?"

"Pour me another mug, an' fill this jug with the blackout mead," Boringer said.

"Wha' d'you wan' a bottle of it fer?"

"I'm going to keep him unconscious."

Bret removed the jug from the bar with a mischievous grin. "Drink yours. I'm goin' ta go fill it."

Boringer drained his mug and tapped the bar impatiently for Bret to return.

"Ye still owe me fer the last five. As well as fer all the mugs ye walk out with!" Bret handed Boringer the filled jug.

"Whine, whine," he tottered from his stool. Then he grabbed the bottle in one hand and a mug in the other and headed for the door.

This should be interestin'. Bret smiled at the thought of the bright orange liquid he had poured into the black bottle.

From the appearance of the battlefield, it was difficult to judge victor and vanquished. Rath scanned the barren plain, littered with bodies, Blood Knight and Dark elf. Riderless horses wandered aimlessly among the dead and wounded. The tattered banner of the Blood Knights hung limply from its pole stabbed into the earth beside its impaled bearer. A few Dark elves tried to crawl away to escape sure death at the hand of the knights scavenging the field for survivors and useful weapons.

Two races trained and primed for vengeance, deadlocked in battle. A horrific combination. Rath shook his head at two crumpled corpses: one of a Dark elven rider and the other a knight ripped apart by one of the Dark One's reptilian mounts. He pulled a strip of parchment from his pocket and scrawled a note. At the sound of Rath's whistle, a hawk swooped from the clouds to land on his shoulder.

"Take this for me, would you?" He tied the note to the hawk's leg and watched it fly away.

Gauntleted arms grabbed him. "Traitor!" The Blood Knight pinned Rath's arms behind his back. "So that's how they knew we were coming."

"What are you babbling about?" asked Rath as he was thrown roughly to the ground, a warhammer held above his head. "You really want to start a fight with me?"

"You have been betraying us to our enemies. I will take you to Ramgis," growled the crimson-and-gold armored knight.

"You sure he's even alive?"

The knight roared and swung at the downed man. Rath brought his legs up, catching the hammer shaft between his feet. He quickly flipped, ripping the hammer from the knight's grip then bounded up to bring one elbow into the man's face. The knight tumbled backward as more Blood Knights charged in to take hold of Rath.

Rath threw up his hands in willing surrender and marched toward Ramgis' hastily pitched tent. Five knights surrounded him. Rath batted the flap aside and entered the commander's tent where Cadegray and two apprentices tended Ramgis' wounds.

"How badly is he hurt?" Rath seemed concerned.

A knight smacked his gauntlet against the back of Rath's head. "You will speak upon being spoken to, traitor."

"Traitor?" groaned Ramgis, struggling to sit up.

"Aye. This one's been feeding the Dark elves information about us this whole time. Uses a hawk as courier. Explains why he and his scouts are so good."

"Is it true?" Ramgis asked, more weary than mad. "You have been trading messages by hawk?" The old commander's shoulders sagged.

"Yes, but——." The gauntlet slammed into Rath's stomach; he doubled over and dropped to his knees.

"To whom were they being sent?"

Rath coughed, catching his breath. "I'm under orders."

"Whose?"

"Can't say."

Ramgis waved his hand dismissively and turned away. "Tie him up and capture as many of his men as you can."

A whistle hung from a strap around Rath's neck. He yanked it from inside his shirt and blew into the mouthpiece. At the high-pitched signal, a horse charged into the tent. Rath grabbed the mane, threw himself astride and galloped out, his riders already heading across the plain. The Blood Knights scurried from their resting places to mount their steeds and make chase.

Rath glanced over his shoulder and smiled ruefully. *Sorry, Ramgis. You can't find out yet. It would ruin everything.*

Stevan stared into the deep, black hole with a satisfied expression. *So this is where he went!*

"Oy, Hannah, we're going in."

"Down there?"

"Aye."

"I can't even see the bottom!"

"I don't mean jumping down into it," he scoffed as he tied a rope to the end of his halberd.

"Why do you have a rope?"

"We were climbing a mountain."

"This won't work."

"Why not?"

"You're going to do it anyway, so I won't bother explaining."

"It'll work. You'll see." Stevan hitched his halberd on the edge of the opening and let the rope drop. He shinnied off the ledge, twisting his leg around the rope while still clinging to the side. "Told you so." He shifted his weight to the rope.

"Problem," Hannah said.

Stevan tilted his head back, eyes up.

"Look at the rope."

Stevan's triumphant grin faded as the knot began to slip down the handle. "Curses!" The halberd held tight, but the rope slid free, and the dwarf tumbled one way and his helmet the other into the blackness.

Hannah shook her head and lowered her upper body into the opening. A smooth, stone pillar, just out of reach, dove into the darkness. Holding the ledge, she made a quick, decisive move. She dropped, swung her legs toward the wall and launched toward the pillar as the ground crumbled away where she had held it. She twined her long limbs around the pillar then, loosening her hold slightly, she glided to the bottom.

Stevan groaned as Hannah came to a smooth landing. Slowly, he climbed to his feet, stretching his wrenched shoulder. "You jinxed it."

"That's ridiculous. It was just a dumb idea."

"Was not."

"Was too."

"Shoulda worked," mumbled Stevan as he tapped a dent out of his helmet and replaced it on his head.

"But my idea was better."

"How was I supposed to have climbed down that way?" Stevan threw up his hands, displaying his considerably shorter limbs. "If you were *really* a dwarf, it wouldn't have worked for you either."

"I am a dwarf," she persisted.

"Only by adoption," said Stevan. The squabble ended when the halberd, loosed from the perch above, tumbled through the darkness for a direct hit to Stevan's helmet. His ears where still ringing when a door squeaked open, and firelight illuminated the space.

"Stevan?"

The cinnamon-haired dwarf spun toward the source. A tall boy, black cape draped across his shoulder and torch in hand, stood in the doorway.

"Boryn?"

"Please tell me . . . ," came another voice from behind the boy, ". . . it is no' another human!"

"There's one human."

"Wha's the other one?"

"A dwarf."

Rogma jangled past Boryn and came eye-to-eye with the young, well-groomed dwarf. After a moment's hesitation, delight lit Rogma's face. "It's the king's favorite cook! Come back ta cook fer 'im?"

"Actually, I was looking for Boryn."

"Where did you and Hannah go during the storm?" Boryn wondered aloud.

"A man in white nabbed us while the one in red was picking a fight with you."

"White? With black edges?" asked Rogma, his face darkening.

"Aye."

"What color were his eyes and his hair?"

"Orange, I believe."

"It was Fernus," Boryn said, recognizing the description.

"First tha' one called Thundrus, an' now another is crawlin' aroun'!"

"Thundrus is gone now," Boryn said without elaborating.

"But there's still another one," Stevan added, "by the name of Glacius, the one who fought the elven king of fire."

"Two daemon generals an' an elven king on our mountain. Tha's no' good. Come with me. Ye must tell King Fazrin what ye saw." Rogma held out one hand. His fingers began to glow with a golden light, and he drew a large rune, leaving a glowing trail in the air. He slid his fist into the pattern and smashed it toward the earth. The rock floor began to crumble into a swirling whirlpool. "Everyone in." Rogma leapt into the whorl, Stevan after.

Boryn held out one arm. "Ladies first." Hannah jumped, and Boryn followed last. The whirling rock felt almost like water, comforting and warm. Boryn opened his eyes as he spilled out face first on a shiny stone floor, but something sharp and cold pressed against the back of his neck, and he dared not move.

"Wha' is the meanin' o' this?" puffed a rather gruff yet refined dwarven voice.

"Forgive me, me lord, fer this intrusion, but there was no' time," Rogma apologized.

"Wha' matters are so urgent tha' you dirty the throne room with human filth?" bit Boringer while King Fazrin watched.

"Daemons. They have found us." Rogma was long faced.

"An' how d'ya know this?"

The red-bearded dwarf stepped forward. "I saw them."

The king mirrored the action. "Stevan?" he squinted into the dwarf's face.

"Stevan, are ye sure abou' the daemons?" Boringer probed.

"Aye. Two generals by the names of Glacius and Fernus."

"The daemons followed him!" Boringer pointed an accusing finger at Boryn. The guard whose blade kept Boryn floored now made it clear that the boy was expected to rise.

"What?" Boryn cocked his head.

"The boy brought 'em down upon us. We all can feel tha' he 'as got the stench of a daemon about 'im."

"Maybe because I kill them!" Boryn replied sharply. The point at his neck pressed harder, breaking the skin.

"Le' us execute 'im, O King," Boringer urged. The guard's blade forced Boryn to his toes.

"He didn't do anything," Stevan insisted.

Without warning, Boryn lurched sideways. Using the moment of distraction, he kicked up and planted his toe in the guard's groin and followed with an elbow to the jaw. The guard teetered and fell. Boryn looked behind him where the rock continued to swirl. He snatched the fallen dwarf's halberd and charged the guard holding Hannah. The guard shoved her toward the upraised weapon. Thinking fast, Boryn hooked his arm around Hannah's waist and swept her out of the way as the guard's halberd came down, nicking Boryn's side. He winced but closed his eyes and pulled Hannah along as he let himself fall backward into the granite vortex.

Together, they fired out of the eddy and tumbled into a wafer-thin sheet of shiny rock. It shattered, opening a passage to a stairway leading up. Camouflaged amidst the silvery debris was something glistening black. The scimitars! Boryn grabbed the handles, rose and sheathed the twin black-gem blades, enjoying their weight at his side.

"Are you hurt?" he asked, helping Hannah to her feet.

"I'm fine. Why aren't they following us?"

"Rogma must have closed the portal." The place appeared undisturbed.

"What of Rogma and Stevan? How do you know they will be all right?"

"I don't."

"Are we going to go back?"

"We can't. All we can do now is follow these stairs." Boryn turned and started up.

A crater on the top *of the mountain! Incredible.* Wenval enjoyed the view despite the chill wind and his captive state. He looked from his own bound hands to those of his companions, and then toward Ranton, fidgeting, an arrow nocked in his bow.

"What's gotten into him? Well, besides the obvious," Laric asked Wenval.

"Boryn is close. Look at your gems," Wenval said.

"You think Ranton will shoot Boryn?" Calny was having a hard time imagining this.

"Ranton, I think they're conspiring to help that daemon escape." Julia's voice was disgustingly smooth.

Ranton looked at her with blank eyes.

"Go die, whore," Laric snarled. "You're lucky Fernus showed up to help you. Otherwise, you would never have been able to tie us all up."

Wenval added, "But Fernus is not here anymore, and when we get free . . ."

A loud pop startled them. Ranton snapped toward Wenval, arrow raised. The ground beside them cracked, and as the crevice widened, rock spilled in, leaving a yawning hole in the crater floor.

"Ranton, he's here!" Julia ran behind him, pointing and encouraging him to re-aim.

A figure, cloaked and hooded in black, stepped out of the chasm. Wenval called, "Boryn, watch out!"

Boryn wheeled toward Ranton.

"Shoot him!" screeched Julia.

Wenval threw his weight into Ranton, knocking the bow high while shoving the muscular archer to the ground.

"Ranton?" Boryn ducked as an arrow whizzed overhead.

"You idiot. Get him!" screamed Julia. Daemons swarmed toward the crater's edge, dropping from the sky with weapons drawn. Boryn unsheathed the black-gem blades.

"What are you waiting for? Get him!" Julia raged.

Boryn closed his eyes as a flock of the red-skinned daemons surrounded him.

"What is he doing? Boryn, look out!" Laric called.

A daemon stabbed at Boryn with a long spear. Boryn jumped up, kicked the shaft and snapped it in two. He spun as another swung its blade. Boryn swatted the blade out wide and shoved his scimitar upward into the thing's chest.

Wenval felt himself roughly pushed aside. It was a girl he'd never seen before—*Whoa!*—taking a knife to the ropes.

"Who are you?" asked Wenval, distracted.

"No time. Go help Boryn," she said as Wenval's bindings fell away.

Wenval got to his feet and scrambled toward his bound companions. "Fair lady, step back," he said to the pretty, fair-skinned girl with exaggerated gallantry and a twinkle in his eye. He aimed his open palm. "*Luce!*" Multiple beams hissed through the bindings, freeing the rest.

"Why didn't you do that earlier?" Emily grumbled.

Emily hurried to the place where their weapons had been piled and dug for her rings. She slipped them on her right hand, ran at Julia and swept her arm wide. The succubus jumped as five deep gashes shredded the ground where she had been standing.

"Aren't you going to save your precious little boy?" Julia taunted, flashing her pink cat eyes.

Glowering, Emily slipped the rings on her left hand. She ran at the succubus again, but the creature took flight and started circling her. It dove in. Emily swung her arm high, but the succubus hovered just beyond reach. Emily ran and leapt, but Julia dropped, held out a terrible arm and clipped Emily's chin in a vulnerable, airborne moment. Emily flipped and fell, landing hard on her back, coughing. Julia alighted at Emily's head and grabbed her arms and pinned them to the dirt.

"You're all helpless now. It's so cute," said Julia. The succubus tugged Emily's hands above her head, crossed her wrists and kept her pinned with one hand. Then, with a free hand, Julia stroked Emily's cheek and brought a haunting face close in. "So cute I could just kiss you."

Emily struggled, but the succubus was strong. The daemon temptress leaned lower, brought its lips even closer, its pink eyes boring into Emily's. Suddenly, Emily felt overcome with tiredness and calm. She shut her eyes, but instead of feeling the succubus' kiss, she heard a screech. Her eyes flew open, freed from the momentary spell, to see the creature called Julia writhing on the ground, a gash down its back. Someone held out a strong hand; Emily grabbed it and was pulled to her feet.

"Emily, are you all right?"

"You saved me again, Boryn . . ."

The boy smiled and turned to see the last of the daemon force cut down by Laric.

"What are you smiling about?" coughed Julia, rising, unfazed by the wound.

"You failed. Nice act at the graveyard. Did you even know the poor woman?"

"No," Julia giggled. "But you forgot someone." In one agonizing moment, Boryn winced and fell, hand clutching an arrow at his breast; and Ranton dropped, released from Julia's trance.

"By the way, your little dwarven friends? They're dead, too."

"Wenval! Help!" Calny cried out.

Suddenly, a massive explosion from deep underground shook the mountain, and a cloud of debris blew from the side. "The daemon army will march from Ranlon and destroy Armorica. Your precious little world is ours now, and there's nothing you can do to stop us!" The succubus cackled its warning and flew away as the mountain shuddered once more.

Hannah ran to Boryn's side and knelt beside him. She placed a green glowing hand on his chest and gently pulled the arrow free, finding it peculiar how shallow it was. Then with healing fingers, she sealed the wound.

"Come out, little ones," the furry, gray creature called. It crept through the opening blasted into the side of Mount Pyr and into Raz Kiri. The creature moved toward the heart of the dwarven city and found its first victim. Afterward, it stroked its fur. *A nice change, I think. Flattering.* It held up its claws and snaked its tongue around one of them, licking it clean. "But I'm still hungry. . . ." Sauntering from house-to-house, it darted purple-red eyes, eagerly seeking prey. When its gore-covered fist smashed through a wall, someone screamed inside.

"I found you," Morpheon sighed with contentment while slowly slitting the resident from throat to stomach. The dwarven victim let out an excruciating cry cut short by blood gurgling from his neck. Morpheon howled with joy and lifted the small dwarf, letting the warm blood spill like a delicious shower.

A whistle screamed through the cavern. Morpheon tossed the whimpering dwarf against the wall and moved toward the palace, growling at the interruption. It smashed through the door to find two dozen or so dwarves on their knees, Stevan and Boringer among them, with Flame elves holding blades to their necks.

"What do you need from me?" snarled Morpheon toward the one dwarf standing among the captors.

"Ye can have yer fun later," Kam chuckled as he tapped his axe edge on the dwarven king's shoulder. "I need a secondary witness ta the execution of the last hope o' the dwarves," laughed the swarthy, mutton-chopped dwarf.

"You're wasting my time."

"I did no' have ta invite ye to this party."

"Just kill them," said Morpheon impatiently.

"Ye'll die fer this, Kam," King Fazrin snapped to the traitorous dwarf. "Sidin' with the daemons is a bad idea, regardless o' the payment they offer ye or the power ye fancy ye'll gain from it."

"Pah! You think so?"

"If it weren't fer tha' damned whelp," grumbled Boringer.

"You mean Mhinbron?" asked Kam.

"Aye."

"That li'l bugger! A snag ta our plans. If only we were allowed ta kill him," Kam sputtered. "Then everythin' woulda been so easy."

"So Boryn led ye here?"

"Actually, Boringer ol' friend, *you* led me here," laughed Kam.

"What?"

"Remember the las' time we fough', I knocked ye out cold?"

"Wha' did ye do?"

"Put a rune on yer weapons so all we had ta do was wait fer the day when we were ready ta bury you. Turns out you brought us to the last of 'em. So when the orders came . . ."

"No . . . ," Boringer dropped his face to his hands.

"If I cared enough, I woul' show ye the rune on yer blade's hilt, neatly tucked beneath the bindings. But why waste me time on a dead dwarf?" Kam rattled his axe against Boringer's helmet.

"Reminisce on your own time. I'm bored with this idle chatter." Morpheon's words came out as hot, raspy air. "Get on with it."

"Farewell, Boringer," Kam said then turned to command the golden-armored Flame elves pressing their blades to the victims' necks. "Slit their throats at the order of—"

Morpheon's eyes darted around the room.

"Why so edgy all of a sudden?"

"Hurry. Kill them now or never," grumbled Morpheon, sensing that the window of opportunity might be closing.

Kam lifted his axe to finish the order, a wide grin forming on his ugly face.

A crescent of energy sliced through the throne room, cleaving a Flame elf in two and opening the door to chaos. The dwarven captives leapt to their feet, grabbing blades from the captors and running them through elven skulls. Lightning seared through the king's would-be assailant, another bolt saved Stevan, and Shadow Crusaders poured in to help.

"Oh, well," Morpheon said under his breath and loped from the throne room, having lost interest. But when he stepped outside there waited a tall boy, two black-gem scimitars drawn. *He looks fun.* The foul creature let out a long wheeze. "Ah! You must be Boryn. The thorn in our side since day one."

"I'm honored to be of service."

"You're soon to die for it, as are your little friends."

"You mean the ones retaking the throne room as we speak?"

"Kam and his moronic Flame elves won't beat them. I will."

"You, by yourself, plan to defeat all of us?" Boryn challenged, laughing in the face of the gray creature's confidence.

Their eyes locked. "I'm starting with you." A raspy, guttural sound rolled from Morpheon's throat as the dry, gray fur began to thicken and take on life. "I am Morpheon, harbinger of carnage."

Suddenly, the creature was wolfish, though its face remained almost human. With blurring speed, it pounced. Boryn jumped aside barely in time to miss the claws that gashed the earth. It spun to face Boryn again.

One sword up to block the vicious claws, Boryn charged toward the creature. He hacked with both blades, but Morpheon raised one hand and stopped the incoming blades with steely claws then kicked out with a powerful foot. Boryn took the brunt of the blow in the stomach. The boy hurtled backward and tumbled into the throne room where the dwarves and the Shadow Crusaders were gaining an edge. Undeterred, Boryn jumped up, ready for more.

Now the creature's voice was shrill and grating. "You underestimate me. I'm nearly amused."

Blood that had pooled on the granite floor sucked toward the creature which it absorbed into its body. The being laughed, recharged, and ran at Boryn again, even faster this time. Boryn raised his blades in an X to block. The beast crashed into them hard, claws first. Boryn's boots scraped the stone floor as he was shoved backward. The beast drew in its claws and exploded them outward, blasting the scimitars from Boryn's hands. It let out a cold, empty laugh while glowering into Boryn's eyes.

"Die," Morpheon breathed. But as the word came out, an arrowhead burst from its forehead and the expression went lax. Morpheon reached up and tapped the shaft as a second arrow pierced its right shoulder.

"Morpheon," came a plaintive squeal for help. Morpheon turned to see Kam pinned against the wall by more loyal clansmen, and a third arrow met its mark. Morpheon hissed, moving toward the dwarven captors, shoved them aside, and grabbed Kam by the nape. Then it turned to Boryn grinning maliciously.

"We will finish this later, hopefully without baggage . . . ," Morpheon tossed Kam over his shoulder like a sack of worthless goods, holding the bulky dwarf by the foot, ". . . or an arrow through my head. So annoying." He chuckled before turning black and sinking into the ground like a shadow.

Boryn turned to the doorway of the palace. Ranton was there, hunched over, breathing hard. Boryn ran to his side.

"Your arrows were aimed at that creature, right?" Boryn queried with a half smile.

"I don't miss," Ranton said. "But how are you still alive?"

"Evidently, I wasn't your target."

"No. From before, when you were. I shot you through the heart with an iron-tipped arrow. No one should survive that," Ranton said, sounding guilty. "I mean, I'm glad you did, because if I'd killed you because of that succubus' spell, I don't know what I'd do."

"Julia took me for dead, so I guess she released you when she left. And the save? Talk to Hannah; she gets the credit. Incredible, huh?"

King Fazrin interrupted, searching Boryn's face. "Ye came ta help us. Why?"

"I couldn't leave you all to be slaughtered," replied Boryn simply.

"Ye know we planned ta kill . . ."

"Leaving you to be executed wasn't the right choice to make."

Boringer went to Boryn and dropped to his knees. "I . . ."

"Don't worry about it."

Boringer shook his head and stood up. "O King, we can no' stay here any longer."

"Fight with me, then." Boryn spoke with confidence.

Boringer's head snapped up in surprise.

"I will gather the armies of the old alliance. Together, we will kill the daemons and send them back to hell," Boryn said.

"You plan an *offensive* strike against the daemons?"

The boy nodded.

"Yer highness, le' us destroy the daemons again," Rogma implored, his mind wandering back to his own part in that war, alongside Fyr Bill and the other heroes.

"Rogma, we are no' equipped nor are we ready fer war. How could we possibly help 'em?"

"We are dwarves! We destroyed 'em once; we can destroy 'em again!" Boringer sounded indignant.

"Waste of time and lives," replied the king. "We will no' be able ta beat 'em. An' with our numbers as low as they are, especially after today's attack, I can no' risk further casualties. Besides, with daemons already gathered at our door, we 'ave ta find a new home." Fazrin's tone was unusually sober.

"Boryn, can ye stay fer two days more?" Rogma sounded hopeful.

"Why?"

"If King Fazrin can no' spare the help o' the dwarves, I will help in me own way."

"You will fight with us?"

"I can no' leave me people, but I will help in me own way."

"So you failed again. No surprise there."

"It's that bugger kid. He and 'is friends go' in the way," complained Kam as he waddled from one side of the room to the other.

"Your problem, like mine, is that you waste too much time toying with your prey instead of killing it. You should have just killed them, not strutted about how clever you are." Morpheon ripped the arrow from his shoulder.

"At least I don't play with my food."

"No point in squabbling now." Xandon shook his head, sagged into his throne and sank his head into his hands. "Of course, all my men are dead, right?" Xandon looked to both of them, stopping at Morpheon. "You still got something there," Xandon said pointing to the disgusting creature's forehead.

Morpheon reached up and tapped the protruding arrow tip. He tore it out, the wound sealing instantly. "I slaughtered a few of the citizens, but I was unnecessarily summoned to 'witness' a failed execution."

Xandon continued. "Tarn won't be happy."

"He should 'ave fought 'is own battle," Kam insisted, "rather than orderin' us aroun'."

"The daemons are too busy transforming the Forest of Ranlon," Xandon pointed out.

Kam's flat face twisted with a question.

"The daemonic version of *beautification*. The trees char and die, the water boils away, the grass is set ablaze and the ground itself becomes ashen and dead. Crevasses break open and ooze with lava flowing in rivers, never hardening. Fires burn but never consume. I personally think it will be a pleasant change for the Wood elves," Xandon chuckled. "Imagine! The pompous Wood elves who think they can guard and protect!" Xandon laughed a deep, resonant laugh.

"Is tha' wha' 'appened in the Black Expanse as well? Did the daemons do tha'?" Kam was interested to learn.

"Yes. During the war, the daemons managed to set up a second fortress, giving them a stronger foothold. The humans and the dwarves, even some of the elves, were in serious trouble."

Morpheon mused. "Ah, yes, the daemons' second fortress—now humble home of the conniving Dark elves."

Ramgis studied the black iron walls looming before him, dawn's early light reflected in the smooth surface. Massive spikes lined the curved corners and shot up from the fortifications in double rows. Watch towers rose at each corner, and in the center stood an even taller tower, forged from solid, black steel and studded with barbs. The tower of the Dark Queen. *How can we possibly take this impenetrable fortress?*

A rider on a dun-colored pony separated from the army and approached the general. Ramgis turned to face Cadegray.

"Formidable, isn't it?" Cadegray observed with deliberate understatement.

"And Rath crowed about blasting through these walls."

"A traitor's boast. Worthless."

"Yes, a strange one, that," Ramgis nodded.

"Without a plan, we are useless here."

"Any way to get through?"

"Unless we find access into their tunnel system and somehow manage to survive down there, no, not that I can see. It's nigh impossible."

"Fortunate I'm here then."

Ramgis turned, warhammer drawn, as Rath, a roguish grin on his face, rode up silently behind them.

"You betrayed us! Why are you here?"

"I am no traitor. I just don't answer to you—which is why you don't pay me. I answer to another commander."

"Kelris?"

"Expecting the worst of me?"

"To whom do you answer?"

"You will know soon enough. Once I'm done here, my contract ends."

"What were you ordered to do?"

"That is between my patron and me."

"You're a shady one, aren't you?" Ramgis grumbled.

Rath motioned his arm forward, and his battalion of mounted archers formed up behind him.

"If you'll kindly wait for me here, I'll put a hole in that wall for you."

Ramgis turned to Cadegray. "Prepare the men to charge. I want to watch this one."

Rath shrugged and cantered toward the walls, his men at his heels. Rath held up an arrow with an unusual silver-colored shaft. His men nodded, recognizing it, and then turned to withdraw their own from their quivers.

"All right, men, unleash hell . . . right . . . there!" Rath discharged the special arrow toward the solid wall. It stuck fast. In a constant volley, hundreds more of the adhering missiles struck the same target, a growing mass generating intense heat. The earth trembled and shook at the detonation, and a wave of heat blasted out, reaching as far as the place where Ramgis waited. He turned his face from the heat then stared in stunned silence as the smoke cleared; the iron wall was breached, molten metal from the hole pooling on the barren earth below. Horns sounded within the walls. Ramgis turned and rode toward his men, ignoring Rath's smirk.

"Men, to arms!" Ramgis roared. "The Dark elves die here!"

"Huzzah!" The knights roared as they galloped past. Ramgis guided his white warhorse back toward the walls where Rath's men were riding back and forth firing with precision into the narrow crossbow slits.

Kelris shot up at the sound of horns blaring inside the fortified city. The elf ran to his balcony from which he could see the void in the wall. Through the gap, Kelris saw an amassing force of crimson-clad knights.

Ramgis, we meet again. Kelris smiled at the prospect.

A quick rap on the door signaled a messenger's entry. "Lord Kelris, you are ordered to escort the queen to the harbor so that she might escape and you with her."

Kelris countered, "Order all troops to move to the harbor and wait while I engage the Blood Knight leader. We will lop off the head of the lion."

While Kelris prepared for battle, Dark elves grouped behind the opening, lowering their pikes so any knight foolish enough to enter would be run through. The Blood Knights continued their charge indifferent to the Dark elves guarding the wall. The knights grabbed throwing hammers from their side pouches and hurled them toward the Dark elven pike men. Ramgis roared encouragement as hammers struck home in elven skulls. The elven formation broke up as many in the center fell.

A second alert sounded across the city, and the formation disintegrated as elves retreated. Ramgis threw his hammer spinning forward to smash a retreating elf in the back, sending it crumpled to the earth. Making chase, he spurred his horse forward, clung to its mane and dropped toward the ground to snag the hammer as he galloped into the Dark elven capital. He pulled up and slowed, a distant, familiar roar of that Dark elf's mount heard in the distance. "Kelris . . . ," Ramgis muttered. He wheeled his warhorse toward the sound then kicked him onward, down the emptied stone streets, galloping toward the sea. Krixlus roared again as a dozen Dark elven archers stepped from an alley, crossbows trained on Ramgis, while ahead in the port, black sails billowed to life and the elven fleet pulled out.

"Damn you, Kelris!" Ramgis roared as the bows clicked. Hooves clattered on the paving, advancing fast from behind, and Dark elves fell or ran for cover in the alleyways but not before their armor-piercing darts were released. Arrows whistled one way and darts rocketed the other. The advancing horse and rider stepped into the crossfire, and dozens of metal darts *thunked* into leather-clad arms and body. The rider fell. The ground sponged the man's blood, and the circle of red grew wide. Rath looked up at Ramgis with a resigned smile.

Ramgis dismounted and crouched beside the mercenary. "Those darts should have been mine—," Ramgis stopped short. Here was one he had hated, sent ahead in hopes he'd be killed, the one he had accused of being a traitor—and the one who had saved the Blood Knights a second time.

Voice weak, Rath spoke kindly. "You still have work to do."

"I am an old man. I've seen my day as hero."

"As have I. Find the hero of this age, and follow him to the death. Protect him at all costs." Rath moved his bloody fingers from his throat where a dart had pierced it. "I'm finished with my mission here. Finally, I'm free . . . ," he smiled through a cough.

"Cadegray can heal . . . We'll get you to the capital."

"My only regret is not meeting my so—"

"Quiet now. Save your breath."

"To think you actually care! I'm touched, commander."

"Cadegray!"

Boringer plopped down on the arena sand breathing hard while Boryn leaned against one of his new iron swords.

"No' bad fer a human."

"Thanks," Boryn gave him a crooked smile.

"But ye need this," said Boringer. While getting to his feet, he tossed out a plain leather bracer embedded with an amethyst the size of a hen's egg.

"What is this?"

"That skill ye use ta make yerself go faster? 'Tis heavily damagin' to yer body; the body is no' made ta move so fast. So charge tha' with energy, rather than yer body, an' see wha' happens."

Boryn slid the cuff on his right arm and straightened it.

"All right, lad, charge the bracer," Boringer said as he moved to attack.

Closing his eyes, Boryn channeled energy into the gem in the same way he did with his blades. The bracer's purple gem began to pulse, and Boryn released the energy as the dwarf came close. Boringer's assault advanced in slowest motion, as if time had stopped. Boryn hopped behind the dwarf. Time righted itself, and Boringer spun to receive a face smash from the pommel of Boryn's scimitar.

Boringer dropped to the sand rubbing his tender nose. "Oww!"

"It's incredible! What is this thing?"

"An artifact. Yer body'll thank ya fer usin' it."

Boryn helped Boringer to his feet. "How does it stop time?"

"It is the stone, actually. It multiplies th' energy sent inta it an' releases it in a way tha' slows everythin' around ya. Not sure abou' all the science of it."

"This thing's amazing."

"Aye, but it is no' a . . . ," Boringer swiveled; a scimitar tapped him on the back of the head, ". . . toy."

Boryn grinned.

"That'll be enough fer today."

"Seen Rogma lately?" Boryn extended his arm, appreciating the look of the bracer.

"Off in the Heaven Forge."

"Where's that?"

"The master's workroom. The other side of Raz Kiri."

"Doing what?"

"Wha' Rogma's doin' is no' my concern. I 'ave got more important things ta do," Boringer swatted Boryn on the back, "like gettin' over ta the brewery ta see who's still around."

Boringer plunged his hands into his pockets, and the pair left the cocoon of the arena for the sobered streets of the city. After the recent attacks, the dwarves were even more resolute of purpose, loading carts, preparing to leave their home.

"Where will you go?" Boryn asked, finding the reality hard to swallow.

"We do no' 'ave a clue, but we'll make it through. We always do."

"May I ask you something?"

"Aye."

"Why does everyone still seem afraid of me?"

"We can talk 'bout tha' later, but now we go' some o' yer friends comin' up behind us."

"Boryn!"

Boryn turned back and smiled to see Wenval and Ranton running to catch them. Laric clomped behind sporting a new suit of armor in very nice, iron plate. "Where'd you get that?"

"The armor's not the best of it," Laric said. "Look at this!" He tugged a gleaming new claymore from its sheath. Golden symbols ran the length of the blade. "Isn't it incredible?"

"Yes, but where did you get it?"

"Laric agreed to sample a few of Bret's newest 'creations,' and the sword and armor were the payment," Ranton jumped in.

"Tha' wadn't too brigh' an idea, now was it?" laughed Boringer.

"It'll be beyond worth it," Laric enthused.

"Somethin' tells me ye'll feel differen' by mornin'."

"Where are the others?" Boryn asked.

"Still at the brewery."

"That's where we're headed. You go ahead. Boringer and I will be right behind you." Boryn turned to Boringer as the other boys left. "The dwarves seem fine with leaving their homes. Why is that?"

"Why do ya think Bret is still pluggin' for business?" the dwarf replied with a good-natured shrug then squared his wide shoulders. "We dwarves are a tough lot. We've been through worse; this is no' so bad."

"Why did Rogma go to the Heaven Forge?"

"Dunno. Probably overseein' a test of a new master smith."

"Rogma never makes anything himself. Why is that?"

"The last axe 'e made was the axe of a traitor. Quit after tha'."

"Kam's axe?"

"Aye. Back at the time o' the Daemon War. Since then he 'asn't forged a thing, except an occasional dagger ta teach a tenderfoot like you."

"I want to see him before I go."

"Li'l doub' ye will. Now, com'on. Le's go see Bret."

"I'm guessin' ye drank tha' brew Boringer gave ye, eh?" Bret said with a wide grin, watching Quaswyn's twitching legs and winking at Calny, his young, new apprentice.

"OhyesIdiditwasgreatIdrankitandIgotallexcitedthenIstarted tobouncemylegatfirstbecauseIwasboredbutthenbecauseIcouldn't stopthenthestonestartedtocrackandthatseemedtobeworkingoutso welllkeptdoingltandeventuallythestonecrackedawayandwewerefree eeeeee!ButthenIwassoooolonesomebecauseBoringerleftusallaloneso hereweare." Quaswyn tugged the head he shared with Marlok as far away from the bar as he could while Marlok flattened their palm against the bar top and jabbed a dagger between their fingers with less coordination than he was accustomed to.

"Be careful with that . . . ," Emily warned, watching the jerky movements along with Stevan and Hannah.

"Oops . . ." The dagger pricked the skin on their middle knuckle.

"Owwwwwwwwwww!" screamed Quaswyn, seizing control over the hand and sucking furiously on the tiny puncture. Laughing, Hannah pulled their finger from their mouth and placed her hand over the wound; the regeneration healed it almost instantly.

"Better?" she asked.

"Um-hmm . . . ," said Quaswyn childlike in a momentary reprieve.

Marlok shifted gears, "Ithinkweshouldgorunoffalittleenergynow. So . . . seeya."

Bret laughed, watching the wound-up character sprint out the door, bouncing off the four returning boys like a pinball.

"Oy, Lari', com'on back 'ere an' try this," Bret called out happily, thrilled to see his willing taster return.

"It's Laric . . . *ck*."

"Alrigh', Lari'. Tha's wha' I said. Now, jus' com'ere." Bret brandished a dark bottle. "Calny, com'an' watch. Ye migh' learn somethin' useful fer tha' tavern'a yers."

Laric went behind the bar and took the jug Bret shoved into his hands. "What is it?"

"Jus' drink it."

Laric stared, uncertain.

"Jus' drink it, or I take back all th' stuff ye bough' with yer early pay."

Laric raised the jug, chugged the thick, odorous liquid and slammed it down on the bar empty. He grinned toward Bret and let out a happy belch.

"Uh, Bret . . ."

"Wot?"

"Will you be still? You're swayin' around too much."

"I ain't swayin'."

"Oh, yes you are. You're toyin' with me, bobbin' all over the place—like a worm fresh uncovered." Laric wobbled.

Bret was not flattered by the description.

"Bret, what did you give him?" Stevan was afraid to learn.

"Dunno. Found two bottles tucked behin' a keg in back. Forgo' wha's in 'em."

Laric wavered and fell backwards, flat out on the floor.

"Maybe I shoul' save the testin' fer dwarves! Bwahahaha!" Bret lifted the bottle and sniffed. "Oy! Smells like a horse's arse!"

The door slammed open. Bret cringed when it banged against the wall ahead of his friend.

"Wha' happened to 'im?" Boringer asked, observing the boy who hadn't budged. "Go fer a bucket a water, Boryn." Boryn did as instructed, and Boringer emptied the contents over Laric's head. The willing taster sputtered awake, at least for the moment.

"Bret, gi'me tha' other bottle ye found."

Bret tossed the jug to his friend and watched with anticipation.

"How d'ya forget wha' ya made?"

"From time-ta-time, me personal testin' dudn't turn out too good," Bret laughed. "Ye might say I get los' in me work."

Boringer shook his head, took a whiff and recoiled but still downed the bitter liquid. He paused, tasting it on his tongue. "Actually idn't bad. Warms ye right up . . ."

"Eh?"

Boringer exhaled. A jet of flames shot from his mouth, setting Bret's beard afire. The two dwarves tore around the bar, Bret fanning to extinguish his blazing whiskers, Boringer trying to cough out the flames. Bret rushed to the barrel by the door and dunked his head, hissing, sputtering and smoking. The others burst into laughter at the dripping, grinning face.

"Dat was amazin'!" Bret fingered his singed beard.

Boryn recognized the distinctive jingle before he even turned toward the door.

"Wha's goin' on here?" called Rogma stepping over the threshold.

"I've been looking for you! Where have you been?" Boryn was pleased to see him. "I'm ready to try getting a shot in on you so I can move on to some real business."

Rogma laughed and patted the boy's back in a friendly, fatherly way. "I'd be little challenge to ye." Rogma pulled a large package, carefully wrapped in hopsack, from behind his back and placed it on the table next to Boryn. "This is for you. Open it." Rogma smiled up at Boryn with a happy, youthful grin, his eyes magnified through his spectacles.

Carefully, Boryn folded back the cloth. Inside lay two magnificent scimitars of gleaming, sky blue metal. The surface of the blades was intricately figured with golden runes glowing with energy. The handles were golden, the grips leather, and in the pommels, blue stones. Almost reverently, Boryn lifted one of the scimitars. "These are for me?"

"Aye. Carry 'em alongside the iron ones ye made yerself." Rogma nodded to the leather sheathes at Boryn's side. "Ye can carry those black ones on yer back. Now grab these, an' come with me."

The Shadow Crusaders and everyone from the tavern gathered in the dusty courtyard, circling to watch.

"Swing 'em and squeeze the handle."

Boryn followed the old smith's instruction. He extended one arm, tightened his grip and made a wide sweep. The blade fired out, propelled from the hilt but held by a chain that recoiled ever-so-slightly at the farthest reach. When he loosened his hold, the chain retracted instantly, reengaging the tang in the hilt.

"Now press the pommels end-to-end."

Boryn did as instructed, and the pommels fused, creating an altogether different weapon. He held the double-bladed instrument out with one hand and began spinning it like a baton; he squeezed the grip, and both blades fired. The cutting swath was wide and deadly. The Shadow Crusaders watched with eyes wide and mouths wider.

"These are incredible," Boryn said as the blades whirred to a halt, and he separated the pommels.

"These swords will likely be th' only contribution the dwarves can make ta yer effort, but I pray it helps ye greatly," Rogma said with a humble bow of the head.

"Are these runes?" Boryn touched the glowing, golden symbols.

"Aye. The blade is permanently enchanted by the runes— meanin' the abilities are passive, always there fer yer use without even callin' on 'em. One is the rune o' *cleavin'*; it allows ye ta cut through almost anythin'. The second is a rune of *enchainment*. Ye can control the length o' the chain, make it as long as ye like, within reason," the forge master explained. "Next is the rune of *air.* Makes the blade light. It can be light as a feather, if it suits yer purposes. An' the last, the rune o' *channelin'*, makes it easier fer ya to control energy in the blade."

"What about the others?"

"Me personal runes," Rogma shrugged noncommittally.

Elated with his gift, Boryn stooped to give Rogma a warm embrace. Wenval, intellectual curiosity piqued, walked over to inspect the pommel, intent on discovering how the merger worked.

"Once ye've won this war, Boryn, come an' find us. We need ta make sure ye do no' get rusty. And I'll show ye how ta *really* forge a blade."

"Count on it." Boryn made a show of sheathing the new scimitars alongside the irons ones at his side then reached back to touch the hilts of the black-gem ones on his back. "Are we ready to go, Crusaders?"

"Let me grab the books the dwarves have given me, then I'm set," said Wenval.

"We'll bring my fool brother," Calny said, though Ranton was the one to hoist the boy, marginally roused, and carry him out.

"Don't lose yerself out there." Rogma scribed a rune, and the swirling stone portal reopened.

Boryn waited; the others jumped first. "Thank you, Rogma, for everything. I'll stop these daemons, and then I'll be back."

Boringer waited to the side, hands in pockets and a hopeful look on his face. Boryn turned to him, "And you, too, Boringer. I'll find you when this is over, friend."

The quarrelsome dwarf smiled, and the boy hopped into the portal. A moment later, Boryn tumbled out on the mountaintop where his friends were already dusting themselves off, shadows long in the evening sun.

"So where to, Boryn? What now?"

"Fernus said he'd see me in Ranlon; that must be where the daemons are hiding out. All of you head there. I'm going to seek help from the Orders."

"From the Knightly Realms?" Wenval clarified.

"Yes, I'm going to Falrik, but I'd like you and the others to gather troops from across the Empire."

"We can't let you go alone! Remember what happened last time? You almost died," Wenval said firmly.

"I'll be fine, professor. Trust me. We have to stop the main daemon army before it leaves Ranlon."

Emily spoke up. "We can do this. Laric and Ranton, you work as a team to gather willing warriors from the western villages. Wenval and Hannah, work the east. Stevan and I will take the northern territories."

"I'll head back to Dusgoroth to handle things and round up a few more recruits there. Bret taught me a few tricks," Calny said with a half smile, "that might be good for business—and recruiting."

Boryn spoke to all of them, "Settle your troops outside the forest and return to Dusgoroth. I'll find you there. Let's rest here for the night, and we'll all start fresh in the morning. It's been a long day." He laughed at his own understatement.

"Sounds like a plan to me," said Ranton. He tossed his pack and bow to the crater floor. "Laric, stop rubbing your head and help me gather some firewood." The pair headed out of the crater and down the mountainside toward the woods.

Wenval set down with his satchel, stacked books for a backrest, pulled out a thin blanket, and wrapped himself in it. Then he spied the new girl perched on the rim of the crater.

Hannah was enjoying the twilight and the view from the mountaintop. A chill wind prickled her bare arms, and she shivered. A blanket enwrapped her shoulders. Hannah turned to see the curly-haired young mage, slightly red-faced.

"I don't believe we've properly met," she said kindly, holding out her hand.

"I'm Wenval. You're Hannah, right?"

"Yup. Care to join me?"

Wenval climbed up beside her and dangled his feet which jiggled nervously beneath his green robe. The sound of Ranton and Laric arguing below drifted up from the woods. A crash, a pause, and more arguing followed. Wenval grinned but found nothing to say, and he and Hannah sat in companionable quiet. At last, she broke the silence. "So how did you learn magic?"

Boryn roamed through the woods and found a clearing where he could try out his new, blue blades. He unsheathed them, getting the feel for the smooth leather grips and experimenting with the air rune. He shut his eyes and squeezed the hilts, letting the blades drop to the ground, hanging by the chain. He retracted then spun the blades, severing a tree trunk and felling the pine. The blades made easy work of slicing the trunk into logs, and he sheathed his scimitars before hefting the firewood to his shoulders.

Wenval arranged some kindling, used a spell to set it aflame, and piled twigs, dry branches and then the logs on top, sorting the dry from the green. Stevan watched, emptying his bag to set up an unusual cooking apparatus.

"How do you do that?" Stevan asked.

Wenval looked at him, puzzled.

"How did you make the fire start?"

Wenval nibbled his lip before answering. "Truth told, I'm not really sure. When I put my mind to it, casting spells seems as natural as reading or writing."

Or as natural as making runes is for a dwarf. . . . Stevan fanned the flame, helping the fire grow, and when it was blazing gaily, everyone gathered around like moths to the light.

"Let me go with you," Emily said to Boryn as she stared into the dancing fire.

"It's too dangerous. I don't know if my reception in Falrik will be friendly."

"Oy! That's hot!" sputtered Stevan almost dropping the steaming pot. He rifled through his bag and pulled out eight dented metal bowls. He poured soup into each.

All stared at him.

"What? So I always travel prepared . . ."

"You must be magic!" Emily teased with good nature.

Stevan smiled, but it was halfhearted.

Boryn eagerly took a dish and gulped the contents, the broth warming his body from the inside out. He smiled to see his friends circled around the fire. *Everything's going to be all right . . .*

After the meal, Boryn stood and walked to the edge of the crater; he turned his face toward the sky, stars blanketing it. Wenval joined him.

"Don't make us have to come save you again," the young mage laughed.

"I'm pretty sure I was doing the saving," Boryn chuckled then paused. "The situation seems to be getting more and more dangerous. . . . Be careful, will you?"

"Same goes for you. You're the one going it alone."

"I made it this far. I'm sure I'll be fine."

"Allies and enemies are not always easy to separate."

Boryn nodded grimly.

"I'll see you in the morning unless you start out ahead of us," said Wenval as he slapped his good friend's shoulder.

Boryn wandered a way down the mountainside and climbed into one of the taller trees. He lay down on a broad, sturdy limb and stretched out his legs, shutting his eyes for an instant.

"Hey!" came a shout from below. Boryn bolted up, nearly smacking his forehead on the branch above. Daylight pierced the foliage, and Stevan stood below waving him down. "We're waiting on you."

Clumsy after his abrupt awakening, Boryn clambered down the tree. He shadowed Stevan back to the crater where they found the Crusaders packed and ready to go. Laric stood to one side groaning and massaging his temples. Ranton sneaked behind him, got close to his ear and squealed, "Time to go." Laric moaned while Ranton, laughing, flung his bow over his shoulder and picked up his bag to leave.

Calny said, "I'll go with you two until the Dusgoroth cutoff."

"Wait! Take these," Wenval tossed each of them a leather strap with crystals tucked into little sleeves.

"New and improved?" Boryn asked.

"Working on it. I made these before we left Dusgoroth. I haven't perfected some of the capabilities, but hopefully I'll have them all working by the time you get back."

"Stay safe, Boryn," called Ranton trailing the twins downhill.

"Goodbye, Boryn," said Hannah, waving as she and Wenval headed off. "Thanks for everything. Take care!"

Stevan called out as he set out behind the others. "Later!"

Boryn hugged Emily. "You'd better hurry; they're leaving you behind. I'll see you soon."

"You'd better." She smiled, squeezed his hand and turned to chase after Stevan.

Lost in thought, Boryn watched his friends go one way. On his own again, the young man gathered his satchel and went the other.

The path descending Mount Pyr was easy; the rising sun warmed his face. He had traveled but a few steps when a rushing noise from behind caused him to turn back. A whirling portal opened in the crater, and a billow of purple cloth spewed out followed immediately by a heavy, leather pouch. A cloud of dust erupted when the man and his bag thudded to the dirt. Boryn dashed back to stand over the mound. A mass of striped hair popped out.

"What are you doing?" Boryn asked.

"Oh! My head is killing me!" Marlok rubbed his temples.

"The dwarves don't want us." Quaswyn sounded brokenhearted.

"If you'd shut up half of the time, we might have been able to stay," Marlok complained.

"Rude."

"Where are you headed now?" Boryn asked.

"No idea. We're from Elemencia. Trying to find someone who knows about magic and orbs and such. . . ." Marlok reached for the bag and got to their feet.

"Head to Dusgoroth. Calny's going there; if you hurry, you can catch him. If you don't, you'll find him at the Strawberry Mug. He'll put you to good use and help you locate whatever it is you need."

"Really?" Quaswyn clapped their hands.

"Yep. Just get going."

"We have a quest, a purpose, and a reason for our journey!" cried Quaswyn bolting with glee.

"We already had a reason for our journey—not sharing a body, remember?"

"Oh, yes . . . that."

"Thank you, Boryn."

"I'll see you when I get there."

Fernus loved the view, floating high above the world. Below him an enormous army of orcs and all manner of greenskins trooped toward Falrik. He grinned. *It's soon to become much more . . . interesting.* The most powerful of daemon generals gazed into the distance where he could just make out the boy running down Mount Pyr.

"Mhinbron, Mhinbron, Mhinbron , , , savior of dwarves. Let's see what you can do for your own kind."

Another general popped from a cloud wiping ice crystals from his pale, blue skin. "What do you want this time, Fernus?"

"Pleasure to see you as well, Glacius."

"What do you want?"

"Impatient, aren't we? I want you to watch this army destroy the humans. Make sure things go smoothly. As for any orc that decides fleeing is a good plan, kill it. A group of our own is coming to meet you and will operate under your command, but under no circumstances are you to take part in the battle."

"Leaving all the fun to the orcs?"

"Oh, you'll have fun. I'm not worried about that."

"You're probably right," said Glacius, a cold smile creasing his frosty-blue face.

"Wait." Sailing toward the open sea, a fleet of Dark elven ships was retreating from their homeland. And separately, sailing toward human shores, were more ships.

Glacius squinted. "What do you see?"

"Is that a Blood Knight in command of the Dark elven ship? Now what would be the story there, I wonder." Fernus considered the conundrum, entertained by the failure of the Dark elves and the tenacity of the Blood Knights. "I expect that means more fun ahead."

"Oh?" The crystalline daemon's grin grew wide.

Fernus burst into black flame and disappeared as Glacius shattered into icy crystals. Both reformed moments later on the deck of the leading iron ship. An armored Dark elven soldier charged the two daemons with a brutally-tipped spear. Glacius grabbed the spear tip with two sharp fingers and laughed as ice fired the length of the shaft, up the warrior's arm and through his body. Glacius flicked the ice-covered elf who fractured and cracked, brittle as glass.

"Kelris!" warned another elven warrior. "We are under attack! It's the humans!"

"Humans?" cried Glacius, horrified by the suggestion.

Fernus wisely leapt up to float above the deck, and Glacius sunk a pale blue hand into the sea. "Could a human do this?" Ice shot from his fingertips, snaking out like a treacherous seine, snaring the fleet as well as all the elves unfortunate enough to be outside.

Glacius threw his arms skyward. Thousands of enormous ice spears splintered up from the deep, skewering hulls and breaking ships apart. "Do I have your attention now? Come out, Kelris," commanded Glacius.

A low growl was heard from below the ice-covered deck. Then the deck heaved and popped; the main mast split in two. An enormous lizard exploded upward. An elf, white-and-gold armored and astride the beast's back, gripped the reins and waved a razor-pointed spear.

Glacius fired a salvo of ice spears at Kelris, but the ice melted before reaching him. The daemon looked up scowling. "What are you doing, Fernus?"

Ignoring Glacius, Fernus turned a curious eye to the Dark elf. "Why are you running from your home, Kelris?"

"Queen's orders." Kelris' mount growled, saliva spraying Glacius' face.

"Which ship is hers?" Fernus pressed.

Kelris smiled and pointed toward the vessel with gilded trim headed out to sea ahead of his.

"Would you mind if I paid the queen a visit, Glacius?" Fernus asked with a malicious grin.

"Do what you want, but if this ugly beast doesn't get out of my face, I'm going to run it through."

Fernus burst into flame and reappeared on the queen's ornamented deck. The elite Dark elven guards charged, but the white-cloaked general smiled in response. He snapped his fingers, and the elves burst into flame, their black armor melting to their skin. The screams were horrible; to end the pain, some leapt overboard, only to sink like anchors.

"Queenie?" Fernus called. "Come out, come out wherever you are!" Fernus held out his hand and burned an opening in the deck. Then a blast of black smoke coughed her out. She tumbled across the floor, her regal, golden robes scorched and covered with soot. "Do you know what happens when you don't follow orders?" Fernus spoke as if talking to a naughty child.

The queen began to speak, but Fernus did not wait for her reply.

"You had specific orders to put an end to the Blood Knights. We practically handed them to you! And still, you failed. So now you are officially more trouble than you're worth."

The queen's mouth opened and closed like a fish, but no words came out. Fernus snapped his fingers again, and the queen settled as a small heap of cinder.

Boryn woke up with a start. *What was that?* A rustle in the brush. His eyes roamed the copse, barely visible in the dying embers of his fire. *A growl.*

He moved slowly to rise and unsheathed his scimitars. Pinpoints of light encircled him. *Eyes.* He touched the bracer on his arm then stood stock still. With low, throaty rumbles, wolves crept from their cover. A pack, eight or so, surrounded him. Behind them stalked a much larger wolf, the leader, with snow-white hair and fearsome, yellow eyes. Boryn waited for the wolves to make the first move. A twig snapped, triggering one to leap, but it backed off as others did the same—dashing in but then retreating just as quickly. *I guess I'm going first.*

Boryn channeled energy into a blue scimitar and held it back, preparing to swing. He gripped the handle, squeezing it, and the blade flew free, cutting into the first wolf. It dropped without a whimper. With the second blade, he made a sweeping arc, releasing a crescent of energy that reached out to slice through another. One sprang; Boryn rolled safely aside, ending on his feet. Then another, and he held the tip up to slice open the animal's belly as it flew over.

Boryn charged both blades and tightened his hold. With a click, the blades fired from the hilts while Boryn spun in a circle. A fourth body flopped to the earth. The remainder of the pack backed away, except the white leader. Boryn turned to face it; its growl was low and threatening.

"Not going to save your life by running?"

The wolf howled in response.

As if fired from a bow, the animal shot forward. Boryn dodged, a hair's breadth away from the fangs that ripped into the loose sleeve of his shirt. *Holy* . . . The wolf landed lightly and lunged around for a second attack. This time it came in low. Boryn back-stepped, but the white wolf nipped his ankle, drawing blood. He tore his boot free and, regaining his footing, swept a blade sideways, releasing it to extend his reach, aiming to slice through the wolf's open maw. The wolf clamped down on the blade with ferocious jaws, halting it mid flight. The wolf jerked, pulling Boryn forward, off balance, then released his bite and sprang toward Boryn's vulnerable throat. The jaws snapped perilously close.

Boryn channeled energy into the bracer as he tumbled to the side. Up fast and stepping back, he swept the blades in wide, slow circles. He let the energy flow as the snarling wolf charged again. Under the bracer's spell, the wolf's momentum stalled, and Boryn advanced, ready to end the fight. He grabbed the wolf by the nape and held the blade to its throat as time resumed its normal pace. The wolf struggled then calmed. Boryn released it, stepped back, hands high. A truce was struck.

"I know. I cheated. Sorry."

The wolf expelled air, less threateningly, as if it understood. Eyeing the boy, it turned toward the bushes and yipped. The pack reemerged, a fuzzy, black furball tangled in the elder's feet. The alpha nudged the pup into the open. Pale blue eyes ringed with white turned toward Boryn. An extra nudge sent the pup toddling forward where it came to rest across the toe of the boy's boot. The other wolves turned and disappeared into the underbrush.

Gently, Boryn extracted his foot and moved toward a tree. He sat, leaning against the trunk to ponder the gift. "Hey . . ." The young wolf, all feet, wobbled toward the boy and nestled against his legs. Boryn scratched behind its ears; the pup nuzzled his open palm.

"Guess we don't have to worry about brigands and rogues sneaking up on us now, do we?"

Ramgis waited outside the captain's quarters in which Cadegray was tending Rath. Their Dark elven ship rocked mightily as it scudded across the strait toward the Realms, and Ramgis held the doorframe for balance.

"Commander Ramgis, we are approaching knight-controlled shorelines. The port has not been repaired since the Dark elves' attack so we are going in to the west."

"Raise the signal flag. Prepare the men to march to the capital."

"If I may ask, sir, why didn't we pursue the Dark elves?"

"It would be unwise for us to chase the elves where they are at their best—on the sea. We've swept them from their capital; for now, we have the upper hand. Another day, we'll see them to their end."

"Yes, commander."

The old knight rubbed a callused hand against his hairless head, rapped gently on the door with the back of his gauntleted fist, and then turned the knob.

"Cadegray, prepare Rath to be moved. We make landfall soon."

"If he's to survive, we must hurry. I'm afraid I've reached the

302

limit of my abilities. Still, the time we gained by commandeering the Dark elves' ships may spell the difference for Rath. I compliment you on your wise strategy, general.

"Do your best, Cadegray. We are close. We will reach Falrik in time." Ramgis turned to face the advancing shoreline, closing the door behind him. He walked amidships where a handler waited with his warhorse, ready to fly down the ramp the moment the ship pulled in. Ramgis heard the cabin door open behind him; Cadegray and an aid emerged carrying Rath on a hastily crafted litter.

Waves slammed the ship's prow as if resisting its approach, but an aft wind won the battle, and the craft slid into the sandy shore. Metal screeched against sand, and the ship stopped with a jolt. Ramgis' mount regained its footing on the wooden deck as the gangplank splashed into the shallows. Ramgis grabbed the mane and vaulted into the saddle. He kicked the mount forward and hurdled across the lapping tide to land on soft, wet sand.

Against Ramgis' direction, the horse trotted toward the inviting, fresh seagrass beckoning from the dunes.

A second vessel pulled alongside, and Blood Knights poured from the decks. "Your orders, sir?" an officer asked Ramgis.

"Get me five of your fastest riders; we will go ahead for help. Assemble the rest of the troops and make your way toward Falrik. The men deserve some rest after what we've been through. We will meet you there soon enough."

"Yes, commander." The officer relayed the orders as knights grouped up on the sand, all struggling to keep their mounts away from the alluring seagrass. Five riders broke from the mass to join Ramgis, and they trailed him inland, galloping in all haste across the plains of the Knightly Realms.

Marlok grinned, surveying the busy marketplace through eyes of experience. *Rich noblemen, overpriced goods, bountiful food, and best of all*—Marlok doffed a phantom cap with a sweeping bow as a lady walked past—*beautiful women. The perfect place for a crime spree.* "Remind me who we're trying to find."

"Calny, one of the twins we met in Raz Kiri," Quaswyn answered.

"That's right. I remember now. At some inn called the Strawberry Mug."

"Oh, I do hope they serve food there."

Marlok felt a shift in the orb-heavy satchel at their side. His hand fired back, capturing a slender wrist. A girl struggled to get away, her free hand scratching like a cat. Their eyes locked. "Nice try."

"Help meee!" she squealed. A boy ran to the rescue, fists swinging. Quaswyn released the girl's arm, and she took off while Marlok grabbed the boy's fist, twisting it painfully behind the boy's back.

"Where did the girl go?"

"I don't know."

"I have an idea!" said Quaswyn with excitement. "Let's report this incident to the authorities. They may know where we can find the maker of this orb," he patted the satchel. "And while we're there, we can recruit some of the guards for the war." Quaswyn used his free hand to slap their side with gusto. "We can be helpful!"

"I knew you were deficient." Marlok rolled his eyes. "I'm not going anywhere near the town guard!"

"Why ever not? After the ruffians so rudely assaulted—"

"Professional hazard."

"But they could give us directions to the Strawberry Mug. It's not like they have your wanted poster in Armorica."

"Not yet," Marlok bragged.

"Just let me do the talking. Come on."

"Well, they may want to know about that little thief. But this one's going, too." Marlok restored their grip on the resisting boy's arm, and they dragged him all the way to Dusgoroth's central watchtower.

The ruckus entered the room ahead of the man, the boy kicking and screaming and wresting to wriggle free. "Lemme go! I didn't do nuthin."

"Excuse me, dear sirs," Quaswyn said formally, holding their arm at full extension and making every effort to ignore the boy's raucous behavior. "I'd like to speak to the captain of the guard, please."

A particularly imposing guard separated from the group of four and approached. "My name is Sir Ferrik. I am second in command."

"I was robbed by a young girl today, and this boy fought to protect her. Do you fine gentlemen know anything about a girl thief on the loose?"

Sir Ferrik turned a sigh into a dramatic event.

"One more thing," Quaswyn continued. "Would any of you be interested in fighting a war against the daemons?"

"Yeah, sure, sounds like great fun. Can I bring my girl along?" said a guard propped on two legs of a stool and leaning against the wall. Laughter wrapped the room.

Marlok tried to hush Quaswyn.

Turning to go, Quaswyn lamented, "I just hate to disappoint Boryn. He would have been so pleased with us."

"That daemon kid? He's still around here?" Sir Ferrik studied the odd visitor. "Belral will want to hear about this."

Sir Ferrik led the pointy-faced visitor wearing a peculiar purple robe up the stairs. At the top, they entered a room furnished sparsely, only a table and a single chair, with a large window overlooking Dusgoroth. An older man and a boy stood silhouetted in front of the window.

"Why do I have to close so early?" the boy argued. "I should be able to stay open all night if I want . . ."

"Because, according to the codes, you are running a tavern, not an inn . . ."

"Calny!" Quaswyn shoved past Ferrik.

"What are you doing here?" was Calny's reply.

"Boryn sent us to Dusgoroth to see you. What a surprise to find you here!" Quaswyn made a broad sweep with their arm. "Boryn said you could help us."

"Boryn? You've seen him?" questioned the steely-haired man.

"Yes. And we're trying to help him by gathering an army of our own for an offensive against the daemons."

"What could have possessed him to think that was a proper course of action?" Belral was eager to hear the answer.

"He thought of it after the dwarves were attacked."

"Attacked? Where?"

Marlok responded. "A place called Raz Kiri, by a fellow named Kam."

"Nasty looking little dwarf, if you ask me," added Quaswyn rather prissily.

Belral paused, frowning at the man's odd change of tone. "Where is he now?"

"Kam? Don't ask me."

"No, Boryn."

Quaswyn became dignified. "We left him at Mount Pyr. He was going to Falrik to solicit assistance from the Knightly Orders."

A crash from the stairway preceded a giggle, interrupting the explanation. Sir Ferrik searched for a weapon. "Left my spear downstairs . . ."

"I'm empty handed as well."

"Hey, I don't carry," said Calny, showing his hands to make his point.

Marlok shook his head and pulled a dagger from their sleeve. The door opened slowly. Marlok instantly recognized the thieving girl from the marketplace, but she looked different, shockingly so. Wearing nothing but a seductive smile and a very revealing robe, the auburn-haired girl glided into the room. The men and the boy stared slack-jawed. Not knowing what to do with his eyes, Calny turned beet-red.

She sidled close to Sir Ferrik and purred, "My name is Julia."

"I'm a . . . uh . . ."

"It doesn't matter," she whispered as she stroked his cheek.

"Wait!" Calny stepped between them and found his voice. "She's a—"

Julia spun and put a finger to Calny's lips to silence him. Then she turned to the one in purple and strode confidently in that direction. "How would you like it if I . . ."

Marlok muttered, but Quaswyn noticed a trickle of blood from the corner of the girl's mouth.

"*Luce.*" A beam of light fired from Quaswyn's palm, piercing the succubus' head, leaving a smoking hole. The corpse fell backward, *thunking* on the wooden floor.

"No, thank you," said Quaswyn, brushing their palms clean as Calny and Belral stared with eyes big as saucers.

"Seems you have a daemon problem of your own here," Quaswyn observed. "We would be ever so pleased to be of assistance to you with your problem—if you promise to go help Boryn," bargained Quaswyn.

Calny stirred and reached up to close the old sword master's mouth.

"Umm, sounds fair," Belral stammered. "But who is 'we'?"

Quaswyn aimed an open palm. "*Luce!*" he repeated. A larger blast incinerated the succubus' body, leaving only a handful of ash. "Now that's a long story, which I'd be pleased to share. But would you have a little something to eat while we talk?"

The Tower of Order made an impressive sight when it came into view rising up above the next hill. Ramgis shook away traces of drowsiness from riding through the night. With rising hope of getting help for Rath, he pressed his heels into his steed's side, urging it onward. In that margin of time between nighttime and dawn, he crested the hill, anticipating a glorious view of the fertile fields sweeping toward the beautiful, walled capital of Falrik. What he saw instead was far from reassuring.

Before him lay the largest force of greenskins he had ever imagined. Orcs, ogres, goblins, and trolls huddled around bonfires but mixed into a single massive force. A mountain backdrop protected Falrik from the north, but as far as Ramgis could see, the rest of capital city was surrounded, the farmlands overtaken by destructive brutes.

"In hell's name . . . ," said one of the Blood Knight riders.

"The death of us all."

Another puzzled, "Orcs never muster in such large groups; they're too busy fighting amongst themselves."

"Whatever brought this together . . ."

Ramgis moved to action. "The fastest of you, ride back and tell the Blood Knight army to hurry. There's no time to lose. These beasts act on base animal urges, and anything could trigger this horde. Orcs aren't much for planning either; they much prefer to smash and burn."

A crimson-clad rider broke off and sped away.

"You others, spread out and scout the conditions. Learn what you can about what's going on here while we await our army. Too bad the Wolf reinforcements never showed up; we could really use their help about now."

The riders nodded and followed instructions. Ramgis found a quiet place in a grove of trees, dismounted, and prepared to wait. *Who could possibly be behind this?* The old commander contemplated the frightening scene before him. *I can't even imagine.*

"We've been at this all night, and we're getting nowhere," moderated the Grandmaster of the Raven. The Wolf rested his head on the table and fiddled with the wax puddled there.

"Perhaps the Horse and the Bear could summon their forces from the provinces to help us out of this precarious situation," suggested the Grandmaster of the Serpent.

The Grandmasters of the Horse and Bear squirmed in their chairs, unwilling to admit that their warriors had been killed or captured.

Finally the Bear offered a plausible excuse, "Too slow. It will all be over before they arrive."

"You are the cause of this predicament!" the Grandmaster of the Serpent hissed toward the Blood Master. "If Ramgis hadn't insisted on picking fights with the orcs, they wouldn't be massed on our doorstep."

"This is not one orcish tribe, nor even a single war band. This isn't even an army completely comprised of orcs! How can you blame the Blood Knights for this sudden alliance of beasts?" challenged the Grandmaster of the Blood Knight Order.

"You awoke them to our presence and our power," growled the Bear.

"Regardless of the cause, we must defend ourselves, or we are all lost," interjected the Raven.

"Tell me, Grandmaster of the Bear, just where is your army that makes it unavailable to help in this fight?" posed the Blood Grandmaster again.

"You lose something?" the Grandmaster of the Wolf goaded. "I would think it hard to misplace an army. Perhaps you and your friend the Horse could help out by misplacing our greenskin enemies as well."

"Dogs should learn their place."

"Grandmasters, please stop and listen."

The grandmasters grumbled but turned to the large, heavily armored Grandmaster of the Dragon. "I shall defend this city as is my duty. Those of you with troops to lend, I would appreciate your assistance."

The Wolf offered, "My troops are off on campaign, but I will attempt to summon them back to assist your effort to save Falrik, Grandmaster of the Dragon."

"I will guard the Tower, fellow Grandmasters, to ensure continuation of smooth governance," promised the Raven.

"My order will support the Raven in that!" said the Bear, feigning bravery. "Rest assured that if either of our esteemed colleagues—the Dragon or Raven—should be ki—," the Bear cleared his throat.

"—the Realms will not be left undefended," the Horse finished the Bear's statement.

"If you have nothing more to offer," the Dragon replied in disgust, "I must leave you to prepare for the battle to come." *Cowards.*

The Grandmaster of the Wolf rose to go. "I'll take my leave as well."

"Running from a fight?" said the Serpent to the Wolf.

"We alone have the courage to support the Dragons in this lopsided mission to save your pompous ass."

"Ah, I forgot you Wolves still function like barbarian packs."

"It's better than enslaving your own people to fatten your personal coffers. And by the way, where is your army?"

"It is otherwise occupied."

"Of course it is. How convenient."

"And where are the Blood Knights, the mighty heroes, to help in this squabble?" teased the Grandmaster of the Bear.

"Off fighting their own fights, settling petty, private scores! As selfish as always," retorted the Grandmaster of the Horse.

The Blood Grandmaster stated with conviction, "I have no doubt the Blood Knights will come. Ramgis has a habit of being timely."

The Grandmasters of the Dragon, Raven, Wolf, and Blood left the room, steeling themselves for the battle ahead.

Raz Kiri was falling, demolished at the dwarves' own hands. A stoic lot experienced with the sad business of resettlement, the dwarves were unwilling to leave anything behind for their enemies. Dwarves climbed atop their roofs, removed the copper caps then smashed hammers into centerpoles, cracking the structures and collapsing them inward. Boringer gazed upon the once great city, sorrow his heavy burden.

"We run like cowards," he grumbled.

"We make a smart move," King Fazrin reassured.

"Smart moves got us 'ere in the first place," came Boringer's sharp retort.

The king shrugged. "Then wha' might ye suggest, Boringer?"

"I'm leavin'."

"Going where?"

"Ta reclaim old treasures. From the dead."

"Ye woul' desert our clans?"

"I'll be doin' 'em a favor by regainin' wha' was lost to us and by purgin' the world o' the unclean at the same time. An' then I'll be back."

"Ye can no' do it alone. Pick twenty lads ta take with ye, then be off."

"Thank you, O King."

The old dwarven king turned toward the palace, his chin to his chest and his shoulders drooping almost as much as his long, white moustache. He pulled his royal battleaxe from the carrier on his back. He hesitated for an instant before slamming it into the earth. A tremor shot through the mighty dwarven palace; it shook then crumbled into a dusty heap. "And so we die in order to live again."

Boringer hurried through the debris-strewn streets toward the brewery. He found Bret standing over a dusty cord, a lighted torch in his hand. Bret's eyes never left the beloved building.

"Been in me 'ands since we firs' came ta Raz Kiri, since the Daemon War . . ."

"An' we can build ye a nice, new one when we settle inta our new home."

"The king won't le' me take any of me creations . . ."

"Why?"

"Too unstable," chuckled the brewmaster.

"Well, since ye're comin' with me on an expedition, you can bring 'em along—a taste or two." Boringer's beard bobbed with a conspiratorial smile.

"Wha' kinda expedition 'ave ye go' in mind, eh?"

"We're headed to the swamps."

"Oy, ye serious? We're goin' fer the treasures?" It was Bret's first genuinely happy smile in a while. He turned toward Boringer, but when he did, his torch-bearing hand dipped. *Hiss.* Bret looked down; a flame snaked along the fuse toward the brewery.

"Tha's no' good."

The tiny blaze slithered under the door moments before a thundering boom. The building exploded, chunks of stone and iron hurtling through the air. Bret and Boringer were tossed like playthings, and the building across the street settled into a heap of dust.

Black with smoke, Bret turned to Boringer and grinned widely. "Tha' was totally worth restartin' all me work!"

"Ye coulda killed us!"

"Nah. We were fine. Wadn't even close."

Boringer pointed to the boulder pinning the tail of Bret's apron to the ground.

Bret tugged the apron free and smiled. "Like I said, wadn't even close."

The Grandmasters of the Dragon, Raven, Wolf, and Blood Knights mounted their warhorses and marched purposefully toward the main gate of Falrik.

"I never thought I'd see the day that Falrik might fall."

"With our generals all away . . ."

"I admit it doesn't look good, but let's consider our enemy," said the wise Blood Knight.

"Indeed. Ravaging bands of mindless beasts that know nothing but brute force. And hundreds of them! How does an army of any size overcome such an adversary? Not to mention that we have only the Dragon's cavalry and the Raven's soldiers here to fight."

The experienced Dragon listened to the discussion before speaking. "Usually in a large force of orcs, you'll find one powerful creature that keeps them all in check. If we can find this leader, kill its bodyguards, then kill it, there is a chance that these bands will fall apart and retreat."

"What tactics shall we use to draw the leader out?" asked the less experienced Wolf.

"No need to worry about that. If we ride out and make enough commotion, the leader will show itself. Orcs can't resist a good fight, and for the leader, the bigger the fight the better."

"I will post my archers on the wall to grant you cover," said the Raven.

"I will ride to my villages nearby and gather the civilians for the fight; they are brave men who'll be proud to help as reinforcements," the Wolf offered.

"How will you make it through the orcish line?"

"Don't worry. The Wolves are the best riders you've ever seen— whether civilian or knight."

The Falrik gate swung open. The green-skinned horde nearest it began grunting, and the message heaved like an ocean wave through the assembled mob. The white-and-gold clad Grandmaster of the Dragon rode out the gate, his cavalry behind, and the Raven's archers lined the fortifications. It was already late afternoon; they would have to work fast to finish this before nightfall.

"Let us cut them down until our last breath," declaimed the Dragon. His knights roared in agreement, lowered their lances and exploded forward. The Grandmaster of the Wolf slipped out behind the cavalry just as the Grandmasters of the Raven and Blood closed and locked the gates.

Orcs and beasts lumbered toward their weapons, shook them in the air, and grumbled, eager to fight. At the same time, the Grandmasters of the Bear, Serpent, and Horse assembled on the wall above the gate, eager to watch.

"If the Dragon should be ravaged by this rabble, perhaps our vote to oust the Blood Knights will turn out differently," chuckled the Bear.

"A shift in the balance of power, no doubt," added the Horse, frothing at the thought.

"A fool riding to his death! He dreams that his measly little cavalry can run off such a horde! His loss, our gain," laughed the Serpent.

Secure within his black armor, the Grandmaster of the Raven approached the men from behind. He grabbed the Serpent by his emblazoned, teal tabard and dangled him over the ledge. "Still your tongue, Snake."

"I . . . I . . . I meant no harm. . . . We s . . . s . . . spoke in jest! I didn't mean it. Hones . . . s . . . tly."

The Raven tossed the wriggling figure to the street. Heads low, the others rushed down after him. They lifted the twisted Serpent and scurried away to hide in the Tower like the cowering rats they were.

The Dragon Grandmaster wasted no time before charging, thrusting his lance through one orc while his mount crushed another under trampling hooves. Arrows whistled overhead, dropping onrushing greenskins in their tracks, and the Dragon struck down more as he shifted back toward the gate to prepare the next foray.

A particularly large orc smashed its way through the lines. It pounded the heel of its axe against its chest. "Fight me!" the warlord challenged.

The Dragon dismounted, preferring the agility of battle on foot, and cautiously approached the mighty, looming orc. The old knight slammed the butt of his wooden lance against the earth. An outer shell shattered to reveal a dazzling, white iron spear hidden within. The knight spun the magnificent spear and waved it, taunting the orc, and he planted both feet, ready for the orc's assault. It roared in reply and charged. Powering forward on bulky legs, it took a wild swing with its battle axe, but the spear came up to smash the creature to the earth before the blade could bite. The orc tried swinging from the other direction, but the attack was easily parried. The orc held the axe above its head and loosed a deadly chop while the nimble knight continued his defensive strategy, skittering behind the orc so the blade embedded in the dirt with a harmless spray of gravel.

The orc warlord jerked the blade free then twisted, knee raised, to slam the old knight's chest. The Dragon stumbled backward but righted quickly, and with mocking eyes, stared down the orc, luring the next charge. Not taking the bait this time, the orc used two hands to slam its axe into the earth, sending up a new cloud of dirt to blur the Dragon's vision. Then, grunting happily, the orc swiped the man's side.

Far in the distance, Boryn was able to make out the Tower of Order in the falling light of day. Though the walls protecting the powerful capital of Falrik were concealed by evening fog, he felt energized with the destination in view, and he hastened his pace. But as he drew closer, he realized it was not fog that shrouded the city walls but roiling clouds of dust.

A battle! He ran, his tattered cape flapping, until he was close enough to see what separated him from the city: a huge army of orcs, ogres, and beasts locked in combat with white-and-gold armored horsemen.

Boryn tucked the yipping wolf pup deep into his pack where he hoped it would be safe and rushed toward the mêlée. With growing uncertainty, he neared the rear line. Suddenly he felt a familiar, though unpleasant, sensation. His head snapped up in time to see a figure dip into a cloud. Several orcs noticed the boy advancing from behind, and they turned to charge.

Boryn unsheathed the sky blue scimitars Rogma had made for him. *No better way to train.* He rolled sideways as an orc swung a massive fist toward his head. His momentum carried him to his feet, and he came up stabbing. The orc had moved in, so the blades met flesh, slicing as easily as a hand through water. Boryn jumped back letting the body flop to the dirt. He held the blades straight out from his side and began to spin before squeezing the grips. The blades sailed out, slicing into the orcs that had moved in to surround him. The orcish lot dropped, but more were coming. The earth trembled, and Boryn turned to see an ogre, blue-gray-skinned and at least twice his height, smashing its way through the ranks. The beast dragged with it an uprooted tree. The ogre brought the tree around like an enormous fly swatter and slapped it against the ground at Boryn's feet as more orcs gathered and cheered.

Boryn channeled energy into his bracer and waited for the ogre to swing again. Grinning and releasing the bracer's time-slowing energy, he dashed up the trunk and on to the ogre's arm. He let the blades fly wide as he swung the scimitars. The chain coiled round the ogre's neck. Boryn squeezed the grips again, but instead of retracting, the blade chain cinched tight. The ogre's gray eyes bulged. Boryn let time return to normal before leaping to the ground without releasing the hilts. The ogre's neck snapped. The beast fell dead; the cheering ceased, the orcs surged toward the boy.

The Grandmaster of the Dragon pushed himself up using his spear like a crutch. He coughed, feeling the pressure in his side where his armor was crumpled by the orc's blow. The warlord laughed and ran at the Grandmaster again. It swung sideways with its battleaxe. The knight blocked with his spear but was still thrown from his feet at impact. The warlord kicked, slamming the knightly warrior in the chest. Before the Dragon had a chance to rise, the orc was over him. It lifted the Dragon by the helmet, tucked the human warrior under its arm, and ripped away the helmet. Next, the knight was tossed into the air before the poll of the axe batted him to the ground.

"You weak for size," laughed the warlord.

The old knight rose like a cripple, unable to straighten against the crumpled armor. One arm had broken in the fall, but with the other, the Dragon held firm to his spear. He pulled his elbow back and fired his arm forward with as much power as he could muster. Fate guided the spear into the orc's vulnerable armpit at the same moment the orc's axe bit into the side of the Dragon's neck, cleaving down his chest. The Grandmaster dropped to his knees, light fading from his eyes. Ripping the bloodied axe from the grip of the knight's white armor, the screech of metal against metal, the orc raised his weapon and roared. It jerked the spear from its armpit then, with a beefy foot, kicked the knight's chest, toppling him once and for all.

The warlord's triumphant roar was cut short by a hammer blow to the gut. It grunted but swiftly regrouped. Beating its chest, it boasted, "Another warrior wants to die!"

A gold-and-crimson armored knight riding a powerful, white warhorse torpedoed forward, warhammer raised. While the mount galloped on, Ramgis leapt from its back to confront the warlord. He stared into the orc's empty eyes.

"Enjoying the daemon's power?" Ramgis raised one eyebrow.

"Power granted by gods," declared the orc proudly.

Ramgis squeezed the hammer's grip. "You want to see power?" The knight smashed his weapon into the earth, and the ground exploded, knocking the greenskin off balance. He sprinted toward it and this time swung upward. The orc blocked the hammer blow with its axe and shoved to the outside, forcing Ramgis' warhammer wide. Hoping to pulverize the knight's unprotected head, the orc made a grand sweep, but Ramgis managed to scoot out of the way, and the battleaxe smashed into the ground instead. Ramgis used the momentary advantage, propelling the hammer for a low blow to the orc's knee. The shot caused the orc to drop, and as it fell, the knight's hammer swatted the axe away. With the warlord kneed, Ramgis lifted his weapon with two hands, reared back and launched a brutal assault on the orc's good shoulder. The shoulder gave, bone shattering, rendering the second of the warlord's arms useless.

Ramgis swung his hammer again, whacking the warlord's skull, then again from the side, snapping the neck so hard that the head was almost torn off. The warlord fell heavily and did not move again.

The surrounding orcs charged in, each eager to slay the warlord's assailant in order to lay claim to the title themselves. Ramgis saw Cadegray and the Blood Knights swarming toward the battle. A bolt of lightning slashed through the orcish line, and those still standing scattered.

Terrible odds. Luthor shook his head seeing the few courageous knights locked in fierce battle with a much larger orcish force. "Dace, ride back and tell our Bear and Horse inductees that they are home, and unless they want to see Falrik burn, they should hurry and go save their capital."

"Are we not helping?"

"We are, indeed. Tell the Red X to prepare for battle."

"Understood."

Luthor spurred his horse into a gallop and dashed toward the capital, strapping on his metal shoulder guard as he rode. Ahead, he noticed a boy dressed as if he'd scrapped with a wildcat and skillfully wielding shining, blue scimitars, holding his own against an assaulting force. The blades whirred in perfect synchrony. Luthor smiled. *Boryn, all grown up and fighting like a warrior.* He urged his horse faster in that direction as the armies of the Bear, the Horse, and the Red X barreled in from behind. *Time to play good guy . . .*

A troll as lanky as the beast Boryn had fought in Raz Kiri came at him, and the youth grinned with confidence. The bracer's amethyst glowed with energy that Boryn released as the troll was nearly upon him. While time crawled, Boryn ran at it with flying blades. Under the bracer's spell and before the troll knew what struck, both its arms were sliced off. Boryn jumped back, loaded the blades with an erratic charge, and swung, releasing crescents of energy that cut the troll like knives. The charge extinguished, and the troll's wounds burst open, spurting blood, and screeching, the creature toppled over.

A powerful footfall behind him caused Boryn to spin just in time to see a new assailant swing. Boryn sidestepped to foil the attack then wheeled out of harm's way. Suddenly, a crack opened in the ground, and the beast tumbled in. Boryn's eyes traced the cleft to its source: Luthor, his massive claymore resting on his shoulder guard. Luthor raised his hand to his forehead and with the slightest move offered a two-fingered salute.

Boryn smiled, and Luthor turned, absorbed in a battle of his own.

"Glacius, we should help the orcs," suggested a young daemon from his lofty vantage point.

"No," replied the irritable commander.

"But we granted them some of our power. Are we really going to let it go to waste? Look at the state of things. Not only have they lost their leader, but human reinforcements seem to be popping up on all fronts."

Glacius watched that Mhinbron boy joined by the Red X. On the other side, a ragtag bunch of ill-equipped but ferocious Wolf fighters were newly arriving. And in the middle, the knights of Dragon and Blood were crushing anything unfortunate enough to be caught between.

"If you move out of the cloud cover, I will kill you myself."

"Forget the orders," urged the eager, young daemon. "This is your time to shine! Stand up to Fernus! Wipe out the Blood Knights and that boy, not to mention his brother—all in one grand move. It's an opportunity we shouldn't pass up!"

Glacius' head lolled, and he turned his frosty, blue eyes toward the overly eager daemon. "You are so very tedious." He held out his hand, and a spear of ice fired out, piercing the minion's head.

Another daemon appeared behind him. "Lord Glacius."

"What?"

"We are ordered to withdraw and return to the citadel."

"Finally," Glacius flung the daemon corpse to one side. "The fun is finished here."

Thick fog and branches brought low by heavy loads of damp, trailing moss made it hard to see anything beyond a dozen strides into the swamp. The dwarf moved by touch and instinct, the sodden ground sucking at his boots until finally he felt cold stone beneath his boot. *Dry ground. About time.* Boringer turned to his boys, all eager to recover the ancient treasures, even if it meant being wet, muddy, and cold.

"We camp 'ere tonight. An' ring the camp with fires," Boringer ordered, an edge to the voice that escaped between moustache and beard.

The dwarves dumped gear from their carts and turned them on their sides as backrests. They stretched and groaned, releasing muscles and minds weary from the day's long journey.

"Who'll be on watch?" one of the hunters wanted to know.

"Jus' me. The rest o' ye, sleep. We will eat as soon as the sun rises an' be movin' on."

"The sun's only jus' goin' down. Should we no' be goin' farther now?"

"Through this?" Boringer made a sweep with his arm that

caused the thick air to swirl and clear.

"I see yer point," the treasure hunter agreed with a low chuckle.

Ring fires cast an eerie halo around the encampment, but the weary treasure seekers cared not, settling down to rest. Boringer approached Bret. "Will ye take watch fer a bit? I need ta take care o' somethin'."

"Wha'?"

"I'll tell ya later. I wan' ta ge' it done while there is still a bit o' light." Boringer thumbed his helmet for good luck then trudged away from the light into the fog, a rope tied around his waist to lead the way back. The dwarven warrior carved a rune in the trunk of the first tree he encountered. Repeating the simple rune, he moved from tree-to-tree until he had fully encircled the camp. Satisfied that the traps would protect them should visitors come, Boringer followed the rope tether back to the campsite, making sure no tree was overlooked. *Hopefully, these won't be needed.*

Boringer sat by the fire, vigilant while his companions nodded off. But his lids grew heavy and he drifted off.

A blast reverberated throughout the swamp, and Boringer shot to his feet. *Bloody hell! The traps!* Tossing off his drowsiness, he grabbed his battleaxe and shouted, "Oy, get up *now!*"

The dwarves sprang up, weapons ready, and more detonations sounded.

"Boringer, wha' is it?"

"Welcome ta the home o' human necromancy."

"Ye mean . . ."

"Yup. Shatter bones or remove the head, and ye should be fine."

"But . . ."

"Boringer, min' if I clobber 'em?" asked Bret eagerly.

"Jus' don't get us killed."

"Alrigh'." Bret cocked his crossbow and grinned, his baggy eyes lighting with mischief.

Boringer faced the outside of the circle. A figure emerged dripping from the swamp and stumbled toward the camp. Boringer barreled toward the decomposing human corpse, its skin loose and peeling from its face and rusty armor dangling by rotted leather straps. Spinning with his axe held out, Boringer first cleaved the thing in two and then, before the lower half hit ground, came over the top and down into its head. The head burst like overly ripe fruit, splattering Boringer's armor with putrid goo.

More of the undead came tumbling out of the swamp. One took a crossbow bolt between the eyes but continued to advance. Boringer ran at it, swinging. When the bolt exploded, it threw Boringer backwards into the slough. *Bloody Bret.* The brackish water began to bubble, and invisible hands from below groped at Boringer's legs and arms. He floundered and struggled to escape. He reached for handfuls of marsh grass to haul himself out. Thick slime dripped from his clothes and beard as more corpses rose to the top, breaking the black surface. He shuddered. *There mus' be an honest-to-goodness necromancer 'ere.* An explosion, closer this time, blasted away the oppressive fog and lit the area. Boringer made out a man, or the remnants of one, with a staff upraised, shielded by a covey of undead.

"Bret, fire there!" Bolts zoomed into the zone, but the figure and its guardians kept coming, lurching straight toward the blast-happy brewer. None too soon, Bret's bolts exploded, clearing the air and obliterating the necromancer's bodyguard.

A blue rune on Boringer's axe blade began to glow as he channeled energy, and he slammed the axe heel into the ground. Ice spears shot from the blade, but the evil lord of the dead fired energy from his own staff to deflect Boringer's salvo. With a clattery laugh, it ran at Boringer.

"Chargin' a dwarf. Well, aren't you rattleheaded," boasted Boringer. He readied a swing at the necromancer's rotting robes but caught his foot in an uproot and toppled face first into the soggy ground. The dwarf tried to roll but long, bony fingers of a skinless hand clamped his ankle. With the haft of his axe, Boringer shattered the wrist. The hand released its grip, and Boringer scrambled to rise, but more hands fired up from the ground and held him down. The hands flipped him face-side up so that he stared into the gruesome face of the necromancer holding its staff upraised and smiling menacingly, ready to bring Boringer into the undead fold.

"Welcome to my army," the necromancer said in a bone-chilling tone. At that moment, something small and orange thumped its chest. The necromancer flinched, and Boringer's arm shot up to shield his face. The bolt exploded, slinging flesh and bone into the air. Their leader downed, the undead released their hold and fell like deflating balloons. Boringer staggered to his feet, swatting out flaming remnants caught in the wires of his beard while enraged dwarves hacked at the bodies to make sure they would not rise again.

Wiping gore from his face on the back of his hand, Boringer walked toward his savior. "Nice timin'."

"Thanks," Bret said, pleased with himself.

Boringer flung his hand, splattering Bret with residue from the necromancer.

"Oy! Tha's disgustin'!"

"Then do no' blow 'em up on me, or I get ta share the experience with ye."

"How does it taste?"

"What is it?"

"It's a 'muffin'!" Stevan exclaimed.

"I've never heard of such a thing," Emily said.

"Well, how is it?"

"It's really good . . . ," she said between distracted bites.

"He's fine."

"Who?"

"You know who," Stevan grinned.

"You suppose?"

"Think about it. Have you ever seen him lose? Somehow he always dodges death." Stevan laughed, "Do you think he's part immortal?"

"Right." Emily chuckled, gazing into their campfire. Then, quietly, "Do we have a chance?"

Stevan moved toward the fire and began to pack his tiny makeshift oven, wiping the coals off the hollowed stone cube. "What do you mean?"

"In the war. Can we beat the daemons?"

"I don't know. Partly, it depends on how many help. Somehow I think Boryn will have a lot to do with it, too."

"How many people do you think agreed to meet us outside Ranlon?"

"Fifty if we're lucky. It will be interesting to see how many of those show up. How close are we to Dusgoroth?"

"I expect we'll make it there tomorrow."

"Great! Then I can really do some cooking!" said the dwarf, rubbing his hands with anticipation.

"How did you come up with the name 'muffin'?"

Stevan let out a jolly laugh.

"One day, I was preparing dinner for the king, but I was sidetracked by something new I wanted to try. I had just stuffed one of my steaming hot creations in my mouth when the guard came in looking for the king's platter. Asked what I was doing. I tried to answer 'nothing.' But my mouth being full . . ."

Emily laughed at the silly tale.

". . . so the guard takes the tray, and serves the 'muffins' to the king."

"Loved 'em, too, I'll bet." Emily lay back and closed her eyes. "A big day ahead, and I'm bone tired. So I'm going to sleep now. It's your night for watch," she grinned, eyes still closed.

"Oy, what?"

"Good night."

Stevan wiped away the last of the coals and picked up his satchel, spilling its contents. A stone disk tumbled out, a red rune carved in its flat surface. He grasped it in his palm. Hoping, he shut his eyes and focused. Nothing happened. He tried again, squeezing his eyes even tighter and wrinkling his entire face. He opened his eyes. The rune remained unchanged. *Should be as natural as reading or writing.* Angrily, he tossed the stone into the shrubbery and repacked his satchel. He lobbed his bag toward Emily's, wincing at the noise it made, then he shuffled toward the place where the rune had come to rest. *Why am I the only dwarf who can't use a rune?*

Laric and Ranton looked at each other, grinned stupidly, threw their legs across the tabletop, and tilted up to the back legs of their chairs. It seemed to be the favored pose of the experienced patrons, and the boys were eager to look the part. In addition to the brews, they savored the visual pleasure: watching beautiful barmaids whose years of practice allowed them to serve drinks unspilled while sidestepping the boisterous crowd.

"So this is the village where Boryn grew up?" Laric commented, more statement than question.

"I think so. From the location and the way he described it," Ranton answered.

"If it is, I have no idea why he left. This place is great." Laric's gaze trailed one woman as she stumbled over a mug on the floor. "I haven't eaten so well in . . . ," he drifted away in thought, patting his stomach. "Kinda nice having no guards around telling you what to do. I could get used to this—freedom."

Ranton thought aloud. "Do you suppose we could we stay here for a while? We're done, and check your crystals; everyone seems to be fine. We even did a swell job recruiting."

"Makes sense to me. This is our last town, after all." Laric held up his mug and clanged it against Ranton's.

"Did Boryn ever tell you why he left this place for Dusgoroth?"

About that time, one customer scuffled with another who tumbled into the lap of a third. The third man came up slugging and launched the first man across the room. The man's sailing figure landed squarely on top of Laric and Ranton's table, breaking it in half. The table tumbled the stools, which in turn spilled Laric and Ranton to the floor, while the second man leapt on the first, now downed. Disregarding the ensuing brawl, most of the patrons continued their merriment.

In the spirit, Laric escaped to the bar determined to start a conversation with a girl he'd been eyeing. Ranton moved out of the way near the window. *So Boryn lived here?* Just then, a man went flying headfirst out the window. *That explains a lot.*

Restlessly, Wenval paced the campsite, eyes skipping from the midnight sky to the dying fire. He checked the crystals at his side as he did many times each day.

"You worry about the others like they're your family," Hannah said quietly.

Wenval turned. "I didn't know you were awake."

"And how is everyone?"

"All right, I think. It's been a long day for Boryn; he's been doing a lot of fighting, but everything looks calm now."

"So how did you get together?"

"What do you mean?"

"The Shadow Crusaders—what brought you together?"

"It was that daemon Boryn roused in Old Town."

"No, I mean originally. How did you meet?"

Wenval walked toward her and lowered himself to the ground. He stacked three books on the ground as a pillow then crossed his hands behind his head and lay back, contemplating the stars and Hannah's question.

"I guess it was Boryn's doing. I first met him when he was hiding under the table I use in the library—trying to lose some guards. What a troublemaker! Scared the daylights out of me," Wenval said fondly, "but still, he's almost as entertaining as my books!" He looked at Hannah with a boyish grin.

"Boryn introduced me to Laric and Calny whom he'd met at the arena watching fights. As for Ranton, I don't really remember the story—only that it had to do with animals in Grinfol Forest. Knowing Boryn, he was probably being chased by a bear or a wolf. Or possibly Boryn was the one doing the chasing."

They laughed together.

"Do you miss your real family, being so far away?"

"Yes, but I'm kind of glad to be away while I work on this spell-casting. When my parents hear about it, they'll probably insist on throwing a party to celebrate."

"What's wrong with that?"

"Doesn't seem right to be pampered and fussed over simply because I have a gift—and one I don't even understand!"

"And Boryn? What about his family?"

"I think they're dead. He doesn't really talk about it. He's been living on the street as long as I've known him, since he came to Dusgoroth."

"How long ago was that?"

"Em, before the winter. So yeah, it was Boryn who brought us together."

"A motley crew you Shadow Crusaders are, too," Hannah teased.

Wenval turned serious. "Funny . . ."

"Huh?"

"I don't even know Boryn's family name. Never thought about it . . ."

"So what's everyone up to now?" Hannah nodded toward the crystals.

Wenval inspected the stones. "I'd guess everyone is sleeping."

"Except you."

"I can't," Wenval sighed.

"You worry too much."

"Possibly. What about you? Do you worry about your home and your family, Hannah?"

"Not really. The only family I know is a clan of dwarves and an old witch. The dwarves took me in when our village was raided and my parents didn't survive. And I'm not so worried about the dwarves; they're a hearty bunch. They can take care of themselves."

"I thought dwarves were practically extinct, and those few that were left live hidden away in caves."

"Mostly that's true. But I was rescued by a clan living on the outside. The king kicked the clan out of Raz Kiri because they kept up contact with the humans."

Wenval's face twisted, and he changed the subject. "Tell me about *your* magic. Did the witch teach you?"

"She taught me the basics, but since then I've been experimenting with different techniques." She shrugged her shoulders. "I guess I have that gift, too, though I prefer to think of myself as a healer rather than a mage," she amended modestly.

"Either way, we seem to make a pretty good team." Wenval's face blushed red.

"Only one village left, and quite a few soldiers following us!" Hannah agreed, her tone light.

"So why aren't you asleep?"

"I don't know. This is all kind of thrilling."

He turned toward her, enjoying the delicate features of her face, the soft blue of her eyes in the firelight. "How so?"

"We are on the frontline of a war that could decide the fate of our world. We might even become heroes! What could be more exciting?"

"Um, a book about ancient culture?" Wenval turned on his side, cradling his jaw in his palm, and smiled.

"Tough contest, no doubt." She laughed a soft, little laugh.

Ramgis approached the gates of Falrik, the lifeless form of the white-armored Grandmaster of the Dragon draped across his warhorse's withers. Cadegray's pony was equally burdened with Rath. "Open the gates! We have wounded. The battle is won; all is safe," Ramgis bellowed.

The Blood Knight commander and his healer looked up at the sound of someone yelling from above. "Here is your leader. Let him help you with your need." Laughter erupted, and in the light of the night torches, Ramgis saw the crimson-robed Grandmaster of the Blood Knights dropped from the wall to land hard at his feet. The old man struggled up, slowly and crookedly but apparently uninjured.

"You hollow-hearted bastards!" Ramgis roared while dismounting. "Grandmaster." He bowed slightly while offering the man his hand.

"General . . ."

The two smiled narrowly, eyes connecting in quiet though mutual admiration.

"It is wonderful to see you, old friend," Ramgis said. "But tell

336

me, what circumstances—"

Cadegray interrupted, "What's going on here?"

Dusting the road from his robe, the Grandmaster of the Blood Knights began, "Anticipating a different outcome to this battle, the Grandmasters who stayed behind voted to revoke our position at Table as well as our rights as knights. The cowards ordered their guards to . . . escort . . . me from the city. The Blood Knights are removed from the Orders as are the Wolf and the Dragon, not that it makes a difference to their fate."

"So we're outlaws in our own land?" Ramgis clarified.

"And the people are left out to dry," the Blood Master finished.

Ramgis wheeled toward the closed gate, his face red with fury. He hoisted his remarkable golden hammer, gleaming in the firelight. He reared back and swung hard, slamming the weapon into the barrier. The wood splintered under the unbelievable force of the blow, and the portal flew open.

"Grandmasters of the Orders! Judgment hath come!" Ramgis roared as a few sentries charged him. He clouted one in the face, a bolt of lightning taking another as Cadegray moved in to shield Rath with a barrage of flashing outbursts. The Blood Knights closed in behind the leaders, intent upon overthrowing the Table. A spear scraped Ramgis' armor but halted mid-strike as a massive blade ran the assailant through.

"I have scores to settle with these bastards as well," the sword-bearer said, dismounting.

The seasoned commander appraised the raven-haired newcomer and saw enough there to trust him—for the moment at least. "Then let us speak to them together," Ramgis said evenly. Continuing, "Cadegray, find the healers and take them along with Rath back to our camp. We are not likely to find a friendly reception here."

Cadegray broke away while the two leaders moved into Falrik, their armies behind. Ramgis glanced toward the tall, black-cloaked man walking beside him, noting the black flag carried by his men. "The infamous Luthor of the Red X, I presume?"

"Guilty." A wry grin crossed Luthor's face before he turned

serious. "Shall we skip the formalities, General Ramgis? We have business to complete."

Ramgis and Luthor marched through the streets, well guarded by Blood Knights. A company of the black-armored soldiers stepped into their path, the captain bearing the standard of the Raven. After a momentary faceoff, the captain stepped aside as did his soldiers, allowing the invading Order and the Red X to pass and then falling in behind them.

The growing force reached the inner wall that protected the Tower of Order. Through the gates it stormed and on to the parade grounds within. Standing at the Tower entrance was the Grandmaster of the Raven, flanked by the balance of his army.

Face-to-face with Ramgis, the Grandmaster nodded. Wordlessly, the Raven force split, opening a passage for Ramgis and Luthor. The visitors advanced toward the Tower, its iron door shut, the cowardly Grandmasters of the Horse, Bear, and Serpent sequestered inside.

Ramgis raised his warhammer and took a swing. Despite the powerful blow, the formidable door merely dented.

Luthor stepped in. "Let me get this one." He growled; his eyes reddened. With both hands, Luthor reached behind his head and clenched the claymore's pommel. He slid the blade up, and with a smooth, skillful move, slung it skyward. Reaching its apex, it flipped, sailing down pommel first. The ruby X on the crosshatch sparkled as the hilt settled into Luthor's readied grip. Luthor snapped the blade downward and rammed the indestructible tip into the ground. A massive tremor shot under the door, and the barrier fell away. Supporting himself against the pommel, Luthor looked to Ramgis and offered, "After you."

"Tha' was entertainin'!"

"Ye 'ave a very strange sense of humor," Boringer shuddered.

"How much farther to tha' mausoleum, eh?" Bret asked. "I can hardly wait ta get me 'ands on tha' treasure."

"I'm hopin' it's as easy as all tha'."

The dwarven band slogged on, eager to be out of the swamp. Mud sucked at their boots like magnets; the cartwheels sunk to the axles, even when mostly empty. The day wore on, bodies and tempers stretched.

After a long while, Boringer was able to make out a building in the distance. *Here we go! We foun' th' place!* The pace picked up, the dwarves buoyed by the prospect of leaving the swamp behind and finding riches ahead. As they neared the home for the dead, its features became clear. It was a porticoed, stone structure, columns all around, with a pitched roof. In the center, behind a plain, iron gate, was a relatively small shrine guarded by eerie statues of human dead staring from placid, stone faces. One of the dwarves fished through the lock, and the gate clicked open. Inside, the shrine was cold and echoey and perfectly featureless save for a single wooden door on the opposite wall.

"Do no' touch anythin' without checkin' with me first," Boringer ordered.

The treasure hunters nodded their assent.

"Now light the torches, and let's get goin'." Boringer opened the wooden door, thumbed his helmet, and started down a cold spiral of stairs; the dwarves trailed behind. He came to another wooden door like the first one, and he tried the knob. The door eased open with little encouragement. Behind it was a long, dark space. In the torchlight, he could see stacked rows of coffins, like berths on a ship, lining the walls. The dwarf shut the door quietly and continued down the curling stairs. The next door stood open. He held his torch in front and peered inside; the room blazed to life, a trove of old weapons.

"Bret, get 'em started shuttlin' this up to the carts."

While Boringer continued ahead in search of greater reward, Bret scurried around the stone chamber piled high with golden staffs and swords and all manner of iron weaponry. With single focus, Bret dug through the riches in search of a new hammer. He rummaged greedily then spied what he sought under a pile of spears. When he reached for the leather-wrapped handle, it was heavier than expected so he tugged harder, dislodging a rack of iron weapons that clattered to the stone floor, burying him in the process. Pushing aside the leaden blanket, the dwarf hoisted the new hammer and crawled out to inspect his find. The handle was tipped with a small, golden skull. *Eew.* He cringed.

"Well . . . I like mine better anyway," Bret said and tossed the hammer aside like a dirty rag.

Meanwhile, Boringer followed a stone corridor to more stairs that led deeper into the catacombs. Another door. He opened it. An unsettling, purple glow spilled into the stairwell. Bending around the doorjamb to peek inside, Boringer recognized the accursed object, a radiant, purple orb about the size of his helmet balanced on a narrow plinth. He couldn't back out fast enough, slamming the door shut and toenailing one of his throwing axes between door and doorframe to seal the opening.

He plunged farther down the endless spiral, opening the next door he passed. The sound alone told him it was a much larger chamber. Torch extended, he stepped in. The light from his torch did not find the far corners of this space, so big it was. Instead, the light was absorbed and reflected in an unimaginable cache of treasure, the huge room overwhelmed with gold and gems and master-crafted weapons.

Boringer spun at the sound of another loud crash. Rushing up the stairs to investigate, he poked his head inside the first weapon room. "What're ye doing up here, Bret? Tryin' ta wake the dead?"

"I most definitely do no' wan' ta do tha'!" Bret grimaced above an armload of weapons.

"Put those down an' follow me."

Bret considered the prizes regretfully then dropped them, sending up a terrific racket.

"I foun' the *real* treasure room."

"This isn't it?" Bret asked, eyes wide at the possibility there could be more. "Wha's with humans an' buryin' treasure?"

"They though' it was safe among th' dead."

Boringer led Bret and his helpers down the stairs, past the sealed chamber and on to the treasure room.

"Will ye look at all tha'!" Bret exclaimed, baggy eyes bright and round with wonder.

"Start carryin' this out, lads."

While the dwarves garnered booty, Boringer followed the chute deeper still. The steps finally stopped at an iron-framed door. He used an axe to pry the lock, and the door snapped open. The space was more corridor than room, flanked with prisonlike doors. At the far end was an ornamented wooden chest, its metal frame glinting in the light of Boringer's torch. Warily, Boringer slid toward it. A finely-wrought latch sealed the chest, but it was no match for Boringer's sturdy boot. He stamped down. The latch broke free. After settling his torch in a wall holder, he bent his knees for leverage to lift the heavy lid. Folded within was a blood-red hide covered with shining scales. The dwarf's brows shot up behind the rim of his helmet as his eyes grew wide. *Dragon scales! Lightweight but harder than metal.* With caution and awe, eyes aglitter in the torchlight, he slipped his arms under the unwieldy bundle to lift it free. *A treasure of all treasures!*

Behind him, a creak. On instinct, he pulled out a throwing axe and wheeled around. One of the barred doors swung lazily, squeaking on rusty hinges, but otherwise the space was eerily still. Suddenly, from out of the cell stumbled a sun-bleached skeleton. Devoid of living parts, the figure was no less animated. Boringer sent the nimble axe spinning. It struck the skull between the empty eye hollows, and the skeleton dropped, shattering into pieces that skittered across the floor. *Rattlehead.*

Boringer collected the bulky dragon hide over one arm while holding a readied axe with the other. More quickly than he had come, he retraced his steps through the hallway as other cell doors squealed open behind him. A scrape against his armor.

"Run! Get out now!" he shouted up the stair shaft while bundling the hide under his arm. He heard clattering from behind but dared not turn and look, and ahead were boots scooting across stone as dwarves hurried to escape. He started up the stairs when an arrow pierced the armor gap behind his knee. He gasped and fell. Turning back, he missiled another throwing axe, smashing the stalking skeleton's skull. Half-dragging himself up the stairs, Boringer neared the room where he'd seen the orb, but the axe he had used to secure the door lay on the floor. The door was open; the room was empty. He sputtered a curse. *No time ta worry abou' tha' now.*

A troupe of skeletons continued the clattery pursuit, and Boringer advanced as fast as his bundle and injured leg allowed. Boringer's head snapped up as a dart *thwacked* the ceiling above him. Recognizing Bret's handiwork, Boringer hastened onward. Boringer shoved the dragon bundle toward Bret's extended reach, then Bret, crossbow still in hand, pulled his leader clear just as the ceiling exploded and collapsed.

Throwing a wiry arm around his friend's wide back, Bret pulled Boringer to his feet and mostly carried the dwarven warrior through the next round of stairs. They passed the uppermost door, past dwarves fighting to hold it closed as rotted hands smashed through. Once Bret and Boringer went by, the rest of the dwarves turned tail for a quick exit, running as fast as they could through the shrine, out the iron gate, past the colonnade and into the yard.

Bret dropped the hide and took aim again, firing into the stair shaft as the last dwarf leapt to safety. The upper ceiling gave way, closing the entrance and sealing the undead below.

Red faced and breathing hard, Boringer turned tight lips to the dwarves. "Who took tha' orb?" he growled, jerking the arrow from his leg.

"Wha' orb?"

"The glowin' purple one."

They searched one another's faces before catching sight of the culprit standing apart from the rest, trying to cover something with his vest. Boringer grabbed Bret's crossbow and fired. The bolt struck the orb, exploding it and propelling the surprised dwarf into a tree. Glittering like gold, ruins of the purple orb rained to the earth.

"I told ye no' ta touch anythin'!" Boringer erupted before tossing the crossbow back to Bret. And to the treed thief, he snarled, "An' I hope fer yer sake tha' wadn't wha' I think it was."

Boryn waited, watching the white-robed healers tend the unconscious man. The camp steward had kindly offered to mend the rags he wore as clothes, and he waited, blanket wrapped, for his garments' return. Absently, he took a morsel of meat from the plate beside him and dropped it in front of the wolf pup.

The pup ate hungrily then frisked at his master's feet. Boryn rubbed behind its ears. "Now what should I call you? How about Shade, mascot of the Shadow Crusaders?" Shade tumbled under the attention before falling fast asleep across Boryn's bare toes. The boy leaned back and dozed, too, only to be awakened by a sharp yip.

The healers backed away, and with a groan, the dark-haired man sat up. Cadegray looked on with a broad smile. Boryn saw that his clothes had been placed next to him, and he bounced up like a spring and hurried into them, pleasantly surprised by the remarkable transformation.

"Where am I?" Rath asked with only a slightly weakened voice.

"In a camp outside the capital."

"Of the Dark elves?" he reasoned, kneading his temples then

combing his fingers through tangled, dark waves.

"No," Cadegray shook his head. "We are well past that."

"The Knight's capital," Boryn rushed to the bedside. "Falrik."

"Who are you?"

Cadegray answered. "A very impressive lad we met on the battlefield. Held his own against the greenskins. Now he claims to have important business to discuss with anyone having command over troops. Since Ramgis is otherwise engaged, the boy waited in hopes of speaking with you."

"How did we come to be in Falrik?" Rath wanted to know.

"After you were injured, Ramgis commandeered several ships from the Dark elven fleet. Frankly, your wounds were beyond my abilities. But Ramgis was determined to save your life. When we arrived at Falrik, we came upon the largest mass of greenskins ever seen in one place, camped around the city, preparing to attack. One thing led to another—it was rather amazing really—and we, along with some others, prevailed—against all odds, I might add."

"Where is Ramgis now?"

"Taking care of business at the Tower of Order."

Rath leaned back wearily, taking it all in.

Boryn moved matters ahead. "I would like to request your allegiance to help in a strike against the daemons."

"No need for the formality. Tell me what you want?"

"Will you bring your men and join us?"

"Who is *us*? And who did you say we are fighting?"

"As of now, only the forces of Dusgoroth. And our enemy is . . ."

"Dusgoroth?" Rath paused thoughtfully. "And who is helping you on this mission?"

"My friends are assembling fighters across the Empire. I'll meet them in Dusgoroth soon."

"Namely?"

Boryn seemed puzzled by the query. "Well, there's Laric and Emily, Wenval, Hannah, Ranton . . ."

Rath smiled and nodded. "I will help you. Expect Ramgis' assistance, as well. I'm still two up in the favors," Rath turned to

Cadegray with a playful wink.

Cadegray chuckled, ushered out the Falrik healers, and left Boryn and Rath alone in the tent. Tentatively, Rath pivoted his feet to the ground and moved to stand, relieved to find his stiff limbs reasonably cooperative. At that moment, the tent flap snapped back, and an imposing, crimson-armored knight entered, shadowed by a taller, younger man whose garments bore the scars of long use. The second man exchanged a quick, knowing look with the boy.

"Ramgissss," Rath exaggerated, his carefree nature returning.

"Welcome back, Rath," Ramgis said warmly. "I'm sure you've heard of the Red X? Meet Luthor, their leader."

Rath nodded in acknowledgment. "Was your business in the city successful?"

"We have new Order at the Tower—only four chairs remain at the Table."

"Whose, may I ask?"

"Governance is in the hands of the Dragon, Raven, Wolf, and Blood Knights."

"Hah. I shall expect great things from this new Order," Rath smiled wryly. "Oh, by the way, Ramgis, you and I are helping him out." Rath gestured toward the sandy-haired boy.

"And how might that be?"

"Seems he needs our assistance in fighting a new war." He paused for effect. "A Daemon War."

"That was fifty years ago . . ."

"Going for number two," Luthor interceded. "Saw them with my own eyes. In Dusgoroth. It explains the orcs getting riled, too." Luthor continued, "I also ran into a rapi chief who prophesized potent darkness headed our way, if you accept such stuff."

"Do we know where the daemons are coming from?" Ramgis raised the question.

"Ranlon," Boryn answered.

"I guess they like it there," joked Rath. "You'd think they wouldn't choose to set up shop in the same place as before."

Ramgis studied the boy, while Luthor observed, smiling. Ramgis said, "I saw you fighting the orcs. You are very skilled for one of your age." A question hung in the air. "Who are you, young man? What is your plan?"

"My name is Boryn."

"Your presentation does not suggest nobility," Ramgis fished, motioning toward the boy's heavily mended attire, "yet those swords. . . . What is your family name?"

Boryn's eyes darted toward Luthor, but he suppressed the desire to grin. "I come from Dusgoroth," Boryn dodged. "I am gathering armies in preparation for our assault on the daemon citadel in the Forest of Ranlon. Beyond that, there isn't much of a plan."

"It's a start. What do we know of this developing war? What's behind it? Why now?"

Boryn outlined the attacks on Dusgoroth as well as his experience with the dwarves. As Ramgis listened, his eyes narrowed, deepening the lines at the corners of his eyes.

"You have the support of the Red X," Luthor said. "I'll gather my forces and meet you outside of Ranlon, on the fields this side of it."

"Thank you, Luthor. Will the other Orders join us?" Boryn looked at Ramgis hopefully.

"The Knights of Blood will be with you. I feel confident that I can pledge the support of the Wolf and the Dragon as well."

"And the Raven, too." A black-armored man, sizeable under any circumstances but consuming considerable space in the compact tent, entered. The Grandmaster of the Raven looked down on the rangy boy; a chuckle rattled within the confines of his helmet. He removed it and smiled pleasantly.

Boryn commented, "You look different than I expected," and teased, "and a lot younger than Ramgis."

"As do you," the Raven followed the lead. "I expected someone more . . . mature to have whipped my renegade general working for that witch."

"Giving mercenaries a bad name, was he?" Rath quipped.

"Grandmaster of the Raven, I thank you for your assistance

in this war," Boryn replied respectfully. "I'll see you when I reach Ranlon then."

"Where are you going now?" Luthor asked Boryn.

"To gather more fighters."

"Alone?"

"I work best that way," he said, leaving the tent. "I'm heading north; I've heard there may be people who will help."

After Luthor had followed Boryn outside, Cadegray turned to Ramgis. "Why are we putting so much trust in this boy?"

"How old were you in the first Daemon War, my dear friend?"

Cadegray's face creased in a crooked smile.

"We led the fight, and we won."

"And now the future is in new hands," Cadegray acknowledged with a touch of melancholy. "A time for new heroes—and retiring of the old. Let's hope the young ones are ready."

"So how old *are* you two?" laughed Rath.

"Far too old to be doing this," chuckled Ramgis, rubbing the small of his back.

Scruffy approached the castle with bold steps and bolder heart. *I told him it wouldn't work, and he refused to believe me.* He entered the throne room after the barest of knocks on the door.

The Emperor, as usual, sat sloppily draped across the elegant golden chair. "I order you to purge me," he said without preamble.

"From what I hear, you've had the . . . pleasure."

"The other healer was a pretender. He didn't know what he was doing. You, on the other hand . . ."

"Precisely."

"I tell you, Edrick, I've made a turnaround. I know that I was wrong, and I truly want to make amends."

The healer eyed Mhinbron impassively. "I will not be a pawn in your game."

"For the sake of Dusgoroth," the Emperor tried.

The healer guarded his silence.

"For my sons." The Emperor dropped his eyes. "I have been an unworthy father."

"No, sir, you have been no father at all."

"Yes! But now I want—I need—to atone!"

"Or could it be that your boys—men now—might be valuable in helping you save your throne?"

"It's nothing of the kind!"

"Pah! I know of the advisors' rumblings. Now that it's no longer to the council's benefit to keep you in power—or in drink—you're having a handy change of heart."

The drunken lord powered from his chair and lunged toward the healer. Mhinbron grabbed the old man by the neck of his untidy white robe and leaned close to his face. "How dare you!" The Emperor smelled foul and caused the healer to turn away. Then Edrick stepped back and chuckled, infuriating Mhinbron further.

"Your devotion is yet shallow, Emperor." Edrick said the title as if it tasted sour. "When these newly sprouted feelings of yours have grown some roots, feel free to summon me again. Until then, I have more important matters to attend."

Noiselessly, Scruffy left the room, and Lord Mhinbron resumed his seat. The Emperor looked out the window. For a brief and rare moment, lucidity crossed his face. *Is there a chance a purge might really work?*

"You are making me fat." Marlok pinched the bulge at their waist.

Quaswyn licked their lips, grinning childishly, a stack of empty crocks in front of them. "A person needs a bit of extra sustenance when traveling."

"Enough to feed a dozen?" grumbled Calny. He grabbed the plates and carried them to the pantry.

"Heh! It was delicious." The chair scraped against the wooden floor as Quaswyn shoved away from the table.

"We've done nothing but eat and sleep since we got here."

"Everything you want to do is immoral or illegal."

Marlok smiled. "Well, we could get to work on the daemon problem. That's what we said we'd do, remember?"

"So much work, so little time," Quaswyn lamented.

Calny, still not accustomed to the bizarre two-sided banter coming from one mouth, returned. "Well, I'm tired of feeding you. You eat enough for two . . ."

"With good reason," Quaswyn said pleasantly.

"It's time you start earning your keep." Calny tossed them a damp dishcloth and pointed to the back room. "You can start there, with your own dishes."

Quaswyn recoiled from the sour rag as if it was a serpent about to strike. "Why I do believe it's almost time for our appointment at the library," Quaswyn began. "A gentleman there has so graciously offered to bestow upon us the benefit of his kind. . . . Isn't that so, Marlok?"

"Whatever."

Amidst considerable flurry, they made a quick escape from the Mug.

"That was disgusting!"

"At least it got you moving. Now which way to the library?"

They wandered through Old Town, now bustling with activity thanks to the success of the Strawberry Mug, and headed into the busy streets toward the main square. When they reached the library, Marlok shoved open the heavy, wooden doors and stepped inside the enormous, though hushed, chamber. Shelves of books climbed toward the soaring ceiling. Marlok had never seen anything so astonishing as this. He marveled, mouth agape.

At the distant end of the room, a double stairway curved to a balcony where more volumes lined the walls. Muttering the words, Marlok read the inscription there: "Magic is governed by the limits of man's imagination and the power of his will." *Hmm. Maybe I should give it a try.*

"It's not as easy as it sounds," Quaswyn said as if he shared the thief's thoughts as well.

"Where should we start?"

"Argh."

"What?"

"We left the orb back at the Mug. We should have brought it with us in case we find someone who knows about it."

"You bloody moron! What if something happens to it? I told you to keep it with us at all times!" Marlok turned on their heel and pushed out the door and into the street.

"I will not bear the burden of this responsibility alone. You could have brought it."

"Shut it," Marlok said, clamping their jaw shut.

"Em! Emm! Emmmmm!" Quaswyn waved his arm and pointed. "What now?"

"Marlok! Look! Smoke!" A charcoal-dark finger spiraled up in the direction of the Strawberry Mug. "You don't think . . . ?"

"No!" Marlok exclaimed, elbowing their way through the crowd on a near dead run. They arrived to find flames pouring from the window of their room.

"Get me inside there," Quaswyn insisted.

"Are you nuts?"

"Just do it!"

Marlok stepped back then sprinted toward the wall and jumped, taking several running steps up the wall before grabbing the window ledge and throwing them inside.

"Pleg Is!" yelled Quaswyn. He threw their arms out wide, encasing the room in ice and instantly smothering the flames.

Heart pounding, Quaswyn clambered to their feet and began a frantic dig through the charred remains. "Where did you leave the orb?"

"You had it . . ."

"Oh, for the love of food, can you just not argue for once and help me here?"

"On the bed . . ." They spun toward the burned-away mattress just as the door crashed open. Calny, club in one hand, bucket of water in the other, fumed. "Now you're trying to burn the place down?"

"We weren't even here!" Marlok protested.

"When we arrived, it was all wrapped in flames." Quaswyn threw his arms around himself to demonstrate. "It was so scary!"

"But I heard someone up here," Calny said.

Quaswyn continued a frenzied search of the blackened room. Calny watched, puzzled. "Lose something?"

"Actually, yes," Quaswyn's voice came in spurts. "A large, purple orb. About so big—"

Marlok interrupted, "Have you seen it?"

As far as Boryn could see, dunes of sand undulated like waves in the ocean. *How is that possible?* He jumped from the plateau that rimmed the Knightly Realms and landed in the yielding sand of the unfamiliar territory. The surface gave like a pillow under his feet and threw him off balance. Noting this, Shade waited atop the small cliff, growling and disinclined to jump. Boryn whistled, and the pup leapt. He caught the wolf and lowered him to the shifting sand, then side by side they advanced into the desert, the swells growing higher with every step. In short order, the boy's legs trembled from the fight with the pounding sand.

Boryn lifted Shade and searched for solid ground. A heavy wave buffeted him, knocked him from his feet and buried him up to his shoulders. The grit scratched his skin as the wave retreated and a second, more powerful than the first, pummeled him, this one burying him head to toe. He looked behind him, reconsidering the wisdom of this mission, but the roiling waves had carried him far from shore. He tried to swim, clutching the pup to his chest, and sputtered up, choking. Blinking sand from his eyes, he scanned the horizon. *What is . . . no way . . .*

A clipper cut though the battering surges like a sharp knife. Boryn waved his arms desperately trying to draw the ship's attention. The sails came around, and the ship tacked to glide alongside him. A pole was extended, and with grateful hands, Boryn grabbed it, trapping the squirming pup between his arms. Like a fish on a line, he was pulled to the wooden deck. The boy lay in a heap, hacking sand, then flipped to his back and coughed some more. Shade shook; a small explosion of sand sprinkled the deck.

A sailor, breathing hard from the effort of hauling in the heavy load, sat next to Boryn. "Are you all right, lad?"

Boryn stopped coughing long enough to nod. He brushed dry sand from his face while his eyes explored the deck of the ship.

"What are you doing in the Sand Ocean?"

"Walking across it." Boryn's sheepish tone acknowledged that the absurdity was not lost on him.

"What would possess you to do that?" the savvy, old sailor wanted to know.

"How was I to know it would be like walking on water?"

"Note the name," the mate laughed.

"I've never heard the name until you just said it."

"So what brings you here?" came a more serious voice. A man with the bearing of an officer approached. The rescuing sailor moved out of the way.

Boryn looked to the older man, seasoned and stern-faced. Boryn rose, the pup tucked into the space between Boryn's feet. "I'm trying to gather soldiers to fight."

"Why would you come here?"

"Didn't know any better."

"You picked a bad time for us," replied the man, softening, as he stroked the black whiskers clinging to his chin. "You'll understand once we reach port." He pointed toward a distant plateau, a small town squatting on its top. "I'm Captain Yarrik by the way."

"Sail ho!" a watchman called from the masthead.

The captain frowned then issued the orders. "Bring the sails around and hold clear until we identify."

"What's wrong?" Boryn was curious, rising to see.

"Few know of this port, and for a ship so large to be here—well, it's worrisome, to say the least."

"Why?"

"Pirates."

"I thought pirates sail the seas."

"Give men a ship that can fly in the sky, and there will be pirates."

"Why not pull into port?" said Boryn, unsheathing a scimitar and twirling it, eager for a fight.

"Cap'n, there is a net cannon on their deck and another on shore. We cannot get in close," called the watchman.

"A net cannon?" Boryn asked.

"It fires a huge seine over a ship, dragging crew and all into the deep."

"How can I get to port?" Boryn asked, a plan hatching.

The captain indicated the rowboat lashed to the deck. "It will be slow."

"What about the catapult?" Boryn nodded to the weapon lashed to the ship's deck.

"It's for hurling rocks at ships, not boys at towns."

"Try it, please," Boryn urged.

"I won't have your blood on my hands."

Without giving it a thought, Boryn wound back the arm of the catapult, climbed atop the launch arm, and braced himself. "Watch my wolf." Boryn sliced the twisted skeins that held the arm down and went hurtling across the sky, his hair and cloak flying behind him. The island came up fast, and he readied for landing. He hit the ground in a roll and planted his feet, skidding sideways and kicking up a ferocious cloud of dust. He slid to a stop near a handful of plain, white buildings overlooking the strange sand sea.

"Ahoy, who in 'eavan an' 'ell's name ere ya?"

"A visitor, only dropping in."

"Ye best be payin' tha great, gran' price fer the priv'lege a stoppin' 'ere then, matey." Boryn heard the rasp of the man's blade leaving its sheath.

"Afraid I can't help you out there." Boryn turned out his empty pockets.

"Then permit me t' be takin' those luverly, nice blades ye got thar."

"This one?" Boryn unsheathed one of the iron blades he had forged at Raz Kiri.

"Them 'nes thar," the scraggly, little man nodded toward the blue scimitars still sheathed at Boryn's side.

"Try and take 'em."

"Arrrr! We go' us a scrapper!" rattled the pirate, baring snaggled teeth in a happy grin and charging forward. Boryn waited for the pirate to take a swing. When he did, Boryn sliced his iron blade up, surprising the pirate and throwing his saber behind him. With his free hand, Boryn cross punched, landing his fist between the pirate's bloodshot eyes, and used the off balance moment to sweep his leg behind the pirate's knee to swipe the legs out from under him. More pirates, brandishing a hodgepodge of weaponry, converged on the action. Boryn smiled and ran forward, the gem on his bracer glowing brightly.

Hearing the commotion outside, a heavyset man with a short scrubby beard rose from his barstool and moved to the window. "Wha' 'as me men up'n arms?"

"Some'ne rarin' ta fight."

"Who's a started it this time? Wer it that squiffy again?"

"It's no' a single one we know. Ya can see 'im from tha roof thar." The first mate pointed.

The scarred, old captain climbed out the window to watch, clucking at the havoc the boy was wreaking among his men. The boy surged into the fray and disappeared in a blink of purple light before reappearing behind the group, more than half of whom were already grounded with injuries.

"Find ou' fer me who is this wil' brave laddie," the pirate captain ordered. He withdrew his two-handed sword and rested it on his shoulder while unsheathing a longsword with his left hand. He leapt from the roof, landing in front of the boy, and smashed his blades against the rocky ground. Shards of stone flew in every direction. The dust cleared, and the boy waited in a readied stance, the iron scimitar upraised. The pirate captain looked the boy head-to-toe.

"Wha's tha point in carryin' six scimitars if'n ye're usin' only one of 'em?" jeered the pirate.

"One is plenty for weather-beaten fighters like you," was Boryn's cheeky reply.

"Me thinkin' yer a mighty bit mistaken thar!" said the pirate as he took a swing at the boy only to have him deftly dodge and the blade swoosh open air.

Boryn powered forward. He sidearmed the pommel of his blade into the pirate's face, sending him sprawling. "Take your men and leave."

"Pah! Heave to yer own fine self, matey!" the tough, old seaman roared, leaping up, fists cocked and swinging.

Boryn vanished, and a heartbeat later, the captain felt the cold, iron blade pressed against his neck. *'Ow did tha' louse get ahind me?*

"I invite you to leave. Now," Boryn said calmly.

Ever so carefully, the grizzled man rotated to face the formidable boy. Their eyes locked, hard as flint. Boryn relaxed the blade's pressure ever so slightly, paused with a final, dark glare then lowered it

The captain took a step back and turned, calling out, "All 'ands on deck, and pr'pare ta set sail. Weigh anchor, me hearties!" The pirate clipped to his vessel, his crew limping behind. Within minutes, sails unfurled, and the ship pulled out.

"The coast is clear," came the watchman's call on Yarrik's ship.

"Into port and dockside all hands," ordered Captain Yarrik. The gangplank dropped, and the captain disembarked, the wolf pup scampering behind him. Boryn waited on the shore making no pretense of containing his mirth. The pup frisked playfully, nipping at Boryn's boot straps.

"Chasing off a boatload of pirates without killing a single one?"

"I'd rather avoid doing that."

"Honorable."

"What do you say now to joining my army?"

"As I told you, it is a bad time for us. We are sorely outnumbered and under constant siege by vicious pirate bands. All available men have been called up to fight this war of our own."

"Is there anyone I can talk to?"

"To fight alongside you, permission would be needed from the council to which all soldiers on the Sand Ocean are sworn."

"Where do I find the council?"

"The capital, northwest of here, but the pirates have had it under control for a while."

"I'll go clear out the pirates and see if I can win the council's support for my efforts." Boryn spoke boldly.

"No shortage of confidence." Yarrik smiled, and Boryn returned a lopsided grin. "It is likely that the council is imprisoned, or dead."

"We won't know until I try."

"I can't take you. Our boat needs repairs. And no, the catapult won't get you there," Yarrick joked.

"Any other way?" Boryn bent to retrieve Shade.

"You can use my sandboard," offered one of the crewmen.

"And that is . . . ?"

"Innkeepers and their directions," Wenval muttered as he held up the hand-drawn map, turning it to ash.

"At least we lost our way on the last day," Hannah laughed. "Any idea where are we?"

"Not exactly. If the clouds weren't covering the stars . . ."

"The road seemed to just end."

"I guess not many travel to Dusgoroth from around here, so the road's state has simply degraded over time."

"Should we wait till morning?"

Wenval stopped, wary. He put a finger to his lips to silence her. "Get down," he whispered. Grabbing Hannah by the arm, he pulled her crouching in the bushes beside him.

The foliage above them stirred, then two figures dropped noisily through the leafy canopy. They landed on the forest floor with a solid thud. Groaning, one stood and arched its back.

The other climbed to its feet more slowly, catching its breath. "I thought you saw them."

"I did. I know I did. They were right here."

"Why do we get stuck with this menial job?"

"Because Julia failed. So we have to clean up her mess," complained the daemon.

"At least these two aren't fighters," chuckled the second daemon as it stretched its batlike wings.

"Let's get finished here and go watch the others. The pain and suffering will be amusing to see."

"Maybe they'll let us help."

With an imperceptible shift, Wenval moved his hand. "*Lux!*" he cried out suddenly. A light fired from his palm, impaling one of the daemons; its body instantly burned to a heap of cinder.

The second daemon howled and ran for the bushes. Hannah stepped into its path, raising her staff. Before she could strike, the daemon laughed and backhanded her, sending her spiraling into a tree trunk. The girl gasped on impact.

Unsheathing its blade, the daemon walked toward her. "Where's the boy, wench?" it asked as it let the blade swing. Wenval leapt between them, his arms crossed in front of him. The daemon's blade *thwanged* as if striking stone, and the sharpened edge bit to the bone. Wenval cried out and dropped to the ground beside Hannah, his arm gushing blood, limp in his lap. She grabbed his hand and aimed it at the daemon. "*Lux!*" he intoned at the last moment; the blast burned the daemon away.

Hannah rose up on her knees above Wenval. He winced in pain. She let her hands hover over his wound, and green light floated down like dust, covering his arm and sealing the gash. He relaxed as the pain dissolved and reclined against the tree trunk.

"Does it hurt?" she asked.

"Not anymore."

"You saved me . . ."

"And you, me."

She hugged him, and he blushed crimson.

Clambering awkwardly to his feet, the young mage turned serious, "We need to warn the others." He offered her a hand up. Reluctantly, he released Hannah's hand to check the crystals, finding that several were darkening at that very moment.

"Wait . . . we can follow Calny's crystal. That will take us to Dusgoroth," Wenval remembered.

"Why didn't we think of that before?" Hannah laughed. "Should we go for Laric and Ranton?"

"I'm more worried about Calny. Let's head to Dusgoroth first. And we should hurry."

Laric stared at nothing through the bleary eyes of inebriation, a half-empty mug still clasped in his hand. Other than Ranton and himself, only the innkeeper remained, cleaning tables and sweeping the floor.

"Don't you think you have had enough?" Ranton asked, piqued and bored.

"Of what?" asked Laric fuzzily.

"Never mind. Let's go to sleep."

Ranton pulled Laric from his stool and helped him toward the stairs. Halfway up, a pounding on the inn's locked door caused them to pause. At first the innkeeper ignored the racket, but it only grew more insistent. Suddenly, the wood splintered and an axe-wielding daemon took long strides into the room; a smaller, wispy daemon strutted behind. Ranton dragged Laric up the remaining stairs and ran into their room, slamming the door behind him. He grabbed his bow and tried to hand Laric his sword, but the twin toppled to the floor.

Ranton left him there and slipped into the hall to peek downstairs. The terrified innkeeper dangled from the daemon's taloned hand.

Nocking an arrow, Ranton took aim. The daemon heard the *twang* of a bowstring and ducked instinctively just as the arrow *thunked* into the wall where its head would have been. The daemon turned a sneering face toward the stairs, tossed the man aside and started up, each tread splitting under its heft.

"Come on down, boys! We only wish to talk to you." Although the words were friendly, the large daemon's voice was anything but.

"Bugger off," said Ranton as he loosed a second arrow at the thing's head only to have the nimble fingers of the smaller daemon pluck it right out of the air.

It considered its catch then snapped the arrow in two. "Brave, aren't you? Stupid, but brave," the wispy one said as it reached the upper landing.

"Where's the other boy?" the first daemon was eager to learn.

Leaning into the room, "The little fool is passed out on the floor." The small daemon let out a devious laugh. "A good time to take care of our business. Keeps the screaming under control."

Ranton planted his boot in Laric's ribs. "Laric! Get up!"

Laric roused, and the smaller daemon stabbed down with the tip of Ranton's arrow, not so much to harm as to pester. The boy rolled over, shading his eyes with one hand. Just as his eyes adjusted, a black line blinked past his face, and blood spurted from the daemon's forehead. The daemon dropped like a loaded sack across Laric's shins.

The big one shook the fallen comrade with its free hand and leaned close to Ranton's face, its breath like steaming manure. "What did you do?"

"Nothing!"

The daemon lurched to slam the boy into the wooden floor, but a second arrow flew in through the open window, piercing up through the daemon's armpit and out the opposite side of its head. The daemon slumped against the wall, blood streaming from face and neck; Ranton dashed to the window.

"What in the hell . . . ," mumbled Laric, struggling to free his legs.

"Stay here, Laric." Gripping his bow, Ranton bounded out the window. He could see the archer sprinting across the field toward the forest. "Wait!" Ranton called chasing after the man. Without slowing, Ranton pulled two hunting arrows from his quiver. The arrows were rigged with cord to trip runaway game. Simultaneously, he fired both. Ranton saw the man jump, his form silhouetted in the light of the full moon, and release an arrow of his own. The man's perfectly placed shot intercepted Ranton's arrows in flight, pinning the trip cord to the ground before it reached him.

"Stop, damn you!" Ranton withdrew a small, ball-tipped arrow. He set a target well ahead of the man, fired the flare arrow and grabbed a second, intent on impaling the ball on the tip of the first. He nocked the second and looked up to see the flare already ignited by a shot from the fleeing archer's bow. Momentarily blinded by the premature detonation, Ranton tripped and landed in the grass. He shook his head, sight restored, to see nothing but a vast, moonlit field; the man was nowhere to be seen. *Who the hell was that? His aim was amazing.*

"We made it!" Stevan grinned as the moonlit walls of Dusgoroth emerged in the distance. "The recruits are on their way to Ranlon, and we finally get a rest—and hopefully a real kitchen to cook in as well!"

"It will definitely feel good to sleep in a bed, but it's such a beautiful night, I almost hate to go indoors," Emily said dreamily.

"It *is* a lovely evening, isn't it, Emily?" The voice came from behind.

The tall girl spun as two heavy figures plowed into and pinned Stevan to the dirt. A third—human in appearance and owner of the voice—held back. Its orange hair and white cloak were almost dazzling as it stepped from the shadows into the light of the full moon. Then it looked up, fiery eyes and sharp, glistening teeth betraying the illusion of humanity.

"Who are you?" Emily demanded.

"Don't you recognize me? I'm hurt!"

Emily searched her memory, looking from the two daemons holding Stevan to the cloaked figure before her. With scarcely a movement, she slid her rings onto her fingers. But despite her stealth, the instant she moved to swing, a vice grip stopped her.

"Protecting the silly little dwarf? He's of no interest to me."

"Run, Emily! It's Fernus, a general! Just *run!*" Stevan struggled to make as much commotion as he could, hoping to distract the general long enough for Emily to escape.

She stripped her hand free and shot off, but Fernus reappeared in front of her, grinning. "Now, now. None of that." His form radiated heat.

She doubled back only to have the daemon block her way again. Trapped, she stopped. An instant later, Fernus was behind her, taking hold of her arms. "Release the dwarf, and go back to Ranlon," Fernus ordered his minions. Then to Emily he said, "You have the pleasure of accompanying me."

The two daemons nodded, spread batlike wings and lifted into the sky, sending a blast of dirt into Stevan's face; at the same moment, Fernus and Emily burst into flame born in hell. She was engulfed in screams, terrible horrifying shrieks, but the black flame did not burn her.

When the screaming died, she opened her eyes to find herself in an elegant, black marble chamber notable first for its oppressive heat. Emily flushed and fanned her collar as she looked to discover where she might be. Two enormous braziers spilling fire into pools below flanked a magnificent, marble throne. Torches lined the walls, their flames dancing in the lustrous marble, and an unusual, black banner with green flames hung above the door.

"Xandon!" called Fernus, his voice bouncing off the walls of the mostly empty space.

As if awaiting the summons, a tall, distinguished-looking figure with flowing, white hair and a fiery, green scar slashing one eye entered from a small doorway to the side. Emily thought his scarlet cloak was the most beautiful she had ever seen.

"What do you want this time?" groaned the elven king, his tone weary.

"Hold onto this for me, will you?" Fernus said as he shoved Emily toward Xandon.

"Must I? Lentz!"

The Flame king's personal guard entered and took Emily by the arm.

"We will keep her safe, Fernus," Lentz assured.

"Any other children you'd like us to watch for you, Fernus?" sniped Xandon while picking a speck of lint from the sleeve of his regal red robe.

"Ask and you might receive," toyed the daemon general who then vanished in a blast of black hell fire.

Xandon turned an appraising eye to Emily, his expression inscrutable. "Lentz, her leather garments remind me of those detestable Wood elves. Find her something decent to wear. One of my old robes will do."

The inn was cheap and sparse, and the food even more so. Boryn considered the unusual offerings on his plate, undecided whether to eat or not. *Too bad it's so cold. Otherwise, I could have gone on to the Sand Ocean capital tonight.* He picked up a meatlike bite; his stomach gurgled. He held it out toward Shade who shied away, evidently sharing Boryn's opinion of the fare. Relatively speaking, the bread seemed safe, so Boryn grabbed it and took a bite. The young wolf growled behind him.

"Well, well, well. Look at you, the brave new warrior."

Boryn spun round, reaching for his blades, but Fernus stepped between the boy and his arsenal. The daemon general smiled and patted the pile of six sheathed scimitars. "Managed to scare off a pirate crew without a single cut with your sword! It would have been better had you not drawn one at all. Far more impressive," Fernus goaded as he twirled one of the iron scimitars then stopped to appraise it like a fine work of art, orange eyes glistening.

"What do you want?"

"It's not what *I* want; it's what you want."

"And that is?"

"I hear that you are a compassionate fighter."

The implied question hung in the air.

"At this moment, those you planned to rescue in the Sand Ocean capital are being massacred by pirates. From subject to victim, just like that," Fernus snapped his bony fingers and chuckled lightly. "It seems you will arrive too late."

"And you want me to go save them now?"

"Your chances of playing the hero, er—shall we say, improve if they are not dead before you arrive."

"Why are you telling me this?"

"Mutual interests," Fernus said with a devilish grin.

Before Boryn could raise the question, Fernus blackened and vanished into his own black shadow. Boryn stepped toward the window. A battering, cold wind rattled the pane and sent a shiver down his back. *No reason to bother anyone else with my leaving.* He grabbed his cloak and scimitars, opened the window to an icy blast and crept out, Shade at his heels.

Pulling the cape tight around him as the only foil to the cold, Boryn hurried to the dark quay. He searched for the sandboard and found it lashed to the rails. The board was half again as tall as Boryn, smooth, trim, and slightly curved like a fallen leaf. In the middle was a small hinged mast wreathed in a furled sail. He loosened the bindings, raised the mast, and released the sail.

Instantly, it caught the wind, and Boryn barely grabbed Shade and the mast before the tiny craft zoomed into the waves. Scrambling for balance, Boryn tucked Shade into the satchel that hung across his body. An icy gust blasted the board forward, scraping across rising waves of sand. Wind billowed the small sail, and stars guided him northward while grainy spray and cold bit his skin. He sailed through the moonlight with single focus—reaching the capital as quickly as possible.

The moon crossed the sky, and an orange glow on the horizon signaled his first glimpse of the city. *Why would the pirates burn a city they already control?* As Boryn drew closer, he could hear the occasional anguished cry of someone within. He hit a large wave and used it to propel himself to the stone plateau upon which the capital was built. The board skittered across the rock before grinding to a halt against a stone walk. Boryn tumbled off.

Long legs carried him quickly toward the city gate. One iron panel lay on the ground, unbroken but still useless; the other had been blasted apart and hung in shreds. Boryn shuddered and entered. Ahead stood two men pushing a terrified woman back and forth between them as if it was child's play. They laughed and slashed at her clothing with their blades. Without thinking, Boryn ran toward them, reaching for his dwarven-made scimitars. The pirates glanced his way but ignored him, continuing their cruel game, ending it, in fact. One extended his longsword toward the woman as the other shoved her against the deadly tip. She stumbled into it, powerless against the force of her tormentors. It looked easy the way the sword was swallowed into her chest. She sucked in, breath blunted, then slumped and fell. The pirate kicked her lifeless form to the street, letting his bloodied blade slide free.

"Nooo!" A badly injured man hobbled from a doorway's shadow. Another pirate tackled the easy prey, stabbing the man in the arm and mercilessly walloping his face to a bloody pulp. Shocked at first by the display of unspeakable violence, Boryn stood frozen. *Humans slaughtering humans?* From his battered face, the injured man's eyes searched and found Boryn. The entreating look was the spur Boryn needed, and he burst into action, a blur of unleashed rage.

He sheathed the blue scimitars and traded them for the black-gem blades on his back. "Leave that man alone," he cried, powering toward the assailants with maniacal fury. "Fight someone who can fight back, you bloody cowards!"

The pirates sized up the youthful adversary and began to laugh. Three charged at once, weapons held above their heads. *Axe, scimitar, scimitar.* Without another thought, Boryn shot forward, diving low beneath the swing of a pirate's axe. With his own blade, he sliced up, cutting the axeman from knee to chest. The pirate cried out and fell against Boryn's shoulder, shielding Boryn from a scimitar assault. Boryn shoved the dead pirate's body away to confront the second pirate's scimitar. Boryn blocked then lunged, sending the pirate weapon flying.

"Let's see how you like it," Boryn said as he ran the man through then kicked him to the ground. He spiraled around to face the third charging pirate. Swerving to keep clear of the pirate's outstretched blade, Boryn swept up with his right, severing the pirate's hand, then even as the villain screamed, lunged with the left to cut the cry short by impaling him in the chest. Boryn pulled his blade free and hurried to the side of the brutally beaten man whose hand stretched toward the woman. But it was too late.

Wherever you are, Emily, I hope you are safe.

"Hey, the big, bad laddie has kilt sum'a our own! Watch an' see!" called a pirate as he rounded the corner. In the light of the burning buildings the menacing scene played out: from buildings and alleyways pirates poured into the road where Boryn stood over his victims.

"You should have been preparing," grumbled the daemon.

"Nary a poin' ta it," groaned the pirate lord reclining in the long-misused council room of the Sand Ocean capital.

"You've grown lazy. You aren't even ready should an army arrive to retake the place."

"If'n tha council leaders wer'n't locked in cells b'low me bein' tortured by yer gran' an' luverly friends, I migh' be worried," was the pirate lord's testy retort.

Suddenly, the chamber door burst open. In flew a raging messenger, madness in his eyes. "Cap'n . . . ," the man cried through gasping breaths.

The lord turned a curious though unalarmed eye to the fellow.

". . . Death . . . is comin'!"

An eerie howl swept across the burning city followed almost instantly by an explosion in the antechamber. The palace door blasted inward, splintering, and the messenger went sprawling. The dust cleared. There stood a tall, slender boy, green eyes flaring, bloody, black scimitars in hand. From his satchel peered a wide-eyed wolf pup. The pup howled again and, spinning the scimitars, Boryn swept them side-to-side, the chiseled blades flashing in the firelight. The pirate lord watched, transfixed; he had never seen such weapons or such display of weaponry—especially by a mere boy.

"Leave this city, or you and all of your men will die!"

"Pah! Threaten'd by a wee whelp?"

The messenger lost his remaining shreds of composure and scrambled to his feet. There was something terrifying about the rampaging boy.

"I'm goin' ta destroy ye, mate. Wanna help?" the lord turned to his daemon sidekick but found it gone. "Cowardly daemon!" he muttered before shouting for his men. Dozens of pirates stormed into the room, surrounding Boryn but standing well clear of the ring defined by his whirring blades.

"It would seem that you're the coward," Boryn taunted.

"Wise 'nuf ta use me advantage."

"Then allow me to use mine." Channeling energy into the already powerful black blades, Boryn swung fast, horizontally, in a wide arc. A full circle of unimaginable destruction sliced out, cutting down any pirate unlucky enough to be in the path. The next line of pirates moved in, demanding blood.

Suddenly, it was as if Boryn was one with the scimitars, a whirl of devastation. He leapt up and sliced, sparking blades and dropping bodies: a scimitar cutting through one pirate's chest; landing, spinning low, amputating legs; popping up, slashing faces; rechanneling into one blade, blocking with the other. *Cleave.* The scimitars glowed with energy, and swinging again, Boryn released a new crescent of destructive power. The blast sliced through most of those still standing, splattering blood and matter like paint on the walls.

Boryn reared back as a monstrous spiked ball smashed into the floor in front of him. His eyes chased the length of attached chain to see the pirate lord, handle in one hand and axe in the other. The few surviving pirates backed away; their leader tugged the chain and started the tethered ball circling overhead.

Boryn charged underneath. The pirate lord's axe sailed moments before the chain ball whistled. Boryn crossed his blades above his head, stopping first the axe and then the gigantic flail. He dropped to the floor and rolled to absorb the impact but let his momentum carry him back to his feet. "You can't even get near me. How do you intend to beat me?"

The pirate tugged back his barbed ball, preparing to swing again. Boryn slid one of his black scimitars into his back sheath and withdrew one of the iron ones from his side. The axe swept in; Boryn parried, but the chain ball followed. Boryn stabbed down with the scimitar tip to pin the chain to the floor.

The pirate lord tugged the captured chain then dropped the handle in favor of a mighty, two-handed chop with his axe. Boryn channeled energy into the black-gem blade, and he shot the blade high. A crescent splintered the axe handle, and the axe head flew free. Not beaten, the pirate unsheathed a saber. His eyes bored into Boryn's. "I'm gunna rip ye limb from slimy limb!" he roared, and his eyes turned hollow and black.

Now Boryn called on the time-slowing power of the bracer. He channeled energy into the purple stone. Though the pirate lord shot forward with incredible velocity, jabbing with his saber, the boy disappeared in a blink of amethyst light. The pirate circled fast, blade out, hoping to connect with the invisible attacker while Boryn, time on his side, repositioned for the next assault.

The bracer charge extinguished. Time returned to normal, but Boryn was in position to pounce from behind. He jumped and landed on the lord's shoulders, severing muscle and tendon with an impaling blade. The pirate's arms hung uselessly at his sides. Crazed and undeterred, the pirate turned and ran at the equally manic boy. He kicked with heavy boots, but Boryn sliced first through the kicking leg and then through the other, and the freebooter hit the ground.

Strange, twisted words spewed from the downed pirate's mouth, and his eyes rolled back, showing only white. A smirking, daemonic aura floated out of the body as the pirate let out a blood curdling scream. The daemonic spirit reached into the man who was paralyzed either by horror or by pain. Slowly, the daemon withdrew its hand, bringing with it the ghostly form of the pirate lord. The body paled and died as the pirate lord's soul was extracted, writhing and fighting. Both of the ghostly forms were engulfed in fire and disappeared with a final, tortured scream.

Boryn stared at the pirate's defiled body. He looked from the bloody scimitars to the desecrated city beyond the door. He dropped to his knees, thoroughly spent.

"What have I done?" he said under his breath. Shade crawled from the satchel and rubbed against Boryn's leg.

Footsteps approached from behind, but Boryn paid them no heed. "You did what you could."

Boryn looked up. It was Yarrik, who had followed the boy with a few of his men, unwilling to let the boy face the pirates alone.

"Yeah, but these were humans, and it didn't even faze me."

"They lived to kill and plunder."

"Does that make it right for me to kill them?" Boryn sat amidst the remnants of massacre.

Yarrik turned away. "Men, go check the dungeons to see if anyone is left alive." Yarrik waited until he and Boryn were alone. "Do you want to know why I became a captain?"

Boryn looked at the man without speaking.

"My family lived on an island not far from here. One day we were attacked by pirates, one of this one's crews, in fact. They killed my wife and little girl." Yarrik paused and stiffened. "No, let me get this right. They didn't just kill them; they pinned me to a wall to watch helplessly and then abused them . . . until they died. They left me with this souvenir." He lifted his tunic to show a small scar near his heart. "The fool didn't even know where the heart is, else I might have had the good fortune to go with my family." His laugh was hollow.

Boryn glanced toward the pirate lord's body then back toward Yarrick. "I'm sorry . . ."

"And I am sorry that we are unable to help you as you have helped us."

"The blood of these men stains my hands."

"Their evil, murderous blood! You saw their leader!" Yarrick raged. "He had made a deal with daemons! You are a hero!"

Boryn rose slowly and walked to the ruined door. "Then why do I feel like a murderer?"

Boryn left the palace, pulling up the hood of his cape, shrouding himself from the world. He walked toward the Sand Ocean, looking neither right nor left, Shade tagging along as if sharing his master's burdens.

Engagement

"There must be something we can do."

"We have no idea where Fernus took her," Calny walked from behind the bar, wiping his hands on his apron, and sat down with his friends.

Wenval sighed, "Too bad Emily doesn't have a crystal."

"I'm telling you, he took her to Ranlon." Stevan slammed his fist on the table, rose noisily and paced the floor. "Where else would a daemon take her?"

"All I know is that even with the troops we've assembled, we don't have a chance against the daemons. Too many of them; too few of us."

"Aren't you worried about Emily?" Ranton asked.

Heads pivoted toward Wenval. "Of course I am," the curly-haired boy replied, "but nothing will matter, including Emily, if we let the daemons win. The dwarves have already said 'no' to helping us . . ."

"So what do you suggest?" Laric asked, sounding a little irked.

"Maybe we should see if the Moon elves will join the alliance again," Wenval mused from his barstool perch.

Calny looked at Wenval as if he was deficient. "Not only have we had no contact with them since the first alliance fell apart, but we also have no idea where they live."

"Hold on," Hannah held up her hands. "Elves? I've *heard* of the Moon elves, but that's all. Who are they?"

"Here's the story as I've heard it. The elves used to be a single, unified race—with a very advanced civilization—living on an island lost in the ocean. Before the Daemon War, a group split off, though not a hostile break, to come to Armorica to be guardians of the mainland. This group became known as the Wood elves while those who remained on their home island became known as Moon elves. Later, but still before the Daemon War, there was among the Wood elves a faction that displayed unusual abilities to control fire. These elves were believed to be destructive and evil, so they were persecuted and cast out and are now known as Flame elves."

"So are the elves our friends?" Hannah wanted to understand.

Wenval stopped to think. "The Flame elves sided with the daemons while the Wood and Moon elves were our allies in war. But Calny is right; there hasn't been much contact with any of them since."

"What about the Dark elves?" asked Stevan.

"The Dark elves split during the Daemon War, initially pirates preying on human ships and siding with the daemons. They are a self-absorbed bunch who think they should rule everything, be the master race. When that proved impossible, they settled in the Black Expanse, eventually forming their own civilization—if you can call it that."

"And the Moon elves live nearby?" asked Hannah.

"That's the mystery. Legend has it that they reside on an island south of Dusgoroth called Mercist Isle. The isle stays shrouded in mist and has never been shown on a map." He paused for effect, "And no one has ever returned from a voyage there."

"What makes you think they would help us, even if we could find them?" Stevan pressed.

"Regardless of what they think of humans, I know they hate

the daemons. The elves' history with the daemons is much longer than ours."

Calny interrupted. "It seems like a big risk with little chance of working."

"I can't disagree," Wenval offered. "But at the moment, I'm fresh out of better ideas. And doing nothing means almost sure death."

"That's a reassuring thought," Laric commented then shrugged. "So since you put it that way, we might as well try."

"I'll hire a boat and crew." Surprised eyes turned to Calny who was grinning widely. "This inn has been a respectable maker of coin."

"What if Emily comes back here? Or Boryn arrives while we're gone?" Hannah asked.

"Hannah and I will stay here in case anyone shows up," Stevan offered. "We'll also take care of the Strawberry Mug for you, Calny."

"Thank you, Stevan. But if we aren't back soon, go ahead to Ranlon. We'll find you there," Wenval said. "All right now, everyone. Let's get moving. Gather what you need and meet at the dock near Calny and Laric's house."

When the others were gone, Wenval reached for the crystal marked with *B*; it was cloudy blue. *Troubled.* The young mage left the Strawberry Mug cloaked in uncertainty. *Stay strong, Boryn . . .*

"Why do you answer to Fernus? You're a king, aren't you?" Emily badgered Xandon.

"It's complicated."

She sprawled on the floor, seeing as the only seat in the room was reserved for the king. "So explain. I have time," she pressed while idly shoving food around her plate.

"No," groused Xandon.

"How long are you keeping me here?" She smoothed the scarlet-colored robe Xandon had loaned her, admiring the feel of the fine, silken threads.

Xandon did not reply.

"No reason to be rude." Emily rose. Taking hold of the fire prod, she poked into the brazier.

"Stop that. Lentz, watch her." Xandon left the throne room through the side door.

"Why?" Emily asked.

"That could be asking so many things," Lentz replied smoothly, almost entertained by the girl's persistence.

"Has Xandon always sided with the daemons?"

"As he said, it is very complicated."

"Where did he go?"

"Does it really matter to you?"

"No. I'm curious. That's all."

"The graveyard of his family line," came Lentz' simple reply. "Now please stop asking questions and eat."

"I'm not hungry."

"Then sleep."

"Not tired."

"Here then." Her ten rings jangled as he tossed them skidding across the floor. "Show me how you use those."

"I wouldn't want to hurt you." Her green eyes danced in the flickering firelight.

"A spar will do."

"What will you use?"

"This," he said taking the fire prod from her. He moved to the far end of the marble chamber where there was plenty of room to maneuver. The taller, thinner challenger checked his weapon's balance and took a stance. "Ready when you are."

"If I win, you explain Xandon to me."

"If I win, you remain still and preferably quiet for the rest of your stay."

Emily smiled and ran at her would-be foe, ducking as Lentz feigned a swing at her head. He reversed direction and took a measured swipe at her ducking crown. As pliable as a willow, she bent, planting one hand on the floor, the robe sweeping as her foot spun toward the royal guardian's chin. Lentz tilted his head away and clamped his hand on her ankle. Twisting fast, she pulled her leg free, swept it down like a pendulum, and up and around. But Lentz grabbed again. She sprang from her hands and shoved off Lentz's chest. He stumbled back on his heels. Emily chose that moment to slide the silvery rings onto one hand. Lentz jabbed with the metal poker, and she spun to the side, robe flaring wide, swinging her hand over and down. At the last instant, Lentz pitched sideways, and the vicious strings whizzed by. Again they came, and Lentz launched the poker into the path. The projectile fell to pieces that clattered to the floor.

Tasting victory, Emily sailed toward her unarmed opponent. Lentz smiled and waited, admiring her perfect combination of timing and technique—as well as her grace and beauty. He ducked. The strings whistled overhead. He moved in low to punch but stopped short as her knee crashed into his face, sending him tumbling backward.

Her hands flew to her mouth. "I'm so sorry!"

Lentz chuckled. He wiped his bloodied lip on his sleeve before taking the hand she extended to help him up.

"Ready to fill me in?" she chirped.

Lentz moved to the polished marble wall, leaned against it and slid down. Emily did the same. They sat, quiet but for the sounds of their breathing. Then Lentz began. "About fifty years ago, shortly before the Daemon War, the time had come when one of the king's children would be chosen as successor. At that time, Xandon's father was the king, and only Xandon and his sister remained in the royal bloodline. By tradition, the rite of ascension required a series of trials, each one more difficult than the last. In a way, it seems a cruel system, because often, the successor earns the spot simply by being the last one standing; the others don't survive the trials. But nonetheless, it is the way of the Flame elves.

"Xandon and his sister finished the first trial successfully. They were, in fact, not only brother and sister but also close companions, and they were celebrating their shared victory, scampering through the halls of the palace as children will do. She was so full of life, his sister. So young—and enchantingly beautiful," the old adviser sounded wistful. "Watching her fight was a sight to behold, how she spun fire, like a halcyon, and used it to her advantage. Somewhat like the way you fight."

Lentz cleared his throat. "Well, the princess rounded a corner and bumped into a nasty daemon general named Glacius. The Flame elves and the daemons were allies then, but Glacius was ally to no one. The ice daemon killed the princess on the spot, without so much as a word."

"How could he do something so cruel?"

"No good reason. He later said the girl had 'soiled his robe with her dirty hands,' and she was unfit to breathe the same air as he. Glacius was always cocky and spiteful; even Xandon's father detested him, but he was also afraid of him."

"So why was Glacius allowed in the palace in the first place?"

"As I said, the daemons and the Flame elves were allies—at least that was the story. In reality, it was more like enslavement, and Glacius had come with a message for the king." Lentz sighed; Emily listened.

"Well, Xandon was devastated. And he wanted his father to act against Glacius, and all the daemons in fact. Xandon blames his father for not acting. But whether that was to happen or not, we'll never know, because only a few days later, the king himself was killed at the hands of our known enemy, the Wood king, Weskin.

"Xandon assumed the reign, but he became known as the Sorrowful Prince. And as you might imagine, his distrust of enemies as well as allies runs deep."

"So why does he side with the daemons now?"

"You will not get that answer from me." Lentz's eyes moved toward the door through which Xandon had left.

Xandon bolted upright, a scream shattering his repose, but the Hall of the Eternal Flame was utterly quiet, deathly still. Exquisitely carved statues stood guard at each grave though Xandon's eyes rested on one alone, the figure of the elven princess, forever young. He could still hear her cry . . .

"She's beautiful," came a gentle voice from behind.

Xandon glanced toward the stairs to see the girl. His anger flared then softened.

"Mind if I join you?"

"What are you doing down here?"

"I wanted to see where you had gone."

"Nosey." He stood slowly, burdened.

"Interested."

Xandon tilted his head slightly and brushed off his robe.

"Why do you join with the daemons that killed your sister?"

"It is not your concern."

"Join Boryn. Avenge her."

"It's not that simple."

"Help us destroy them."

"Please, just leave me alone."

"How long until we reach the camp, Luthor?"

"I expect it will come into view very soon."

"You know I've been excited to get there," Dace admitted.

"And why is that?"

"We are about to join the army for the world's last stand!" Dace was earnest. "I guess it just feels . . . important."

Luthor looked toward his clueless second. "What are you expecting? Siege weaponry, honor guards, and multicolored tents?" Luthor bantered.

"Siege weaponry, yes. And tents, of course, but not those fancy ones."

Overhearing the exchange, Ramgis rode alongside them. "A comfortable place to sleep is all I ask," the old general laughed, rubbing his travel-weary back.

"Dace, ride ahead and make sure the accommodations are suited to the esteemed general's tastes," Luthor teased. Turning back to Ramgis, he continued, "I'm sure you will find the armies of the noble Empire to be quite imposing indeed."

Rath joined them. "Do you suppose Boryn and his young flock

have actually been able to recruit many warriors?"

"Warriors, no. Fighters, yes," Luthor answered.

"What do you mean?"

"The imperial villagers are a scrappy bunch but none too fond of staying with a battle plan," Luthor observed. "Plus, so many have been slaughtered by marauding rapi, the ones left tend to be the most . . . unrestrained of the lot." He shook his head. "If the incompetent Emperor had any control over the regular army, maybe we wouldn't have to depend on unruly villagers," Luthor amended with more venom than seemed necessary.

"A miserable leader, that one," Rath agreed.

The Forest of Ranlon emerged in the distance, a finger of black smoke trailing up from its core. The idle chatter ceased as the three leaders came face-to-face with the reality of the challenge ahead. They rode in silence, burdened with anticipation and heartened with hope.

Nearing the gathering place, they noticed a swirling cloud of dust.

"Could the daemons have attacked already?" Ramgis spurred his horse into a gallop. Rath and Luthor chased after.

"Let's hope not."

The fight seemed rowdy, but no weapons were drawn, and there was no sign of daemon or orc, or for that matter, foe of any sort. The recruits were simply brawling among themselves.

"Is this their idea of a good time?"

"Maybe we should join in," Luthor ribbed, and he began rolling up his sleeves.

In disbelief, Ramgis pulled to a halt and wheeled toward the mob. "Men!" he barked. A few men paused, but only for a second.

Grumbling, Ramgis dismounted. He hoisted his golden warhammer and slammed it to the ground. The earth quaked beneath the powerful blow, and the untrained warriors regarded the red-clad knight with new respect. Luthor, Rath, and Dace rode through the crowd, attempting to maintain the momentary calm.

Ramgis called out. "What were your orders?"

"To move near Ranlon and wait."

"You call this 'waiting'?"

"He tried to take my food," hollered one man.

"He punched me for no good reason," said another.

Before matters erupted again, Ramgis demanded, "Who is in charge here?"

"I am." Six hands shot in the air.

"I'd guess that means no one," Rath said under his breath.

"My name is Ramgis, and you will be taking orders from me beginning now. Anyone object?" Ramgis scanned the life-hardened faces. A hand patted his bald head. The old commander wheeled angrily; Luthor sat on his horse, grinning.

"You were right, Rath. It is really smooth."

Nails against steel, Tarn drummed his claws on the arm of his imposing black throne. Here in the presence chamber, the light slanting through the single window was long and harsh, and colors in the glass dome were dimmed by the shadow of late afternoon. Three daemon messengers stood before the daemon king, grinning weakly and knees quaking, with hopes their leader would appreciate the news they brought to the citadel but terrified in case he didn't.

"So the humans are gathering outside Ranlon? Interesting."

"That Mhinbron boy is orchestrating it."

Tarn laughed. "Hmm. Well, in that case, I suppose we owe him our gratitude. Bringing them all together—serving them up on a platter, one might say. It only makes our job easier."

"Tarn, what if they defeat us?"

"Are you daft?" Tarn backhanded the trembling messenger with a tattered, outstretched wing. "Hah! A ragtag bunch of humans?" He snapped each word.

"Many pardons, lord and master." The messenger wilted beneath the king's reprimand.

"And when do your sources say the attack by this motley crew will begin?"

"As early as tomorrow, perhaps."

"With unlimited numbers of daemons at my beck and call, and five portals at the forest edge to give us continual flow of reinforcements, our line is . . . invincible. Yes, we are ready. Let them come."

"Tarn, what of this boy Boryn?" The unusually even voice came from the far, dark side of the presence chamber.

"What of him? He's nothing but a nuisance to me. A fly to be swatted." Tarn sniffed to underscore his disdain.

"You know, of course, that the boy has struck down two of our generals and now carries their black blades. Does that not give you pause?" chuckled the flame-haired general, heels clicking as he crossed the room to stand before the daemon king.

"I know all about that firebrand. Do you think me the fool? We have been watching his every move. Frankly, I'm sick to death of him. I'll be glad when this is over."

Fernus' silence and wry smile spoke volumes.

"You dare to suggest a human should put fear into the king's heart?" the messenger blurted.

Fernus snapped his fingers, and the messenger burst into black flame. "I am merely saying," he continued unabated, "the boy is rather . . . tenacious. He has a habit of not dying."

"Yes." Tarn held a clawed hand to his chin, "But it has come to my attention as well how often your path crosses his. What game are you playing, Fernus?"

"There is no game." Fernus held out his hands in deference and bowed his head. "I would never betray my own king."

"Your loyalty is noted."

"Well," Fernus said, wrapping it up, facetiousness veiled. "Right as always, Tarn. Allowing the humans to assemble on your own doorstep was a stroke of brilliance. One could not imagine a more propitious situation."

"I assume you and the generals will be present?"

"Of that you can be sure." Black flames crept up from the floor and engulfed Fernus' body. The daemon general blackened and disappeared into his own shadow.

Boryn elbowed his way through the tangle of vines and trees, plunging deeper into the jungle. Shade nipped at his heels, bedraggled and ready for a rest. *So much for 'just head south and you'll get back.'*

Having no clear options, Boryn decided to yield to Shade's request. He folded his long legs and sat down at the base of a giant fig tree. He crossed his arms and propped them atop his knees. But rest proved elusive. Rather than twisted foliage, he saw broken human limbs. Instead of swirling mist, he saw ghostly souls wrenched from tortured bodies. In place of calming warmth, he felt raging fire. Instead of a way out, he saw only darkness. *And he called me a hero . . .*

"Accept the compliment and move on."

Alert, Boryn scoured the dense growth for the words' source. Seeing no one, he said, "Hello? Where are you?"

Silence was the only reply. Just then, a strange boy dropped from the leafy overhang, landed lightly, and sprang upright, turning glittering, golden eyes to Boryn. "I don't see the problem here. You saved a country." The oddly familiar visitor waved his arm grandly.

"And so you're called a hero."

"But all those men I murdered . . ."

"Get over it. Bad stuff happens to bad people."

"Still, they were human beings, just like me!"

"That's right—just like you. They'd have done the same to you, given the chance. No difference."

"What? That's not what I meant," Boryn protested. "Of course there's a difference! Those men found joy in torture."

"Well—"

"When I fight, I fight for what's right!"

"That's what you always tell me."

It was an odd reply. Boryn looked at the boy closely. "Who could say that ridding the world of daemons is not a just cause?"

"Through your eyes, or those of the daemons?"

"You're twisting my words. It's so confusing. Nothing is a clear as it seems."

"Ah."

A heavy quiet lingered.

"Are you saying that with my fighting and my blades I'm no different than the pirates or the daemons?"

"That, my friend, is your question."

Boryn jerked, his face buried in mud, a warm tongue licking his ear. He sat up, wiped his face on his sleeve, and examined the strange exchange. *Was that a dream?*

The wolf's hackles rose, and Boryn instinctively scooped Shade and scrambled up a thick, woody vine. Moments later, the ground cracked open. Boryn vaulted higher, grabbing a tree limb to pull up to a higher perch. From out of the cleft climbed an enormous dark-skinned figure. A strong, thick hand brushed back the hood of its fitted, white cloak, uncovering a shiny, hairless pate.

Boryn sat breathlessly still, but without hesitation, the giant turned his eyes directly to the place where Boryn crouched among the boughs. *Don't be distracted.*

"Who are you?" Boryn demanded.

"I am Tharrus." The daemon spoke with pride.

"I killed that sadistic swine."

"You killed the last one. I am the new general of earth."

"So if you're a mere replacement, doesn't that make you lower still in the pecking order?"

"You shouldn't talk about things that you don't understand," replied the daemon with studied calm. The daemon, bigger and bulkier than an orc, held out his arm and uncurled his fingers. A colossal, black crystal fired out in the shape of a battleaxe.

Boryn unsheathed his dwarven scimitars but held back. Tharrus drove the axe into the ground, clods of dirt sprayed into the air. Boryn did not budge. Next, Tharrus swept his axe upward back-to-front, gouging the earth and firing the excavated rock toward Boryn. The rubble reformed as a solid pillar that clouted against Boryn's perch. The impact caused the boy to lose his balance, which he regained, but not before he lost his grip on the blue scimitars, and they went flying. Tharrus was gaining a foothold up the vine when Boryn withdrew the black-gem blades, but as the daemon spidered toward Boryn, his general's cloak became ensnared. Boryn, prepared to use the advantage, shot to the ground like a released spring while Tharrus struggled. But the more the daemon fought to get free, the more the vines twisted round him until he hung like a bloated moth in a web.

Confusion crossed the daemon's wide face, and he gave up the fight. Suddenly, hanging upside down but still face-to-face with Tharrus was a wiry little man, his head clean shaven except for a narrow brush of blood-red hair running forehead to nape. His torso was unclothed, and his breeches were little more than shreds.

The giant daemon bent his head back and used his sturdy neck like a firing mechanism to slam his head toward the man's sharp but placid face. The nimble figure swung to the side in the nick of time, and the daemon's forehead slammed into the pillar instead, and the daemon's body plunged to the dirt.

The little man, agile as a lemur, dropped to his hands while the daemon wobbled to his feet then lumbered toward Boryn with a mighty hand set to grab the boy's throat. At the same instant, the wiry man scampered up Tharrus' back and vaulted from his shoulder to the top of the daemon's upraised axe. Tharrus roared and flung the butt of the axe against the pillar. The man spiraled to the wrist that wrapped Boryn's throat and smashed the hand to the ground, shattering the bones.

"Quit jumping around!" The daemon boiled, veins bulging in his thick neck.

The wild, little man dove to the side as Tharrus' good fist punched the air where had stood the man moments before. Springing off of his hands, the man twisted and kicked, one foot rocketing into the side of Tharrus' head to propel the far larger but significantly outmatched daemon through the rock pillar. With that, the dark-skinned daemon dropped like a rock before vanishing into its own shadow.

The oddity landed on one hand and spun around until he was sitting on the ground, legs wrapped together. He brushed his hands together as if to say, "That's done," then looked at Boryn wordlessly.

Boryn was equally speechless but finally found his voice to say, "Well that was interesting."

The man replied with a jerky little nod.

"Who are you?"

"I am me."

"Who is *me*?"

"Not you."

"I'm not in the mood for riddles," Boryn muttered as he stooped to retrieve his dropped scimitars.

"Nor am I."

"So what is your point?"

"Not all problems are solved with a blade."

"Yeah, I know."

"Do you?"

Boryn fixed his gaze on the impassive man. "Maybe not."

The edgy little man paced in front of Boryn. He didn't say a word for several minutes. At last, he spoke.

"Lulz."

"Huh?"

"Name's Lulz."

Boryn nodded.

"I suppose you like fast?"

"Yeah, why?"

"Want to be as fast as any steed?"

"Sure."

"I call it 'nature walk,' but to do it one must find the center of energy within oneself."

"Sounds like a pain."

"Sit."

Begrudgingly, Boryn sat and watched Lulz.

"Now pay attention to the way this feels. I will balance for you, and if you prove to be a suitable student, you will remember the way the energy flowed through you." Lulz placed his hands on Boryn's shoulders and closed his eyes. Boryn felt nothing—really nothing—around him, not even the ground upon which he was sitting. Then he felt everything: the soft earth beneath him, a whisper of air brushing his face, the even distribution of energy in his core, and a penetrating peace.

"Now stand and do it yourself."

Boryn stood. He shut his eyes and let the power flow. Making miniscule adjustments, he found the spot of perfect equilibrium.

"Now, take what you feel, force it all into your legs and come to me."

Boryn followed the instructor's orders. Before he could blink, he was in Lulz' face.

"You are smart. You learn fast—fast," the jungle man chortled at his own wit.

If I have to be a prisoner, *this isn't so bad.* Emily lounged on the silken chaise in the elegant antechamber where Lentz had locked her. Her eyes roamed the luxurious accommodation, the lustrous red rug and gleaming black marble walls, then circled up to the ceiling's golden dome where flickering firelight painted moving pictures. She stretched, basking in the pleasant warmth imparted by flaming torches. *I hope Stevan isn't too worried . . . and Boryn, too. Mostly, I hope everyone is safe.* The door rattled behind a peppering of short, fast raps.

"Emily, may I come in?" She recognized Lentz' voice.

"Of course."

"Gather your things," he said with urgency while waving her out the carved doorway.

"Why?"

"You're leaving."

"What if I like it here?" she said, lingering on the soft cushion.

"So you don't wish to return to your friends?"

"I can't go like this," she said, holding out the sides of Xandon's old—though beautiful—robe.

"You don't have any choice. Xandon burned the leather you arrived wearing. Couldn't stand the sight of it. Now, you must hurry."

"You're betraying the daemons, aren't you?"

"To be precise, it's Xandon, but he's gone ahead to divert attention."

"Why are the two of you taking such a risk?"

"Hold on." Abruptly, Lentz grabbed the girl around the waist, encircling her fully in his strong arms, at which time, the arms became flames. The fire engulfed her, but it was different than when Fernus did it. This time, she felt an overwhelming sensation of comfort, and she burned away to reappear a heartbeat later at the gates of Dusgoroth.

Her smile was genuine as she turned to the Flame elven guard. "Thanks to Xandon, and to you as well, Lentz. I hope we will meet again."

Before Emily could say more, Lentz burst into flame, leaving her behind when he rematerialized at the rim of a steaming volcano deep in the Fyrfang Mountains. Through waves of intense heat, Lentz could see his king and the daemon general on an isle in the magma basin. They stood together, Xandon and Fernus, surrounded by bubbling, red lava, separated by no more than a sword's length.

Rapid, wavering strides carried Lentz to his king's side where he knelt respectfully.

"Where is the girl, Xandon?" Fernus demanded.

"A trade, perhaps?"

"What do you have to offer that I could possibly want more than that girl?"

Xandon withdrew a large object from beneath his cloak and extended it toward Fernus.

Fernus' face clouded, and for the blink on eye, he hesitated before the glowing, purple orb.

"The Morpheic Orb as a trade for a girl's freedom?"

Xandon arched one eyebrow.

"You do remember what this orb releases?" Fernus laughed,

finding it funny.

"Indeed."

"How did it come into your unworthy hands?"

"That is none of your concern," Xandon replied.

"Personally, I would rather you hadn't found it. But it *will* be of great use to us."

"As suspected."

Fernus reached for the extended orb. "And you remember, of course, that we are all ordered to stay away?"

"And you, Fernus, are worse than a nagging wife."

"There are those who make a habit of *not* following orders."

Xandon offered a defiant salute, but Fernus had already vanished into a shadowy swirl of black flames.

"We were worried sick!" Hannah exclaimed, thrilled to see Emily return unharmed. The fair-haired girl smiled with relief. "And where did you get that robe? It's magnificent!"

"I'll tell you all about it, but first tell me . . . where is everyone else?" Emily asked, concerned to see only Hannah and Stevan at the Strawberry Mug.

"Boryn we have yet to see," Stevan answered. "The others went looking for help, and I don't want to alarm you, but they should have been back by now. Tomorrow, we're moving on to Ranlon to wait there."

A brief shower left the jungle sultry, a condition well-suited to Boryn's foul humor. Brooding, he sized up the knee-high monkey gamboling in front of him.

"You want me to beat up a cute little monkey?"

"Only if you can."

"Shouldn't I fight something bigger?"

The odd, little man called Lulz stuck two fingers in his mouth and whistled. An enormous, black-haired ape came crashing through the wet underbrush into the clearing. "Is this what you had in mind?"

"I'll stick with the monkey to start."

As solid as a boulder, the ape plopped to the ground, watching the monkey and the boy.

"Then begin," Lulz said.

Boryn tilted his head to the side, appraising the spindly, brown animal. In like manner, the monkey cocked its head, examining the boy. Boryn was thinking he was almost glad the man had taken his blades when the monkey sneezed and shook its little head.

"Why do you want me to hurt it?" Boryn wanted to know, eyeing Lulz suspiciously.

The monkey fired forward and coiled its tail around Boryn's ankle. Boryn's legs shot out from under him when the monkey tugged, and before he knew what hit him, he was seat-first in a mud hole. The monkey pranced backwards and clapped its hands together, chattering with glee. Not amused, Boryn climbed to his feet, wiping the slime from his breeches.

"Always keep your eye on your opponent."

"I figured that out, thanks."

Three swift bounds, and the monkey scrambled from ground to tree to Boryn's back where it clung with piercing nails. Boryn let out a sharp, pained yelp.

When the monkey dropped at his feet, Boryn stepped toward it and kicked. The nimble creature dodged aside and like an electric shock, circuited up his leg, torso, and shoulder before delivering a surprise poke to the eyes with tiny balled fists. Boryn teetered backward to the tune of the man's annoying words.

"Become the monkey."

The monkey shinnied down the same course, halting at Boryn's feet. Patiently, it awaited Boryn's next move. The boy kicked, and the monkey jumped. Under the foot and out with the planted one it went, and Boryn was mud-bound again.

The odd man reiterated, "*Be* the monkey."

The boat rocked mightily, and Wenval held his churning stomach. His cloak hem jiggled as he bent over a small work desk in the captain's meager quarters. A hanging lantern swayed overhead, struggling to keep its light on the map open across the table's pocked surface. *Where would that mist-clad isle hide?* He searched for clues.

The cabin door slammed against the back wall when the ship lurched. Wenval's head snapped up, but Ranton, reclining on the berth in a trancelike state, didn't move.

Laric bound in on steady sea legs. "Can you believe it? Just us four on our own adventure!"

"I just hope we can find the elves," Calny said.

"Hey, Ranton!" Laric called with childish exuberance.

"Ranton's not home right now. Can I take a message for him?" Wenval teased.

"Where do you suppose he goes when he looks like this?" Calny really wanted to know.

Laric shrugged and grabbed Ranton by the shoulder and shook him.

"What?" Ranton asked, blinking his eyes and joining their presence.

"Do you think we'll find them?"

"Who?"

"The elves, you oaf," Laric *thwacked* Ranton on the head.

Ranton snapped, "If you let me and Wenval focus."

"Wenval and me . . . ," muttered the scholarly, young mage.

"How much do you know about this crew?" Laric turned to his twin.

"Not much. Why?"

"Well, I found this flag." Laric held up a black banner, emblazoned with a bright, white skull.

"Calny, you hired pirates?" Wenval exclaimed.

"It's not exactly the kind of thing a crew promotes when they're trying to get hired."

"'Scuse me, lads." There was a tap on the doorframe. "The cap'n'd like a word wit' ya."

Almost immediately, a handful of sailors surged in, cutlasses in hand, followed by a particularly wizened pirate wearing a once-distinguished black cloth hat atop his balding head.

"Well, now, I'm ta be givin' ya two options. Giv'us the rest a yer gold and join us, or we take th' rest a yer gold—an' yer lives. Now, us? We're preferrin' th' second option." The crew mimicked the captain's hearty laugh.

"Cap'n?"

"Aye?"

The first mate pointed to their feet. Thick fog frothed through the open door and enshrouded their feet in its puffy blanket. The pirate faces paled.

Turning the moment of distraction to profit, Wenval ever so slowly backed toward their weapons. Keeping his hands hidden in the rising fog, he pushed blade and bow toward Laric and Ranton.

"Oy! Ye scalawags! They be makin' fer th' weapins!" The pirates ran at them, and Wenval wobbled. All of a sudden, he felt dizzy, disoriented. He heard whispers all around him. The room went black, but the drone continued. His imagination swirled in a kaleidoscope of color, and the whisper swelled to rhythmic chanting. The language was unknown to him, and yet the voices seemed to say his name. Lights fired in his body, and he felt an incredible, arcane energy surge through his limbs. He blinked his eyes open. The cabin was blasted away, leaving him exposed on the deck. A rippling half-sphere of water mushroomed over the four boys, and Wenval saw Laric, Calny, and Ranton looking around wide-eyed.

"What in the world was that?" Calny asked. They looked from one to the other with equal parts confusion, fear and awe.

The barrier dissipated, and the boys found themselves ringed by tall, slender figures dressed in pristine, white armor, clouded in mist, bows up, and arrows nocked.

"We found 'em!" Laric whispered.

"Or they found us . . ."

Wenval glanced at the gems at his side and noticed that Laric's and Ranton's were blackening. "We mean no harm," Ranton, the most powerful looking of the boys, said. "We only wish to find help."

"Elves helping humans? Perhaps long ago, but we'd never stoop so low now."

"Please just listen to us," pleaded Wenval.

"You trespass on our lands, and now you must die to protect the safety of our people."

A black figure shot out of the fog. A foot crashed into the side of an elf's head, sending it overboard. Another elf turned as the nimble figure landed in a spin, swiping the elf's feet out from under it. An elven arrow fired wayward when its archer was tossed into the deep. And others ran for cover as the dervish spun to a stop in front of the human group. As if on cue, the fog cleared, revealing a ship pulled alongside—an elven one by the look of it—the entire crew incapacitated. Wenval reeled as the figure in the long, tattered cape slowed into focus.

"Boryn?"

"Wenval?"

"Boryn!"

"Where am I?" laughed the boy, steadying himself.

"Didn't take you long to spring into action!" Wenval teased. "We're somewhere near the isle of the Moon elves."

"But wait a minute," Laric squinted. "You don't know where you are? So . . . how did you *get* here, Boryn?"

"I have no idea . . ."

"Wenval, what are you grinning about?" Ranton asked.

Wenval's grin held a healthy measure of guilt. "Remember when I replaced all of our gems?"

All nodded and waited expectantly.

"I was trying to integrate a teleportation spell. I thought it might come in handy if someone got into trouble." Wenval looked only a little sheepish.

Boryn slapped Wenval on the back, and lively greetings passed all around. About that time, Shade popped his head from Boryn's satchel and bounded clumsily to the ground.

"And who is this?" asked Ranton stooping as close to the wolf pup's level as his bulky frame would allow.

"The newest Shadow Crusader. Shade's his name. Mind if he joins?"

Delighted with the attention, Shade tumbled and frisked for his new friends.

"Wenval, I am truly amazed by your blossoming magic skills. But can you do anything—productive—with these tricks of yours?" chuckled Boryn.

Wenval waggled his eyebrows and cracked an impish grin, "You never know!"

"What are we doing here?" Boryn inquired.

"Searching for the Moon elves. Thought they might be of some help."

"Judging from my reception on their ship, I'm not sure how eager they'll be to lend us a hand," laughed Boryn.

"I see the isle in the distance."

The others followed Ranton's pointing finger, seeing nothing.

Intrigued, perplexed, they turned back toward Ranton who grinned, "I'll guide the way."

"Maybe we should take the elves' boat," Boryn suggested. The pirate ship on which they stood listed dangerously. "What happened here, anyway?"

"Wenval blew everything apart," Laric answered.

"New spell, professor?"

"It was so incredible!" Ranton described. "Wenval didn't say a word. Just floated up in the air and curled up in a ball. When he stretched back out, a blast of energy ripped through the ship!"

The group turned its collective head to Wenval, expecting explanations, to be greeted instead by a hearty shrug of the shoulders and a nibble to the lip.

"What's *that* all about, Wenval?" Boryn probed.

"Truth be told, I haven't a clue. But you can be sure I'll be digging into the old magicians' manuscripts as soon as we get home," he said, eyes twinkling with anticipation.

Head bowed and bandaged leg extended like a pole to one side, Boringer knelt before King Fazrin, "O King, I am mos' pleased ta present ta ye the treasures we reclaimed fer th' livin'."

Pushing wooden carts heavily laden with gold, the treasure hunters approached the makeshift throne, a wooden bench beneath the canopy of a tent. Bret, separate from the others, came forward with the precious dragon hide draped across his forearms.

Fazrin stared speechless and reached out to stroke the exquisite scales. "Ye've done well. How can I repay this gift?"

"I did replenish me axe supply," Boringer smiled modestly and touched the pouch on his back. "And there is a li'l somethin' else I woul' like ta ask o' ye."

"Ask it now."

"O King, I humbly beseech thee t' answer me two requests."

"How coul' I deny ya when ya present gifts such as these!"

Boringer continued. "Me first request is that some o' me boys and me be allowed to assist in fightin' the daemons, and second, that you pay a visit to the Moon elves requestin' their aid in the fight as well."

"Ah, me friend Boringer, ye seek much. Las' time a dwarf spoke to an elf, t'was with our axe." The king shifted in the hard chair.

"I beg that ye set yer grudges aside as we did fifty years ago. More'n our race is at stake; the whole world's in peril."

"Tell me, why is it ye're so eager ta stand alongside the humans, Boringer?"

"Boryn already saved our race from sure death—even after we tried ta execute 'im for bein' with the daemons. He deserves our respect."

"Does 'e deserve our lives as well?"

"If we do no' stop 'em, the daemons'll find us, too. 'Tis only a matter of time. Far better it is ta destroy one enemy in the field than face two at our door."

"A second enemy?"

"I believe 'The Four' are released."

Fazrin's expression telegraphed his dismay. "Yer reasonin'?"

"I found the Morpheic Orb at the mausoleum we raided. One o' me boys was fool enough ta take it. To me own good fortune, I realized tha' it was a copy. A mere glass replacement . . ."

"How is it tha' ye discovered this?"

"I broke it, and nothin' happen'd."

"Such a risk!"

"I can assure ya t'was no brave act. It was an acciden' and a mighty frightenin' one at tha'."

"The unpleasant result is the same—"

"—except fer the bystanders." Boringer heaved a sigh of relief. "So I'm figurin' the real Morpheic Orb has been found and taken."

"Tha' is most troublin'; I see yer poin'. I will alert the Moon elves ta the possible danger and request their aid. Perhaps they'll be so grateful fer the warnin' that they'll give us wha' we seek. And you, Boringer, ye may join with the human forces but with no more than the warriors ye took inta th' swamp. The rest are needed here to protect us in our search fer a new home."

"But tha' is hardly twenty warriors—"

"'Tis all I can spare at this time, Boringer."

"Thank you, O King." Using his axe handle like a crutch, Boringer pushed himself up and hobbled away.

Bret rushed to his side. His voice was muffled and shaky. "Boringer, are ye serious tha' 'The Four' are ou' an' abou'?"

"Aye, it's comin', and there's no doub' abou' that." Boringer's hands crawled deep into the comfort of his pockets.

Bret sputtered and spewed and grabbed a loose stone off the ground. Angrily, he sent it skittering. "Why can no' the dead jus' stay bloody dead, eh?"

Boringer's whole body was involved in the shrug. "I do no' know." Then he straightened as tall as possible and thumbed his helmet for good luck. "Now, be off ta tell the boys ta gather their gear and get ready ta march. We're goin' to Ranlon. It's time we slay us some daemons."

"Finally, some real fightin'!"

Boringer turned back to the king. "Permission to Stone March, O great King?"

"If ya think yer boys can handle it."

Boringer beamed, ripped the dressing from his leg and ran limping to join the dwarves gathered around Bret. "For . . . mation!" Boringer barked. The dwarves grabbed their weapons and linked arms to make a tight box, Boringer in the middle. "We're ta be the proud representatives o' the entire dwarven race in this figh' against the daemons, so le's send 'em righ' back ta hell and show those humans who the real warriors be!"

The small dwarven force roared mightily, pounding chests and shields with courage and pride.

"Stan' clear!" cried Bret.

"Stone March Rune!"

Each using his own weapon, the dwarves drew individual parts of a single, large rune on the ground.

"Ready. And . . . Stone March!" Calling out as one voice, they slammed their hands upon the glowing, golden rune. The ground exploded upward in an enormous cloud of dust and debris.

Shadows swirled *around the man and filtered through his cotton-white hair and beard, embracing him in a blanket of darkness. His body slammed to the floor, the blackness of his nightmare twisting his white robes, tangling them around him. Before him stood a tall, lanky figure holding two scimitars. The entire being was black, not a single detail was visible. But then from the blackness appeared piercing golden eyes. "See what you let live. Look what you created!"*

"He is not evil," the old man insisted.

"Then why are you dreaming that I am?"

"This is not a dream. I am a healer; I know all about these things. Someone is manipulating this dream. Plus, I recognize you. You are not the boy I rescued from the streets and sent outside of this city to be protected. Nor are you the Boryn who's off again fighting daemons."

"He is not the one manipulating. I am." An orange-eyed, flame-haired figure emerged from the depths.

Scruffy turned toward the white-cloaked daemon general whose arms were outstretched as if in supplication. At his waist was wrapped an orange cincture hung with keys. "Who are you?" Scruffy asked.

"Fernus . . . General Fernus. . . . I want information about young Mhinbron."

"Why should you care? You only want to kill him."

"If you were speaking to any other daemon, you would be correct. I, however, have more interesting plans for that boy."

"You want to make him into that, don't you?" Scruffy pointed to the golden-eyed, scimitar-wielding creature.

"Heh! Not exactly, although that would be a possible outcome."

"Boryn will never turn into that; his will and spirit are too strong."

"But if the sole purpose of his enemies is to break him, find his triggers . . . Who knows what might happen?"

"I venture to guess you intend to use him."

"Yes." Fernus' voice rolled like thunder. "We have the same goal, Boryn and I, so I think we ought to work together despite our disparate loyalties," Fernus said as a chair lifted out of the floor behind him, and he reclined comfortably.

"What is your goal?"

"It would spoil the fun if I told you now, wouldn't it? So, tell me, am I to learn anything about him from you, or shall I seek elsewhere?"

"I refuse to help you. Forgive me if I refuse those who wrest control of my dreams and kill for pastime."

"A pity, really. Well, even though you won't help me, I'll be nice enough to show you something interesting. Enjoy the show." Fernus stood and bowed, bursting into black flame and burning away along with the dark world.

The healer was in an open meadow at the edge of a road. A rock flew past his head, striking a tree ahead of him. Reflex caused the healer to duck, then he turned to see a boy, young and well shy of manhood, wandering alone down the road, kicking rocks and tossing a few.

Boryn came to a place where two roads met. He stopped at the crossroads; ahead lay the quiet town where Scruffy had arranged for him to live. The boy grinned impishly, and turned right. "I'll see what's that way." And he set off.

Then Scruffy was awake. *Headstrong even then.* He shook his head, his smiled tinged with concern. *That strength will serve you well, Boryn.*

What's taking Boryn so long? Ramgis was tired of the wait as were the other warriors in camp. The veteran commander sensed that time was growing short. He looked toward the distant forest; the infection spread farther each day. Fire-charred skeletons of chestnut, beech, and oak stood like crippled sentinels safeguarding the daemons' evil citadel. Blackened branches twisted against a red sky, not from the setting sun, but from the fire raging in the forest's heart, always burning but never consuming, held at bay until . . .

An explosion startled the waiting warriors. Men leapt to their feet, weapons drawn, and turned backs to the forest in the direction of the sound. A dusty cloud erupted on the ridge of the knoll, and Emily, Stevan, and Hannah hurried over to see what the commotion was about. When the dust settled, a small force of heavily armored soldiers came into view.

"Rath!" Ramgis called.

"Got it." Rath jumped astride his horse and cantered toward the group.

Ramgis watched as Rath stooped to talk to the visitors. With a wry grin on his face, Rath returned to camp, the new arrivals assembling to march behind. "At least they're on our side," Rath said, approaching Ramgis.

"Who are they?"

"Ever heard of Ones-of-the-Earth?"

"As in dwarves?"

"Yup."

"Those are dwarves?"

"The bearded wonders in the flesh," laughed Rath.

"I thought dwarves were all but gone from our lands . . ."

The stubby, yellow-bearded leader of the dwarven company came running into camp, his horned helmet cockeyed, closely trailed by another, wiry in build, baggy-eyed and mousy-bearded. The rest of the dwarves followed, and the lot fell to the ground, laughing and panting.

"Boringer?"

The dwarf calmed his breathing and looked skyward into the face of a husky man with a familiar, hairless head. Boringer's bushy, yellow eyebrows popped skyward. "Ye're still alive?"

"Hell of a way to greet an old friend!" chuckled the Blood Knight.

"Ramgis!" exclaimed the dwarf. He leapt up to clang his armored gauntlet against the Blood Knight commander's. "How 'ave ya been?"

"Fine. But tell me, what are you dwarves doing here?"

"We wan' ta be a help to that fella Boryn. Ye know 'im? Is he hidin' out someplace near here?" It was then that he saw Emily, and a smile of recognition lit his face.

"Have you seen Boryn," she asked, "or the other Shadow Crusaders?"

"No' since ever'one left Raz Kiri."

"We're all waiting for him, as a matter of fact—and at least some of us are wearying of the wait," Ramgis said peevishly.

Rath slapped Ramgis on the back with characteristic good humor. "Boryn will be here soon enough, the action will begin, and then you'll be whining about your old, aching back, pleading for just a few more minutes in the sack."

"Well, good then. At leas' we're in the righ' place. We'll 'ave time ta catch up an' prepare, an' maybe while we wait, we can build somethin'," the dwarf kindled with excitement.

"Build something?"

Boryn led the way, plucking a path up the treacherous slope, moist and slippery in the mist. Every few steps he stopped to help the others, except Ranton who made out just fine on his own.

"I told you he couldn't sail a ship." Calny's accusation was blistering. The elven boat, a gaping hole in its hull, lay far below, piled against the rocky shore.

Laric barked back. "I got us here, didn't I?"

"Yeah, into the side of a cliff."

Boryn reached the bluff and braced himself to pull the others the final few steep steps.

"What are we going to do about the elves we left tied up in the captain's quarters?" Wenval asked climbing over the brink.

"Bargaining power?" Boryn suggested while pulling Laric to the top. "I have no intention of letting them free if all they want to do is kill us."

"What's with elves and wanting us dead?" Calny asked, meaning it rhetorically, but Wenval, still on all fours and looking ahead, spoke in earnest.

"Meaning?"

The others wheeled around to see cocooned in cloudy vapor a corps of well-armed Moon elves, weapons drawn and ready to attack. The boys stood perfectly still, facing the small company.

One of the elves, his white armor ornamented with gold and holding his golden sword high, took a step forward. In a loud, high-pitched voice, he announced, "You desecrate our lands and slay our soldiers, and for that you will die."

The officer lowered the weapon, and the elven archers drew back their bowstrings.

"First you lose the orb, and now you get us lost!"

"That's very unfair of you. It was not my fault. Someone took it."

"Until we figure out where it went, the results are the same. We're scr—"

"I won't hear such talk!" Quaswyn threw their hands to their ears. "And why am I responsible for our whereabouts, unaccounted as they may be?"

"You're the one who said Ranlon's this way." Marlok pointed with the right hand. "Calny said any fool could find it."

"No. I pointed that way." Quaswyn swung the arm around.

"It doesn't matter now, because neither of us has a clue where we are."

"I do."

Marlok waited.

"We are in a forest."

"An observation of a true genius!"

"Now we'll never find the others," Quaswyn wailed. "I miss them sooo much."

In the distance, Marlok noticed something shining through the trees. "What is that?" he pointed.

"A shiny tree?"

A shadow shot through the bushes behind them.

Marlok shut their eyes then reopened them in search of heat signatures. A bright, white light whizzed by, blurred even in the thermal vision.

"Did you see that? What was it?"

"I haven't a clue," Quaswyn said petulantly. "I have never seen, heard or read of anything like it."

Marlok blinked back his regular vision to see a tiny creature similar to a goblin but golden skinned, cleaner, and with a less pointed nose. The impish being tilted its head sideways, scratching its head with a bony, little finger.

"On further inspection, I believe that would be an olan."

"Olan!" squeaked the thing, pointing behind it and shaking its head as if to say no.

Marlok strode past the creature toward the glistening area, but he was stopped by a solid club to the knee. He shrieked, and they fell to the ground while the olan waggled its head.

"Olan . . . ," repeated the golden-skinned creature crossing its arms, club in hand.

"This must be one of their sacred groves," Quaswyn conjectured. "They guard them ferociously."

"Evidently," Marlok replied, rubbing their aching knee. "So what's an olan?"

"Olans are creatures of the forest and relatives, but only distantly, of the goblin; that's why they look so similar. Each 'tribe' lives in its own grove, each one with a sort of spiritual quality. Humans deemed olans a threat and burned their groves, slaughtering the olans along with their homes."

"The little bastards are so fast—how did the humans catch them at home?"

"Set the grove aflame, the olans die, for the magic of the grove fuels them. Without the grove, the olans cannot survive."

"So this one is defending its grove?"

"So it would seem . . ."

"There's another interesting way they have of protecting themselves."

"And what's that?"

Before Quaswyn could answer, the olan held out a bony little hand, and purple energy spiraled around its arm and poured into its palm where it formed into a tiny, vaporous ball. The glob smacked them in the forehead; their vision twisted inward like the turn of a kaleidoscope before righting itself, except now they were lying face up in a meadow of tall grass. Before moving, they circled their eyes trying to see where they might be but spied nothing familiar. Off to one side they could see part of a building. Warily, they lifted up on one elbow to see a small stone fort surrounded by tents rising from an open field.

"You were saying?"

"They teleport intruders away, sending the intruders wherever they wanted to go."

"I wonder where on earth that might be?" Marlok stood up and limped toward the unfamiliar fort.

They backed as far as they could, a mere sliver of ground separating the Shadow Crusaders from the cliff, the rocks and the swirling sea below.

"Bloody elves," muttered Calny.

"*Stop!*" boomed a voice through the fog. The elven army spun, a few dropped their weapons immediately, and others simply stared.

"Boryn!" the familiar voice warned. The battalion parted, affording a wide berth between the Moon elf officer, who stood pat with sword drawn, and a short, white-bearded newcomer backed by a small but fearsome-looking force.

"These humans have spilled elven blood," the elven officer announced, "and destroyed one of our ships. They must die, and no dwarf will stop us."

"I'd recommend ye drop yer sword."

"I shall not!" declared the elf, at which time the earth melted out from under his feet, and he sank into a pit of liquefied stone. Before the elf's head went under, the stone hardened in response to the white-bearded dwarf's glowing fingers.

"Now, I'd like ta speak with yer king. So if yer men coul' take us to 'im, it woul' be greatly appreciated." The tone was as friendly as the words.

The elven ranks scattered as the sturdy, armored dwarf moved toward Boryn and friends.

"King Fazrin!" Boryn called, taking first a relieved breath and then a relieved step away from the cliff. "What are you doing here?"

"Came ta talk a bit o' diplomacy with the King o' the Moon Elves."

"I owe you one for the timing!" Boryn laughed. "Did you find a new place to hole up?"

"No' yet. Tha's fer later. Now, le' us go see the Moon king."

The elves formed up ahead of the dwarven soldiers and marched across the grassy headland into the fog. Boryn motioned for Laric, Ranton, and Wenval to come along, too.

"Why is there so much fog?" Boryn asked, noticing for the first time that all the colors here were paled, as if milky-white fog had tinted them.

Oddly enough, Ranton knew the answer. "It's the Moon elves' defensive system. They are literally lost to their enemies; enemies can't find them in the fog. I'm guessing the reason they're so jumpy is because the daemons found them; they've taken the brunt of this invasion already."

The others turned to him, questioning this insight.

"Wenval, launch some fire in that direction." Ranton pointed.

Wenval snapped his fingers and a fireball sailed, burning away the fog and revealing a faded field littered with tortured elven and daemon bodies.

"They haven't even had time to clear away the dead."

"How did you know about that?" Laric puzzled.

"I could see it." Ranton gave a "no big deal" shrug.

Calny posed a new question. "Wenval, don't you have to say a spell before you can use it?"

"Yes, why?"

"Because you didn't say anything just now."

"Sure I did. I said '*Fyr.*'"

"No. You just snapped your fingers, and there was fire. Do it again."

Wenval snapped his fingers and stared astounded at the fire that formed. "All I did was *think* about it."

"Try something else!" Laric urged.

Wenval spotted an outcropping of rock barely visible in the enshrouding white mist. He lifted two fingers and held his hand over his head. The hand whipped forward, and a bolt of lightning flew. Shards of rock fired into the air. He dropped his hand to his side then snapped it toward the sky. A pillar of stone shot up from the ground where the rock had been.

"Since when could you do that?" Laric asked behind the widest of eyes.

"I don't ever . . . I can't . . . er," Wenval stammered. "I didn't know I could!"

"Do you think this is what happened when you blew apart the ship—you *thought* about it?"

"Now that's a scary thought, er, well . . . it's getting more and more interesting all the time," Wenval said to himself, and his imagination took flight.

"King Fazrin!" called the sentry. "Hurry up. We can't keep the king waiting." The dwarven king hustled in the direction of the voice, the Crusaders at his heels.

"Here it is!" The sentry stepped aside and made a wide, sweeping presentation with his elegantly armored arm.

They stood before two white trees woven together in a high arc. A mystical blue light filtered between them.

"The Moon king's portal," Fazrin said simply. "Boryn, me and you'll stay 'ere to meet with this king. Me boys'll take yer friends ta prepare the forces at Ranlon."

Boryn's questions spilled, "So there are fighters at Ranlon? Have we been successful in gathering forces? What about Emily?"

Fazrin patted the eager young man's back. "More than ye can

imagine, I suspect."

Boryn turned to Wenval. "Tell everyone we'll be there soon. Be ready."

"Follow me." The elven sentry stepped in front and led Boryn and Fazrin into a wide corridor. Boryn felt himself bathed in cold, blue light that seemed to wash away all color. The light faded as they descended deeper into the passageway, but then they arrived in a white marble chamber so radiant by comparison that they blinked their eyes against the glare.

"Wait here," ordered the arrogant guard. "I shall advise King Silvaros of your unsightly presence." The guard's face twisted as if sniffing something rancid, and he left through a side door.

Fazrin and Boryn took in the room, grand not only in scale but in features as well. It was brilliantly white, spotlessly clean, lavishly ornamented, and extensively gilded. Boryn, dressed in little more than rags and road dirty, and the dwarven king, whose standards of splendor were far different from these, looked one to the other and chuckled.

A pair of soaring, white doors, bookended by liveried guards, swung open noiselessly on golden hinges.

The chamberlain stepped through the doorway. "You may now address his highness," sniffed the elf. He stepped aside to admit the motley visitors. When Boryn and Fazrin entered the throne room, they found it to be dazzlingly bright, though the colors were pale. At the far end, Boryn could see a gleaming marble baldachin with a gold-encrusted moon suspended above it.

Fazrin and Boryn ascended a short but grand rise of stairs and padded down the carpeted aisle, flanked by guards in silvery-blue heraldic finery. The king, attired in golden robes, appeared both regal and serene upon a gilded, white marble throne.

"Pah!" Fazrin waved a dismissive hand. "Seems they sure 'ave a liken' fer th' gold."

"What brings you out of your hole, King Fazrin?"

"The same as wha's killing yer people, Silvaros."

The guards leveled their spears toward the dwarven king. The pompous elf who 'granted' this audience cleared his throat before speaking. "You shall address the king with respect."

"As ye ough' ta respect me, fairy," growled King Fazrin.

The elf sputtered and fled.

Now it was Silvaros' turn to speak. "I regret the rudeness of my aide, but please refrain from insulting us, Fazrin. Some of the races still value decorum." After an appropriate pause, he continued, "So, to what do I owe the honor of your visit? Last we spoke, we weren't exactly friends."

"This boy wished ta meet with ya. Then I have a more private matter ta discuss."

"Who are you, boy?"

"Boryn Mhinbron, son of the Emperor."

Fazrin eyes snapped to the boy's face though Silvaros took no notice.

"And what do you humans want from us after all this time?"

"We have assembled forces for an offensive attack on Ranlon."

"That would be a first," Silvaros' tone was even.

"And we would like your assistance. We intend to drive the daemons out of Ranlon and back into the pit. Judging from the looks of your field, you must be aware of the threat."

"Is your father behind this mission?"

"My father is a mindless fool."

The Moon king stroked his chin and looked the boy over. "You carry odd blades for one who claims to be against the daemons." The hilts of the black-gem scimitars were just visible over Boryn's shoulder.

"I agree it looks strange, bu' he's true ta 'is word," testified the dwarven king. "We tried executin' him, yet still he chose ta save us when we were attacked by these daemons."

"My regrets, Mhinbron, but I cannot pledge my soldiers to your battle."

"But, sir, we cannot do it alone! And we must act fast if we are to stop them before they become too strong!"

"Your plan is naïve, and my troops are spread thin. None can be spared without endangering the safety of my own. Now if our business is concluded, my guard will escort you to a portal and off the isle," the Moon king said quite formally. "And please, do not come'back." It was not a request.

"Wait." King Fazrin drew a golden rune that reflected in the gleaming, marble floor. He charged the rune; the place outlined by the markings began to swirl. "Jump in, Boryn. That'll take ye d'rectly to the forces at Ranlon."

"Thank you."

"And next time we meet, I'll be more tha' a bit int'rested ta hear more about yer . . . heritage," Fazrin winked. "Meanwhile, consider us even once again, Boryn Mhinbron."

"Just plain Boryn suits me fine."

Fazrin acknowledged the unspoken request, and Boryn leapt into the whirlpool of stone.

"Now about that other matter . . . ," Fazrin began, speaking to Silvaros.

The streets were cloaked in darkness, allowing the large man to pass unrecognized. He approached the wooden door. Above it hung a small sign painted with a green cross. Reluctantly, softly, the man rapped. When the knock went unanswered, he tried again more forcefully.

A candle sputtered within, spilling yellow light from the window and casting a crooked square on the street. The man waited, and the door cracked open. The healer recognized his visitor and pulled the door back to admit the man, despite his own disheveled appearance, having been roused from sleep.

Lord Mhinbron entered. He lowered his bulk to the long bench beside the healer's table; the bench groaned under the strain. Something about the man seemed different, and the healer observed carefully, trying to put a finger on it. Edrick moved to the table, sat across from the man and waited.

"What have I done?"

"Meaning?"

"I am a failure."

"That is the popular opinion."

Mhinbron turned remorseful eyes to the healer, but his head remained low. "It has nothing to do with the people of Dusgoroth or my council or even my rule."

"What then?"

"I am Emperor only because of my father's influence."

"That, of course, is history. I'm well aware of your father's machinations on your behalf."

"He never believed in me—only wanted to get me out of his hair," Algyer reflected for a moment then added bitterly, "or make me into something I never was."

"Or perhaps make you what you might have been?"

The Emperor's head snapped up. His eyes met the healer's. Then he looked down at the tattered robe he'd worn to disguise his passage through the streets. He fingered the frayed hem of the sleeve. "I beg of you to take me through the purging," the man said without looking up. "Could it be that I am a good man and a bad drunk, or am I simply—"

The healer cut him short. "I honestly don't know."

"I must find out. It's long past time." Algyer paused. "Will you do it?"

"It will not be pretty."

Mhinbron released a soft, rueful chuckle. "So I've heard."

"And even then, it may not . . ."

"It will work this time."

A measure of silence passed, and the healer rose and walked to an inside room; the Emperor followed. Gently, Edrick closed the door behind them to shield what might happen within.

Ramgis tossed back the flap and stormed into the tent. Brilliant light poured through the opening, spotlighting Rath on the floor tangled within the bedclothes. The mercenary groaned and tried a glance toward the door but, snapping his eyes shut against the brightness, decided otherwise and took a swig from the jug behind him instead. Another head popped up from the coverings.

"You brought a woman to a war camp?"

"Huh? Oh . . . yeah . . . that," said Rath grinning.

"Get her out of here. And you are needed. Now."

"Why?"

"There is a boy—more accurately, a young man—out here. Belral and the men say he is a better shot than you."

"Not possible," said Rath, turning over to return to sleep. "And who is Belral?"

"A sword master who showed up this morning about the time the boy and several more of Boryn's comrades arrived," Ramgis explained.

Rath sat up. "So Boryn is here?"

"Not yet. They said to expect him soon, tomorrow perhaps."

"So the time is nigh." Rath mused. "Tell me more about this archer."

"A fellow by the name of Ranton. I have to admit, he is good. But nevertheless, since you have no interest in defending your honor, I'll pass along your message." Ramgis stepped from the tent and bellowed for all to hear, "Sorry, everyone. Rath's afraid to take him on."

Wearing only his breeches and with bow in hand, Rath burst through the flap before the sentence was finished. "Where is he?"

Ramgis pointed to the dark-haired boy who was shooting at a target almost indiscernible in the distance. The Shadow Crusaders and all the dwarves had gathered round to watch.

Rath marched toward the boy and broke through the circle of rapt observers, Ramgis close behind. "Are you the reason I am up so early?" Rath asked, looking the muscular young man top to bottom.

"It's well past early," laughed the boy, his hazel eyes flaring in anticipation of a challenge.

Before anyone even registered the movement, Rath launched an arrow that sliced through the shaft of the last one fired by the boy. *Got him!* Rath rubbed his eyes with the back of his hand to clear the remnants of sleep. The boy, meanwhile, raised another arrow, aimed and fired, impaling the nock of Rath's arrow.

"That young man is very good," Ramgis observed to no one in particular.

"And I never thought I'd see an archer equal to Ranton."

Ramgis looked at the bald-headed boy standing beside him. "There are things much more important than being flashy with a bow."

Ranton fired again; mid-yawn, Rath loosed another, directing it high into the sky. Rath's arrow arced then torpedoed to the ground, pinning the boy's in flight. Less than a heartbeat later, another arrow popped through the center of the impaling shaft, slicing it cleanly in two.

Rath turned to the boy and studied his face.

"Your name is Ranton?"

"Yes."

"Your mother is a hunter?"

"Is this an inquisition?" retorted the boy.

"I guess that's your answer," Ramgis said, bemused by the exchange.

Rath, uncharacteristically, stayed quiet.

"He's here!" Boringer's excited call rang out from the camp's far side; he was thrilled to be first to see him. Boringer's boys poured out of the small fort they'd built to keep themselves busy, and everyone else ran from the archery match to converge on the figure lying in the grass.

But suddenly, Boringer skidded to a halt, those behind him too close to stop. *Don't let it be true!*

A purple-robed man with tousled orange-and-black striped hair popped from the tall meadow grass and bounded—though limping—toward the dwarf. "Boringer! It's you again! I'm so happy to see you!"

"You're making us look stupid." Marlok slowed the pace.

"Argh!" The joy in Boringer's face burst like a bubble. "Wha' are ya doin' here? I though' I lost ye."

"We came to help," Quaswyn chirped.

Boringer turned and stomped away, wagging his horn-helmeted head while the Shadow Crusaders moved in for a warmer welcome.

"How did you get here so fast?" Marlok turned to Emily. "You were still in Dusgoroth when we left."

"I came straightaway with Hannah and Stevan. I've been here for days. What took *you* so long?"

Marlok scowled.

"Is Boryn here yet? Did we make it on time? I can hardly wait. This is so exciting," Quaswyn rambled and tried to clap his hands while Marlok struggled to keep them coolly at their sides.

"Boryn is not here yet, but you'll be happy to hear, your timing is perfect. We were just about to eat," Wenval said.

"Oh, goody."

Plates filled, Wenval seated himself next to the Elemencian mage and utterly ignored the thief's necessary presence. "Have you met Hannah?" Wenval asked as she joined them. "She's a healer."

"How wonderful!" Quaswyn seemed genuinely delighted. "One who chose the regenerative tree of magic! Where would we be without the healer's skills?" he mused.

"My abilities are nothing compared to Wenval's."

Eager to learn what he could from the seasoned mage, and squirming under Hannah's praise, Wenval diverted, "So tell me, Quaswyn, do you have a specialty?"

"Magnification glyphs and light magic."

"Will you teach me?"

"Gladly. And what about you? What is your specialty?"

"I'm not exactly good at anything yet, but I've dabbled in all the elements."

"Control of *all* the elements?" Quaswyn's eyes grew wide.

"Is that unusual?" Wenval wondered.

"It's rare to control three, much less all. Sounds like you may be vying against Prizzadar to become archmage one day!"

Wenval chuckled. "I doubt I'll be able to rank among the highest mages of all the races—"

"He's really here this time!" Boringer shouted. All heads turned to the rune-built defensive structure and then back to their meal; no one moved. "Hurry, I promise. Boryn is really here."

Reluctant to put plates aside, the troops moseyed toward the fort. Something in Boringer's urgent manner won them over, convincing them, and anticipation mounted; the long-awaited arrival was at hand. The Shadow Crusaders shoved to the front.

Waiting inside the fort and relishing the build up, Boryn held back. Chuckling at his own mischief, he lowered Shade to the ground and nudged him forward. "Go get 'em!" he whispered.

The fluffy, black furball, no bigger than a minute, tumbled over the threshold, landing on too-large paws with blue eyes narrowed and face twisted in his best attempt at a ferocious growl. After a heartbeat of hesitation, the big-eyed onlookers burst into laughter. Boringer slammed his helmet to the ground and blustered into the fort. Faceless bellows and the word "clobber" spilled out just before a hearty laugh. Boryn stepped into the light and strolled out. Shade yipped at his master's feet.

"It's about time," Ramgis was first to speak.

"Glad you could make it!" Ranton smiled warmly as the others converged, questions, slaps on the back, and shaking of hands all around.

"How'd the situation with the Moon elves play out?" Wenval was eager to hear.

"Turns out they are too self-absorbed to consider the larger world around them," Boryn was saying when he was tackled to the ground from behind. Sensing a friendly attack, he still flipped over quickly. His face broke into a wide smile. "Emily!" and he stood to wrap her in his long arms. "I'm really glad to see you."

"Same to you."

Wiping dirt from his ragged clothing, as if it would help, he asked, "Did you have any trouble?"

"None worth talking about," she deflected.

"So has everyone made it here?" Boryn held on to her hand.

"Present and accounted for," Wenval said.

The crowd stepped back, eager to see and hear the words from the boy they had awaited for so long and whose feats were growing to legendary proportion. Boryn climbed the outside stairs to the fort's flat roof and called out in a clear, strong voice, "Protectors of Armorica! Tomorrow, we take the offensive and send our unwanted guests home!"

Cheers erupted, and the unlikely alliance was forged: a few old heroes, a motley throng of would-be warriors, a mixed company of renegade leaders and their men, and a handful of eager youth.

"They actually think they might win?" The raven-haired daemon rolled her eyes. With skin as white as her cloak, shadows of darkness playing along its folds, and eyes and lips as dark as her hair, she leaned back in her chair. She let her eyes drift, alighting briefly on each face crowded into the dim room where the ignoble fraternity convened.

"So right you are, Noctas. Humans with groundless assumptions of victory are so . . . unsightly," said her similarly attired companion. Aquus ran long fingers through his rippling, blue hair and blinked his watery-blue eyes.

"Noctas, Aquus. Come now. Just think of all the fun we'll have pulverizing those humans," laughed the hulking general Tharrus who slammed one fist against his palm for emphasis.

"Sheep for the slaughter." A smile cracked Glacius pale blue face.

Kelris snorted, "Sheep are more valuable than dead humans."

"Oh, stop it. You're getting me all excited," Morpheon said with delight.

"That's certainly creepy," Kam groused.

The door opened, spilling light into the dark room. In the

doorway stood the flame-haired general, an equal by title but in reality much more. His manner decidedly nonchalant, Fernus asked, "A bit too eager to massacre the humans, aren't you?"

"Why do you say that?" Glacius responded, suspicions piqued.

"We have separate orders. We will not be fighting in this battle." In unison, the assemblage protested and sat straight.

"Wait. Do you mean we are leaving? Are we nothing but puppets on Tarn's stage?" Noctas wanted to know.

"Our own armies get to have all the fun, and we do not?" Aquus was incredulous.

Fernus raised an eyebrow. "Is that a problem?"

"Yes, it's a problem! I've been itching for this bloody battle since I set foot in this accursed world! You've already called me off one battle!" Glacius raged, his words sharp and icy cold.

"Sorry to disappoint you, but we have specific assignments."

"You're trying to give the humans a chance, aren't you, Fernus?" Noctas, the white-skinned one and daemon of darkness, accused.

"Want to see your little pet shine?" Tharrus said in a whiny, singsong voice.

Kelris answered the charge. "Humans make bad pets. They tend to misbehave."

"Young Mhinbron is more like an intriguing human than a pet."

"So what are we to do, Fernus?" Aquus was blunt despite his washy appearance.

"You are to assassinate only certain members of the opposing force—those select few and no others."

"However we'd like?" Tharrus inquired.

"Kill them any way you please, so long as you do it."

"That helps a little," Glacius sulked, tiny ice crystals forming on his forehead. "I suppose the ones we're after are the old heroes?"

"You're quick to catch on," Fernus chuckled.

"As it stands, the main force of the dwarves and elves offer no assistance." Ranton poked at the fire that the leaders of the new alliance had gathered round.

"How do you propose to take on a limitless army?" Rath raised the crucial question.

"Ranton scoped out the daemon line," Boryn said.

Unrolling a small sheaf with drawings on it, Ranton pointed. "The daemons have five positions, each with its own portal to hell. They are set up on the outskirts of the forest, in a zigzag pattern, three on the perimeter, two a little ways in. The portals will be easy to spot. Look for a tall ring of fire encircled by stone. The gateway is protected at the center."

"There is a sixth portal, here, that is nothing more than a chasm to hell—directly from Tarn's citadel. If we manage to take out the five, that will stop the flow of reinforcements and, no doubt, dishearten the daemons."

"Who will take out the portals?" Ramgis asked. Cadegray listened intently.

"We plan for Rath and Ramgis to take the two left of center,"

Boryn outlined. "And Luthor and Belral, you take down the two on the right."

"And in the middle?"

"That will be mine. Once you close off your portals, we'll all move toward the sixth, here," Boryn pointed. "Take any chance you can to break through the lines to Tarn's citadel. The only hope we have of winning this fight is killing Tarn, and the more of us there to fight him, the better our chance of winning."

"And what of our men?"

"They will reinforce you in closing the portals."

"And the dwarves and the Empire's warriors?"

"Boringer, The Shadow Crusaders, and Quaswyn and Marlok will lead them in a stand against the ground forces—the daemons who strike from the forest rather than through the portals. And one more thing—name a second in command in case . . ."

"When does the fun begin?" asked Luthor, his tone more serious than his words.

"Daybreak, at the sound of the horn."

Ranton inquired of the veterans. "Have we overlooked anything?"

Rath looked Ranton in the eye. "It is a plan to be proud of. Now go tell the others so everyone will be ready."

"We'll move into position tonight," Boryn continued. "No fires. No talk. There will be no preparation in the morning. When the horn sounds, be ready to fight without delay."

Boryn stood and made a clicking noise with his tongue; Shade hopped up and trailed him obediently. He motioned for Emily to join them.

With sober spirits, each leader retreated to own his space and thoughts.

"So will the strategy work?" Ramgis pressed his trusted tactician.

"There is a chance," Cadegray replied.

"You're not overwhelming me with confidence," Ramgis chuckled. "So whether or not the world as we know it ends tomorrow is a big 'maybe'?"

"Does it ever really change?" Cadegray grinned, his face lined by experience. "Age is a great teacher, but at times, the blind courage of youth is more valuable."

"You know, Luthor, you're at risk of losing your bad-guy reputation."

"How's that?"

"We might be saving the world tomorrow," Belral said.

"If I don't do this, there will be no one left to rob," Luthor replied, elbowing his old teacher in the side.

"Always been about the coin with you, huh?"

"Well, yes. Gold is the only love in life," laughed Luthor, "except maybe my sword."

"I suppose there's always hope. Even the worst can find redemption," the wiry sword master observed with a fond smile. "We'll be fighting side by side tomorrow. Your form had better not be rusty, or you're in for it," he teased.

"It's *you* who should be worried about getting rusty, old man." Luthor turned serious. "We will fight together, and we will put an end to this daemonic madness . . ."

"I'll cover your back, Luthor. Count on it."

Boryn and Emily passed nearby.

"Are we interrupting your chummy reunion?" Boryn quipped.

"Eh, little brother. I hear loyal, old Belral's covered for you a few times, too," Luthor swatted the sword master's wide shoulders.

Boryn stopped, smiled and nodded with heartfelt sincerity, "And for that, dear Belral, I am most grateful to you."

Boryn and Emily continued toward the knoll that provided a view of the whole scene. In one direction was the quieting campsite; in the other, the hellish forest, glowing red from an unconsuming fire, a curl of black smoke rising from its center. Boryn sat down and dug his fingers into the thick black fur at Shade's neck. Emily lowered herself to the ground beside him.

"What shall I do tomorrow, Boryn?"

"I want you to watch Shade. Stay in the camp."

A bit indignantly, she said, "I can fight."

"I know you can. But I don't want you to."

"Does it matter to you?"

"Yes." Then less sure of his footing, Boryn continued, "I don't want to save a world without you . . ."

She smiled.

"Besides, Shade may need you to protect him!"

"I'll stay . . . on one condition. Promise me you won't die."

He laughed. "I promise."

"You might have some unexpected assistance."

"Hm?"

"While you were away, I was taken prisoner."

Boryn looked at her, surprised and alert.

"It was fine, really. But they took me to Xandon's palace. An incredible place, but that's a different story. He wouldn't tell me straight out, but I think the Flame elves would like to see the daemons stopped as much as we would."

Boryn took her hand and lay back, staring at the star-blanketed sky. "To think I was once so naïve I thought daemons were imaginary. And the biggest of my worries was my next meal. And now I feel like the fate of the world rests on our shoulders."

"You've handled the move from imperial exile to hero quite gracefully," she said, her mouth smiling but her eyes heavy with worry.

"Let's not get ahead of ourselves," he laughed. "But don't worry about me. I'll be fine. I always am, remember?"

Emily pondered the immense sky, stars glistening like the tears that welled and threatened to spill from her eyes. "Do you think they are watching us?"

"Who?"

"Our mothers."

"I like to think so."

"Me, too," she said and snuggled close.

Boryn rested his head on the soft grass, moved his closer to hers and shut his eyes. *I will not die tomorrow, I promise.*

The war camp slept, or more likely, was simply quiet, waiting. Creeping away from the place where Emily lay sleeping, Boryn stared across a yet-still battlefield, an empty slope that separated the camp and the tormented forest.

The sun bobbed on the horizon like a tiny cork in the ocean. Boryn nudged the signal master. "Oy. Time to sound the horn." The soldier groaned and rolled over. Boryn grabbed the small trumpet from the lazy bugler's bag, squatted beside him, and blew into the mouth reed. The hollow blast punctuated the quiet and bounced across the plain just ahead of the clamor of rising warriors who had slept dressed and ready for action. The sound, no doubt, alerted the daemons as well; screeches and howls erupted from Ranlon.

Allowing only enough time for battle-ready warriors to rise and grab weapons, Boryn unsheathed his blue-bladed scimitars and twirled them in his hands. He stabbed the indestructible blades into the ground, and soldiers began to form up around him. When it was time to move, Boryn turned to his allies, raised the blades and sparked them. He slid them into their sheaths and drove directly toward the daemon host.

Behind Boryn, Belral extended his longsword. He raised the blade and touched the edge with an appraising finger, making sure it was sharp and clean. He turned to the rabble of imperial regulars, deserters and militia that comprised his daemon-fighting force and cried, "For humanity!" And forward he charged. The teaming body swelled and followed. With an explosive shout, as if from one voice, the horde of humanity thundered toward the gates of hell.

An overpowering weight descended upon Boryn as he scanned the field of battle, and daemons poured from the forest. His eyes came to rest on the white-cloaked General Fernus standing in the center, in front of the first portal, with arms outstretched in an oddly welcoming pose.

Boryn's hands cupped the pommels of the blue scimitars. *Let's see how strong I am now.* Then he remembered his lesson with Lulz. *And how fast.* He focused his energy to balance then forced strength into his legs. Wind whistled past his ears he moved with such speed, pulling well ahead of his allies. He slowed as he drew close to the place where Fernus stood. The daemon general laughed, bemused.

Boryn unsheathed one blue scimitar and squeezed the hilt to fire the blade. With scant effort, Fernus batted it aside with the flat of his own black-gem sword. "You felt overwhelmed when I appeared, didn't you? Imagine how you'll feel in front of Tarn. He's even stronger than I am—for the moment, anyway."

"I thought the daemon king was a poser—a figurehead enthroned only by lucky birth—and you and your generals hold the real power." Boryn stepped close, face-to-face, separated only by the width of Boryn's upraised blade. He could feel the heat that Fernus radiated.

"Generally that's true," said Fernus grinning and forcing Boryn's blade out of the way.

"And what about you? Where is your power?" Boryn withdrew his second blue scimitar.

"Don't concern yourself with me; there's simply no need to waste full power in a quarrel with a mere human boy. Don't flatter yourself."

Boryn took an awkward step backward but charged one scimitar with energy before sweeping it upward. A crescent of energy flowed from the length and width of the blade like a knife spreading butter.

"You missed. . . ." Fernus jumped aside, making no move to parry.

"But I put you right where I wanted you." Boryn crossed his arms in front of his chest and pointed the blades over his shoulders.

The forces of humanity split, surging left and right toward the forest's edge. Without slowing, Ramgis rode past, admiring the duel in which Boryn and Fernus were engaged. He came close enough to feel the tremor when the ground upon which the two accomplished swordsmen stood blasted skyward in a cloud of swirling dust.

"Rath," Ramgis shouted over his shoulder to the man running behind him, "take your men wide. Give those two some serious distance."

Ramgis hoisted his mighty warhammer and kicked his steed into a gallop. "Blood Knights and the Alliance of the new Table! For our world! For our people!" The mounted knights raised a mighty huzzah and galloped behind their commander, trailed by Rath's men who broke off to lodge a first, deadly volley along the front lines.

Cadegray waited until he was alone at the rear. "*Zulon!*" he called, holding out his palms. *Grant me a small bit of your power, if for only this moment.* The response was immediate. Lightning flashed across the sky, striking Cadegray's open palms. His body lifted into the air and floated, infused with newfound power—the wrath of a storm cloud at his command.

Splintering from the others, Luthor fired off a friendly salute. "Red X, charge!" he roared to his men, and the Red X swarmed down the slope intent on destroying the northern daemon portals. He lifted his bone horn to signal the second wave, Belral and his men.

Daemons dropped in their path, and more, in countless numbers, kept coming. Luthor sprinted ahead of his men, claymore high, eyes reddening, and his face twisting into an unusual smirk.

The smoke cleared, and Boryn smiled. Dozens of gashes scarred the earth, and there was no sign of Fernus, though in front, he faced a daemon stampede.

"That was impressive! Good luck with getting through that next daemon line," came a taunting whisper from behind.

"Have you given up already, Fernus?" Boryn challenged, keeping one eye on the approaching horde.

"My job was only to help you warm up," Fernus replied before bursting into black flame and disappearing.

A maelstrom of arrows whistled in as the daemon mob neared. Boryn pressed the pommels of the dwarven scimitars end-to-end. A snap told him the bond was solid. Twirling the double-bladed weapon like a windmill on its side, Boryn squeezed the conjoined hilt to release the blades. They sailed wide, slicing through the daemon mass. The boy retracted and separated the blades then pointed them over his shoulder, X-ing his arms across his chest.

From the top of Boringer's fort, Rogma observed the unfolding battle. *Thank ye, Fazrin, fer changin' yer mind.* He scanned the scene, searching for the best way to help. He lifted his short arm and swept the widest possible arc, casting a glowing, golden rune in the air while twenty or so rune makers repeated the pattern in the sand below. Rogma smashed the glowing symbol into the earth. The ground quaked, and hundreds of boulders shot up, each becoming the arm of a stone golem pushing out of ground. Rogma made a new rune, and slammed it to the ground. This time when the earth trembled, it ruptured, and a crack snaked past Boryn toward the daemon portal. The gateway split and crumbled into the crevice, and the first daemon portal flickered and died.

"Aw right, lads. Le's go get the bastards!"

The golems tromped forward, the dwarven reinforcements behind. Boringer and Bret grinned proudly when they caught sight of their dwarven comrades joining the fight.

"Bret, try not to die out there."

"I'll bet ye all tha money tha' ya owe me tha' I kill more'n you, eh?"

"Deal," said Boringer, thumbing his helmet for luck and shoving his way past the golems to the front line.

Already, the ground was splattered with blood and deeply scarred. Battle cries rose as armies of human, dwarf and daemon clashed. Boryn shut his eyes and focused all energy to his legs. He shot forward, hacking a swath through the daemon lines. Bracer glowing, he advanced toward the innermost portal, heavily fortified by swarming daemons. He released the bracer's power. Time slowed. Boryn leapt while charging one of the blue blades. The crescent of energy fired and smashed the portal and all the daemons around it. Boryn charged onward, Tarn's iron citadel, dark and foreboding, in his sights.

Quaswyn hastily drew a glowing, blue symbol in the air. He pressed a hand to it, and the aura became blindingly intense. "*Lux*," he intoned. An enormous blast of energy discharged from the symbol. It carved a deep trench to the pulsing portal, incinerating any daemon in its path and collapsing the gateway when it reached its target. The groove was deeper than a man is tall.

"What in the world was that?" Marlok asked. "That was far more than a '*lux*' spell."

"The symbol magnified . . ."

"Holy . . ."

"We might want to move."

"Gimme control of our legs. I run faster." Marlok jumped into the smoking trench while Quaswyn shot down daemons with spears of light. They sprinted the length of it to enter the desecrated forest: ashen trees, lava crevices, fire, and bones. Surely this was as close as Armorica could get to hell.

Boryn rushed toward the citadel rising like a beacon of evil before him, blind determination fueling his steps. A narrow figure stepped in his path. Boryn stopped in front of the white-cloaked daemon, its blue hair slicked back, straight and stringy. The daemon grinned, but there was nothing friendly in his icy stare.

"Well, well, well. If it isn't Boryn Mhinbron himself, Fernus' little plaything!"

"And you are?" Boryn asked the blue-skinned impediment.

"Call me Glacius, the one to end your bout with heroism." Glacius raised a crystalline limb that clutched a black-gem spear.

"*General* Glacius, I presume?"

"How observant! The coat must have given me away."

Boryn withdrew a black-gem blade from his back sheath. Elbow raised and arm crossed in front of his chest, he held the deadly edge poised to slice the daemon's throat. "Get out of my way."

In kind, Glacius brought his spear tip in line. "Try to pass." Before either could move, flame burst from the point of Glacius' spear; puzzlement registered on his pale, blue face.

"Boryn, step aside. This one is mine."

Boryn spun to see a tall, slender elf with flowing white hair and flowing scarlet robes. A green scar slashed across his right eye, and it pulsed with energy.

"Xandon, you betray your allies?" Glacius seemed amused.

"What better time to kill one than in the midst of battle when no one will notice." A blade of fire swirled out from Xandon's hand.

Glacius stepped aside. "Run along, Mhinbron. I'll catch up with you later."

Boryn turned quizzical eyes to Xandon. "Why are you helping me?"

"Not your concern. Now do as you're told, and run."

Boryn glanced from the Daemon of Ice to the King of Fire, their eyes locked. It was clear his absence or presence meant nothing to these two, already clinched in a battle more intense and primeval than the one in the forest. Boryn broke away, headed for the citadel to find Tarn, his own nemesis.

With Boryn out of earshot, Glacius began. "At last, we blot out your annoying line for good!" And the daemon's lips cracked with malice.

They waited. Frustration and anger had settled into morose silence; no one was happy sitting in the dark room while the battle raged in the forest. Finally, General Fernus rose from the seat where he reclined. The others took note and sat straighter, listening. "It's time for you to make your appearances."

"Aquus," Fernus said to the watery-eyed daemon who was radiating pale blue energy and fingering his rippling hair. "Rath is your target. Rath and none other."

"I will kill that arrogant archer," Aquus promised. "Fear not."

"Kill? Unlikely, but good luck trying." Fernus stated dismissively. Next he turned to the conniving dwarf Kam. "I give you the pleasure of eliminating your clansman, Boringer."

Kam smiled and nodded.

"Now, Morpheon, we are honored that you have chosen to join our fun. Would it be to your liking to exterminate any two heroes of your choice?"

Morpheon lounged in his chair, rolled his eyes to the ceiling, and hung one claw from his lower teeth. "Why, yes. I think I could enjoy that."

"Tharrus, your job is to destroy the places of earth—camp and fort—all of it, and everyone in it. And while you're at it, pick off those silly Shadow Crusaders and their little tag-alongs. We might as well simplify matters," Fernus seemed to think out loud. "And it will be a nice surprise for Boryn."

The giant, dark-skinned daemon smiled at the prime assignment. "Gladly."

Fernus continued. "Now just where are Kelris, Glacius, and Noctas? Tsk, tsk. Leaving before they receive their orders? Oh, well, can't say I'm surprised by that."

Ramgis ordered his men to destroy the southernmost portal then circle back to the nearer one set deeper into the twisted forest. First portal down, the knights looped back, but suddenly, Ramgis' warhorse skidded to a halt. It whinnied and shied and stamped in circles.

An elf, armored in white with gold trim and astride a terrifying, scaled mount, barreled toward Ramgis. "So you've made it farther than we planned," Kelris clapped, hiding behind his white helmet.

"Planned? You cannot *plan* human actions."

"Actually, I did rather well considering that you are close enough that I could find you."

"So this is the place of our showdown? I've waited long to avenge my family, you evil, dark bastard."

"We are in the midst of battle to decide the fate of the world, and you fret about petty, personal grudges?"

Ramgis kicked his mount into a gallop and drove toward Kelris who chuckled and spun, spear extended.

"Snack time," Kelris said, stroking Krixlus' scales. Ramgis tugged his reigns, and his steed reared to clear the reptilian mount's tail, armored with deadly, metallic spikes and swinging at its hooves. Krixlus snapped at the horse's neck while Kelris deflected a swing from Ramgis' warhammer.

"You Blood Knights and your horses! Useless beasts in battle," laughed Kelris as his mount's tail clipped Ramgis' shoulder. Ramgis reached for a smaller hammer behind his back, then sent it spinning toward Kelris. It found its mark, hitting the elf square in his helmet's visor, crumpling it. Dazed, Kelris lost hold of his reigns and fell. "You have dismounted me; the advantage seems to be yours." Kelris jumped to his feet as Ramgis dropped beside him.

"A battle of honor! We shall fight to the end on even ground."

"Ha! If you say so, Ramgis. Even ground."

The spear jabbed forward but the agile Blood Knight circled his hammer to knock the spear wide. The elf whirled around, smacking his spear like a club against Ramgis' head. Ramgis almost fell. Kelris kicked him hard in the chest, and the off-balanced knight dropped to the dirt.

"Sorry, Ramgis. Your honor is your downfall." Kelris held his spear high above Ramgis' fallen form. Kelris jabbed down with all his might. At the final instant, Ramgis rolled to the side, but the razor point still pierced the general's crimson breastplate.

Boryn continued his forward assault heedless of battle around him. But a different kind of movement drew his attention, and he wheeled right. A whirlwind spun through the daemon ranks, and when it stopped, daemon slurry covered the ground. In the center grinning was a speckle-bearded, bespectacled dwarf.

Boryn's eyes widened and a smile lit his face. *Rogma!* Boryn lifted a blue blade in tribute. The old dwarf bowed slightly, eyes twinkling, raised his staff, and charged into the fray.

Rogma ran to the trench Quaswyn had carved and leapt on an assailant that had a companion pinned to the ground. A quick rune from the master smith's hand, and the creature fell away. Rogma recognized the foul being—purple eyes, mangy hair and skin that looked like it was dipped in wax—from the attack at Raz Kiri. If anything, it looked even more awful now, its rubbery, pinched features speckled with gore.

"I feel so lucky! My target's so juicy and weak," Morpheon

wheezed, spying the dwarf.

Rogma scribed a rune, and a wall of rubble fired up to separate him from the beast.

Those damned dwarves and their runic magic! Morpheon transformed into a half-man, half-wolf form.

The old rune master shot his staff up into the thing's chin then down against the ground to form a stone crate, boxing it inside. A third rune caused the box to implode and crush the contents.

The dwarf tipped his head as if to say, "There." But before he could turn to go, the ground beneath him crumbled. Morpheon's claws raked Rogma's chest and flipped him into the air. The dwarf's spectacles flew one way and his staff the other.

"I'll do you the courtesy of letting you rot, dwarf," Morpheon rasped as Rogma's limp body hit the dirt.

Broken, Rogma tried to lift a rune-drawing finger. The glow was dim.

"Still alive? Forgive my incomplete work." Morpheon kicked the half-finished rune.

Guess I will no' be teachin' ye after all, Boryn. . . . Good . . .

Morpheon raised his pincers, slashed down, and impaled the rune master's heart.

Glacius laughed maniacally from behind blue lips, and a blast of frigid air sent hundreds of ice spears firing toward Xandon. Xandon swept with his flaming blade, vaporizing the ice weapons before colliding with the daemon's spear. The chiseled, black gem easily swatted the fiery blade aside then was twirled and thrust forward.

The black spear struck, and cold infused Xandon's chest. He fell forward as Glacius jerked the spear free. Glacius booted the downed Flame king in the face, sending him tumbling across the burnt ground.

Running through the throne room behind the elfin princess. Reaching out to tag her, falling short. Scrambling to my feet. Rounding a corner, headlong into a white cloak.

Eyes glistening, icy, the cloak swivels toward the girl. Guards frozen in their stances. Shrieking from the girl's mouth, ice slithering up from her feet. Someone dragging me away. "Xandon!" she screams. Ice creeping up her body, her neck—silencing first her shrieks and then her life.

Chaos swirling. Tongues of white flame licking out from the abyss. White flame—soul fire—the most powerful of all. "Soul fire cannot be created by hate; hate produces hell fire. Soul fire requires an emotion more powerful than hate . . ."

Lentz's words tangled in Xandon's waning consciousness.

The dwarf stuffed the small, black keg into a slightly larger, black tube then snapped his fingers, sparking small stones tied to the ends. The short fused hissed. "See ya la'er, eh?"

A thunderous boom, clearing smoke, and a heap of daemons at his feet. *Twen'y six . . . twen'y seven . . . an' an even thir'y.*

"Well, that'un worked." Bret crashed his hammer into a daemon skull while tossing another small keg.

Suddenly, a blade sliced into the explosion-happy dwarf. Bret turned a scorching eye to the daemon then pounced on its back, smashing gauntlets into the evil thing's face. He dug a small red vial from his vest pocket and downed the contents to seal his own wounds. He looked up. A blade rocketed toward his face, but just in time, a rocky hand interceded. Bret smiled and held his thumb high. The stone golem looked befuddled then answered with its own thumb up and a happy grumble.

Lunging sideways, Bret grabbed the shaft of a spear hurling toward him. He snapped the shaft in two and used the tip to pin a daemon's foot to the earth. Then he tossed another keg into a fresh onslaught. *Boom!* it went.

"Aw, bugger. I lost coun'."

A river of lava flowed through the forest, and Boryn followed it toward the citadel. A glint of metal flashed ahead; he stopped, looking closely, but saw nothing there. Scoping defensively, he continued on, but a whirring sound caused him to spin back. Behind him was a form bizarre beyond description and unlike anything he had even imagined. It stood on two chunky legs, like a man, but twice as large and bulky. It seemed to be made of interlocking, black-metal plates connected by glowing, orange crystals. Slits in the metal suggested eyes and mouth. One arm held the other, and a ball of energy cannoned from a chute where a hand would be. *What in the . . .*

Boryn lunged sideways, the blast narrowly missing him. He ran at the strange form, swinging his scimitar, but the thing vanished. Seconds later, a metal forearm crashed into his back. He hit the ground face first but rolled to the side in time to see the iron tube smash into the earth beside his face. The ground cracked. *It's unbelievably fast! Charge the bracer.*

The bracer's purple gem glowed brightly, and Boryn released the garnered energy. Time slowed, and he charged forward, his blades absorbing the energy and glowing as well. Under the bracer's spell, the thing moved at the rate of a normal man—still fast, but not inhumanly so. It tried to dodge a powerful strike, but Boryn's scimitars were too fast. The sharp blades glanced off the slick metal body, but the blow still knocked it from its feet. The thing plowed a black iron fist into Boryn's stomach, sending him hurtling. He looked to his bracer. *Think fast; it's almost out.*

Scrambling to his feet, Boryn sidestepped near the lava river. Heat seared his lungs, so he tried to hold his breath. The thing shot forward, and Boryn launched one of the blue blades. The chain entangled the thing's legs, and Boryn jerked, toppling the beast headfirst into the churning magma. The bracer charge ran out, time's passage returned to normal, and Boryn ran clear, gasping for air. He looked downstream to see the creature's feet waving above the surface. *What in the world was that? No time to worry now.* And he continued on his single-minded mission, eager to encounter Tarn.

Kelris lifted his spear to let the Blood Knight commander's body drop heavily to the ground. A blade whooshed over Kelris' head; the elf turned to see a strong, bald boy brandishing a two-handed claymore.

"Run, Laric. Don't fight with this one," Ramgis' voice was weak.

"I'm not about to let you die. The world needs more heroes; I can learn from you."

Kelris spun around to finish Ramgis, but the old knight scrambled to his feet. Heartened by Laric's confidence and a few deep breaths, Ramgis surprised Kelris with a mighty blow to the chin. The Dark Lancer dropped his spear as the visor collapsed into the helmet and his neck snapped back with a sharp crack.

Laric, too, was surprised. "I thought you were a goner!"

Ramgis smiled and said, "You want to learn? Start now. In battle, always wear mail under your armor. Sometimes you'll get lucky and the mail will deflect a shot that gets past the armor." Ramgis bent to inspect the injury that failed to reach beyond his metal mail. "Now help me destroy this evil beast." Ramgis moved toward Krixlus, the beast snorting and pawing the ground.

"Wait!" Laric held out a hand to stop Ramgis. "I don't think it's evil. Look at the amulet chained around its neck. Help me remove it."

"What is it?"

"You'll see." Laric circled the mighty beast, watching for a chance to move in.

Why won't Boryn let me fight? I'm just as strong as the others—probably stronger than Wenval. Emily stared into the feeble campfire, appreciating Shade's company as a foil to the unrelenting sounds of battle.

A breath of air stirred her hair and wisped a strand into her eyes. Absently, she swept it away, realizing it had been oddly still. A feathery touch brushed her ankle. She swiped at it, but the tickle persisted. The wolf slid from the comfort of her lap, hackles raised. Looking down, Emily saw a hand's shadow stroking her leg. She shrieked and swatted at it, jumping back, searching in vain for the shadow's source.

"Where are you?"

"If I told you it would spoil all the fun." The voice was like that of a young girl. "You're so pretty," it said.

Emily felt a soft hand stroke her cheek. She slapped at it, but there was nothing there. She looked to the sky and spun away from the sun.

"That would be clever if I was normal."

"What are you?"

"You could say I saved you. You see, Tarn expected Boryn would leave you here, so he sent a few daemons to kill you. But I killed Tarn's weaklings first."

"What are you?" Emily demanded again, hands in pockets, sliding on her rings.

"One of the generals. We weren't allowed to partake in the main fight, so most of us are simply watching—except for Glacius. He doesn't like to follow orders." The shadow slid in front of Emily and swirled up, forming into a gossamer-pale girl with intensely black hair and deathly white skin. The daemon's red eyes shone with joy as she moved very close to Emily's face and smiled. "My name is Noctas. And I plan to drag this out as long as possible."

"And you are dead!" Emily whipped her hands from her pockets, sweeping wide her slicing cords.

Lightening fast, the daemon grabbed Emily's wrist and encircled her waist, pulling her close. "This will be fun." A shadow crawled down Emily's hand and along her fingers, gently sliding off the rings and dropping them one by one to the ground.

Boryn covered the last few yards of protective coverage at a dead run, stunned by the sight before him. Razor-sharp blades jutted from each corner and aligned the roof like deadly crenellation, as if the black, iron fortress itself was prepared to slay any attacker. *Tarn's citadel.* Boryn crossed a bridge that arched across the cauldron-like moat rimming the outer wall. Intense heat burned through the soles of his boots, and gaseous vapor assaulted his eyes and nostrils. He stepped into an unpaved courtyard—barren ground landscaped with gruesome remains.

The black-caped boy approached the massive, iron entry, his steely resolve unbroken despite the dreadful scene. The doors stood open. He stepped inside. Down a long, stark hallway he could see the presence chamber, Tarn's enclave. There the mighty daemon king sat, clacking tongue and talons like a clock. Dapples of colored light from the stained-glass ceiling above the throne cast odd patterns on the horrifyingly majestic, red-skinned figure.

Quietly, Boryn moved down the long hall then entered the chamber, stopping in a sharp square of light slicing through the single soaring window. While his eyes strayed up to meet the gaze of the daemon king, his body felt crushed under the being's glare. The oppressiveness was overwhelming.

At first, Tarn seemed disinclined to take an interest in the boy. Casually, he remarked, "You must be the one I've heard so much about, the illustrious leader of the Shadow Crusaders." Then Tarn stood, spreading membranous, red-black wings that spanned almost the width of the chamber. It took this for Boryn to comprehend the daemon's size. More than five times the boy's height, Tarn loomed. The daemon bared sharp fangs and let out a menacing chortle. "You've caused quite a bit of havoc, boy."

"Glad to be of hindrance." Boryn appeared stolid in the face of the awesome daemon. "What nasty business brings you back after so many, long years?"

"Business? This is pleasure!" Tarn corrected. "Now tell me, did you intend to face the King of Daemons all alone?"

"My allies were with me, but I'm guessing you figured that and set traps so they wouldn't make it before you killed me. Was that your plan?"

"Bright one, you are! And I see you carry the two black scimitars . . ."

Boryn cocked his head without speaking.

"I'll be taking those back."

"I won't let you do that, not that you really could. But once dead, you'll have little use for them. So all is not lost."

"You imagine that you can kill me alone?" Tarn laughed loudly, a deep boom that ricocheted off the black, iron walls.

"Along with others, should they arrive in time."

Tarn bellowed, "Our fight shall not be within my chambers. Let us fight outside so I won't soil my citadel with your sour blood." Tarn leapt into the air, flapped his wings and crashed into the ceiling glass, shattering it and spraying colored shards across the presence chamber. Boryn covered his head and ran for the exit as iron plates in the floor began to separate, revealing a glowing, red pit flowing with lava. Boryn couldn't see where the fissure flowed, but his heart quickened as the boiling river grew wider beneath the retreating plates. He backpedaled then took a flying leap before the gap became too wide to cross. Rolling to his feet when he landed, Boryn dashed out the iron door. Tarn waited in the grisly courtyard, wings flapping. The daemon grinned and licked its deadly fangs with a pointed tongue.

"Ah, such a sapling you are, young Mhinbron. Hardly worth my trouble." Tarn flicked a long, bony finger into Boryn's chest, surprising the boy and sending him tumbling across the dirt.

"Go back to the hell you came from, daemon," Boryn spat, brandishing a blue-blade scimitar and exploding toward the daemon king. Tarn laughed as a dark shape formed in his own hand, solidifying into an enormous axe. The axe chopped down; Boryn rolled sideways then snaked in close to slip between Tarn's ankles. Boryn fired his blade, opening a deep, stinging cut. Reflexively, the daemon's knee jerked up, then deliberately, Tarn stamped down, intent on crushing the boy underfoot. Boryn corkscrewed around Tarn's back to swipe the other leg. While it was raised, Boryn impaled the tip of his blade in the daemon's planted foot and used the set point to vault upward. But the daemon king was ready, and Boryn collided with Tarn's clawed hand. The grip tightened like a vice on Boryn's shoulder. Then it tossed him. Airborne, Boryn managed to twist and flip to land on his feet. His expression smug, he glared at the daemon king.

"I'll give you something to grin about!" roared Tarn. He pointed two long fingers toward the sky. "*Awestan!*" The oath summoned a powerful explosion. First, it forced the air from Boryn's lungs, a wave of intense heat blasting him backward. Then the recoil, equally powerful, sucked back the emptiness. His lungs burned, seared by the air-turned-fire. He covered his eyes until the burning subsided, and when he reopened them, even the charred trees surrounding the citadel had vaporized.

"Time to cool off," toyed Tarn. Tarn raised his axe, steadied it and chopped, slamming it into the dirt just shy of Boryn's position. The sweeping blade released a glittering ice-blue powder that dusted Boryn. Instantly, Boryn's body slowed, and he began to shiver. The daemon laughed, and the blade whistled again. This time the icy cold blade sliced into Boryn's shoulder. The boy screamed, dropped to his knees, and with blood spurting, fell flat to the ground.

Get up. The real battle is just beginning.

"You always were the cocky one," Glacius smirked at his prey and turned to walk away. Suddenly, heat radiated up his icy spine. He wheeled back. Xandon's body floated in the air, limp and lifeless. But then, the Flame king's body went rigid, and white flames erupted from nowhere. The inferno licked and twisted then spiraled around Xandon and lowered him to his feet.

Xandon's glare penetrated Glacius. "My goal is no longer driven by hate or revenge but the desire of peace for my sister." The scar striping his eye pulsed a furious green.

"Ha! It's too late for that!" Glacius laughed uneasily as hundreds of needle-sharp, ice darts splintered toward Xandon.

The Flame king swept his arm, the full sleeve of his cloak splashing out a wave of white flame that pulsed and melted the ice, dousing the daemon first with water and then drenching him with flame. Xandon turned his hand toward Glacius, and the white flames coiled down his arm and fired forward. An enormous, roaring pillar of flame swept up like a tornado to engulf Glacius' pale blue form. When the flames died back, Xandon saw that Glacius glowed with black, daemonic energy.

"Released the power of your spear," Xandon observed.

"You're going to *die!*"

Spears of ice and black energy formed in midair, surrounding Xandon then firing inward.

"There's the problem with you young daemons. Way too hot-headed. Melt darkness and ice!" cried Xandon as he swung both arms to the sky, flinging impenetrable white fire in all directions.

Glacius reared, preparing for a deadly jab. Faster than the blink of an eye, the spear stabbed forward, propelled by black daemon energy. But Xandon kept clear. Again, the spear fired forward. Xandon shut his eyes. An enormous blade of white flame burst from his palm. With his right hand, he swept the white blade backwards in a full circle. Up and over it came. When it was in line over Glacius' head, the momentum slowed, but the power did not. Xandon slid the searing blade down, burning through Glacius' skull with white fire from the soul. Slowly, it burned its way down, incinerating Glacius' form as it went. When there was nothing left but a pile of ash, the screams stilled.

Xandon opened his eyes, free from torment at long last.

Emily stumbled backward, breaking away from the shadow of the girl. She bolted, but Noctas still managed to grab her ankle and topple her to the ground.

"You're getting slower," the daemon advanced. "Better pick it up before I get bored."

Emily was tired, her arm hurt, and she was bleeding, but she would not give up. Reaching behind her, she grabbed a rock and pulled back to throw, but a shadow scampered up her arm and forced it to the ground whereupon the daemon fell across Emily's shins and grabbed her other arm so that she was fully pinned.

"You lose," the daemon of darkness purred.

A discordant symphony of yipping caused Noctas to whirl. Running full bore, a pack of wolves was closing in on the campsite, a huge, white one with fierce, golden eyes at the lead. It howled, mournful and loud, and the daemon rose while keeping Emily pinned with her shadow.

"Bad puppies shouldn't attack *me*," Noctas trilled. Noctas sidestepped, leaving Emily vulnerable, exposed. "And no rescue by the animal kingdom for you," the daemon said as her face turned daemonic, twisted with venom, snarling and dark. For an instant, Emily saw a face that was terrifying beyond words. Yelping, the wolves turned tail, retreating from the horrifying figure.

Thinking the danger past, Noctas shrugged, but suddenly, a fury of white fur, claws, and teeth tackled her to the ground, fangs biting into her shoulder. She screamed and threw her arms around the attacking beast's neck. It took all of her daemonic strength to overpower the mighty wolf, but finally, fueled by unhuman strength, she lifted it dangling by the neck. The wolf snarled and pawed and snapped at her face, but the stranglehold tightened, and the wolf began to go slack. Emily watched in horror, unable to escape from Noctas' shadowy spell.

Powered by rage, Emily jerked her arm free. "Stop it!" she screamed, running to the animal's aid, but this time it was no shadow that stopped her but powerful, dark hands. She struggled but soon realized the futility.

"Thanks for joining in, Tharrus," Noctas purred. "I didn't know your orders brought you here, but your strength may come in handy."

Suddenly, the daemon girl's head spun backwards in a half-circle. The wolf dropped from her grip and flopped to the earth whimpering. Stunned, Noctas snapped her head face-front and cocked it side-to-side, popping her neck as if she were merely working out a crick. A wiry, shirtless man, bald save for a red stripe of hair down the center, crouched on the ground behind her. Noctas scowled.

"That hurt," she whined.

Emily eyed Noctas suspiciously. "That should have killed you."

"Sticks and stones might break my bones, but these shall never kill me."

Ignoring the chatter, the narrow man said in an expressionless voice, "To hurt man is one thing, but to cause pain to an animal is simply unforgivable."

"Punish me then," Noctas taunted.

Recognizing the spritely form from the jungle, Tharrus growled, "I owe you some pain from last time, human." The earth daemon's veins bulged.

"I am Lulz, the Force of Nature," the little man intoned, disregarding the audience. His body glowed with green energy. He shut his eyes and tensed; the ground buckled beneath his feet. "And you, Noctas, shall be the first to fall."

Tharrus released Emily and shoved Noctas and her shadow toward Lulz. Lulz' energy exploded outward, the earth beneath him shattering, and he shot toward the sky. Then whistling down, he flipped to bounce like a spring off a chunk of airborne earth and rocket toward Noctas. She blocked with her arms, but the man dove low, bulleting into her stomach. The daemon gasped and doubled over. Rebounding, Lulz thundered forward and slammed his fist into the side of her head just before a final sweeping foot sent her tumbling.

Lulz landed lithely, as if nothing had happened, and turned glistening eyes toward Tharrus. "Your turn."

Brandishing his mighty claymore, Luthor cleaved a daemon in two. The assault was so ferocious that the advancing daemons stopped in their tracks. "Heh! That's right," Luthor said. "Be afraid!"

"Am I missing something? Because even in the . . . unusual . . . red-eyed state in which I find you, there's nothing about you that makes me even slightly afraid." The voice was shallow and raspy, like nails on glass, and it came from behind. Luthor felt a needle-sharp claw press against his throat. Then, the creature to which the claw was attached—a spindly, manlike being with long, gray hair and earthworm gray skin—wheeled in front and locked his purple eyes on Luthor.

"Who the hell are you?" Luthor growled.

"Shouldn't matter. What does matter, however . . . ," a furtive glance to the side, and the creature reared back.

At that moment, Luthor began to feel dizzy, then sick, and his legs fell out from under him. He coughed, choking, and clutched at his throat as if he couldn't breathe. He held his hand to his mouth and noticed blood in his spittle, and then he passed out.

Belral shot forward, slicing his sword where the creature had just stood.

"You're getting slower, Belral."

"I didn't think worms had such a long lifespan."

"Well, let me be the first to tell you: we outlive the heroes!" Morpheon cackled.

"What did you do to Luthor?" Belral demanded.

"I made sure he wouldn't get in our way. It makes my job so much easier."

"I won't let you hurt him, Morpheon."

"Him? I couldn't care less about him; it's you I'm after. Oh, and since you mentioned 'worm' . . ." Morpheon reformed as an enormous, purple-gray snake, its tongue darting and slicing. The snake slithered underground, disappearing from sight.

Instinctively, Belral stabbed into the ground, but his blade only scraped hard earth. Then the snake fired up, its head transformed into a monstrous hawk's. The powerful beak clamped Belral's sword arm, snapping the bone and almost ripping hand from wrist. Belral cried out and stumbled back on his heels, cradling his mangled arm. Regaining his balance, he unsheathed a blade with his left.

Morpheon complimented his opponent. "How very tenacious."

"Go to hell."

"You know I have friends there. They aren't big fans, but let me know what you think," laughed Morpheon as a scorpion stinger shot up and lanced Belral's spine. Crying out, Belral arched forward. He nearly fell to his knees but refused to give Morpheon the satisfaction. Morpheon extracted the stinger, shot up out of the earth, and reassumed an almost-human form. The being moved very close to Belral who trembled as the poison coursed through his veins.

Morpheon pressed his forehead against that of the sword master, propping him up. Belral's eyes burned with pain, and sweat poured from his brow. "Now tell him to go on without you," Morpheon gestured toward Luthor. "And do it convincingly. Or I'll take both of you after all."

Luthor roused and looked around, puzzled, eyes normal.

Quickly, unsteadily, he leapt to his feet. Belral sidled next to him, without meeting his eye, and whispered. "I have this under control. The daemons are hording ahead. Go on; help Boryn. I'll be right behind you."

Still dazed, Luthor gave a small nod and jogged onward into the smoldering forest. Belral took a swing at the beast, but it was empty; there was no power behind it, and Morpheon easily stepped aside. The invincible swordsman fell to the earth face first.

"It really is a shame to see you go, Belral. I so enjoyed watching your heroism through the years," laughed the repellant creature. "Ordinarily, I'd accept your invitation to dine, but alas, the sacrifice must be mine. I'd hate to deny the humans the fun of finding you."

"Why are you so eager to fight daemons?"

"Think of the pain they cause, the bodies they've torn and souls they've tortured. I just want to stop them."

"But you are only a boy."

"Doesn't mean I can't protect, fight, or even die for what's important."

"Maybe you'll share your secret—show me what you've learned to become so brave, Boryn."

"Ha! I've always known my skills were second to none! It will be my honor to teach the old master some new tricks."

You have taught me, Boryn. You remind me what it means to be a hero . . . to keep fighting—no matter what.

Belral battled the paralyzing poison that clogged his heart and airways and numbed every fiber in his body. With will beyond measure, he stabbed upward, the longsword slicing cleanly through Morpheon's retreating back and out his stomach.

Morpheon rotated his head without turning his body, the neck cracking. "Come now, Belral. You know better than that."

The sword hilt slid from Belral's enfeebled hands.

Boryn forced himself to his feet.

Tarn chuckled. "I have to admit, to still stand after such a series of blows is truly impressive!"

Boryn eyed the daemon king, so arrogant, leaning against the outer, iron wall of his citadel. A glint of light from the daemon's chest caught Boryn's eye. *Doesn't look like a breastplate.* Embedded in Tarn's chest was a large, black crystal, the diameter of a man's head. **Break it.** Boryn charged the daemon, his dwarven-made scimitars at the ready. Tarn's axe sliced across this time, but Boryn's bracer slowed it so the boy was able to spring up, land on the flat face and grab the axe's shoulder before the blade could whoosh out from under his feet.

"Worse than an orc," Boryn grumbled as he pulled up and sprinted along the handle to reach the daemon's arm. He flipped his own blade, tip down, edge out, and zipped up Tarn's axe-wielding arm, laying it open like game being dressed. Boryn jumped to the ground. Pressing the scimitar pommels together, he charged the blades with energy and let them fly. The first blade glanced off the crystal at Tarn's neck; the second struck it dead center. The black gem cracked, and Tarn roared. *A weak point.*

Anger blazed in Tarn's red eyes. "I hope you kissed that little girl of yours goodbye, because you won't be seeing her again."

"What are you talking about?"

"How many stayed behind, besides her?"

"What did you do to her?"

"Me? Nothing. I did, however, order a rear attack on your army—but only after they ravage the camp and slaughter everyone in it," Tarn laughed.

The air around Boryn grew heavy, and he stared at the ground. "You know I can't let you do that." He said it so quietly it was almost a whisper, and he switched his dwarven scimitars for the daemonic ones. Suddenly, Boryn cackled, an inhuman sound, his voice altered—two competing tones in a dissonant pitch. "So now, rather than just killing you, I will make you suffer, too."

He looked up, eyes red. The changed boy smirked, a black aura emanating from his tense form.

Tarn stepped back. "What are you?"

"The dead have no reason to know," the being inhabiting Boryn's body teased, and he phased behind the daemon. Tarn wheeled in search of the vanished being, and as he turned, a blade sliced across his back. Stumbling forward, Tarn roared, and the blade shoved up into his chest.

"What's wrong, Tarn? You seem scared," the oddly discordant, disembodied voice taunted as the blade pulled free. The red-eyed boy showed himself again.

Bellowing, Tarn shook his head, knowing that he was encountering something altogether different. "What are you?" he asked again. Tarn's whole body trembled. He raised a taloned hand to invoke the spell from his fingers.

"Nope. Sorry," the odd voice said, and faster than the eye could see, Boryn's black-gem blade sliced upward, cleanly severing the fingers from Tarn's right hand. The black blades emanated darkness. The aura pulsed and grew, and Boryn, or a semblance of him, rematerialized. He laughed like a maddened beast before running at Tarn. Tarn swung but now Boryn had the upper hand, and he parried with a glowing, black scimitar.

"I'm going to make you scream," Boryn cackled, his entire being engulfed in the raging black aura.

Stop!

His hands dropped the black blades and flew to his face, fingers spread wide, covering his eyes. The aura faded, and Boryn shrieked, his voice and eyes returning to normal, his fists clenching and unclenching. He reclaimed the dropped scimitars and straightened, sheathing them on his back. The bracer's gem began to glow with purple light.

Tarn swiped at the boy. Releasing the time-slowing energy from the bracer, Boryn rushed the daemon. He sent a massive concentration of energy into his legs, jumped up and kicked off Tarn's knee. Unsheathing a dwarven scimitar, he coursed as much energy into the blue blade as he could, preparing for a massive cleaving. Time returned to normal as he came even with the cracked black gem on Tarn's chest. From close range, Boryn drew back his arm and slammed the pommel into the gem.

A blast of intense energy fired out, a gigantic crescent of brilliant, blinding light. The concussive force tossed Boryn's body across the courtyard like a child's doll then slammed it to the ground. Tarn's roar went unheard over the deafening silence of the light.

At that moment, time itself became nothing, engulfed in the whiteness of the light.

Then it blasted back, an implosion of massive force as if it had ricocheted off the ends of the earth to fire back into the single point where the gem had been. For a split second, reality itself seemed to be sucked into the shattered gem and the blinding, searing light that vaporized Tarn's body.

The light and silence came as one. Luthor's head jerked up, but the brilliance of the pure whiteness forced him to turn away. As suddenly as the light had come, it faded, and when he was able to look up, Luthor searched the sky for the source of the powerful blast. Instead, he saw daemon forms swallowed in the whiteness. The sounds of battle ceased, replaced by an eerie stillness. Luthor saw armies of man and dwarf stunned and confused but standing in a forest that seemed at peace. *I need to get to the citadel fast.*

Deep into the Forest of Ranlon he ran, into the heart where the citadel reigned. Stopping in his tracks, he marveled at the cataclysmic sight before him. The grinding jaws of the earth reached upward, devouring the towering iron palace and all that was within. The preternatural wail of metal against metal was so loud that Luthor wanted to cover his ears; instead he stood frozen, motionless, as the massive structure was swallowed in boiling lava. The piercing screech waned and died, and the abyss closed. A final hiss, then all fell to utter quiet.

Oh, the joys *of not requiring the king's anchor to stay in this world.* Floating above it all, Fernus inspected the results. No sign of Tarn; the citadel and its bubbling moat, a memory and a wasteland. *It seems the boy was successful.* Fernus smiled with self-satisfaction. *And how did young Boryn fare?*

In the heart of the tortured forest, where the citadel had stood, the tail of a tattered, black cape fluttered in the breeze. The black, daemon scimitars lay thrown to the side, the blue, dwarven ones as well. Fernus dropped from his lofty perch toward the stilled figure.

A gentle rain began to fall, a drizzle at first but then heavy, pelting drops. Water gathered in puddles, and with each raindrop, signs of life returned. But the boy did not move.

Quite suddenly, elves clad in elegant, white armor trimmed in gold surrounded the flame-haired general. One stood straight and tall, and tipped his face back to take in the full pleasure of the healing rain.

"Ah, Silvaros. I'm afraid you're a tad late. Were you lost in your own fog?" Fernus chortled.

"You dare address the King of the Moons?" King Silvaros'

guards raised arrows toward the daemon general, but Fernus only laughed and turned back to the body of the boy.

"Sad, isn't it? If not for the expendability of youth, I wonder how willing the humans would be to protect themselves?" the daemon chuckled. With that, Fernus burst into hellish, black flame and disappeared.

A stir at the rear guard, and the elves stood aside as Luthor pushed his way through. He knelt at his brother's side then turned suspicious eyes toward the Moon king. "Why are you here?"

"The Moon elves do not hold humans in high regard. But the Wood elves are our friends, and we could not stand back and leave their home destroyed. We bring the healing rain to remove the scars of the daemons." The Moon king waved his arm beneficently, as if that took care of everything.

Luthor stood, anger flaring. "Forget the damned forest! Save him!"

"Perhaps he is beyond saving." The elven king, a diamond, crescent moon in his helm, stepped closer.

Luthor grabbed Silvaros by the collar and lifted him up; the king's guards stepped in, multiple weapon points pressing against Luthor's neck.

"I've heard you hate the humans. Why, I don't know. But Boryn just saved us all—even you and your kind—no matter how much you want to ignore it."

"Lower your weapons," the Moon king commanded. Arrows dropped, and Luthor released his hold on the king and stepped back. The elven king approached Boryn. He held out his slender, gold-ringed hands, and glistening powder floated from them, cloaking Boryn's form in silvery dust that turned pasty in the falling rain.

Luthor watched and dropped to his knees, overcome not only with battle fatigue but also by the scene before him. Silvaros reached toward Luthor to help him to his feet, but Luthor ignored the gesture. Then Silvaros said, "You are correct. Go check on the others. I will take care of this," and he stooped to lay a cautious hand on the silver enshrouded boy.

Luthor rose slowly and deliberately. He took a final look at Boryn's deathly still form then turned and marched from the place where the daemons' citadel had been. Already he could see signs that the black curse of the forest had begun a slow retreat, as if sucked into the abyss along with the citadel.

He passed through the wet forest, boots squishing in a blanket of ash. Fresh, new growth gave evidence of restored life and hope, yet amidst the emerging rebirth were countless reminders of the cost to humankind. The battle was won, but the losses were great. He stepped across grim piles of bodies: human, dwarf, and daemon entwined in a gruesome dance stopped in time.

Ahead, he noticed a remnant of red, a cloak by appearances. Luthor's heart pounded. *Belral.* With reverence, he approached the body of the downed warrior, hemmed by slain daemons, his sword just out of reach. *Did he save me from the gray one? From this horde?* A wave of guilt washed over Luthor, and he withdrew the cloak, dripping rain mixed with blood, and laid it across the man's shell.

From his watchtower perch, the captain of the guard squinted toward Ranlon, eager for any sign of hope. Sir Ferrik held the glass to his eye to be sure his vision was not fooling him. *Yes, the black smoke has stopped!*

A rider approached at full gallop. "We've defeated Tarn! We are victorious! The daemons are vanquished!" the rider called.

"Open the gates!" Ferrik ordered his aides, "and sound the horn." With three, sharp blares, the joyous message tumbled across the rooftops and filtered into the roads and windows of Dusgoroth. The rider tore through the streets announcing the good news.

Doors flew open, and citizens spilled out, cheering the breathless rider, tying robes to standards and waving them like so many banners. Musicians brought out instruments, and taverns poured out brews. Before long, the market was filled with celebrants, dancing and singing.

Ferrik's watch returned to the forest. At last he caught sight of the first returning warriors, bedraggled and jubilant. He pulled the imperial flag from his holster and held it high, waving it for all to see. "Huzzah!" he yelled, soldiers and citizens gathered along the wall cheering likewise, a mighty chant that echoed across Dusgoroth.

One by one, the Shadow Crusaders and aging heroes returned, filtering throughout the throng. No one told them to gather at the Strawberry Mug, but everyone knew that's where they would meet. The stories flowed; they told what they had learned of fear and pain and uncertainty and, ultimately, of success. And they waited for all to return.

Tsk, tsk, tsk. The daemon clucked as he removed the ash-
covered cloak from Glacius' smoldering corpse. He used the garment
to wrap the black spear, careful not to touch it. *Should have listened to
me.* Then, Fernus snapped his fingers, and darkness reached up from
the ground and tugged him under.

Instantly, he reappeared in the dimly lit room where the dark
alliance gathered, now nursing its wounds. The snarling dwarf Kam
snapped his shattered nose into place, while Morpheon was already
self-healed.

Fernus tossed the wrapped spear aside, a satisfied smile on his
face. The spear tumbled from its soiled, white wrapping and clattered
against the wall.

"Moron," groaned Aquus, his robe rippling as he flowed to his
feet and withdrew the arrows that pierced his limbs and made him
look like a pale blue pincushion.

"Indeed." Fernus cut off discussion, his voice cold and hard. "So
who else fought without orders?"

Noctas stood.

"And Tharrus? Where is he?"

Noctas answered. "Lulz destroyed his physical form. So I'm guessing we won't see him for a while."

"I believe you fought as well, Fernus." A thin but well-toned man stepped from the shadows. His familiar voice was chirpy, and he scratched his head, weaving his fingers into his short, charcoal hair. He slid a dagger from a black-leather weapon belt.

Fernus held up his hands in protest. "I simply was watching and blocking attacks from the boy. I myself never made a move on him."

"Allow me to recommend that you keep your distance to avoid suspicion," sneered the man.

"So who exactly did we lose?" Fernus asked.

"Obviously Glacius . . ."

"I saw Kelris' body. The helmet was crushed; had to be dead," Kam said.

"That's too bad. He was rather clever." Fernus stepped across Tharrus' spear to rest against the wall then addressed himself to the gray-haired human who watched him with keen, marble-gray eyes. "So have things been handled on your side of the world?"

"Actually, things are moving along smoothly, thanks to Prizzadar's fine work. Only a few minor setbacks."

"And our next move?"

The stranger turned toward Fernus, the exchange businesslike. "Take the orb, and reunite the The Four with their bodies."

"The undead?" Noctas asked, surprised.

"None other. Their spirits have been wandering since the orb was broken, and they are eager for a reunion," the man told her.

"So you believe it's time? Are you sure you wouldn't prefer to let them rot for a little longer?" Fernus posed. "But then again, restoring The Four does provide us some interesting opportunities."

"How many of yours are left in this world?"

Fernus was quick with his answer and light, matching his smug expression. "Only the generals. The rest were too weak and pathetic to stay without an anchor."

"And Tarn?"

"Boryn destroyed his spiritual form by destroying the anchor. So unless we actively pursue his resurrection, Tarn is gone for good. Why Tarn thought it was a good idea to implant the anchor in his chest is more than I'll ever understand."

"Nice of him to do us the favor of ripping his own soul apart. Saved us the trouble. And what of the other daemon fallen?"

"Their physical forms are destroyed and can no longer be held in the physical realm until their bodies regenerate. But we'll find a way to bring back the pawns when we need them."

"Good. . . . And the boy?"

Boryn tried to look around, but he was enveloped in black, nothing else, not even a hint of what he was standing on. Or was he even standing? *Where in hell am I?*

Not there.

At least some good news.

Welcome to your mind.

Boryn peered into the darkness from which emerged a pair of golden yellow eyes. *Who are you?* He said no words, but still received an answer.

Shouldn't you ask what am I, and what am I doing in your head?

Yeah, that—

I'll leave you to figure out the first part on your own. As for the reason I'm here—your mind houses your soul. If you look around, you might see your other house guest.

Who are you?

You repeat yourself. But don't worry about me. Worry about him.

Boryn turned to see eyes that were blazing red and colored

black where the white should be. He stared into them and somehow recognized a terrifying side of himself.

It's time you awoke anyway.

A light flashed, and Boryn roused. He felt soft linen against his skin. He opened his eyes to a familiar window. Creaking, the door opened, and his fuzziness cleared. A wolf pup slipped through the crack of the door, and seeing Boryn awake, bounded to the bed top and licked his face. The picture of jubilance, Shade howled, and footsteps rushed the door.

"Scruffy!" said Boryn with a fond smile.

"I told you to stop trying to get yourself killed, didn't I?" the healer teased. Scruffy moved to the side of the bed and sat down on the single wooden chair. "You really put me to the test this time. If the Moon el—"

Wenval barged in.

"Professor!" Boryn's face lit.

"Glad to see you made it!" Wenval teased as the twins and Ranton made space for themselves behind him.

"We won, right?" Boryn scanned their faces, arching one eyebrow.

"Last time I checked," laughed Laric.

Boryn smiled and turned toward the door. Emily leaned against the frame, a shy smile behind weary eyes. Relief washed her face. "Boryn, I was so worried," and she ran to him, knelt beside the bed, and draped one arm across his chest.

"Ow . . . oh . . . ouch!"

She moved her face in front of his and smiled. Lifting his head, he touched his lips to hers. She pressed in and kissed him. Boryn chuckled, knowing his friends were nudging one another, seeing their smirks in his mind's eye. "That was definitely worth waking up for," he said, wrapping his good arm around her.

"I'd hope so." She squeezed him again.

Hannah and Stevan arrived to crowd the room to overflowing, but that didn't stop two guards ahead of a large man wearing regal, blue robes.

"Boryn."

"Emperor." Boryn held a steady gaze, his manner turned cold.

Wenval ushered the others out the door to leave the two alone. "We'll see you when you're up, Boryn."

Lord Mhinbron spoke haltingly. "I wish to speak with you."

Boryn raised his brows as if to say, "Well?"

"If you will come to my keep later—"

Boryn cut him off. "If you command it, m'lord."

About that time, two dwarves came bustling in, unconcerned about barging in on the Emperor. They paused to bow, but the Emperor departed without another word, permitting the celebration to resume.

"What were all of you doing? Camping outside the door?" Boryn smiled, overwhelmed by his friends' attention.

"Oy! Ya di' it, boy, eh?" said Bret excitedly.

"*We* did it!" Boryn protested.

"I guess we did 'elp a wee bit," Boringer admitted, grinning.

"Why are you still wearing your helmet, Boringer?" Boryn wanted to know. "It's over, isn't it?"

The golden-bearded dwarf shrugged and removed the horned helm. When the others saw the frightful hair beneath, everyone laughed. Boringer scowled and slammed the helmet back in place.

"Great timing on finishing it, boy," said Ramgis as he stepped through the door with Cadegray, Rath and Luthor.

"My life was passing before my eyes—and then that amazing light just before the rain started!" Rath swept his arm in dramatic fashion, smiling happily.

"Come to think of it," Ramgis turned to Rath, remembering to ask, "just who were you working for?"

Rath smiled. "The honorable Grandmaster of the Raven dispatched me to help you."

A question crossed the old general's face. "And tell me, pray, why the Raven would pay a mercenary to aid the Blood Knights?"

Rath grinned broadly, a Cheshire-cat grin, before moving to Boryn's side—ignoring Ramgis' question—and hurrying the conversation forward. "Now, Boryn, I want you to know we had everything under control all along," Rath smiled. "What a grand alliance it was," he added wistfully.

"I'm glad to hear it," Boryn replied, "because, to tell you the truth, there's a good bit I don't remember."

"Look at me!" A rail-thin, carrot-headed man wearing billowy purple robes entered next.

The man seemed familiar, but Boryn couldn't place him. "Can you help me out here?"

"I'm Quaswyn, of course!"

"What happened to Marlok?"

"He's here." The mage reached behind him and tugged the rogue forward. "His nasty scars no longer mar my ravishing body," Quaswyn preened like a peacock.

"What happened? How did you get separated?"

"Don't have a clue. We were right in the middle of the battle when all of a sudden there was a huge blast of light. And voila! We were separated!"

Boryn smiled at all the friends gathered to see him, glimpsing for the first time what "family" might mean.

"Oh, brother," Luthor said, "you ought to know you're an official hero of Armorica—now known as 'The Shadow Saint.'"

"Nice title! I can't wait to hear what I did to deserve it!"

"You'll always be the leader of the Shadow Crusaders, as far as I'm concerned!" Laric added, poking his head back through the doorway.

Boryn raised himself on one elbow and, feeling steady enough, continued to sit up on the side of the bed. "Where are Rogma and Belral? Everyone else is here." Boryn looked up, expecting the two to pop in like all the others.

Instead, everyone except Boringer and Luthor left the room.

"Tha's actually somethin' we needed ta tell ya . . ."

Boryn waited, willing the anticipated words to be untrue.

"I think Rogma would wan' you ta 'ave these." Boringer held out Rogma's pendant, the silver man of stone he'd made for his son. Boryn slipped the cord over his head and tightened it at his neck.

Then he held the charm between his fingers, warming it.

"An' this." With two hands, Boringer extended Rogma's staff.

Boryn took it and laid it across his lap. He ran his hand along the length of the knotty wood, its length short for a human, recalling its slap, remembering his time with Rogma training and smithing. With a rueful chuckle, Boryn lifted the rune-covered stick and snapped the shaft across his thighs, saddened to realize he will miss the *thwack* of it. *I promise I won't get rusty, master smith.*

"And Belral?"

Luthor simply nodded.

A large stone box rested in the center of the graveyard awaiting return to the dwarves' new home. Boryn walked to the stone vault and ran his hand along the side. He heard a faint jingle. *Rogma's keys.* He looked up, but realized it was only his imagination that brought the smith here. Unable to hold back any longer, he dropped to his knees, and tears washed his face. He unsheathed the two iron scimitars he had forged and set them atop the stone coffin. *I have your staff; you take my scimitars.* It seemed like a fair trade.

"I'm so sorry," Emily said, eyes filled with sadness, as she walked up behind him. Lowering herself to the ground, she touched her hand to his back. Boryn turned to the fresh mound beside him, two swords at the head.

"Why did they have to die?"

Luthor joined them, his eyes welling at the gravesite of his teacher, the man who had been like a father. Luthor shook his head as if to deny that the powerful man and steadfast friend had fallen to some sadistic beast.

"Are you going to see the Emperor now?" Luthor asked.

Boryn climbed to his feet and helped Emily to hers. "Emily, I have to go to the castle. I'll see you later at the Strawberry Mug."

Wondering what would come next and in no hurry for an encounter with the Emperor, Boryn wandered through Grinfol Forest. He thought about the people who were lost, the ones who died helping him. Suddenly, Lulz was in his face, hanging upside down from a low-hanging bough.

"For you." The strange man with a brush of red hair thrust a furry, white bundle toward Boryn. The bundle unfolded as it exchanged hands. "Gave his life for the fight, for Emily."

Boryn stroked the thick fur of the mighty alpha wolf, a worthy opponent. With respect and regret, he threw the pelt across his shoulder.

"Once you pass Mount Pyr, go apart from the others."

"Who says I'm going to Mount Pyr?"

"Go into the jungle. There's someone you need to meet."

"And that is?"

"A Force of Nature."

"Like you?"

"Except she sees."

"And you don't?"

"She has foresight beyond all others."

"What if I don't want to know?"

"You must."

Boryn walked through the castle gates toward the Emperor's keep, forcing down the taste of bitterness, willing one foot in front of the other. He hesitated for an instant, guards watching, before opening the door to the throne room without knocking. The carved, wooden door opened silently, but still the Emperor heard and rose as if he had been watching for Boryn to arrive.

"Boryn." A clean-shaven man rested clear eyes on the boy. Neither moved, and then Lord Mhinbron walked toward his son.

"I've called you here——," he began in a commanding tone. But then he stopped, softening. "You have accomplished what I thought impossible. You saved the world from the daemons. And you made me realize that perhaps there is yet hope." Lord Mhinbron paused and searched his son's eyes.

The hall echoed with silence.

"Thank you, Boryn."

Boryn remained silent, and time crawled. At last, "I like it," he said with a half-smile, apparently for something to say.

The elder looked questioningly.

"You look nice without a beard."

Stiffly, the Emperor laughed, unsure if his son's remark was meant as ridicule or if, perhaps, it was meant to open the tiniest of chinks in the wall between them. He truly had no idea how to become a father to this boy who was a stranger to him.

"It would be my honor to welcome you back."

Boryn walked to the window: a glorious view of the city, the healing forests of Grinfol and Ranlon, and the harrowed fields beyond. He heard a warbler's song and considered the possibility that far more than a forest had been healed.

"Kind of you." Boryn remained formal. "But I have no desire to stay."

"And where will you go?"

"Away from here." He shrugged, "Wherever the wind takes me."

"If I can offer you any assistance——"

But Boryn didn't wait for him to finish.

Boryn left the castle without regrets, glad that the conversation had taken place but not sure what he wished to do with it. He chose an indirect route to the Strawberry Mug, continuing his contemplation. *Why would I go to Mount Pyr?*

"Boryn, sorry to bother, but may we have a word with you?"

Boryn turned to see Marlok and Quaswyn running to catch him.

"Of course! It's funny now that you two are physically separated, you still stick together."

Marlok seemed serious. "After the battle, we found some troubling remains in a river. You might have seen it. It was a large being, more metal than man, black, with glowing, orange, crystal connectors."

"And why does that matter?"

"It was a tecn, a construct from our land."

"I've never heard of a tecn or a construct. What is it?"

Quaswyn marched like a soldier and recited the singsong chant, "They do not feel. They need not heal. Perfected to kill and carry out thy will."

Marlok added, "That's how the tecn was first introduced in Elemencia."

"Sounds like a real charmer. Any idea what it was doing here?"

"Other than a possible alliance with the daemons, no clue."

"Marlok and I are fearful for our homeland. You may recall that the daemons were marching straight for Elemencia when Fyr Bill stopped them. We are ever so hopeful that you might assist us in exploring this matter."

"By . . . ?"

"Going to Elemencia with us!" Quaswyn was enthusiastic. "I know you'll love it there, beautiful fountains, wonderful food . . ."

"Where's Elemencia?"

"Past the Knightly Realms and through the Draeor Strait. We know the way," Quaswyn promised. Marlok rolled his eyes.

"And I have this lovely tower there, very comforta—"

"Sure."

". . . but I don't think we can pay you . . . ," the mage rattled on.

Marlok swatted Quaswyn with his new cap. "Shut it, you peahead. He said 'yes.'"

Quaswyn stopped and looked from Marlok to Boryn and back. In unison, they said, "Yes."

"Oh. Goody."

Boryn shrugged. "I don't have anything better to do. Might as well set out on a new adventure. Besides, I just can't shake the feeling that this threat is far from over."

"Hopefully, this is the end," Quaswyn said.

"In a perfect world . . . ," Boryn sighed deeply. "Yes, I will help, but for now, let's head back to the Strawberry Mug."

Boryn stood on top of a rickety wooden table, the daemon fighters gathered round. "Marlok and Quaswyn have asked us to go with them to their country to make sure that the daemon corruption is truly over. I plan to go to Elemencia to learn what I can, and I hope that some of you will join me."

"What do you need?" Wenval was ready to help.

"I'd like the Shadow Crusaders plus Emily, Boringer, Bret, Stevan and Hannah to go with me. Come to think of it, you should all be official Shadow Crusaders now!"

"What about the Mug?" Calny asked.

"Leave it to the barmaids; they've been doing a fine job."

A moment of hesitation crossed the young innkeeper's face. "It'll be their lucky day!" Calny said with a wistful half-smile.

Boryn continued, "The rest of you," he turned toward the more mature members of the crowd, "remain in Armorica and protect the people at home; make sure nothing goes wrong here. Besides, it's time you old heroes got to take it easy." Boryn teased with a lopsided grin, "You know, bask in past glories."

"Old!" Rath protested. "Luthor, are we standing for this?" The two ran at Boryn, pulled him from the table and pretended to pommel him.

"Yep, little brother, go make sure we really saved the world!" Luthor said. "You can count on us 'old' ones to hold down the fort here."

Cheers of support mixed with merry laughter.

Boryn finished, "Those who are leaving, gather what you need for the journey. We won't be home for a very long time, so make your goodbyes and meet at the stables in the morning."

It was late when Boryn returned to the Strawberry Mug after going to tell Scruffy goodbye; it was the only thing he'd felt a need to do before leaving Dusgoroth again. The customers were gone, and most of the candles were extinguished. He climbed the stairs to the room where he was staying, pausing at the door to his brother's room. He peeked in to find Luthor asleep, but judging by appearances, the slumber was not peaceful. Boryn waited to see if the rousing would awaken him, but when it did not, he opted not to disturb him. "Farewell, brother . . . I'll see you when I return," the younger sibling said in a low voice. And he backed away from the door, leaving Luthor to the torment of his dreams.

Black and red swirled in emptiness, twisting around his body like countless, writhing snakes trying to snare and squeeze him. From the dimness emerged the ghostly form of a woman.

"Mother?"

"Son," she said tenderly. A heavy, black gauntlet with sharpened, metal fingers burst from her chest. She coughed; blood trailed from her mouth. In slow motion, she dropped to her knees. He ran to catch her, dissolving to the ground alongside her, and he held her close.

"Mother, don't leave me!"

"Get up!" An armored boot shot from the darkness and kicked him hard, away from his dying mother.

He jumped to his feet and reached for the claymore on his back. "Why did you kill her?"

"Required sacrifice. Of no consequence in your equation. But imagine how powerful you would be if she had died when you were born instead."

"I have no desire for more of your power; I don't want what you've already cursed me with."

"You never hesitate to draw on the power when it suits your purposes. You have used it to turn . . . how many battles?"

"It's true, you know." Another figure approached Luthor. As ethereal as a shadow, it draped its arm over Luthor's shoulder like an old chum.

The first man pointed to the shadowy figure whose red eyes shone from the darkness. "That one," the man said, "has saved your hide every step of the way. And after all its hard work, you never leave the poor boy out to play."

Luthor turned, trying to see the shadowy figure, but found it was cloaked in darkness except for the red eyes.

Then the shadow spoke. "Admit it. You enjoy it when I use you!" The voice became a whisper, quiet and deathly. "But soon you'll have used me without appeasing me so many times that I will gain permanent control."

"That will never happen."

"It's inevitable," said the first figure, its tone kindly, fatherly. "One day, that one will take over," he gestured toward the other. "And even if you stop drawing on its power, the power itself will one day take over. And you won't be able to stop it."

"I will find a way to harness you," Luthor said to the red-eyed shadow.

The first man said. "You were a failure as a test subject, and you will simply continue to fail. You cannot harness it."

"I can, and I will."

Ranton saddled the bay and pulled the leather strap to tighten the two large packs on its back. He checked the bridle, closed the stall's wooden gate and turned toward the yard. In the doorway stood the silhouette of a man, his unruly, dark hair aglow from the sun behind him, and a fringe of feathered arrows at his shoulder. The man observed the hazel-eyed boy, almost his own height.

"Rath! So you want to go for round two, is that it?" Ranton asked with a puckish grin.

"Ha! Nah, I'm fine. I just wanted to . . . wish you luck . . . ," Rath paused as if he wanted to say more.

"Well?"

"And let you know . . . I'll watch over your mother."

"That's kind of you, Rath." Ranton put his boot in the stirrup and thrust himself to the horse's back.

"Oh, and you want a piece of advice?"

"Anything."

"Paint your arrows in dark colors. They'll be harder to counter at night," said Rath with a wink, and he turned and left.

Ranton smiled and continued his preparations. A hawk's cry caused him to look up. He held out his arm, and the bird landed softly on his leather gauntlet. "Where have you been? I've missed you." Ranton spoke to the bird like an old friend.

"What are you, the bird whisperer?" joked Boryn as he entered the stable carrying only one light pack and wearing a new, black coat.

"Traveling light for an Emperor's son," Ranton goaded.

"Suits me best."

"Nice coat. And the horses are nice, too. Hanging around with royalty has its privileges," Ranton winked.

Boryn only half-smiled in acknowledgment.

Laric called from outside the wide stable door, "Hey, you think you're special riding horses? Check this out!" Boryn and Ranton moved to the light just as Laric stepped into the frame of the door mounted on an enormous and powerful lizard—three times the size of a horse. Laric patted its now-green scales. "It's amazing what the enemy has to offer."

"Nah . . . it couldn't be."

"See and believe. My new best friend, Krixlus."

"How did that happen?" Ranton quizzed.

"Goodness prevailed when freed from the stranglehold of an evil master," Laric announced. Boryn and Ranton exchanged looks then laughed at Laric's surprisingly philosophical outburst.

"There will be plenty of time for stories while we're on the way to Elemencia," Boryn urged, itching to be off.

The side door to the stable came crashing in, which didn't startle the horses as a much as did the tumble of dwarven fighters that rolled through it.

"I beat ya 'ere." The brown-bearded brewer stomped his foot.

"No' so, Bret. Tha' bloody door was jus' locked, so ye caugh' up, tha's all," Boringer insisted, picking up his horned helm and straightening his wiry, golden beard.

Stevan stepped in. "It was a tie. Saw it with my own eyes." He put out his hands to the two grounded dwarves; they eyed each other suspiciously, scowled, then took the proffered hands.

"All ready to go?" Boryn asked.

"Ready, eh? We're always ready," laughed Bret, swatting Boringer on the back hard enough to make him stumble.

"Stevan, have you seen Hannah and Wenval?" Boryn asked.

Emily answered, stepping out of a stall leading a magnificent, white steed. "They went ahead. Said to meet them outside the gate." Emily smiled beneath Boryn's admiring eyes and mounted, ready to move out. Boryn threw the wolf pelt across the horse's flank. Emily looked at him, a question hanging.

"To keep you warm on a cold night," Boryn said simply.

"I'll carry it for you, but it's yours. You need to keep it."

The instant they moved from the castle yard into the streets of Dusgoroth, a deafening cry arose. Roads, alleys and rooftops were jammed with people eager to catch a glimpse of the royal procession and pay homage to the Shadow Crusaders, the fresh, young heroes, as they departed for a new mission.

At last, they reached the city gate. Boryn stepped through, Emily riding beside him. Ranton on the bay, the hawk perched on his arm, and the rest of the Shadow Crusaders, on foot, followed. The silence of the vast country ahead replaced the jubilant cheers behind.

One hand on Shade, content in Boryn's satchel, and the other on the pommel of a dwarven scimitar, Boryn looked back once then turned to the future. "All right, then, we're off."

Epilogue

Almost invisible in the jungle's growth, the shabby, green tent was shrouded in pale, green mist.

"Wenval, wait here. I won't be long." The place appeared to be deserted, but Boryn left his friend and went into the clearing. Boryn leaned his head through the flap; the place was dark and gloomy and filled with pungent aromas emanating from layers of settled smoke. Cautiously, he stepped through the tattered flap.

"So you came!"

The voice startled him, but he took another step into the smoky den.

"Stop there."

"Where are you?"

"I am all around you."

"Your voice is familiar."

"You've heard it then."

The smoke converged, swirling, and formed into a woman, eyes clouded with age, wrinkled, and bent. Boryn studied her. A tattered and bloody cloth was tied above her eyes; grizzled limbs protruded from loose rags. She raised a gnarled staff held by an equally gnarled hand and slammed it into the earth. "And I suppose you want to hear your fate."

"Must I?"

"Watch closely."

The old seer held out her hand, her body lifted from the ground, and the staff moved freely from her hand to float lengthwise in front of her. It smashed to the ground then began to rise up, a slab of stone following it. The seer reformed as swirling, green smoke and was inhaled into the stone. The large stone rose waist high before it shattered. Inside it was a palm-sized square of perfectly smooth, black rock. It hung suspended in the air. The stone moved toward Boryn and passed through his chest twice, leaving no mark, causing no pain. Green colors and blurred images swarmed in his mind. He tried to make sense of the images but found it impossible.

From the dust of the exploded encasement, the seer reshaped in human form. She reclaimed her staff and held it aright. She clenched her fist, and Boryn heard a crack behind him. She looked up into the tall boy's eyes, her face troubled. The disk hovered between them.

"Your fate lies on the stone. Gaze upon it."

Expecting the disk to drop at any moment, Boryn reached for it. It felt warm and velvety and surprisingly heavy. He inspected it closely, running a finger across the smooth surface to feel the etching there. The inscription read: 05 ♆ 20 ⚕ 21.

He looked up, his expression showing confusion tinged with anger. "That's my fate?"

A crooked finger waggled toward the stone. "That is your power. That is who you are."

"A strand of meaningless numbers?"

"It is when, where, who, and what you are, Boryn Mhinbron."

"You're very strange."

"Many have thought so, only to be proven wrong."

"But it doesn't make sense."

"You will understand. That is your destiny: one of heroism, pain, joy and deception. Your path will cause the very world to fall to its knees, as it is you who will bring about end times . . ."

"How, exactly, am I going to do that?"

The old woman shut her eyes and wisped away like a dry leaf in the wind.

Boryn left the tent as a drizzling rain began to fall. He paused at the flap, took a deep breath and then shoved the stone deep in his pocket.

Wenval, who waited reclining against a tree, leapt up and ran to meet him. "What did you learn?"

"Nothing," Boryn said, and he walked deeper into the jungle.

About the Author

While most sixth graders sat through English class, Joseph Hughes lived a fantasy that begged to be told. Over the next several years, he outlined a series of books in a world he imagined and wrote the first, *Armorica*.

When not writing, Joseph enjoys creating musical soundtracks, building and painting fantasy models, playing video games, and anything Irish. He will begin college in the fall of 2009 where he plans to study English. He lives in Dallas, Texas, with his family and two Brittany spaniels.

Contact the author at jh@ARMORICAworld.com